Praise for Gra

"Her Husband's Harlot is a ple[...] read."--*Dear Author*

"Erotic historical romance isn't as plentiful as many would think, but here you have a very well-written example of this genre. It's entertaining and fun and a darn good read."--*The Book Binge*

"I devoured this book in a couple of hours! .... If you love a story with a heroine who is a wallflower with a backbone of steel or a damaged hero then you will love this one too."--5 star review from *LoveRomancePassion.com* on *Her Wanton Wager*

"I found this to be an exceptional novel. I recommend it to anyone who wants to get lost in a good book, because I certainly was."--A Top Pick from *NightOwlReviews.com*

"I thoroughly enjoyed this story. Grace Callaway is a remarkable writer."--*LoveRomancePassion.com* on *Her Prodigal Passion*

"The depth of the characters was wonderful and I was immediately cheering for both of them."--*Buried Under Romance*

"Grace Callaway is one of my favorite authors because of her fearlessness in writing love scenes that truly get the blood pumping."--*Juicy Reviews*

Books by Grace Callaway

HEART OF ENQUIRY
The Widow Vanishes
The Duke Who Knew Too Much
M is for Marquess
The Lady Who Came in from the Cold
The Viscount Always Knocks Twice (2016)

MAYHEM IN MAYFAIR
Her Husband's Harlot
Her Wanton Wager
Her Protector's Pleasure
Her Prodigal Passion

CHRONICLES OF ABIGAIL JONES
Abigail Jones

THE DUKE

WHO KNEW TOO MUCH

Heart of Enquiry Book One

GRACE CALLAWAY

Acknowledgements

The creation of every book needs a village, and this one was no exception. I am so blessed to have the best peeps in the world supporting my endeavors. Tina, thank you for our Fridays and for being the best critique partner and friend—and for supplying a much needed plot element (you know which one!). Diane and Candace, your editorial feedback was invaluable as always. Thank you for understanding and supporting the worlds that I strive to create.

Carrie, you bring my vision of my characters to life with your beautiful art—thank you! Lindsey, hugs for your assistance and making my life easier. Brian, my books (and life) are better because of you. Kisses!

To my family, who has supported my dreams, especially during this transitional year. Your love sustains me. And for Brendan, my little warrior, who inspires me every day.

Lastly, to my readers ... because none of this would be possible without you! I'm so grateful that you've joined me on this adventure. Here's to our continued travels together!

Prologue

As the carriage passed the massive stone gates, Alaric McLeod leaned out the window, trying to get a glimpse of his new home. It was a rare show of excitement for him. At nine, he'd already learned the value of self-discipline, of guarding his responses to the world around him. 'Twas a simple fact: what people couldn't see, they couldn't hurt.

Yesterday, he hadn't flinched when his da tossed the single, ratty travelling case—the only one the McLeods owned—onto the carriage and said tonelessly, "That's that, then. Be a good lad and no trouble to my cousin."

He didn't move a muscle when his stepmother bid him a cool farewell.

Yet when his younger half-brother Will cried, "Why is Alaric leaving? I want to go with him!" something hot and unexpected pushed behind his eyes.

He pushed back, forcing the heat to retreat.

"Good bye, William." He was proud of how grown-up he sounded. "I'm the ward of a duke now, so I shan't be returning here." He glanced at the tidy cottage with its blooming hedgerows and vegetable garden—and the old, stupid yearning pierced him. Though his confidence wavered, he lifted his chin. "My new guardian lives in a castle. I'll have my own bedchamber. And servants to fetch me anything I want."

"I want to go with you," Will insisted.

Will's mother intervened, her arms folding protectively

around her little son. She'd never once held Alaric that way. The knots in Alaric's chest tightened—and he ignored that too. He told himself he didn't care if his father's new wife was young and beautiful with her shining chestnut hair and dark brown eyes—Alaric's own mama had been *more* beautiful. And his stepmother was a mere milliner's girl whereas his mother had been a true lady, the youngest daughter of an earl.

Though his mama had died when he was three, she still visited him in fragments. The fading scent of gardenias. The whisper of silk behind a closed door. Dampness upon a cheek as cool and smooth as alabaster. *We don't belong here, Alaric. We deserve better ...*

"You'll stay here, Will," the new Mrs. McLeod said firmly, "where you belong."

Alaric understood his stepmother's message. Truth didn't need to be spoken aloud: he knew who belonged and who didn't. As if to prove the point, his da came to stand behind his stepmother and half-brother. His chest chafed at the picture the three made. Brown-haired and robust, a proud, loving Scots family. He bore no resemblance to them with his black hair and awkward, gangling build, the pale skin and eyes he'd inherited from his English mama.

You've eyes like the blessed cat, his stepmother had once said.

Aye, he had more in common with that mangy stray than the portrait-perfect McLeods. Resentment swelled. They didn't want him? Fine. He didn't want to be here anyway. He hated them all—and this backward village, too. The bullies and lack-wits, offspring of farmers who would sooner start a brawl than attempt a math problem. Who'd bloody a lad's nose just because he had a head for numbers and sums.

Da cleared his throat. "It's time you're off. Mustn't keep your guardian waiting."

Can't wait to be rid of me, can you? The dark, swirling thoughts burst through the barriers of his control. Confusion and anger swept through him. Even as his fists balled, ice came to his rescue, flowing through his veins, numbing everything else.

Don't let them see. They can't hurt you.

"Yes." His voice frosted over. "I don't want to keep His Grace waiting."

"I'll miss you, Alaric." Eyes glimmering, Will tugged on his sleeve. "You'll come and visit soon, won't you?"

What for? They have you. Their son ... the one that matters.

"Goodbye, William," he said flatly.

He'd boarded the carriage without looking back. What was the point? He already knew what was behind him—what mattered was looking ahead. His hands cold and clammy now, he gripped the window frame of the carriage. If his eyes stung, he told himself it was because of the dust clouds stirred up by the clattering wheels.

Put the past behind you. There's no looking back—the future is what matters.

The dust settled and then, like magic, a vision appeared. His jaw slackened. Surrounded by lush green hills and cloudless skies, Strathmore Castle sprawled with the grace of an ancient behemoth that had fed off time itself. Sunshine gilded the stone walls, glinted off stained glass and mullioned windows. Power infused the building's every line from the rugged towers to the sweeping wings. 'Twas a place that could ward off any attack—and provide refuge to a chosen few.

As the carriage rolled onto the circular front drive, two figures emerged from the arched entryway. The tall, black-haired man with hawkish features was Henry McLeod, the Duke of Strathaven, Alaric's first cousin once removed and now his guardian. He'd met the duke only once before, when the latter had come to offer guardianship to one of the sons of his poor relation. Amidst the clutter of the McLeods' cottage, the duke had seemed like a king with his fine clothes and pristine elegance. Surrounded by the wealth and power of his ancestral estate, His Grace dazzled like a god.

Beside Strathaven was the duchess, thin and slight as a sparrow, lace quivering at her breast. Alaric had never met her. He knew only that her own son had died of a fever, and she could not bear another.

When she waved her handkerchief in welcome, the ice in Alaric's gut began to thaw. Relief trickled through him.

They want me here. I'll belong. I've come… home.

His lips found the tentative shape of a smile, and he waved back with a boy's eagerness.

Chapter One

Twenty-seven years later

As the strains of a waltz emerged from the orchestra, Miss Emma Kent took leave of her sister-in-law Marianne, who was chaperoning her this evening, and wove through the mirrored ballroom. Her purpose wasn't to find a dance partner. With all the ladies eagerly convening like a kaleidoscope of butterflies upon the dance floor, she saw a prime opportunity to visit the necessary without waiting in line.

Born and bred in the country, she was practical by nature. As she nudged a path through the heavily perfumed throng, she thought—not for the first time—that the night's endeavor was rather pointless. She didn't belong here amongst the champagne fountains and rarefied guests. Not only did she lack the requisite blue blood, she was also too old, too independent, and too unsophisticated to attract a husband.

These were facts and did not bother her overmuch. She knew her strengths: having managed a cottage and four unruly siblings since the age of thirteen, she was resourceful, efficient, and competent in an array of skills. She loved her family dearly and had never met a man who'd made her want to relinquish her place there—or her firmly established autonomy.

Hence, marriage was not a top priority.

She had bigger, better plans.

The orchestra began to crescendo, eliciting a swell of emotion beneath her peach silk bodice. Her papa had passed over a year ago, and she still missed him with every fiber of her being. As the village schoolmaster, Samuel Kent had dedicated his life to educating the young minds of Chudleigh Crest, and he'd been the wisest man she'd ever known.

It is not living that matters, he'd taught her and her siblings, *but living rightly. Follow the wisdom of your heart, and it will lead you to the truth.*

The twirling dancers and opulent surroundings faded as Emma contemplated how to put her papa's moral philosophy into action.

After their father's death, her eldest half-brother Ambrose had insisted on moving her and their younger siblings from Chudleigh Crest to London. Emma knew that he wanted to give them opportunities not found in the country. Marianne, Ambrose's beloved wife, had been a wealthy baroness prior to marrying into the middling class Kent family, and she was more than happy to use her social cache to give her husband's younger siblings *entrée* into the *ton*.

Marianne had taken them in hand, polished them up. She'd put in effort and expense, and Emma hadn't the heart to dissuade her sister-in-law's good intentions or puncture the bubbling excitement of her younger sisters Dorothea, Violet, and Polly, who'd taken to city life like ducks to water. Tonight was Emma's first outing in the *beau monde*, and she was supposed to set a good example for her sisters, who would soon be introduced to Society as well.

She didn't want to let her family down ... but she didn't want to be here either. For she'd already discovered her true passion; the problem was how to gain her older brother's support for her plans. As she contemplated the conundrum, she passed through the arched entryway and suddenly tripped, gasping as she hurtled forward. She braced for impact—collided with something firm and solid ...

Blinking, she found herself staring up at the countenance of a ruthless god.

She was far from being a fanciful sort, yet there was no other way to describe the stranger with the dark, gleaming black hair and face sculpted with savage perfection. He looked to be in his thirties, his edges chiseled by jaded experience. He had high cheekbones, a blade of a nose, his chin and jaw arrogantly jutting. Beneath the dark slashes of his brows, his eyes were a startling shade of silvery jade, fringed by the thickest, longest eyelashes she'd ever seen on a gentleman. She stared, mesmerized.

Those arresting eyes narrowed. The brooding mouth twisted into a cynical smile.

"If you wanted to dance, pet, you might try asking."

The deep, mocking tones held a faint lilt, something not entirely English. Then the words themselves penetrated her dazed brain. With dawning horror, Emma realized that she'd literally fallen into the stranger's arms—and he thought she'd done so *on purpose*. That she was deliberately throwing herself at him!

Mortified, she tried to disentangle herself. "Let me go."

"Easy there," he drawled.

His scent permeated her senses, a blend of wood spice and soap that was ineffably masculine. His muscular arms surrounded her, held her closer than any man ever had. Placing her hands against his silver grey waistcoat, she pushed to no avail. Even through the layers of fabric, his chest felt as hard and unyielding as a slab of marble.

Immobilized, she became aware of his heartbeat, the strong rhythm surging beneath her palm. Its dominant cadence flowed into her, overtaking her own wild pulse, harnessing it. Her eyes drew to the sensual curve of his mouth, and her insides gave a strange flutter. Liquid awareness rushed from her center.

With growing panic, she struggled and said, "Release me at once!"

"If you insist."

His hold loosened at the same time that she shoved against him with all her might. She toppled backward in a cascade of silk, landing with a thud on the hallway floor. The wind knocked out of her, she tried to gather her breath and the remnants of her dignity.

"Need help?" he inquired.

He towered over her, his broad shoulders tapering to a lean torso and narrow hips. Nary a wrinkle marred his elegant black and white evening wear. His cravat was a study in perfection, a large emerald winking in its snowy folds.

Flustered, she swatted a loose dark curl out of her eyes. "Not from the likes of you."

His expression turned sardonic. "Just so you know, these ploys of yours have been tried before, and they won't work with me. I don't play with innocent misses. The untied slipper ribbon?" He glanced pointedly at her left slipper, where the peach satin lace indeed dangled undone. "'Tis the oldest debutante trick in the book, sweet."

His mind-boggling arrogance rendered her speechless. Before she could unknot her tongue to give him a proper set down, he swept her a mocking bow, and his tall, virile form disappeared into the ballroom.

Emma stared after him. *Unbelievable.*

He embodied everything she disliked about the upper classes: superiority and sophistication, contempt toward those deemed below their notice. A man such as this was guided not by morality or purpose but his own jaded amusement and self-gratification. Fuming, she rose and dusted herself off.

The bounder. That better be the last I see of him.

An hour passed in which, thankfully, Emma saw no more of the rude stranger. The event had turned into a crush, however, and the ballroom was more sweltering than ever. When she saw her sister-in-law swamped by a circle of admirers, she took the opportunity to get some air, escaping through the French-style doors that led into Lady Buckley's famed maze garden.

Outside, she inhaled deeply, the jasmine-scented night air invigorating her senses, and she couldn't resist wandering farther into the empty garden. Her skirts whispered over the manicured grass as she followed the winding wall of hedges, her pearl-studded reticule swinging from her gloved fingers.

Surrounded by moonlit darkness, she continued to mull over her dilemma: how could she convince her brother to let her join the family business?

The seeds of her destiny had been sown when Ambrose's private enquiry firm, Kent and Associates, suffered a fire several months ago. Luckily, no one had been injured, but the entire office had needed to be rebuilt. Seeing the strain the situation put on her brother, she'd offered to help organize the new premises; besieged by so many responsibilities, he'd gratefully accepted. With her trademark energy, she'd set about getting everything shipshape, and even after the dust had settled, she'd stayed on to assist the clerk, Mr. Hobson, with the day-to-day tasks.

It felt good to help. She liked supporting Ambrose and his business partners, Mr. Lugo and Mr. McLeod, in their noble enterprise. Then, last week, an astonishing event had occurred, making her destiny bloom into vivid clarity before her eyes.

She'd brought tea to Mrs. Kendrick, an anxious widow returning for the third time in as many days. The lady had tearfully shared that she was losing hope that her lost engagement ring, a memento of her beloved husband, would ever be found. Filled with empathy, Emma had asked the other a few questions—and the conversation had unexpectedly led to the recovery of said ring! Mrs. Kendrick's joyful gratitude had filled Emma with satisfaction, a momentous sense of achievement. Then and there, she'd had twin revelations.

First, Kent and Associates needed a female investigator.

Second, *she* was the woman for the job.

Emma reasoned that she would bring a unique and valuable perspective to the work of detection. In the case of Mrs. Kendrick, she'd instantly suspected a culprit whom neither Ambrose nor his male colleagues had considered.

Moreover, Ambrose always said that success in investigation relied upon observation, deduction, and creative thinking. Emma had raised four younger siblings, all of whom claimed—ruefully—that she had eyes in the back of her head. She couldn't count the number of times she'd figured out the location of a missing hair ribbon or boot lace or resolved some knotty household problem. And when times had been lean for the family, she'd relied on ingenuity and determination to see them all through.

Emma *knew* she had the skills to succeed as an investigator.

Yet how could she persuade her overprotective older brother of her plan's merits? It was one thing for Ambrose to let her assist in mundane office tasks—and it would be quite another for him to agree to train her as an investigator. What would it take to prove her worth to him and his partners? Perhaps if she were to solve another case, demonstrate her initiative and resourceful nature ...

A noise cut through her musings. With a start, she realized that she had meandered deep into the heart of the labyrinth. She heard a murmur from around the next bend— then a cry scraped the night. Heart pounding, she instinctively backed against the nearest hedge, twigs and leaves prickling the exposed skin between her shoulder blades. She waited in the shadows, breath held.

Voices emerged from the other side of the leafy barrier.

"Are you going to hurt me?" a female voice said tremulously.

"I'm going to do whatever I want. And you're going to enjoy it."

The coolly arrogant statement jolted Emma. The hairs on her nape shivered to attention, her palms growing clammy within her gloves. Dear God, she *knew* that deep male voice with the faint lilt.

"Please, I beg of you," the lady whimpered.

"You like to beg, don't you? Perhaps if I'm in the mood later, I'll have you do so ... on your knees."

At the silky menace of the words, Emma's eyes widened. What did the fiend intend to do? With shaking hands, she searched for a gap in the foliage. There was none. Only dark leaves in the dark night—an impenetrable wall to accompany the sudden, taut silence. Emma's senses strained for any hint, any sign of what was happening on the other side. Her pulse skittered; her thoughts raced.

Should I call for help—who will hear me out here? Mayhap I should run for assistance?

A feminine plea rent the night. "Oh God. Please, Strathaven, I can't bear it—"

Oh my goodness, I have to do something. The bounder is assaulting her!

Fear for the woman's safety propelled Emma into action. She dashed to the other side of the hedge; her frantic gaze landed on the pair by the gazebo. In the silvery moonlight, their profile formed a terrifying tableau. A tall, slim redhead stood trapped against a column, her hands bound above her head. A blindfold covered her eyes, the black silk a wicked contrast to the whiteness of her face and throat, her heaving bosom. A broad-shouldered man towered over her, his hand fisted in her skirts—

"Stop, you blackguard!" Emma cried, rushing at him.

"What the devil—"

He swung around just in time for her reticule to connect with his jaw. His head snapped to the side; he stumbled back with an oath.

Emma wasted no time. She ran to the woman, tore off the blindfold. "I'll get you out of here!"

"Who are *you*? What are you doing?" The lady's frantic blue eyes darted around the clearing. "Be quiet or someone will hear you!"

Emma had to stand on tiptoe to reach the lady's wrists. She succeeded in untying the rope, which slithered to the ground, coiling like a snake in the grass. A sardonic voice emerged from behind her.

"You again," he said.

Emma pivoted as the stranger advanced toward her, rubbing his jaw. Only now he wasn't a stranger—the lady had called him Strathaven ... a lord of some sort? She regretted not paying attention to Marianne's review of *Debrett's Peerage*. It was best to know one's enemy.

Emma's skin prickled as Strathaven's gaze roved over her, his icy, intense eyes penetrating her layer by layer. Palpitations gripped her heart. No one had ever looked at her this way before. Had ever made her feel this exposed and bared ... Shaking off the alien sensation, she pulled her shoulders back and stood at her full height. Unfortunately, he dwarfed her by nearly a foot; she had to tip her head back to meet his gaze.

"Take one more step, and I'll scream," she warned.

Given the volume of the orchestra and party as well as the present location deep in the garden, she thought it unlikely that her cry for help would be noticed. She prayed the rogue wouldn't realize it.

"Oh?" One black brow lifted. "Who do you think will hear you?"

Dash it. "I have extremely capable lungs," she informed him.

"Somehow that doesn't surprise me." His lips gave a faint twitch, drawing her attention to the hard line of his mouth and the faint grooves that bracketed it. "Well, pet, you have succeeded in getting my attention, I'll grant you that."

The *nerve* of the man. "Of all the arrogant, asinine—"

"*Please* keep your voice down." The lady inserted herself between them. "I beg of you, Miss …?"

"My name is Emma Kent. And you needn't be afraid because I witnessed everything." Emma angled her chin up. "I shall be happy to provide testimony to the magistrates."

"The *magistrates*? You mustn't," the lady gasped.

"The scoundrel was attacking you. Of course I must."

"Attacking her? Why would I do such a thing?" To her disbelief, Strathaven gave a harsh laugh. "Do you know who I am, Miss Kent?"

"I don't care who you are. Your rank doesn't exempt you from rules of conduct, my lord," Emma retorted hotly.

"Your Grace."

"What?"

"Your Grace is how one addresses a duke."

She gritted her teeth at his cool correction. "The point is, *Your Grace*, I heard you assaulting this lady and—"

"You have no idea what you heard." The duke's mouth

formed a humorless smile. "Now run along, pet, and leave us be."

Pet? As if she were a spaniel trained to do his bidding? Before she could summon a scathing reply, the lady gripped her arm.

"Strathaven is right," the redhead pleaded. "Nothing happened."

"But he tied you up and was about to ... hurt you." Had the rogue meant to beat the woman—rape her? Both? Quelling a shudder, Emma said, "If you're afraid, you needn't be. My brother is a former member of the Thames River Police, and he knows the Chief Magistrate of Bow Street personally—"

"*No.*" Her face draining of color, the lady whispered, "I implore you, Miss Kent. If anyone catches wind of this, I'll be ruined. Lord Osgood, my husband ... he'll never forgive me." Her voice hitched on a sob. "There *cannot* be a scandal."

"Surely if you explain to your husband—"

"My reputation will be destroyed. I would rather *die.*" Tears streamed down Lady Osgood's beautiful face, her fingers digging painfully into Emma's flesh. "If you truly wish to help me, swear on everything you hold dear that you'll never breathe word of this matter."

Emma hesitated, darted a glance at Strathaven. He'd propped one velvet-clad shoulder against a gazebo post, his pose utterly unconcerned. Frustration smoldered in her chest. It wasn't fair that Lady Osgood had to worry about her reputation whilst he didn't have to answer for his misdeeds. Why should he should get away with assault just because he was a man—a duke?

'Twas injustice of the *worst* sort.

"*Promise me*, Miss Kent." Lady Osgood fell to her knees.

Shocked, Emma tried to pull the other up. "Please

don't—"

"I shan't move until you give me your word." More tears slid over the lady's sculpted cheekbones, her lips trembling. "If you don't, I shall be forced to do something drastic. I'd rather end it all than—"

"I won't tell anyone," Emma said desperately. "*Please* get up."

"Truly?" Lady Osgood whispered. "You swear it—on everything you hold dear?"

With lingering reluctance, Emma gave a nod.

Lady Osgood rose, her gaze flitting to Strathaven. Emma couldn't decipher the duke's expression. What hold did he have over the lady? Would he threaten or hurt her in the future?

"Stay away from her," Emma warned, "or I *will* see justice done."

Lightning flashed in the duke's gaze, his expression that of a wrathful god ready to wage war. The air seemed to crackle with his aggression. Swiftly, Emma took Lady Osgood by the arm and dragged her back toward the house. As they traversed the twisting maze, Emma's heart thudded, sweat dampening her unmentionables even as she kept a quick, determined pace.

With an adversary like Strathaven, it was best to keep going and never look back.

Chapter Two

"You're not angry with me, are you, darling?" a husky feminine voice asked.

Alaric James Alexander McLeod, the eighth Duke of Strathaven, cast a cool glance over at Lady Clara Osgood. They were alone in his private cottage in St. John's Wood, and she was naked, waiting on her hands and knees on the black satin sheets. For their mutual pleasure, he'd kept her in that pose while he disrobed. He was taking his time about it, noting how she shivered at the sound of his garments being removed, her bottom angling subtly and suggestively higher in the air.

Clara enjoyed assuming an obedient role in their bed sport. As he was an unquestionably dominant lover, this had made for a good fit ... for a while, at least. He was aware of his restlessness, the *ennui* that remained untouched by the games he and Clara played. Less than a month into their *affaire*, he was already tiring of her company.

"Why would I be angry?" he inquired.

"Because of what happened in Lady Buckley's garden." Looking over her bare shoulder, Clara aimed a pout at him. "How could I have predicted that our game would be interrupted by a countrified chit? And I could hardly admit it *was* a game—I do have my reputation to protect."

"Appearances are everything," he said in sardonic tones.

He didn't fault Clara for not spelling out the truth of the situation to the intrepid interloper. His first marriage had taught him not to expect integrity from the fair sex. Although Laura had been dead for over two years, her shining blond hair and beautiful, spiteful face blazed in his mind's eye before he snuffed the image out. The past was done with, and he would never repeat those mistakes again.

It had been foolish of him to be lured out into the garden by Clara and her little "surprise." He'd let boredom get the better of him. Jaded curiosity had prompted him to see just how far she'd go to incite his lust. In truth, he hadn't been all that impressed or aroused by her antics. Ropes and blindfolds—symbols only, with no inherent appeal. Not when the heart of challenge was missing.

For Clara had no real spirit to submit ... unlike Emma Kent.

From the moment she'd tumbled into him, the obstinate miss had captured his attention. It wasn't just her looks, which were fresh and wholesomely pretty rather than beautiful in any classical sense. Her dark sable tresses complemented her cameo skin and clean features. Her eyes were a sparkling, clear brown and had a slight feline tilt at the corners. Petite and curvy, she'd felt soft as a kitten, too.

The memory sizzled through his blood. Aye, she was a toothsome lass, but more than that it had been the way she'd melted, for an instant, in his arms. That moment of exquisite, instinctive surrender—which he'd wager his stables on that she hadn't even recognized as such—had betrayed unplumbed depths of feminine passion.

He'd turned hard immediately.

Yet he wasn't a fool. He'd learned long ago to stay away from virgins.

A good thing, too. As fate would have it, he knew of Miss Kent's brother and his private enquiry firm. From all accounts, Ambrose Kent was an honorable fellow and a true crusader for justice. It seemed the apple didn't fall far from the family tree. Miss Kent practically gleamed with virtue, her "rescue" of Clara both valiant and reckless.

Assaulting Clara, indeed.

For an instant, he considered what might happen if Miss Kent followed through with her threat to report him to the magistrates. He dismissed the notion. No miss would go so far as to involve herself in a scandal. In his experience, women had a habit of saying one thing and doing another. She wouldn't dare take him on—he was a duke.

You're nothing. A deficient weakling. How I regret taking you in.

With indifference borne of habit, Alaric brushed aside the old duke's scorn. Instead, he imagined the magistrates' reaction if Miss Kent did go to them with her half-baked accusations, and his lips curled with derision. They would laugh their heads off to hear a sexual game being reported as a crime. The chit's innocence was absurd ... and perversely intriguing. As he removed his trousers, his erection bobbed in agreement. His smile grew self-mocking.

Wasn't it just like him to get aroused by defiance?

"Strathaven." Clara's throaty plea drew him back to the task at hand. "How long are you going to make me wait? I'm mad for you, darling."

"Do you get to dictate events?" he said.

"No. Are you going to ... punish me?"

He didn't miss the hopeful edge to her question. Nor the way her slim thighs trembled, spreading wider to show him the swollen lips of her sex. Fully disrobed, he went to the bed. He drew a finger through her soaked thatch, and Clara arched her spine, moaning.

"What did you have in mind?" he inquired.

"Well, I *have* been naughty." Tossing her red curls over her shoulder, she fluttered her eyelashes at him. "A spanking, perhaps?"

Because she asked, he would not indulge her. He could have concocted his own version of retribution for Clara, a way to extend their sexual play, but he found he didn't have the desire to draw things out tonight. She was wet and ready. He gripped her narrow hips, pushed her knees farther apart, and drove his cock into her cunt as she squealed in surprise.

He regulated the tempo of fucking. He knew what Clara liked; after all, she made little secret of it, being as noisy during the act as he was silent. As she begged for *harder* and *deeper*, he kept his thrusts measured and shallow, holding her climax from her, building it with methodical precision. As his body mastered Clara's, his mind was drawn inexorably back to Miss Kent.

Her simple dress had clung with subtle eroticism to her curves, its blush color evoking images of the skin beneath the fabric. His pulse quickened as he imagined her enticingly full breasts beneath him, jiggling as he plowed her. Her nipples would be a plump dusky rose to match her impudent lips. Gripping her sweetly rounded hips, he would tame her with pleasure, pound her tight, wet quim until she screamed her surrender ...

The pressure in his bollocks startled him. A warning sizzle shot up his shaft.

"Yes, ram me with your big cock!" Moaning, Clara ground against him, meeting his thrusts. "I'm going to spend—"

What would Miss Kent be like in her crisis? Would she beg for her release? More likely than not the little termagant would demand it. Well, if she was a good lass, he would give it to her. He saw her big brown eyes melting with desire, heard her breathless voice chanting his name as he drilled himself inside her snug sheath, deeper and deeper still, taking what was his, what she'd never given to any man before ...

He gritted his teeth, held on until his partner reached her zenith. Only then did he join her, shuddering, biting back an involuntary groan. He disengaged himself moments later, physically spent ... and flummoxed by his fantasy. By its nature and intensity.

Emma Kent is trouble. Put her out of your mind.

He exhaled and forced himself to do just that.

Tying on his robe, he went to pour himself his routine nightcap. The single dram of Tobermary whiskey before bed was an indulgence. He'd suffered from a digestive ailment in his youth, and physicians had diagnosed him with everything from sensitive nerves to an imbalance of humors. One quack had gone so far as to accuse him of faking his symptoms.

That verdict had earned Alaric countless beatings from the old duke, followed by periods of enforced starvation to rid him of his "deviousness."

That hadn't helped his illness.

It wasn't until after his guardian's death that he'd managed to conquer the disease. At Oxford, he'd met a pugilism instructor who'd not only helped him to hone his physical condition but also placed him on a diet used by fighters to build muscle and endurance. To this day, Alaric's daily regimen included exercise and eating healthful foods.

He'd be damned if he lost control over his body—over his life—ever again.

Clara raised herself languidly against the headboard, stretching like a cat. "After a tup like that, I need something more fortifying than ratafia," she said with sultry satisfaction. "I believe I'll join you in that nasty stuff you prefer."

Wordlessly, he brought her a glass. As Clara sipped on her whiskey, he settled into the leather wingback by the fire. Clara's main drawback was her tendency to linger after their purpose together was done.

"What *did* you think of Miss Kent?" she said.

Though the muscles of his belly tensed, Alaric flicked a glance over. "Not much."

"I found her rather amusing myself. A provincial little mouse and Good Samaritan rolled into one." Clara's smile had a razor's edge. "Do you know that she continued to pester me about reporting you to the magistrates?"

This didn't surprise him. Miss Kent had struck him as both virtuous and determined: a troublesome combination if ever there was one.

"I'm sure you managed to dissuade her. Your turn as the browbeaten wife was quite affecting. Comparable to the great Mrs. Siddons, I should say."

"'Twas no act. Osgood is frightfully afraid of scandal," Clara said petulantly. "He doesn't care what I do—only that no one knows about it. He's such a bore."

"Who makes up for it with jewels and a generous allowance." Alaric's lips twisted in a cynical smile. "You signed on for your marriage, my dear."

Clara made a moue. Finishing her drink, she strutted naked over to the cabinet of spirits. His brows raised as she helped herself to another generous helping of the whiskey and tossed it back. Good God, he hoped she didn't plan on getting a trifle disguised. He would never be rid of her then.

Clara dribbled more amber liquid into her glass, spilling some in the process. "Speaking of marriage, how is your wife hunting coming along?"

"Fine," he said curtly.

"All those ladies pining to be the next bride of the *Devil Duke*." Clara waved her glass drunkenly. "They're even willing to accept your scandalous requirements."

In his rounds of the marriage mart, he'd made his prerequisite clear: no virgins need apply. Nothing was more deceptive than innocence, and he wasn't going to replicate the disaster of his first marriage. This time, there would be no talk of love, an emotion that he neither wished for nor was capable of. His next duchess would be worldly, prepared to give him what he wanted: an heir and complete obedience—in and out of bed. In return, she would want for nothing, would have everything his wealth and status could provide.

A fair exchange, all in all.

Alaric flicked lint off the sleeve of his robe. "I believe in making expectations clear."

I'll not be betrayed again.

"You're quite the challenge, you know. Rich, handsome—and then there's that legendary cold heart of yours. All the ladies dream of making you fall in love with them."

"Do they?" he said indifferently.

Clara smirked. "They don't know the hot-blooded man I know."

Actually, she didn't know him at all. He didn't bother to disabuse her of the notion.

"The topic grows tiresome." His temples were becoming tight.

"I wish I wasn't married to Osgood," Clara said suddenly. "Then I'd be free to marry you."

Alaric stilled in his seat, the ticking of the ormolu clock uncomfortably loud in the silence. He did not wish to show her disrespect, but he would not lie. The possibility had never crossed his mind.

Clara's brittle laugh broke the silence. "Don't look so horrified, Strathaven—I was just jesting. I have no need of another husband. Speaking of whom," she said, her words slurring, "I still have a few hours before Osgood returns home from his evening's depravity."

Alaric had no desire to couple again with her tonight. It struck him that he felt more than tired. He was oddly off-balance, his mind cloudy. His stomach suddenly churned, and the sharp, familiar wrenching cut short his breath. Memories flooded him: bedclothes twisted and damp with his disgrace, the stifling sickroom, vile medicines poured down his throat ...

What the devil? It can't be. I haven't been ill in years.

Fighting panic, he blinked at his glass. The crystal facets winked in a dizzying manner. The whiskey? It had never affected him this way before. His forehead burned; his palms were clammy.

"Strathaven, I don't ... feel well ..."

He could barely make out Clara's mumbled words. Her image suddenly split into two, a disorienting blur of red hair and lips. Her arm swept out, knocking the whiskey decanter to the ground with a smash. She followed, collapsing in a heap.

"Clara!" Alaric stumbled to his feet. He took one step, and pain tore at his midsection, the world spinning. The floor hurtled up toward him, and he tumbled into a pit of darkness.

A gull's shrill cry stirred him.

Sleepily, Alaric burrowed deeper into the sandy mattress. He was in his cave, the secret grotto he'd discovered along the loch's sandy shores, and here he was safe. Here, the illness that twisted his stomach into agonizing knots, that weakened his muscles and earned him the duke's disgust, seemed to fade for a short while.

Alone, things were better.

But the duchess ... she would worry. Flit about her gilt and velvet-lined sitting room like a canary trapped in a cage. He felt her small hands fluttering over his hot forehead and cheeks, bathing him in cool water. Making it better. Making it worse …

Mama, why did you leave me? Da, why did you make me go?

Seabirds shrieked—or was it Laura? Her tantrums lashed at him even in his cave, no escape from her mad accusations, her volatile behavior. God, he wanted only to rest, yet her screaming grew louder—

He jolted awake, blinking. No Laura and not the loch … a room? The cottage—why was he lying on the floor? The ormolu clock was chirping with mad insistence. He drew his hands over his face, and they came away slick with sweat. Groggily, he pushed himself to sitting, orienting himself. His gaze circled the room—and shock slammed into him.

"Clara?" He stumbled to his feet. Staggered over.

She lay splayed on the floor like a washed up mermaid, her hair a stiff red fan littered with shards of the decanter. Her wide, unblinking eyes stared up at him. She didn't respond—it was clear she never would.

Chapter Three

Two days later, Emma left her bedchamber just after dawn. Living in Town hadn't changed her habit of rising with the sun. Unfortunately, she felt less than bright-eyed; for the last two nights, her sleep had been plagued by vague, menacing dreams. In the light of day, the worries took explicit shape.

Was I right not to report Strathaven to the proper authorities? What if something happens to Lady Osgood? By keeping silent, am I colluding with a terrible injustice?

Anxiety quickened her pulse, yet there was nothing she could do about it now. She'd given Lady Osgood her promise, and a Kent never went back on her word. She could only pray that she'd chosen the right course of action.

Releasing a breath, Emma descended the sweeping staircase. The tranquil house meant that her three younger sisters were still asleep; since moving into Ambrose and Marianne's Mayfair residence, Dorothea, Violet, and Polly had adapted quickly to their new lives. Emma couldn't say the same. As she passed the priceless paintings and exotic furnishings, she felt as out of place as a tin cup next to a fine Limoges setting.

On the first floor, she stopped to greet the maids who were dusting and polishing the immaculate atrium. The maids chimed "Good mornin', Miss Kent" in unison and bobbed curtsies. When she'd first moved in, Emma had made the mistake of trying to pitch in with the household tasks. Idle hands performed the devil's work, after all, and she was used to maintaining her family's home.

It had taken Marianne's gentle admonition to make Emma see that her behavior was having the opposite of its intended effect. She was actually *upsetting* the staff, who took her actions to mean that they were not doing their jobs properly.

Horrified, Emma had stopped the lifelong habit of making her own bed. She'd allowed a maid to be assigned to her to help her dress and do her hair. And she never offered to help Chef Arnaud with meal preparations again.

To her, leisure was a foreign concept and one that, frankly, did not sit well. She had no idea how upper class ladies managed all that free time. Thank goodness she had Kent and Associates. She would go mad if she didn't have a meaningful purpose and something to *do*.

When she entered the breakfast room, Ambrose looked up from the sideboard. Marriage suited her big brother well. Emma saw his wife's hand in the simple yet fashionable charcoal cutaway and trousers perfectly tailored to his tall, lanky frame. His unruly dark hair had been wrangled into an expert cut. Most importantly, where haggard lines had once aged his appearance, he now looked younger, happier, his amber eyes warm with contentment.

That, Emma thought with gratitude, had been Marianne's true gift.

"Good morning, Em," he said. "You're up early."

"No earlier than you." She joined him at the buffet, eyeing the bewildering display of breakfast options.

The Kents hadn't always lived a life of luxury. Before he met Marianne, Ambrose had worked in London, supporting the entire family on a policeman's wages whilst Emma managed the cottage back in Chudleigh Crest. For years, she and her brother had been a team, together taking care of their elderly father and younger brother and sisters.

As if sharing that memory, Ambrose gave her a rueful smile. "It still takes getting used to, doesn't it?"

She didn't need to ask what he meant. "Yes, it does." Taking a plate, she chose some coddled eggs and said thoughtfully, "The girls are doing well with the new comforts, though. Thea's health has improved, and Violet is excelling in her riding and dance lessons. Even Polly is flourishing." She experienced a glad pang thinking of how their shy sixteen-year-old sister, the baby of the family, was coming out of her shell. "She's delighted to be reunited with Rosie, who gives her confidence, I think."

Primrose—Rosie to all who loved her—was Marianne's daughter from a youthful affair. It was the search for Rosie that had brought Ambrose and Marianne together eight years ago. While all the Kents thought of Rosie as one of their own, Rosie and Polly shared a special bond. They were of the same age and had been devoted to one another since their first meeting.

"Rosie certainly has confidence to spare." Though his tone was dry, the smile in Ambrose's eyes spoke of his love for his spirited adopted daughter. "But there's someone else you've yet to account for."

Emma took the chair that the footman held out. "Well, Harry is Cambridge's problem now. I'd wager it's a great deal safer for him to be tinkering in their laboratories than here."

Their younger brother had gone off to university the year before. An aspiring scientist, he had quickly established himself as a bit of a genius. Professors lauded the dear boy's tendency to blow things to smithereens. He was spending the summer abroad, at the Université de Paris, learning advanced techniques from a famous French chemist.

"I shudder to think of Harry's expanding arsenal,"

Ambrose said as he cut into his ham. "But I wasn't referring to the lad."

Emma's brow furrowed. "Who, then?"

"You, Em. You haven't said much about that ball two nights ago."

Beneath her brother's scrutiny, Emma tried not to squirm. That was the thing about Ambrose: he didn't miss a thing. He'd always said that, as an investigator, his main job was to observe and let the truth reveal itself. Images bombarded Emma—Lady Osgood helpless and bound to the gazebo, Strathaven, ducal and menacing—and she quickly dammed them off.

You made Lady Osgood a promise. A Kent's word is her bond.

Ambrose requested fresh coffee from the footman. The latter left the room with the well-trained discretion that characterized all of Marianne's staff.

"That bad, was it?" Ambrose said when they were alone.

Emma heard the undertone of sympathy in his deep voice. He, of all people, understood the challenges of living in a world in which one did not fully belong. Ambrose attended *ton* affairs without complaint because he loved his wife. It didn't mean, however, that he liked them.

"It was memorable," Emma said truthfully.

For an instant, she was tempted to tell her brother everything—but Lady Osgood's hysterical threats rang in her head. She had given her word and couldn't risk the other doing something foolish.

Swallowing, she said, "The truth is that I'd much rather go to work with you than to any ball. Shall we leave soon? There's much to do and—"

"About that. We need to talk, Em." Ambrose cleared this throat and set down his utensils. "You've been a marvel, and the partners and I are extremely appreciative for all you've done to help us recover from the fire. But a young woman like yourself shouldn't be holed up in an office. You've known enough burdens, caring for the family all these years. I want more for you. Now is the time for you to enjoy yourself, to find happiness—"

"I know what I need to be happy," she blurted out.

"Do you now?"

Her heart pounded. Ready or not, she had to lay out her proposal.

No time like the present—follow the wisdom of your heart.

"I want to work with you. As an investigator, I mean," she said in a rush.

It wasn't often that she saw Ambrose flummoxed. "You can't be serious."

"I've never been more serious. With the new office and growing clientele, you need help. And I,"—she gave her brother a pleading look—"I need a purpose."

"You have plenty to do." Ambrose sounded bewildered. "You look after the girls."

"They're grown. They don't need me like they once did." Sorrow flickered at the reality. "They have lessons and fittings and outings to occupy their time now. When it comes to fashionable ways, Marianne is a far better mentor than I."

"Then spend your time meeting eligible gentlemen. Don't you want a husband, Em, one you could have your own family with?"

"I've not met a man whose morals I truly admire," she said honestly. "If I were to marry, I would want a husband who shared my values and treated me as an equal partner."

All her life, she'd looked up to her father and brother, men of principle and character who were devoted to their families. Although Ambrose had wed a wealthy woman, marriage hadn't altered his essential nature. He continued to work, no longer out of necessity but because he believed in the pursuit of justice. His pride was such that when his office had burned down, he'd refused to take Marianne's money to rebuild it. He'd gone from one lender to the next, trying to secure a reasonable loan. Just as things had begun to look hopeless, he'd received backing from Hilliard Bank.

'Twas proof, he'd said, that perseverance was the key to success.

"That's because you haven't met enough eligible gentlemen," was Ambrose's predictable reply. "You've been so busy taking care of everyone else that you haven't had time to think of yourself."

"Even so, the fact remains that I'm hardly marriage material." Prosaically, she counted off the points against her on her fingers. "I'm managing, forthright, not to mention practically on the shelf—"

"You're only four-and-twenty!"

"In the *ton*, that makes me a spinster. Please, Ambrose," she beseeched, "won't you at least consider letting me join the family business?"

Ambrose sat back in his chair, his features somber. "It's one thing for you to organize the office, another for you to engage in my line of work. It's not as if I'm a greengrocer, and you'd be helping me to sell lettuce. The private enquiry business is fraught with peril. I won't risk exposing you to danger, Em."

"I helped with Mrs. Kendrick, didn't I?" she said desperately.

"That was an anomaly. Most cases aren't solved by giving an emetic to a ring-eating cat," her brother said in exasperation.

Yes, but Emma had been the *only one* to suspect Snowball, Mrs. Kendrick's long-haired Persian. Having cared for cats herself, she knew all about their penchant for gobbling up shiny objects. Tabitha, her own feline, had once swallowed a brooch; its removal had not been pretty, and for days after Tabitha had given her sour looks.

Thinking quickly, she said, "What if I only worked with elderly ladies and widows? How much trouble could I get into?"

Her brother gave her a baleful look. "Your question reveals your innocence."

"You can supervise, and I'll do whatever—"

"No, Emma. I cannot allow it."

She opened her mouth to argue further, but the door opened.

"Good morning." Pitt, the butler, bowed. "I'm sorry to interrupt, but you have a caller, sir."

Ambrose frowned. "At this hour?"

"It's Mr. McLeod. He says it's urgent."

"Send him in," Ambrose said.

Frustrated, Emma knew the conversation thus far was going as badly as she'd feared. Perhaps the arrival of William McLeod, one of her brother's business partners, would be a good thing. Emma knew Mr. McLeod to be a fair and reasonable man. He'd praised her work at the office. Mayhap she could convince him to take her side ...

The spacious breakfast room seemed to shrink as the brawny Scotsman strode in. Mr. McLeod was as tall as Ambrose and more muscular besides. Despite his fierce, outsized exterior, the ex-soldier was a gentleman. The Kents had supped at Mr. McLeod's home, and he was clearly a devoted husband to his wife Annabel and doting father to their two children.

Today, however, Mr. McLeod's handsome, rugged features were set in severe lines. An air of agitated energy emanated from him. His thick brown hair mussed, he gripped a newspaper in one hand. Emma knew something was wrong when the typically polite Scotsman barely scraped her a bow before going straight to Ambrose.

"What's amiss, McLeod?" her brother said.

"I need your help," the Scot blurted, shoving the newspaper forward.

Ambrose took the paper, shook it out. His eyes narrowed as he scanned the lines. "Dear God," he said under his breath. He aimed an alert glance at his partner. "You've spoken to Strathaven?"

Emma jerked in her chair. *Strathaven? What is going on?*

Mr. McLeod raked a hand through his hair as he paced back and forth. "No. He and I—we haven't talked in months. But I bluidy well know he didn't do this."

Do what? Emma's sense of foreboding burgeoned. *How is Mr. McLeod acquainted with the duke?*

"We'll go to him now." Ambrose left the paper on the table, clapped his partner on the shoulder. "We'll offer our assistance and do whatever we can to help."

"Thank you, my friend. I hope it'll be enough," Mr. McLeod said heavily.

As the men made arrangements for the carriage to be brought round, Emma went and snatched up the paper. Shock jolted through her as the headline swam before her eyes:

DEVIL DUKE DISCOVERED WITH MURDERED WOMAN.

"Oh no," she whispered.

Mr. McLeod turned swiftly. "It's naught but circumstantial evidence and conjecture, Miss Kent. Just because Lady Osgood was found with Strathaven doesn't mean that he—"

"But it's true. I know it is," she said through numb lips.

Guilt and horror swirled inside her. *This is my fault. Lady Osgood is dead ... because of me. Because I didn't do the right thing ...*

"What are you talking about, Em?" Ambrose's tones pierced her dazed state. "And why are you pale as a ghost?"

She took a shaky breath, gripping the back of a chair. Whatever promise she'd made to Lady Osgood was null and void. The lady was dead ... there was no more need for secrets.

I failed her once. I cannot fail her again.

"Ambrose, we need to go to the magistrates," she said, her voice trembling.

"What? Why?" Her brother frowned.

"I have proof,"—she pushed the words through her constricted throat—"that Strathaven did indeed kill Lady Osgood."

"The devil you say."

Her gaze bounced to Mr. McLeod. Gone was the good-natured gentleman she knew. In his place was a fierce Scotsman who looked ready to do battle.

She exhaled. "I witnessed an incident. Two nights ago, between Strathaven and the victim."

"Give her a chance to explain, McLeod." Ambrose's tone held an edge of warning.

William McLeod nodded, but the fire didn't leave his eyes. "Go ahead and explain then, Miss Kent," he said grimly. "Tell us why you would accuse my brother of murder."

Chapter Four

"You have visitors, Your Grace."

At the sound of Jarvis' voice, Alaric's deerhounds, Phobos and Deimos, stirred from where they lay dozing by the fire. They cocked their grey, grizzled heads; noting no promise of food or an outdoor romp, they settled back onto the plush Aubusson. At his desk, Alaric put down the mining report that he'd been reading to distract himself from darker thoughts and gave his ancient butler a hard stare. Stooped and wrinkled, Jarvis returned his regard with unconcerned eyes.

"I gave you instructions to say that I'm not at home," Alaric said.

"I thought you might want to make an exception in this case." The old retainer's weathered face was set in its usual imperturbable lines. "'Tis Mr. McLeod who has come to call, and I've put him in the main drawing room."

William. Just bloody perfect. As if I don't have enough to plague me.

Alaric slapped the sheaf of papers down onto the blotter and shoved irritably away from his desk. "In the future," he said acidly, "I'd advise you to think less and follow orders more."

Jarvis didn't bat an eyelash. "I'll see to the refreshments for your guests."

"Wait a minute. Guests—as in plural? Who the devil ..."

Jarvis had already exited. The butler pretended deafness

whenever he didn't want to hear what Alaric had to say. His selective hearing ought to have gotten him dismissed, but both he and Alaric knew that would never happen. Jarvis had served the Strathavens all his life, his loyalty as steadfast as the rock upon which Strathmore Castle had been built.

During the years of the prior duke's reign, Jarvis had broken with his master's rules in only one arena as far as Alaric knew: the butler had shown kindness to a sick boy. With his antipathy toward any kind of weakness, the old duke had tried to cure Alaric's "malingering" by forbidding all pleasures from the sickroom. Windows were bolted shut, diversions removed. Meals of gruel and water were eaten by the light of a single candle.

By smuggling the occasional treat onto the supper tray or a book under Alaric's pillow, Jarvis had won Alaric's loyalty forevermore.

"Doesn't make him any less of an interfering codger," Alaric muttered.

In canine agreement, Phobos made a chuffing noise and rolled onto his back.

Letting out an aggrieved breath, Alaric stalked toward the drawing room. His foul mood deepened with each step. He could scarcely credit the hellish events of the past two days. Helpless rage burgeoned within him at the thought of Clara. She'd been murdered under his roof—because of him.

Someone had laced his whiskey with poison. Because the decanter had been smashed, its contents lost, he couldn't prove it, but it was the only explanation he could think of. With his one customary drink, he'd gotten ill and lost consciousness. With her three, Clara had paid the ultimate price.

Who had killed Clara? Who wanted him dead?

Possibilities whipped through his mind. Like any powerful man, he had his share of enemies, yet only one had threatened his life: Silas Webb. Alaric's fists clenched as he pictured the portly bastard with the piggish face, sparse black hair, and spectacles.

Around four months ago, Alaric had taken over a failing mining company. He'd formed a consortium of investors and sold stock in the company to raise additional capital. Within weeks, he'd turned United Mining around, and the venture was now poised for success. In the process of overhauling the dilapidated company, Alaric had fired its longtime man of business, Silas Webb. Webb's overwhelming incompetence—which had ranged from inaccurate ledger keeping to heinous expenditures—had sabotaged the already floundering enterprise.

Webb had been none too happy about his dismissal. He'd uttered threats as he'd been forcibly ejected from the premises. The week after Webb's dismissal, a rock had shattered the front window of the office.

To Alaric's mind, Silas Webb was the prime suspect in the poisoning, and he'd given the man's name to the investigating magistrates.

Fat lot of good that has done, he thought in disgust.

It had been two days since Clara's death, and the magistrates had made no progress. Their post-mortem examination had yielded "inconclusive" results on the cause of her death. Nor could they find any trace of Webb, who'd apparently gone missing. Finally, they'd failed to capitalize on the other possible lead: Lily Hutchins, one of the maids at Alaric's cottage, hadn't shown up for work since the murder, and none of his other staff knew of her whereabouts. Her sudden disappearance was too much of a coincidence to be overlooked.

Grimly, Alaric knew that he would have to take matters into his own hands and hire his own investigators. As if finding a killer wasn't enough, now he had to deal with his sodding half-brother.

Shoulders tensed, he entered the drawing room. Will stood by the windows facing the outside square. As always, the sight of his sibling stirred up a potent mix of emotions he didn't care for. Yet he cared even less for the shock of seeing Miss Emma Kent sitting there. Dressed in yellow, she looked as fresh as a daffodil on his green velvet settee.

What the devil is she doing here?

She appeared deep in discussion with the gentleman sitting beside her. They had their dark heads bent together, and Alaric couldn't make out their conversation. Whatever they were talking about, he didn't like the intimacy of their pose.

"To what do I owe this sterling pleasure?" he drawled.

They all turned to him, Miss Kent and the stranger with her rising from their seats.

"Hello, Alaric." Will's cautious tone underscored the uncomfortable state of affairs between them, half-brothers who'd lived most of their lives apart. Who had nothing in common but one parent and a history of animosity.

"I think you know why I'm here," his brother went on.

"Actually, I haven't the faintest idea ... Peregrine."

Will stiffened at the use of his hated first name.

A petty satisfaction, Alaric acknowledged, but one had to get one's pleasures where one could. Arching one brow, he added, "And you've brought guests along on this uninvited visit. What exceptional manners you have, little brother."

"Damn you, Alaric—" Will bit out.

"Please forgive the intrusion, Your Grace." Standing, the stranger was tall, close to Alaric's own height. He looked to be in his forties, and his most distinguishing feature was his gaze; the clear golden brown irises conveyed a disconcerting keenness.

"I'm Ambrose Kent, Mr. McLeod's partner in a private

enquiry business." The man bowed. "This is my sister, Miss Emma Kent."

"His Grace and I have met," she said.

The hostility in her voice, in her big, tea-colored eyes sliced into him. The reason for her presence dawned upon him. Incredulity spread like frost over his insides.

The bloody chit wouldn't dare.

"If memory serves, I didn't extend an invitation to call at our prior meeting," he said icily.

Miss Kent lifted her chin. "This isn't a social call."

"I asked the Kents to come." Will came toward him, bristling with temper. "To help you, you stubborn bastard!"

It never failed to amaze him that he and Will shared a father; in looks and temperament, they were nothing alike. Will was the golden child, the one everyone had fawned over. Robust and sturdy as a lad, he'd grown into a strapping Scotsman with a hot temper to match.

Alaric, on the other hand, had learned to control his impulses with a cool head. No one had spoiled or coddled him; like the god Ares of Greek lore who'd been trapped for years in a bronze jar without his parents noticing, no one would have missed Alaric if he disappeared. He'd been the dark horse all his life, and, aye, he knew how to play the role well enough.

Alaric infused his tone with amused condescension. "Why would *I* need their help?"

"Lady Osgood." Will spat the name, his hands on his hips.

"What about her?"

"You were found with a dead woman, Alaric—bluidy hell, it's all over the papers!"

The papers, as far as Alaric was concerned, were full of shite. The half-truths were worse than lies. Gossip raged about Clara's death; nothing was said of the attempt on his own. Since there'd been no witnesses and he'd suffered no lasting effects from his single shot of the adulterated whiskey, the world's collective ignorance of the facts wasn't surprising.

The magistrates had advised him to keep silent about his poisoning and not add fuel to the wildfire whilst they conducted their enquiry into the matter. He'd done so, not out of compliance with the useless bastards but because he wasn't going to sink to the level of the gossips. He was a nobleman; he wasn't about to give credence to scandal, plead his innocence to the ignorant masses.

Nonetheless, the rumors that he might somehow be involved in Clara's death infuriated him. The notion of Miss Kent adding to the misconceptions made red flicker at the edges of his vision.

He iced his temper. Strolling over to the hearth, he propped one arm against the mantel in a deliberately indolent pose. "You shouldn't believe everything you read, little brother."

"'Tis only because I *am* your kin that I'm giving you the benefit of the doubt," Will said darkly. "Miss Kent has told me she witnessed an incident two nights ago. 'Twas at my behest that she agreed to come today and clear up the misunderstanding instead of going straight to the magistrates."

"There is no misunderstanding, Mr. McLeod," Miss Kent said.

Her conviction tested his self-control. *Stupid, meddling chit.*

"Then why are you here?" he said scathingly.

"To say what I ought to have said that night." Though her cheeks were pale, she lifted her chin. "'Twas my fault for not insisting that Lady Osgood report you to the authorities. I was swayed by her fear for her reputation ... and my own fear that she would succumb to hysterics and do something she might regret. But I was wrong, and she is dead. And now the only thing left for me to do is see justice served."

His jaw ticked. "How, precisely, do you hope to accomplish that?"

"By demanding your signed confession," she said steadily.

By God, the termagant had pushed him too far. He stalked toward her. Kent blocked his path, but she held her brother back.

"Let His Grace say what he has to say to my face," she said.

"You want the truth, Miss Kent?" Alaric said with lethal softness. "Here it is for the last bloody time. I've never hurt Clara. I most definitely did not kill her. But I am going to find out who did and your interference will only get in my way."

"I *saw* you. You tied Lady Osgood up. You were *assaulting* her, and she begged you to stop!"

Damn her and her accusations. To make matters worse, he couldn't deny them without further besmirching Clara's reputation. Bad enough that she'd been found dead with him, a man not her husband; was he now to tell the world that she *enjoyed* being bound and, aye, spanked on occasion?

His chest tightened. Nay, he would protect her honor.

The way he ought to have protected her life.

"Is that true, Alaric?" Will bit out.

Devil take it. Why had he been under siege his whole life? Why was he now being attacked in his own home by his holier-than-thou brother, a righteous virgin, and some damned investigator? He was a duke, for Christ's sake, a bloody peer of the realm. He didn't have to answer to them—or to anyone.

"Miss Kent, as I said to you that night: you have no idea

what you're talking about. Lady Osgood told you nothing happened. You will leave it at that," he decreed with glacial finality.

"Do *not* tell me what to do. I know what I saw, and if you won't admit to it, I'll tell the magistrates myself!"

His temper surged. "Test me, pet—and I promise you won't like the results."

"Don't call me that. I'm not anyone's *pet*."

"Aye, and there's your problem."

Her eyes narrowed. "What is that supposed to mean?"

"It means that you need a man to keep a rein on you. To keep you occupied with your own damned life so you won't have the energy or time to meddle with mine," he said succinctly.

"How *dare* you."

Flags of pink stood out on her cheeks, and her eyes flashed rebelliously at him, her bosom rising and falling in swift surges beneath yellow silk. They were standing nearly toe to toe, neither backing down. Her defiance, her clean, feminine scent maddened him. His fingers flexed. He wanted to shake her for being so stubborn, so *wrong*. To haul her into his arms and kiss her until she admitted the error of her ways, surrendered to him completely—

"That's enough, Your Grace." Kent's warning pierced his haze of enraged lust.

Will gripped his arm. "Alaric, stand down."

He shook Will off, took a step back. Straightening his jacket, he got himself under control. "Get out." It took every ounce of self-discipline not to snarl the words.

"Emma, we're leaving," Kent said sharply.

Her cheeks blazing, she looked as if she might refuse. Then she took the arm Kent held out. If looks were daggers, her departing glare would have left Alaric full of holes.

Alone with his brother, Alaric felt the tension in the

room rise even higher, a warring miasma of past and present that clouded his faculties. The bitter fog sucked him into battle even as he struggled to master himself.

"You haven't changed one bit," Will said in disgust. "I don't know why I bother trying."

"I don't recall asking for your help."

"Ma was right. A leopard won't ever change his spots," Will shot back.

Words catapulted reflexively. "I suppose your mother died an uppity bitch then."

The next instant, Will had him by the lapels. "You take that back, you bastard! My ma was the kindest, most loving woman who ever lived."

Alaric shoved his brother off with equal force. "To *you*, maybe. Although we shared a household, we grew up in different families, little brother."

"What the bluidy hell is that supposed to mean?"

The fact that Will remained ignorant to the truth enraged Alaric further. How pleasant it must be to wear a halo that blinded one from life's ugliness.

"It means one of us had a loving home and the other didn't," he said tightly.

"You chose to go to Strathaven!" Will threw up his arms. "It was *your* choice. You went because you wanted money and prestige more than a real family."

Better to be hated than pitied. Let him think what he wants.

With utter sangfroid, Alaric said, "Can you blame me for preferring a castle over a cottage?"

"Even that wasn't enough for you," Will said bitterly. "After our parents died, you had the chance to take me in, to make things right between us. God knows there was room to spare in that bluidy castle you lived in. But *you* talked our uncle out of it, made sure that I wasn't extended a welcome. Thanks to you, I had no place to go but the regiment!"

You think the army was bad? You think you know the first thing about violence and brutality? At least on the battlefield, little brother, you could see the bayonets and bullets coming ...

"Are you quite finished with your rant?" He buffed his nails against his sleeve. "I have appointments to attend to. The business of being a duke, you know."

Will looked ready to explode. "I'm finished alright. Finished with you for *good*."

Alaric let him reach the doorway before speaking. "By the by, do send my regards to that lovely wife of yours. 'Tis a shame I don't see more of Annabel—more than I already have, that is."

To his grim satisfaction, his barbed reference made Will's oaths echo through the halls. Moments later, the front door slammed. Alaric exhaled harshly. He raked both hands through his hair, willed the pounding in his temples to stop.

A rattling tray heralded Jarvis' arrival. His rheumy eyes scanned the empty room, the wrinkles on his face deepening. "Where has everyone gone?"

"To hell for all I care," Alaric snapped back.

Chapter Five

That evening after her bath, Emma collapsed on her bed. For one of the rare times in her life, she was too tired to do anything. As if sensing her exhaustion, Tabitha came to curl up against her side. Emma stroked the cat's soft, striped grey fur as she stared up at the pink canopy, her thoughts as swirling as the damask.

Accompanied by Ambrose, she'd given her testimony to the magistrates that afternoon.

She'd had a moral duty to make that report. Her chest tightened as she thought of poor Lady Osgood. There was nothing more that Emma could do, yet her nerves were as tightly strung as a clothesline.

If Strathaven thinks he can intimidate me into silence just because he is duke, then he is in for a rude awakening, she thought fiercely.

As far as she was concerned, justice knew no class distinctions. A murderer was a murderer, whether he was a duke or a crossing sweep. And the *nerve* of the cad, telling her she needed to be kept under rein! Her life had plenty of purpose, and she didn't need any man—least of all *him*—telling her what to do. Never had a person angered her so much—or affected her so strangely.

Just the thought of him sent a buzzing awareness through her. In his presence, all her senses were heightened. She recalled the crackling hostility between them in the drawing room. As he'd towered over her, his lean, muscular frame had radiated leashed power. Silver had flashed in his pale eyes, illuminating for an instant the tempest of emotions he'd held in check. Barely.

What would happen if he lost control?

A rapping on the door jerked Emma back to the present. Her breath was puffing from her lips, her skin misted with perspiration. As she sat up, her breasts brushed against her nightclothes, the tips oddly sensitive and tingling.

"Emma, are you awake?" Her sister Dorothea's gentle voice drifted through the door.

"I—I'll be right there," she said.

She took a moment to compose herself; she had no wish to worry her sisters. When she went to unlock the door, Thea, Violet, Polly, and Primrose filed in like a troop of cheerful ghosts in their voluminous lawn night rails.

"Aren't you supposed to be in bed?" Emma said to the two youngest.

While Polly looked abashed, Rosie's emerald eyes sparkled with mischief.

"Yes," the latter said merrily. "So hurry and close the door before Mama catches us!"

With her flaxen hair and flawless face and form, Rosie Kent was a stunning miniature of Marianne. At sixteen, the spirited girl was already beginning to turn heads, and Ambrose joked that he dreaded the day of Rosie's coming out for surely he'd have to start carrying a shotgun to fend off her suitors.

As Emma closed the door, her middle sister Violet declared, "Last one to the bed is the rotten egg!" and, amidst muffled squeals and giggles, the four girls made a mad dash for the destination.

Relieved for the return to normalcy, Emma dragged a chair to the side of the bed. She sat and found herself under the scrutiny of four pairs of bright, inquisitive eyes. Her sisters had arranged themselves along the length of bed, with Violet at the foot, Polly and Rosie in the middle, and Thea at the head.

As usual, Violet spoke first. She sat cross-legged, her chestnut hair tumbling down her back. Agile and energetic, she gave the impression of constant motion.

"Start at the beginning, Em," she said, "and don't leave anything out."

"The beginning of what?"

Vi rolled her caramel-colored eyes. "Your visit to the magistrates' office today, of course."

For the time being, Ambrose and Emma had both agreed to keep mum on the subject of Lady Osgood's murder. They'd thought it best to protect their younger siblings from the gruesome details for as long as possible. Protecting a Kent from her own curiosity was never an easy task, however.

"How did you find out?" Emma said with a sigh.

"We didn't mean to snoop." Thea's hazel eyes were soft with apology. She rested against the headboard, her hands gracefully stroking Tabitha who lay belly-up and purring in her lap. "We found out by accident."

A year younger than Emma, Dorothea was the gentlest of the Kents. Emma attributed it to Thea's constitution, which had been frail since childhood. Although her health had grown more robust, Thea continued to favor more sedate pursuits, and Emma thought proudly that her sister's performance at the pianoforte could compare with that of any fine London lady.

"Thea found out by accident. *I* snooped," Vi said with aplomb. "I asked Millie the chambermaid to ask John the groom where you and Ambrose had gone all day. Since John has eyes for Millie, he told her straightaway. Thea overheard me telling Polly and Primrose about it."

"You're not supposed to encourage gossip amongst the servants, Violet," Emma chided.

"Pish posh. Stop trying to change the subject," her incorrigible sister replied.

"Yes, do tell." Rosie's smile could charm a bird from a tree, and her tone was just short of wheedling. "You wouldn't want us to perish from curiosity, would you?"

"You should tell us, Emma, for your sake if not ours," Polly put in.

Emma's youngest sister sat with her arms hugging her knees. The womanhood which had begun to blossom so radiantly in Rosie hadn't yet unfurled in Polly. At sixteen, she was still a small, thin girl with wavy hair that was neither blond nor brown but a range of shades in between. To Emma, her baby sister possessed a unique beauty: Polly's solemn features exuded quiet dignity, a blend of wisdom and innocence in her aquamarine eyes.

At times, those remarkable eyes seemed to see too deeply. Back in Chudleigh Crest, there'd been whispers about Polly being "odd," which had made the sensitive girl retreat into shyness. As a result, Emma and the rest of the siblings were particularly protective of her.

Family always stood together.

"Why for my sake, dear?" she asked.

"Because something's bothering you," Polly said with her quiet perceptiveness. "You've always said that we could come to you with anything. So you should feel free to talk to us in return."

"You haven't been yourself, Em. Even *I* can see that," Vi added.

"We just want to help," Rosie chimed in.

"But only if you wish us to," Thea said.

"For heaven's sake, you win." Amused and touched at the same time, Emma shook her head. "What was I thinking?

Trying to refuse a band of Kents?"

"And Harry's not even here." The gruff wistfulness in Violet's voice gave away how much she missed their brother, her favorite sibling rival. "He would have added a barrage of logic to the mix."

"What happened, Emma?" Rosie prompted.

Emma debated what to tell them. She wouldn't lie—that wasn't the Kent way—but she didn't want to spoil the girls' innocence, either. In the end, she compromised, acknowledging that she had witnessed an altercation between Strathaven and Lady Osgood and carefully omitting the explicit details of what she'd seen.

"What a blackguard!" Vi exclaimed nonetheless. "I'm glad you walloped him with your reticule. If I'd been there, I would have planted a facer to finish him off!" Her fist swung to mimic the motion.

"Why hasn't Mr. McLeod mentioned having a duke for a brother?" Thea asked, her brow pleating.

"I don't think Mr. McLeod and Strathaven are close." Considering the animosity Emma had witnessed between the two, that might be the understatement of the year. What had driven a wedge between the brothers? she wondered. "According to Ambrose, Mr. McLeod wants to find success on his own merits and doesn't want it bandied about that he's heir presumptive to a duke."

"And Strathaven's not just any duke, he's the *Devil Duke*." This came from Rosie, the resident Society expert. "According to the gossip rags, he's as wicked as they come. As I recall from *Debrett's*, he wasn't even the next in line for the duchy—he only got the title after two distant relatives ahead of him in the succession mysteriously died."

"Gadzooks," Violet breathed.

"There's more." Rosie's voice lowered to a dramatic timbre. "There were whispers of cruelty during his first marriage. To this day, some say the duchess was fleeing from him when the ship she was on went under."

Gasps went up in the room.

Emma's nape tingled. "Why is a man like that still welcomed in Society?"

"He's more than welcomed—the *ton* panders to him," Rosie said. "People might say things behind his back, but they don't dare give him the cut direct. He's too rich and powerful. Now he's looking to secure his dynasty with an heir, and according to the *on dit*, his requirements for a wife are rather peculiar."

Emma frowned. "In what way?"

"He's made it clear he expects complete obedience from his wife. An heir and no trouble. Some say that the marriage contract spells out specific *consequences*,"—Rosie's green eyes were very wide—"for any violation of his rules."

"Consequences?" Violet said in puzzled tones. "Does he plan to send her to bed without supper? Take away her riding privileges?"

"I have no idea. They don't tell the really good details to girls," Rosie said with a sigh.

Emma scowled. "And what about him? Is he proposing to be a model of husbandly propriety in return?"

"The *Devil Duke*?" Rosie rolled her eyes. "I think not. He's notorious for his paramours."

Emma shook her head. "Why would *any* woman in her right mind accept such terms?"

To her, marriage ought to be a meeting of equals. A coming together of minds and hearts. She'd seen the strength of the bond between her parents and between Ambrose and Marianne. Although she'd never known such a connection with a man, she'd settle for no less if she ever married.

"Um, jewels? Untold wealth and privilege?" Rosie's

moon-bright tresses rippled over her shoulders as she shrugged. "Prior to the Osgood scandal, ladies were lining up in droves."

"At least the duke is frank about his expectations." Thea, bless her heart, always thought the best of everyone. "One cannot fault a man for being honest."

"Only for being a *murderer*," Vi said with a snort.

"If the duke is a dangerous man and you've crossed him," Polly said anxiously, "do you have anything to worry about, Emma?"

Emma gave her youngest sister a reassuring smile. "There's no need to fret, dearest. I've already given my testimony, and the matter is in the hands of the magistrates now. In all likelihood, Strathaven and I will never cross paths again."

Quelling a sudden shiver, she prayed she was right.

Chapter Six

"We've been through this before," Alaric said coldly.

On the other side of his desk, the pair of magistrates shifted in their seats.

"Yes, Your Grace." The one on the right was named Dixon, and he was plump and prone to sweat. He patted a handkerchief against his shiny pate. "In light of new information, however, we'd like to ask you a few more questions, if we may."

New information—supplied by Emma Kent, no doubt.

A muscle ticked in Alaric's jaw. The blasted chit had wasted no time in making good on her threat. Thanks to her testimony, the magistrates' office was now interrogating *him* instead of investigating Silas Webb or other possible suspects. Before the authorities had merely been incompetent; now they were actively wasting his time.

Alaric's temples throbbed, anger and frustration battering at his self-control. It didn't help matters that he'd slept poorly for the past three nights. Images of Clara, unmoving upon the carpet, made him toss and turn. That he could understand; he wouldn't rest until he saw justice done for her.

What he couldn't comprehend was *Emma Kent* showing up in his dreams as well. He'd woken up sweating, his fists clenching the bedclothes. His heart pounded with fury while his erect cock tented the sheets. In the crazed twilight, he hadn't known what he yearned for more: to wring her neck or fuck her senseless.

What the devil is the matter with me? Why do I lust for a chit who's done nothing but wreak havoc in my life?

His obsession with her was madness itself.

"Get on with it," he clipped out.

"Thank you, Your Grace." Dobbs, the other magistrate, was tall and thin, his papery-looking skin stretched tight over his bony features. He held a notebook and pencil in hand. "How would you describe your relationship with Lady Osgood?"

"Be more specific."

"Would you say you were on good terms with the victim?" Dobbs rephrased.

For Christ's sake. I'd just fucked her. Is that good enough terms for you? "Yes."

"No trouble of any kind between you?"

"No."

"You didn't have an altercation with Lady Osgood at,"— Dobbs consulted his notebook, "Lady Buckley's ball earlier that evening?"

Goddamn Emma Kent. This is all her fault.

Alaric's fists clenched under the desk. "I did not. I will consider any rumors to the contrary slanderous—and take legal action against all who repeat such libel."

"Understood, Your Grace." Clearing his throat, Dixon said, "And there were no witnesses during the time you and Lady Osgood were, ahem, together at the cottage? No servants who might have noticed anything?"

"As I've said before, the purpose of the cottage is privacy. The staff leaves at dusk and does not return until noon."

"Beg pardon, Your Grace. We were just confirming that there were no witnesses to the victim's poisoning—or, ahem, yours," Dobbs said.

Incensed by the speculative glances exchanged between

the pair, Alaric said cuttingly, "You do not need witnesses. You have my word as a peer of the realm. Now have you made any progress on the missing maid or Silas Webb?"

"No, Your Grace." Dixon wiped his brow. "That is, we've nothing new to report on Miss Hutchins. We have, however, searched Mr. Webb's office."

"And?"

"It appears he has vacated the premises—and rather hastily, I might add. He didn't take much with him, and, according to the landlord, he left no forwarding address."

"We'll keep looking for him, of course," Dobbs mumbled.

Capital. Now I can sleep at night. Disgusted, Alaric stood to signal the end of the interview.

The pair of blundering idiots scrambled to their feet.

"Thank you for your time, Your Grace—" Dixon began.

"Then do not continue to waste it," he snapped.

After the magistrates' departure, Alaric stood, hands shoved in his pockets, staring out the window at the immaculate green square surrounded by townhouses. Typically the sight calmed him, reminded him of how far he'd come. Once he'd only dreamed of such privilege; now, through a combination of fate and hard work, he had an ancient title, estates in England and Scotland, and the power and wealth to do anything he wanted.

So why did peace *still* elude him?

Why was he always under siege? Why did everyone—his family, Laura, the *ton*, even these magisterial lack wits—try to bring him down? What was so loathsome about him that he invited continual attack?

Bitterly, he wondered if contentment was destined to remain beyond his reach. Perhaps happiness was a mirage, the way Strathmore Castle had appeared like a refuge ... and Laura had seemed like love. As he looked out into the empty green expanse, a pair of well-dressed children—a dark-haired boy and girl—entered his field of vision. They skipped ahead of their nanny, laughing as they ran past the gate into the park. A pair of happy, pink-cheeked imps.

Something in his chest throbbed. An old bruise that never healed.

Or a foolish longing that wouldn't die.

Cursing, he scrubbed a hand over his face. *Pull it together, man.* Being targeted for murder was no excuse to turn into a maudlin fool. The world be damned: he would take matters into his own hands as he'd always done. If he'd learned anything, it was that the only one he could rely upon was himself.

Take control and take action: that was his motto.

He'd already retained Runners to hunt for Silas Webb and the missing maid. He'd hired on extra footmen for personal security. At this point, there was naught to do but carry on; he wasn't going to let the threat of murder interfere with his routine.

He was considering a stop at Gentleman Jackson's or the newer Apollo's Academy for a round of boxing when a carriage led by matched grays stopped in front of his steps. The man who descended was tall and fit, dressed with puritanical severity in a dark jacket, trousers, and an unadorned waistcoat. The only note of color was the tawny hair curling beneath the brim of his plain hat.

Minutes later, Alaric received his visitor in the study.

He'd met Gabriel Ridgley, the Marquess of Tremont, at Oxford, and the two had become fast friends. Back then, Tremont had been the spare to the title, and he'd left midway through his studies to live with some wealthy relative abroad. He and Alaric had lost touch; not until last year had they come into contact again. Alaric had been surprised by how somber his once mischievous friend had become.

Now Tremont didn't game or drink to excess and dedicated himself to the restoration of his estates. Although his wife had died some time ago, there were no rumors of him taking a lover or mistress; he was either a monk—which Alaric doubted—or perfectly discreet. Owing to his exemplary behavior, the *ton* had dubbed Tremont the *Angel Marquess*.

Time hadn't eroded all of Alaric and Tremont's commonalities, however. They discovered an avid shared interest in business. Unlike other peers who didn't deign to dirty their hands in business matters, the two spent many a night at their club discussing the merits of various financial schemes. When it came to money, they had a similar philosophy: the more the better.

After exchanging greetings, the men settled into the wingchairs by the fire.

"How are you, Strathaven?" Tremont said.

"I'm fine," Alaric said curtly. "Why shouldn't I be?"

"Because of the scandal." Tremont leveled a grey gaze at him. "The gossips are saying someone stepped forward with proof that you were involved in Lady Osgood's death."

Bloody Emma Kent. I'm going to wring her neck.

"The testimony is utter claptrap."

"I don't doubt it." Tremont steepled his hands. "Unfortunately, it's having an impact on our venture."

Hell's teeth. The news pierced Alaric's gut like an arrow. Tremont had been one of the first investors he'd tapped to join the United Mining venture, and their partnership had proved fruitful. In just over a month, they would hold a General Meeting to finalize an expansion plan that would include the purchase of several key mines in Scotland. When the vote went through, Alaric was certain stock prices would hit the roof.

Everything had been going according to plan ... until now.

"How bad is it?" he said grimly.

"We've lost a half-dozen investors, Surrey and Burrowes amongst them."

"*Damnation.*" Alaric's hands clenched the arms of the chair at the mention of two of their scheme's largest investors.

"That might only be the start. Noblemen catch a whiff of scandal, and they bolt like it's a fire. No one wants to be caught in a burning house." Tremont paused before saying bluntly, "You should know that the current business has also resurrected talk about your previous marriage."

From the grave, Laura's twisted beauty taunted him.

You don't love me—you're not capable of it! You're selfish, cruel, and black-hearted. Her cornflower eyes glimmered with rage, her red lips taking on a malignant curve. *I'm going to make sure everyone knows what a bastard you are.*

Cold, unadulterated fury clawed at Alaric. Control was slipping from his grasp, chaos swirling around him. Clara was dead, a murderer on the loose. His business plans were suddenly in jeopardy. And now his past was rising like a dark tide ...

All because of Emma Kent—the lies she'd told about him.

All of this was *her* doing.

"I'll see to it that my name is cleared," he vowed. "Whoever poisoned Clara and me will be brought to justice."

The marquess' brow furrowed. "An attempt was made on *your* life as well?"

Alaric hesitated before saying, "Yes."

Both he and Tremont were men who valued privacy, and they did not typically discuss matters outside of business.

Given the scandal's impact upon their venture, however, Alaric decided to make an exception and gave Tremont a brief summary of events.

Tremont's frown deepened at the mention of Silas Webb. "I recall Webb was irate when you dismissed him. But would he resort to murder?"

"I intend to find out."

"You must take care. Murder is a dangerous business."

"Evidently so is scandal. Try to keep the investors placated. In the meanwhile, I'll put a stop to the rumor that I killed Clara."

Tremont's eyebrows went up. "How do you plan to do that?"

By dealing with the cause of the fiasco herself.

Jaw taut, Alaric said, "I have my ways. Let's leave it at that."

"As you wish. For what it's worth, I am sorry for your misfortune."

If there was anything Alaric despised, it was pity.

"What do you know about misfortune?" he said in cool tones.

Tremont's gaze darkened, grooves forming around his mouth. Standing, he executed a stiff bow. "Good day, Your Grace."

After the marquess departed, Alaric was reminded that he and Tremont did have something other than business in common: they were both widowers. The resemblance ended there, however. Tremont's lady had been known for her charity and kindness, and their marriage had been accounted a happy one, with an heir to show for it.

Whereas Alaric's duchess had been a lying bitch whose efforts to manipulate him had led not only to her own demise but that of their only child. His son, Charlie ...

He felt a warning cracking inside, like the rushing of

dark water under ice. The currents dragged at him, pulled him toward the vortex. He struggled for purchase, for control against the raging chaos.

No—the past is done. Look forward. Address the problem at hand.

His fists clenched. Yes, that was what he needed to do.

Fix the problem.

All he had to do was find her.

Chapter Seven

"Do you have a minute, Emma dear?" a husky female voice said.

At the escritoire, Emma looked up from her book as her sister-in-law entered the drawing room. As usual, Marianne exuded glamour. Caught up in an elegant twist, her silver-blond curls framed her flawless features, and her emerald promenade dress—which matched her vivid eyes—clung lovingly to her willowy figure.

"I have all the time in the world." Emma tried not to sigh.

Why can't Ambrose give my dream of being an investigator a chance?

The business with Strathaven, she thought darkly, hadn't helped her cause. Ever since she'd reported the duke to the magistrates, her brother had become even *more* overprotective. The authorities had promised to keep her identity confidential, but aspects of her testimony had leaked nonetheless. Rumors that the duke had killed Lady Osgood were running rampant, and Ambrose had insisted that she stay at home until the business blew over.

Ever astute, Marianne said, "Ambrose wants what is best for you."

"I know." Now Emma felt disloyal on top of it all.

All morning, she'd been as restless as a gypsy. She knew she'd done the right thing where Strathaven was concerned, yet the thought of him made her feel on edge, filled her with a disquieting, buzzing energy. If only she could bury herself in tasks at the office—she needed something to *do*, a distraction. Out of desperation, she'd dug up her book of household remedies.

She waved to the open volume in front of her. "I was researching a salve for Mr. Pitt's joints and the second footman's back. I hope you don't mind my using your desk—"

"Of course I don't mind." Marianne frowned. "As I've said before, my home is yours."

Marianne *had* told her this many a time, yet Emma couldn't quite squelch the discomfort of residing in another's woman house. She supposed she'd grown too accustomed to running her own household. Back in Chudleigh Crest, the cottage had been her kingdom; she'd arranged things to her own design, had come and gone as she'd pleased.

"I wanted to catch you whilst we have a few moments' privacy." Marianne sat on the snowy chaise longue, her skirts fluttering gracefully around her. "The girls are with the dancing master, and Edward is still sleeping."

Plopping herself on the adjacent settee, Emma said with sympathy, "Did he have another bad night?"

Edward, Marianne and Ambrose's seven-year-old, had recently started having night terrors. During the episodes, the little lad was inconsolable and difficult to wake.

"Poor thing was beside himself. I stayed with him until dawn," Marianne said ruefully.

"I remember when Polly suffered a similar bout of nightmares. The only thing that helped was a glass of warm milk and a biscuit."

"I'll keep that in mind." Clearing her throat, Marianne said, "What I really wish to discuss with you, however, concerns the Duke of Strathaven. Ambrose told me everything last night. I do wish the two of you had consulted me before bringing the matter to the magistrates."

Emma's shoulders stiffened. Not because her brother had shared this information with Marianne—she knew he and his wife kept no secrets from one another—but because of the judgment she heard in her sister-in-law's tone.

She lifted her chin. "All I did was report a crime that I witnessed."

"I know you meant well, dearest. You always do. But this is London, and things are different here than in Chudleigh Crest."

"I'm aware of that."

"Are you?" The hesitation was uncharacteristic of Marianne and put Emma on guard. "I can't help but wonder if you acted too hastily. No, don't look so put out, dearest—I mean no insult to you. Or to Ambrose, for that matter. I know you both believed you were right to go to Bow Street. I do have some information, however, that might have influenced your decision."

"What information could change the truth? I know what I saw," Emma said stubbornly.

Marianne's lips formed a faint smile. "How you remind me of Ambrose, dear."

"I'll take that as a compliment."

"As it was meant to be. The integrity that runs in the Kent bloodline is a quality that I admire greatly." Marianne's shoulders lifted in an elegant shrug. "Until Ambrose came into my life, I did not concern myself greatly with morality or living by anyone's rules but my own."

"You're a wonderful wife and mama. And you've been nothing but kindness to the rest of us Kents," Emma argued.

"I am glad you think so."

Marianne's sincerity sent a squiggle of guilt through Emma. Since moving to London, Emma had felt a slight degree of tension toward her sister-in-law. It wasn't the other's fault; all Marianne had done was take the Kents under her wing, treating them to luxury after luxury. Yet in doing so, she'd inadvertently made Emma ... extraneous. When it came to leading a fashionable life, Marianne was an expert guide—and Emma as necessary as a fifth wheel.

Shame suffused Emma. She didn't want to be ungrateful; she did love her sister-in-law.

"I know you have our best interests at heart," she said, flushing.

"I do," Marianne agreed, "which is why I must talk to you about Strathaven."

"What about him?" Emma said warily.

"While I cannot lay claim to being as honorable as you and Ambrose, I do have my areas of expertise, and one of them happens to be the *ton*. Simply put, I have access to a surfeit of gossip. In this instance, there are things I know about the duke that you do not."

With trepidation, Emma said, "Such as?"

"First off, his so-called victim was not a stranger to him."

"I know they were acquainted. In fact, I believe Strathaven might have had some hold over Lady Osgood. He probably forced her to his cottage and—"

"They were lovers, Emma."

Chill trickled down Emma's spine. "Lovers?"

Marianne nodded. "From what I gather, their *affaire* was not longstanding. They kept it discreet owing to the fact that Lady Osgood is married."

Emma's mind was working furiously. Goodness, Lady Osgood and Strathaven had been amorously involved? "But it doesn't change what I saw. He was hurting her," she blurted. "I saw the duke restraining Lady Osgood. He tied her up, said he would make her *beg*."

A pause.

"As to that, there might be another explanation,"

Marianne said.

"Such as?" Other than the obvious, Emma couldn't think of a single one.

"There have been a few whispers. About Strathaven's proclivities." Peachy color stained Marianne's high cheekbones. "You see, dear, sometimes the relationship between a man and a woman can take … unusual forms."

"I don't understand."

"I don't suppose you do." Marianne sighed. "I should hate to spoil your lovely innocence. Suffice it to say that, in hurting his lover, Strathaven may not have actually been hurting her. Do you see what I mean?"

"No." That explanation was as clear as the mud on London's streets.

"Good lord, this is more difficult than I thought," Marianne muttered.

They were interrupted by a knock. Mr. Pitt appeared. "Good morning, madam," he said with a bow. "Mrs. McLeod wishes to see if you and Miss Emma are receiving at present."

Emma's unease grew. Mrs. McLeod wanted to see her? It was too early for a social call.

Marianne waved her hand. "Send her in. And do bring some tea—the Ceylon, I think." When the butler departed, she said, "We'll continue this conversation later, Emma."

As Marianne rose to greet their guest, Emma hung back shyly. In the presence of the older ladies, she felt like an awkward miss. Her sister-in-law was a celebrated beauty, and Annabel McLeod, with her fiery tresses and smoldering violet eyes, possessed an aura of sensual femininity.

What would it be like to possess such mystique? Emma wondered.

She saw herself as a sister, daughter, even a mother of sorts, but as a … woman? A wife? Mundane and forthright, she'd never attracted much male attention. Never inspired passion in any man except, on occasion, over her cooking (the one marriage proposal she'd received, from the village vicar, had been motivated by his ardor for her Sunday supper). In truth, back in Chudleigh Crest, she'd had a reputation for being a bit of a termagant, and it hadn't boosted her allure.

Was she supposed to stay silent when the butcher tried to sell her an overpriced cut of meat? Was she to just accept the thatcher's word that the flimsy excuse of a roof he'd put on would hold up against the elements? Her strong will had been forged by years of taking care of her family, her determination a trait that had helped her cope with poverty, illness, and loss.

Nonetheless, she'd begun to suspect that her managing nature might preclude her from falling in love. As she'd told Ambrose, she had yet to meet a man who made her want to relinquish her independence. Who tempted her to give up control over her own future.

Out of nowhere, Strathaven's face appeared in her mind's eye, his slashing cheekbones and gleaming jade eyes. Her belly quivered at the memory of his lean physique, so close to hers that she'd felt the heat emanating from him, his spicy male scent infusing her senses ...

Her heart raced. *That's just ... fear. You were afraid of him and rightly so.*

"To what do we owe the pleasure of your visit, Annabel?" Marianne said when they'd all seated themselves.

Mrs. McLeod's gaze settled on Emma. "I won't beat around the bush. It's about Strathaven."

Though the declaration came as no surprise, Emma tensed, her hands clenching in her lap.

"Mr. McLeod doesn't know I'm here," the lady went on, swishing her russet skirts into place. "He's quite irritated with his brother at the moment."

"I can't blame him. From what Ambrose told me, the meeting between them didn't go well," Marianne murmured.

Mrs. McLeod sighed, shaking her head. "Men can be such foolish creatures."

"On that, we cannot agree more."

The ladies shared a smile before Mrs. McLeod turned to Emma. "It's always been that way between McLeod and his older brother," she explained. "Since I've known them, they can't be in a room together for more than a few minutes before they're at each other's throats."

"Strathaven started it," Emma said. "He was rude. Mr. McLeod was only trying to help."

"Yes, well, that's why I'm here. Once my husband's temper wears off, I am certain he will regret not doing more to help his brother. They are kin, after all, even though they were raised apart. To a Scotsman, blood is thicker than water."

"Why were they raised apart?" Emma couldn't help but ask.

"It's a lengthy tale and not mine to divulge. Suffice it to say, those two have had a long and difficult brotherhood—but it doesn't mean that they don't care about each other. And for all Strathaven's ..." Mrs. McLeod waved a hand, as if trying to summon an accurate description of the man.

"Arrogance? Conceit? Holier-than-thou attitude?" Emma suggested.

Mrs. McLeod's lips twitched. "Given your short acquaintance, you seem to know him well."

"One doesn't have to be acquainted with His Grace long to glean those facts."

"Be that as it may, arrogance doesn't make a man capable of murder. Strathaven is McLeod's brother, and I cannot believe a man who shares my husband's blood could do anything so vile." Mrs. McLeod's expression grew somber. "Furthermore, the duke once did me a great favor, one I'll never be able to repay. I do not speak of that time,"— shadows flitted through her violet gaze—"but in truth, McLeod and I owe him our very happiness. Strathaven does have a heart; he's not as wicked as he likes to have others believe."

Emma tried to digest that notion. Could that be *possible*? Uneasily, she turned the facts over in her mind, saw the duke overpowering his victim in the garden, heard Lady Osgood's pleas for mercy ...

"Sometimes things are not as they appear." Mrs. McLeod gave a delicate cough. "Lovers, for instance, might engage in, er, behavior that could seem ... odd. To an onlooker, I mean."

Perplexed, Emma said, "Marianne was trying to explain this earlier."

"With no more luck than you, Annabel." Briskly, Marianne said, "To be blunt, Emma, some men have a need for control more than others. The duke is said to be such a man."

Strathaven's voice echoed in Emma's head. *I'm going to do whatever I want. And you're going to enjoy it.* She shuddered. She had no doubts whatsoever that the duke was a dominating brute.

"Which is why he must be stopped," she said fiercely. "So he cannot hurt anyone else again."

"But, you see, there are ladies who don't, ahem, mind such behavior from a man," Mrs. McLeod said, her cheeks reddening. "In fact, they might welcome it."

Incredulity and confusion filled Emma; what the other was saying didn't make an ounce of sense. "That's ridiculous. Lady Osgood was *begging* for mercy. I heard her."

"Are you certain it wasn't part of a lovers' game? Perhaps

you misunderstood—"

"I misunderstood nothing." She might not be as sophisticated or beautiful as the other two, but her senses were fully functioning. "I know what I witnessed. Nothing can change those facts, and I'll not take back the truth."

The ladies exchanged glances.

With a sigh, Mrs. McLeod said, "My brother-in-law is an odd, haughty gentleman, one who does not march to anyone's drum but his own. I urge you, however, to reconsider what you witnessed and to ask yourself if you *truly* saw the duke hurting Lady Osgood in any way."

Emma frowned as the events replayed in her head. Lady Osgood had *begged* Strathaven to stop, and she'd been tied up, blindfolded ... Yet had Emma seen any real evidence of injury? Had she witnessed the duke lay a hand on the lady?

No, but that is because I prevented it ... didn't I?

Mrs. McLeod leaned forward, took one of Emma's cold hands in both of her own. "A man's life is at stake. Despite his faults and devil-may-care attitude, Strathaven has suffered much. A little over two years ago, he lost his wife and son in a grievous accident."

Emma's heart skipped a beat. He'd had a *son*? "But they say he was cruel to his wife," she blurted. "That she died fleeing him."

"Where did you hear that?" Marianne said.

"Rosie," Emma admitted.

Marianne's gaze cast heavenward. "My daughter may think she's an expert on the *ton*, but she is only sixteen. At that age, she and her friends are as impressionable as wax. Believe me, she doesn't know half as much as she believes she does."

"So the rumors aren't true?"

"Years ago, I met the Duchess of Strathaven. She was undoubtedly beautiful: a blond, blue-eyed angel. The *ton*—

and gentlemen in particular—adored her." Marianne's eyes narrowed. "Beneath Lady Laura's charming exterior, however, I sensed a manipulative nature. I cannot say whether the vitriol she spewed about the duke was true or not, only that her own behavior was far from blameless."

Leaning forward, Mrs. McLeod added, "It is a little known fact—and I would prefer it remain that way—that the duchess was once engaged to Mr. McLeod."

Emma's jaw slackened. "What?"

"She met Strathaven at her own engagement party to Mr. McLeod and promptly jilted one sibling for the other. The duke must shoulder his share of the blame, of course, yet what sort of a woman would come between two brothers?" Mrs. McLeod said with distaste.

Mind whirling, Emma struggled to absorb the new facts. She recalled something else Rosie had mentioned. "What about the heirs? The two who were ahead of Strathaven in the succession and who mysteriously died?"

"My daughter was your source again?" Marianne said dryly.

Emma nodded.

"While murder and mayhem make for excellent novels, rarely is real life as exciting. People die all the time." Her sister-in-law shrugged. "Heirs included."

Could it be true? Could the rumors about the duke be nothing more than hearsay?

Excited voices and footsteps sounded outside the drawing room.

"The dancing lesson must be over," Marianne said.

"And I must return before McLeod suspects anything." Rising in a rustle of silk, Mrs. McLeod took Emma's hand and gave it a squeeze. "Promise me you'll think about what we discussed?"

After Mrs. McLeod departed and Marianne went to shepherd the family to their various activities for the day, Emma decided to go out for a short stroll. Needing solitude, she didn't call for a maid. She walked along the tree-lined streets of Mayfair, the sun beating down upon her bonnet as thoughts ricocheted in her head.

What on earth were Mrs. McLeod and Marianne talking about?

How could Strathaven's hurting of Lady Osgood be part of a *game*? How could his controlling behavior be anything but dangerous? And why would any woman welcome being forced to submit to a man? 'Twas ludicrous and yet ...

Perplexed, Emma considered whether her perception of what transpired in Lady Buckley's garden could have been distorted. Had her dislike of Strathaven's arrogance somehow prejudiced her, made her misjudge the situation? But, no, she *knew* what she saw. From the time she was thirteen and her mama had passed, she'd relied on her own judgment to take care of herself and her family. Her ability to make sound decisions was one of her few virtues.

She could hear her papa's voice: *The only good is knowledge, and the only evil is ignorance.*

Until now, she'd never found it difficult to discern right from wrong, fact from falsehood. She'd viewed the world in black and white, yet where Strathaven was concerned, everything seemed to be ... grey. A stormy, turbulent shade that made it difficult to know what was what.

Was he a wicked rake or a grieving father? A coldhearted aristocrat or the caring brother to whom the McLeods apparently owed their happiness? An arrogant, abusive brute—or a lover who'd been engaged in some sort of incomprehensible game?

Chewing on her lip, Emma turned the corner onto a quiet street lined by sleepy mansions. What if Mrs. McLeod

and Marianne were right, and she had somehow
misunderstood the situation? Goodness, she couldn't live
with herself if she had wrongly accused an innocent man of
murder ...

At the clip-clop of approaching horses, she absently
looked up. A black lacquered carriage pulled up beside her,
its thick navy drapes drawn. She barely had time to note the
painted gold crest on the door before it swung open. A large
arm reached out, catching her by the waist. A gloved hand
stifled her startled cry, and she was hauled into the carriage.

Chapter Eight

Alaric regarded his captive calmly. Despite her pale cheeks and heaving bosom, Miss Emma Kent's eyes shot sparks at him. He was certain that if he removed the silk strips binding her mouth and hands, she'd be shouting the roof down and clawing his eyes out as well.

Which was why he'd had to resort to present measures. She gave him no choice.

"Listen carefully, Miss Kent," he said. "I am not going to hurt you. You have my word."

"*Mfm mph gm.*"

"I will release you," he conceded, "after you give me an hour of your time."

She muttered something darkly.

"It is your own fault. I told you not to test me, and yet you have. I told you I had nothing to do with Clara's death, and yet you have persisted in making false accusations, in interfering where you have no business doing so. In short," he concluded, his jaw tight, "you have succeeded in making my life a living hell."

"*Gmmd.*"

His eyes narrowed. "On the contrary, Miss Kent, it *isn't* good. For me or for you. Therefore, you leave me with one alternative."

The carriage drew to a halt.

"You wouldn't listen to reason. So I shall have to show you the truth," he said.

Emma should have been terrified. At the very least, her sensibilities ought to have suffered some sort of damage. After all, there she was, bound and gagged, a victim of kidnapping, standing in a room of what might possibly be a house of ill repute. Having never been in one before, she couldn't be certain, but several clues supported the hypothesis.

First, they'd entered together through a gated back entrance flanked by a pair of guards. By "entered together," she meant that she'd refused to walk and Strathaven had consequently acted like a savage, tossing her over his shoulder and carting her inside. Even from her topsy-turvy perspective, she'd deduced from the richly decorated and quiet corridor that this was an exclusive, secretive place.

Second, another guard had led them to the present chamber which was decorated in alarming shades of scarlet and gold. A fresco on one wall dominated the room: it depicted a naked woman, her nipples painted a lurid red, her body chained to a rock overlooking the sea. The tubular (and rather phallic) head of a giant sea monster thrust ominously from the foamy waves.

Finally, the proprietress of the establishment who greeted them now had a distinctly disreputable look about her. Introducing herself as Mrs. Roddy, she was a handsome, voluptuous blonde who wore more rouge than clothing, and she leered when Strathaven set a bound and furious Emma on her feet.

"Welcome to Andromeda's," Mrs. Roddy said. "Games are underway already, are they?"

Games? What games? What does the infernal woman mean?

"I'm being kidnapped!" Emma said indignantly.

Unfortunately, it came out as "*Mmf bemf kdmgf!*"

Truthfully, she was more angry than frightened. Never in her life had she been manhandled in such a manner—or *any* manner. She wasn't used to being told what to do, never mind being forced into places against her will. Strathaven was acting no better than a barbarian!

When she tried to get away from him, his arm circled her waist like a steel band, trapping her against his side. She struggled and succeeded only in rubbing herself against his rigid form. Again, the blighter's proximity had a queer effect on her senses: her belly quivered, followed by a molten feeling lower down. Her breath hit the linen in quick, successive bursts.

Ruddiness stained the high ridges of the duke's cheekbones.

"Stop wriggling about," he ordered.

She glared at him. *Then let me go, you heathen!*

Ignoring her, he said, "Has everything been arranged, Mrs. Roddy?"

"Yes, Your Grace. And if there's *anything* else you need ..."

With a suggestive flutter of her sooted lashes, the proprietress performed a curtsy that showed rather too much of her charms. In fact, the robust mounds nearly spilled out of her non-existent bodice. *Why bother wearing a dress at all?* Catching herself, Emma frowned at the uncharitable thought. Nonetheless, she couldn't resist darting a look at Strathaven who looked unimpressed by the display.

Not that she cared, of course.

"See that we're not disturbed for the next half hour," he said dismissively.

The simpering proprietress departed.

Alone with Strathaven, Emma was torn between fury ... and burning curiosity.

Why did he bring me here? What does he hope to prove?

Her instincts told her that he wouldn't hurt her; if he wished to, he could have attacked her in the carriage. He'd sworn that he didn't intend to harm her, and Emma hoped that Annabel was right in saying that his wickedness hid an honorable character.

Honorable is a definite stretch, Emma thought darkly. *What does the blackguard want?*

He went to a set of crimson drapes and parted them in a bold sweep. Emma blinked as a door was revealed. He opened it, and curious in spite of herself, she craned her neck for a better look. A pulse fluttered at the side of her neck as she glimpsed flickering dimness.

"'Tis your choice, Miss Kent," Strathaven said. "You can either walk through this door on your own two feet or we can have a repeat performance of our earlier entrance."

Some choice, she thought in disgust.

She assessed the situation. Standing there in his immaculate charcoal cutaway and trousers, his lean form radiating taut power, Strathaven looked ducal. Merciless. A man who didn't issue threats idly. If she didn't make a decision in the next few seconds, she had no doubt he would once again toss her over his shoulder.

"Not afraid, are you?" Now his words held the taunting edge of challenge.

Did he think to intimidate her? She was no wilting violet who was going to faint at the sight of a dark room. Squaring her shoulders, she set forth through the doorway.

She entered the enveloping darkness and heard the door click shut, sealing her and Strathaven inside. The air turned heavy and humid in her lungs. As her eyes adjusted, she saw that they were in a narrow, dead-end corridor. Flickering wall sconces illuminated a row of wooden slats set at eye level on both sides of the hallway. Peculiar, muffled sounds raised goose pimples on her skin, her heart beating a furious staccato.

"I'm going to free you now," Strathaven said in a low voice. "Be quiet if you don't wish to be discovered—and I assure you, you don't."

The instant he removed the binding from her mouth and hands, she whispered fiercely, "What is this? Why are we here?"

"To relieve you of your innocence."

His reply sent a tingle over her skin. Before she could argue that she wasn't a naïve chit—that she'd run a household, raised a family—he placed his hand on the small of her back, guiding her toward the wall. He slid one of the panels open. Emma blinked as a glowing hole appeared, her breath catching as the sounds took on a human quality.

"You wanted to know the truth, Miss Kent. Have a look ... if you dare."

Not one to back down from a challenge, she leaned forward.

A wave of shock crashed over her.

The room was cell-like, starkly furnished with only a plain wooden bench and a table next to it. A fully dressed blond gentleman sat upon the bench whilst a brunette lay on her belly across his lap ... and she didn't have a single stitch of clothing on! Emma swallowed as the man smoothed a tanned hand over the pale hills of the woman's bottom.

"Have you been a wicked girl?" he said.

"Yes, sir," the lady replied in a breathy, cultured voice.

"Do you deserve to be punished?"

"If it pleases you, sir."

Calmly, the man reached to the table next to him. Emma made out an array of odd implements upon its surface. He selected an object ... a paddle? In a swift motion, he brought it down against the woman's backside. The loud *slap* made Emma jerk back in response.

Her back collided with Strathaven, her pulse leaping wildly at the contact. She was acutely aware of his rock-hard frame caging her, his spicy scent curling in her nostrils. Her fingernails dug desperately into her palms as the sounds of slapping flesh filled the chamber.

Breathe. Remain calm.

"Keep watching," he murmured.

Shivering at the brush of his breath against her ear, Emma saw that the woman was writhing on the man's lap now. Her face conveyed not pain, Emma registered with confusion, but ... pleasure? How could that be? The lady was being abused, was she not?

"Oh, yes, spank me harder, sir!" the lady cried. "Don't stop. I'm almost there!"

She wishes *to be spanked?*

As the brunette's cries grew in volume and desperation, Emma became keenly aware of her own physical state. Her limbs were quivering, and sweat trickled beneath her bodice, slickening the valley between her breasts, the tips of which had stiffened, throbbing like pulse points. She felt giddy, lightheaded—not like herself at all.

She trembled when Strathaven's hands closed around her upper arms. He steered her toward the next viewing panel; like one caught in a dream, Emma peered through the revealed hole. Air whooshed from her lungs as she struggled to put two disparate and equally shocking facts together.

First, she was looking into a dungeon.

Second, the people within it were taking part in a wild bacchanal.

The chamber had iron bars in place of walls, and its scantily clad occupants were enthusiastically engaged in debauchery. If Emma had thought that growing up around farms and livestock had given her a general idea of the sexual act, then in that one astonishing instant she was proven *wrong*. Like a veil, her innocence was ripped away, and she stared at the writhing bodies through wide, disbelieving eyes. Her heart jammed in her throat as her gaze flitted around the cage ...

Oh. My. Goodness.

Her cheeks blazed as she beheld the first human phallus she'd ever seen in the flesh. A shirtless man sat upon a wooden chair, his member thrusting upward from the opening in his black buckskins like a crimson *flagpole*. If that wasn't shocking enough, he held a black leather strap, which was attached to the matching collar worn by the naked blonde kneeling between his muscular thighs.

When he tugged, the woman gave him a saucy wink and shuffled closer on her knees. She bent her head. Dizzily, Emma watched as the blonde slowly licked up and down the turgid column of flesh before swirling her tongue over the mushroomed dome.

"Suck it," the man commanded, "Swallow my cock."

The blonde's mouth opened obediently, his member disappearing betwixt her lips ...

Heart palpitating, Emma tore her gaze away, only to have it land on three—Good God, *four?*—undulating bodies. A woman was on all fours, bookended by two men. The one behind her was on his knees, his expression salacious as he pumped his manhood into her. The one in front lay on his back, the woman's head bobbing over his groin. Emma couldn't see his face because another woman was sitting upon it, grinding her hips and rubbing her breasts ...

Sweat misted over Emma's brow as her eyes shifted to an auburn-haired lady. Her wrists were bound above her head to the iron bars. She stood, her breasts quivering, a black silk blindfold covering her eyes. A man strode over, his fleshy member aimed at her like a lance. Without further ado, he grabbed one of her thighs, hitching it over his hip. The muscles of his buttocks flexed as he entered her in a deep thrust, and the redhead moaned, "Oh, *yes*. Fuck me harder. Make me beg for mercy ..."

The images swam in Emma's vision as past and present collided. Lady Osgood tied to the gazebo, her voice filtering through bushes. *Are you going to hurt me? Oh Strathaven, please, I beg of you ...*

"Can you take more of my rod, wench?" the man demanded.

"Yes, master, screw it in deeper. Do whatever you wish to me!" the redhead said.

Realization cut like a knife through Emma's shock; the truth bled out.

A depraved sexual game—that is what I witnessed.

Lady Osgood was a willing participant, and Strathaven, he's innocent ... so to speak.

The scene suddenly vanished, the panel closing. She was whirled around, her back pressed against the wall. Strathaven's palms planted on either side of her shoulders, trapping her.

In the flickering dimness, a wild, silver fire lit his eyes. Controlled savagery burned beneath his polished facade. Waves of tension rolled off his powerful frame, and every fiber of her being responded to his potent energy. Her skin was hot, sweaty. Her limbs trembled.

"Now do you understand?" he demanded.

She couldn't look away from his gaze, the heat and the ice. A magnetic force hummed in the sliver of space between them. Her heart thumped, the tempo reckless and uncontrolled. Wordless longing tumbled through her. She wet her lips.

His eyes honed in on the movement of her tongue. His nostrils flared. A sound left him—a groan or a curse—and his mouth crashed upon hers.

She couldn't breathe, couldn't think. Strathaven's firm, hot lips roved over hers with masterful intensity. Sensation overrode everything, a tide of pleasure washing over her, so strong that she lost her bearings. Her lips clung desperately to his, and his kiss grew even more potent and seductively demanding. His drugging male flavor weakened her knees, and he caught her, held her against the wall. She shivered when his tongue swept against her bottom lip.

"Open for me," he whispered. "Let me in."

Senses spinning, she obeyed, and his tongue plunged boldly inside. Somewhere in the far recesses of her mind, she registered that her first kiss was unlike anything she could have imagined. He tasted her as if he *owned* her, and his unapologetic possession sent a strange, singing sweetness through her blood. Her awareness of anything but him faded. Instinctively, she followed his lead, letting him in deeper, meeting his tongue with her own.

A sound tore from his chest, and the kiss grew even more torrid. He penetrated her mouth with a stabbing force that made heat bloom at the center of her being. Fire unfurled over her skin, the tips of her breasts pulsing, itching for contact. She pressed herself against his hard strength and moaned at the sublime sensation, needing more ...

His hands found her breasts, and she panted into his mouth as he found the aching tips, teasing them, causing them to rise against the layers of fabric. When he gave a sharp tweak, liquid rushed between her legs, a frantic need rising in that same place. As if he were attuned to her every desire, his thigh wedged into her skirts, and she moaned, rubbing herself against the hard trunk of muscle, desperate for the friction, release from the sweet ache—

"Dearies? Time's up."

The words sliced through the moment like a guillotine. It took a moment for Emma to recognize Mrs. Roddy's voice. Before she could gather her senses, she was shoved behind Strathaven. His broad back to her, he faced the approaching bawd.

"Ah, there you are." A knowing gleam lit the bawd's eyes. "Enjoy the show?"

"We're done," Strathaven said.

Dazed by the sensations still coursing through her, Emma watched as he dropped a small purse in the bawd's waiting palm, the coins landing with an ignominious *clink*.

"*Thank you*, Your Grace." Fluttering her lashes, Mrs. Roddy said, "If there is anything else—"

"That is all," the duke said imperiously.

The bawd curtsied low.

He turned, and Emma's lungs constricted as she saw his expression. 'Twas as if a curtain of ice had fallen over him, his face frozen in hard lines, his eyes a glacial jade. She flinched when his large hand closed around her arm like a manacle.

"We're leaving," he grated out. "Now."

Chapter Nine

The next evening, Emma wondered what in mercy's name she was doing. Given all that had transpired in the past day, the *last* place she should be was here in the foyer of Strathaven's palatial townhouse. On her last visit here, she'd been distraught over the news of Lady Osgood's death, her assumption of Strathaven's culpability; she hadn't taken note of the surroundings. Now she saw that checkered marble gleamed beneath her half-boots, crystals dripped from the tiered chandelier overhead, and in front of her, the twin wings of the mahogany stairwell seemed to float up toward the paneled ceiling.

Surrounded by the incontrovertible proof of her host's wealth and power, she couldn't feel more ill at ease. Yet her honor had demanded that she come. Ambrose and Marianne had taken the rest of the family to a performance at Astley's tonight, and pleading a headache—plausible, given her return visit to the magistrates earlier that afternoon—Emma had stayed home. Soon after, she'd slipped out of the house and hailed a hackney to the present address.

As much as she hated deceiving her family, she had no choice. She had a debt to settle and the sooner the better. The catastrophic mistake she'd made—the man's reputation that she'd recklessly ruined—gnawed at her insides.

As did the memory of what had happened yesterday at Andromeda's.

The kiss washed over her, thrill and dismay swirling in

its wake. Of all the times for her to discover that she was indeed capable of feminine passion, of all the men she might have discovered it with ... why in God's name did it have to be *Strathaven*?

The butler returned, and she noticed how shuffling and painful-looking his gait was.

"His Grace will see you in the library, Miss Kent," he said with a thick Scottish burr.

For an instant, Emma was tempted to flee—but she'd never been one to shirk duty, no matter how unpleasant it might be. She'd made this mess; she would tidy it up.

She straightened her shoulders. "Thank you, sir."

"'Tis Jarvis, miss." His countenance was kindly.

She gave him a small smile and followed him down a long corridor hung with gilt-framed paintings. She had no idea how Strathaven would react to seeing her. The carriage ride home from Andromeda's had taken place in silence. He'd been white-lipped, foreboding, and she'd been too dazed to say anything herself. He'd deposited her at the corner of her street; the moment she'd entered the house, his conveyance had sped off.

Jarvis held open a door. "In here, miss."

"Thank you." Emma heard the uncharacteristic quiver in her own voice.

Pull your chin up. A Kent always takes responsibility for her actions.

Expelling a breath, she entered the large, high-ceilinged chamber. Only a few lamps were lit, and in the flickering dimness, she saw shelves of books lining the walls and leather furniture clustered around a glowing hearth at the center of the room. At the far end was a desk framed by tall bow windows. Strathaven stood there, staring out into the dark gardens.

His still, solitary pose wrought an oddly resonant pang in

her breast. Juxtaposed against the starry night sky, he looked ... alone. As if he carried the weight of the dark heavens upon his broad shoulders.

At that moment, two shapes darted from the shadows, and Emma let out a startled breath as large paws planted onto her thighs. She found herself looking into the shaggy, grinning faces of two Scottish deerhounds. Their cheerful welcome was infectious.

She scratched them both behind the ears. "Friendly boys, aren't you?" she murmured.

"Phobos, Deimos—*down*."

At their master's sharp command, the dogs obeyed at once, padding off to curl up in front of the fire. She looked up, her smile fading. Before now, she'd never seen Strathaven in anything but impeccable attire. In his shirtsleeves, his potent virility was even more pronounced. The fine lawn shirt stretched across his wide shoulders, draping over his narrow hips. It was partially unbuttoned, revealing the corded column of his throat, an intriguing glimpse of his muscled chest ...

"Why are you here?" he demanded.

She dragged her gaze up. Strathaven's pets were aptly named after the companions of the mythical Ares. With his face set in harsh lines, his eyes cold and glittering, the duke looked every bit as ruthless as the God of War.

Pulling back her shoulders, she said, "We have unfinished business to discuss."

"Is that so?" He took a casual sip from the glass he held.

While his indifference grated, she reminded herself that she *had* wrongly accused him of murder, and thus probably didn't deserve a warmer welcome ... even if they had shared a kiss. To a rake like Strathaven, such intimacies probably meant nothing. He probably kissed women like that all the time. Besides, she knew that his purpose in kissing her had

been to demonstrate his superiority—and her inexperience—
when it came to sexual matters.

He'd succeeded spectacularly.

Her lips pressed together. *Fool me once.*

She'd learned her lesson. Even as she now recognized
that her disturbing awareness of him was sensual in nature,
she knew she was no wanton. 'Twas a boon, actually, that
she'd gained a better understanding of carnal impulses.
Knowledge was power. She now knew what to guard against.

After all, attraction was just an appetite like any other.
Curbing urges had never been a problem for her. During the
years her family had been mired in poverty, there'd been
plenty of times when she'd practiced stringent economies,
chose practical options over indulgent ones.

*Just because one craves a piece of cake doesn't mean one has to
have one.*

Resolved, she said, "I wanted you to know that I
withdrew my testimony today. I told the magistrates that I
misjudged what I saw between you and Lady Osgood in the
garden."

His dark eyelashes veiled his gaze. "Why?"

"I was wrong," she admitted. "About what I thought I
saw. I came to offer my sincere apologies for the hardship I
have caused you."

"My forgiveness. That is why you've come?" Sarcasm
dripped from his voice.

It wasn't the only reason. In truth, she'd come with a
proposition in mind.

Anticipation took root as she considered her brilliant
plan to grow two trees from one seed. She could make things
right with Strathaven *and* secure her own future. The
proposal was perfect, would benefit all parties involved.
She'd spent the last day strategizing how to broach the
subject; she didn't want to repeat her failed negotiations with

Ambrose.

Consequently, she said with care, "Actually, there is another reason as well."

"I thought so." Strathaven's mouth had a hard, cynical bent. He tossed back the contents of his glass and set it down with a *clink* on the desk before advancing toward her.

Although her heart pounded like a drum, she held her ground. He stopped mere inches away, his hands on his lean hips, his booted legs set in an aggressive stance. His clean, spicy musk drifted to her, and her body reacted of its own accord. Her breathing quickened, her mouth pooling as the memory of his dark masculine flavor tingled over her tongue.

One dark brow quirked. "Well, Miss Kent? If you've come to exact the devil's price, you'd best get on with it."

Devil's price? What is he talking about?

She marshaled her wits. "I have a proposal to make, Your Grace. A plan that I believe will benefit both of us."

"Save your breath. You'll get no offer from me."

She stared at him blankly. "An offer ... for what?"

"Well, now, there *are* other kinds of offers, are there not?" His pale gaze roved insolently over her. "I didn't think you were in the market for that sort of arrangement, Miss Kent."

His meaning sunk in.

"You're either foxed or mad," she said in outrage. "I wouldn't marry you—much less consider the other ... Not if we were the last two people on this earth! It's absurd to even suggest—"

"On that we agree." His freezing accents cut her off. "So what is this *proposal* of yours?"

Her fists balled at his unbelievable arrogance. "I'm offering to help you find the murderer, you conceited nodcock!"

"What?" he bit out.

"You heard me." She tilted her chin up. "Since I got you embroiled in scandal, I'm going to help you get out of it. By conducting an investigation into who killed Lady Osgood."

Chapter Ten

For once in his life, he had no words. None.

The chit rendered him utterly speechless.

He was already furious at himself over the way he'd lost control at Andromeda's. He'd brought Miss Kent there to teach her a lesson, to show her the full extent of her ignorance. Devil take it, she ought to have fainted after a minute or two. Or slapped his bloody face.

Instead, she'd tempted him ... *melted* for him.

He still couldn't believe that he'd kissed her, couldn't believe how close he'd come to doing much more. If the bawd hadn't interrupted, he might have found himself well and truly caught in the Parson's snare for even his tarnished sense of honor wouldn't permit him to deflower a virgin without accepting the consequences.

He'd assumed that she'd come tonight to demand that he pay the matrimonial piper. The notion of being manipulated by her feminine wiles had enraged him. Savagely, he'd recalled how Laura had seduced him with virginal glances and shy smiles. Aye, he'd paid dearly for losing his head over a so-called innocent, and he'd sworn never to do it again.

But apparently Miss Kent wasn't interested in marrying him.

This ought to have improved his disposition. For some reason, it infuriated him *more*.

What does the chit have up her sleeve?

'Twas best to know one's adversary. Waving a hand to

the divan by the fire, he said caustically, "By all means, shower me with your pearls of wisdom."

With a huff, she went and perched on the cushions. He followed and took the adjacent wingchair. Despite his suspiciousness, he couldn't help but notice how her velvet cloak set off her creamy skin and rosy lips—lips that he'd sampled. She'd tasted as delicious as she smelled, like an apple tart, wholesome and spicy sweet ...

"I have a plan," she announced, and he instantly grew warier. "For the last several months, I have been working at Kent and Associates, and I've learned something of the trade."

What the devil?

He stared at her. "You have been employed ... as an *investigator?*"

She cleared her throat. "Not exactly. I was assisting my brother in more of, er, an organizational capacity. I have, however, learned the ins and outs of detection work. In fact, I recently solved a case on my own."

The chit was unbelievable. Cracked. Possibly unhinged.

"As a female investigator," she went on in a determined manner, "I may be uniquely positioned to assist you."

Specific positions in which she could assist him flitted through his head.

Scowling, he said, "That is the most demented thing I've ever heard. What special female talents do you bring to bear, Miss Kent? Your skill wielding a reticule as a weapon? Or perhaps your remarkable ability to jump to the wrong conclusions?"

"I already apologized for my mistake and have rectified it with the magistrates." She narrowed her eyes at him. "Are you always this difficult when someone tries to help you?"

"I wouldn't know. I've never had the experience," he said shortly.

He didn't trust it either. The only one who'd ever tried to do anything for him was the dowager duchess, and he didn't know which had been more stifling, his illness or Aunt Patrice's overbearing anxiety.

"That can't be true," Miss Kent said with a frown. "Everyone has relied upon another at some point. What about your mama?"

"She died when I was young," he said curtly.

"Your papa then—"

"I do not discuss my family."

She looked as if she might argue ... and apparently thought better of it. "Well, *I* am trying to help you," she said, "and I've been thinking: according to the papers, Lady Clara was poisoned. Poison is oft said to be a woman's weapon. Given that the victim was a woman as well, it seems that a female perspective is warranted in this case, don't you agree?"

He couldn't resist bursting her little bubble. "The poison wasn't intended for Clara. It was in my whiskey. She had the misfortune of drinking with me."

She blinked. "*You* were poisoned too? But you're ... not dead."

"Disappointed?" he said acidly.

"The papers never mentioned—"

"The fewer who know the better. I don't want the integrity of the investigation tainted."

Miss Kent's gaze widened, firelight dancing in the faceted depths. Most brown eyes he'd encountered gave the impression of opacity, but not hers: they were as clear and dark as the finest tea, reflecting her rippling emotions.

"This changes *everything*," she said.

"It changes *nothing* where you're concerned," he said with emphasis. "You're not to get involved. In fact, I want you as uninvolved in my life as possible."

Keeping her away from him, he concluded, was the only way to preserve his sanity. Emma Kent possessed an uncanny talent for pushing him to his limits. Her willfulness was infuriating—and bloody arousing. He wanted to shake some sense into her. He wanted to yank her into his arms, taste her honeyed surrender again ...

She leapt to her feet, which obliged him to rise as well. He suppressed a grimace as his stiffening cock butted against his trousers. Praise God his shirt covered the bulge.

"But you could still be in danger!" She bit her lip, pacing in front of the divan. "This is my fault. I misled the magistrates into focusing on you instead of the true killer."

Her concern was ... befuddling. In his extensive experience with the fair sex, he couldn't recall a single instance where a woman had been answerable for her actions. Where a female had shown a sense of honor and fair play. As he recalled Laura's tears and denials, her baseless accusations, his jaw tautened.

"Actions have been taken," he said abruptly. "I've hired investigators."

"You've spoken to Mr. McLeod and my brother?"

The last thing he wanted was to be in Will's debt. "There are other agencies in town."

"But none as accomplished as Kent and Associates. They're the best." Her head canted to one side. "Why wouldn't you trust your own brother?"

Because I don't deserve to.

"It is none of your concern," he said irritably.

"Can't we let bygones be bygones? If your life is in peril, we must work together—"

"There is no *we*, Miss Kent."

"I am sincerely sorry for my mistake." Her eyes pleaded with him. Just as he began to thaw slightly, she added, "And it is not as if you're entirely in the right. You did kidnap and drag me to Andromeda's after all."

"I did that because you were too pigheaded to accept the truth," he gritted out.

"And I gave the testimony because you were too arrogant to explain what really happened." She had the temerity to lift her chin. "When it all boils down, I'd say we're equally in the wrong, wouldn't you?"

His grip on his temper slipped. "Like hell we are. You spied on me and falsely accused me of murder. Then you instigated that kiss—"

"What?" she said indignantly. "You're the one who started it."

"You licked your damned lip in invitation!"

"If I did so, 'twas because of nerves. Unlike you, I'm not accustomed to debauchery."

Her prim, virtuous reply caused the pressure in his veins to shoot up. A muscle by his left eye twitched. "Nerves my arse," he said. "If you possess any, they are clearly made of iron. The truth is you were bloody *eager* for my kiss."

Uncertainty flitted through her eyes—the first of it that he'd seen from the bullheaded chit.

She recovered quickly. "Circumstances being what they were, it is understandable that we were both somewhat overwrought. What's done is done, however. There's no sense arguing about it," she said in annoyingly brisk tones. "If your reluctance to accept my help stems from fear that we'll end up in another compromising situation, I can assure you that will *never* happen again."

Her naive confidence, the flippant way in which she dismissed the attraction between them fueled his need to prove how wrong she was. The termagant needed a lesson, and he needed to rid himself of her once and for all. He knew exactly how to accomplish both goals.

Kill two birds with one stone.

"You think you can control yourself around me?" he said silkily.

"Of course. And there's naught to control. Truly."

The slight wobble in that last word betrayed her.

"So if I were to sit on that wingchair right now,"—his gaze directed to the furnishing in question—"with you on my lap and my mouth on yours, you'd be indifferent?"

"Don't be ridiculous."

He stalked toward her, and she retreated immediately. When the back of her knees hit the wingchair, she lost her balance, her bottom smacking softly against the leather seat. He planted his hands on the back of the chair, caging yet not touching her.

Leaning down, he mocked, "Then don't be a liar. You said you had full control of yourself around me."

"I do. In that hypothetical scenario, I would be trying to get away from you," she shot back.

"What if I held you tight, kissed you deeper, licked your sweet lips until you let me in?"

Her cheeks turned rosy. "I—I'd bite your tongue!"

"Ah, but then I'd have to punish you." He let his words sink in, saw her pupils dilating—not with fear, but ... *arousal.* Devil and damn. His trousers grew instantly tighter.

"You wouldn't dare." She didn't sound so full of conviction now.

"To the contrary, pet, I dare most anything," he purred. "Now you saw quite the variety of punishments at Andromeda's; I wonder which you would most prefer? For instance, would you enjoy being bound and helpless as I took my pleasure? As I touched and kissed you however, wherever, I wanted to?"

A choked breath left her. Beneath her cloak, her bosom surged.

"Perhaps you'd like to pleasure me," he said

thoughtfully. "On your knees, taking everything I give you."
His cockstand, already turgid, pulsed at the idea—and even
more so when her teeth sank into her lower lip. Sweat
dampened his collar; he forced himself to finish what he'd
begun. "But I think you'd most like being turned over on my
knee. Raising your pretty bottom up for me."

His senses flooded with the beauty of that image: her
supple, white skin beneath his palm, her beauty entirely in
his hands. He knew she was not a miss of half-measures;
when Emma Kent submitted, she would give ... everything.
Heat sizzled through his veins, and he burned to know the
generosity of her ardor, to show her ecstasy that she'd never
known before.

In a hoarse voice, he continued, "You could let go of fear
and worry, Emma. Put yourself into my keeping." He
cupped her downy cheek, her quiver travelling straight to his
prick. "You could trust me to give you everything you need."

She made a strangled sound, and he saw his own dark
desire mirrored in her eyes. Her cheeks were flushed with
arousal rather than disgust. She swayed toward him, her
breath panting through her lips, her passion like a seed
poised to sprout through virginal inhibitions ...

Virgin—a trap.

His mind sounded the alarm over his roaring lust. *Laura
seemed sweet and passionate, and she played you for a fool.* His gut
clenched as her betrayals flooded him, the humiliating
memories. The loss ...

Never again.

Control is everything.

Somehow, he mastered himself. Pushing away from the
wingchair, he straightened and lifted a brow. "Well, pet? Are
you unaffected now? In complete control?"

She blinked, paling as the words struck home. "You're a
bastard," she whispered.

"I'm honest," he corrected coolly. "This is what will happen if you play games with me. Now this is your last warning: stop meddling or face the consequences."

She shot to her feet. "*Fine*. If you wind up dead, see if I give a farthing!"

Phobos and Deimos leapt up, ready to give chase to her departing figure.

"Stay," Alaric commanded.

The deerhounds came over to him, whining at the loss of a visitor.

"Trust me, lads," he said darkly. "It has to be this way."

Despite his victory over the indomitable chit, Alaric felt bedeviled with restlessness. The dark fantasies he'd used to warn off Miss Kent continued to plague his lustful imagination. Visions of her kneeling in front of him, her lips parting so sweetly as he fed her every inch of his throbbing shaft ...

He paced the library like a damned prisoner in his own house. Either he could go upstairs and frig himself like a blasted greenling or he could find some distraction. His club—that was the ticket. He hadn't gone to White's since Clara's death, and his continued absence would add fuel to the gossip.

Best to nip it in the bud. He had naught to hide.

Summoning his carriage, he made the short trip over to St. James Street.

As Alaric entered White's, that bastion of male comfort, all eyes turned to him. The scent of leather and cigar smoke curled in his nostrils as he returned cold stares and polite greetings in equal measure. Nothing like strife to separate friends from foes. He made mental note of who fell on which side: the Scot in him valued loyalty above all else.

"Strathaven, I am surprised to see you here."

At the pompous drawl, Alaric turned to see the Earl of Mercer approaching, accompanied by his usual pack of dandies. With his wheat-colored hair immaculately pomaded and his trim figure clad in embroidered velvet, Mercer was a handsome Pink of Fashion. He was also a snob, the kind of fellow whose sole purpose in life appeared to be flaunting his wealth and position—neither of which he'd earned—and spewing "wit" with his viper's tongue.

"Why would you be surprised?" Alaric said in even tones.

"The passing of Lady Osgood—so very shocking to the sensibilities." Mercer shuddered. "It appears you've managed to escape unscathed. Must be those *hardy* Scottish sensibilities of yours."

Mercer's cronies tittered.

"I had nothing to do with Lady Osgood's death. Anyone who claims the contrary can meet me at dawn," Alaric said coldly.

"At dawn? How uncivilized an hour. Lord knows I have plenty of engagements," Mercer said with a brittle laugh, "and cannot possibly rearrange my schedule to fit you in."

"Well met, gentlemen." Gabriel, the Marquess of Tremont, came up to them. If Tremont's astute grey gaze took the full measure of the tense situation, his pleasant expression showed no signs of it. "Mercer, I believe some friends of yours are looking for you. Something about an entry in the betting book."

"A gentleman's work is never done." Sketching a bow, the earl sauntered off, his entourage tagging at his heels.

Alaric said in low tones, "I'd like to rearrange more than that bastard's schedule."

"Mercer's just looking to stir trouble. Don't give him the

satisfaction." Tremont slapped him on the shoulder. "Let's have a drink and talk of more important things."

They managed to find prized seats by a private hearth.

"They don't make chairs like this anywhere else," Tremont said, stretching out his legs.

"They do if you pay them enough." Alaric had commissioned furnishings from the same manufacturer for his study at Strathmore Castle, and it had cost him a pretty penny.

Tremont regarded him with a dry smile. "We aren't all as rich as Croesus, you know."

While the marquess had improved the financial situation he'd inherited, apparently he still had a ways to go. Alaric understood the other's predicament. After all, he'd spent his tenure as duke replenishing the coffers left empty by his guardian's profligacy.

"You will be once our venture is settled at month's end," Alaric assured him.

"I do have some good news on that front. I spoke with Burrowes today, and he's decided to stand firm with us. His show of support should help us cauterize this wound yet."

"Well done," Alaric said. "That is the best news I've had all day."

"What are you two up to now?" said an amused voice. "Whatever it is, may I join in?"

Marcus Harrington, Lord Blackwood, was another friend from his Oxford days. Blackwood had been the spare to the title back then and after University had bought a commission in the army. His training was still evident in his militaristic bearing, the precise cut of his golden brown hair. After his brother's death, he'd acquired a marquessdom and a marchioness soon thereafter.

All three stood and exchanged bows.

Alaric said, "Care for a hand of cards, Blackwood?"

"Why not? I could always do with some of your gold."

At one o'clock in the morning, Alaric left the table with heavier pockets, bowing to the good-natured groans of his friends. Outside, he descended the steps of the club, aware of an edgy energy that the night's distractions had not quelled. As he headed toward his carriage parked up ahead, he considered making a stop at a bawdy house. Mayhap a fuck was what he needed to rid himself of his inexplicable itch for Miss Kent once and for all.

Yet for some damnable reason, he didn't feel like bedding a whore.

The oncoming rattle of wheels made him look to the road. A black carriage was flying over the cobblestone; the driver, a fellow obscured by a dark hat and greatcoat, must have bacon for brains for driving that fast down St. James. Trash fluttered from the open window. As the vehicle passed him, Alaric glimpsed whipping curtains, a face split by a scar into two menacing halves, metal glinting—

Even as he threw himself to the ground, the shot rang in his ears. He lay on the pavement, blinking up at the stars. Muffled shouts came from the distance. Scorching pain flamed over his arm, and the night descended upon him.

Chapter Eleven

The stillroom, with its bottle-lined shelves and large work table, was a refuge for Emma. Claiming that remedies were not her forte, Marianne's housekeeper generously allowed Emma use of the space below stairs whenever she wished. At present, Emma was working on a salve for Mr. Pitt's aching knees and the second footman's bad back. She added drops of camphor to the bowl, stirring it into the thick concoction of beeswax and rosewater.

"The new gowns came for me and Polly," Violet said. Perched on the table next to the bowl, she swung her legs idly.

"That's good, dear," Emma said absently.

Thank God she had a few mundane activities to occupy her. If not, she might have been driven mad by her thoughts. *Do not think about him*, she reprimanded herself.

"There's ribbons and slippers to match," Violet went on.

"Mmm."

As Emma concentrated on giving the salve a good mix with the wooden spoon, she kept hearing Strathaven's seductive voice, the wicked things he'd described last night. The pale fire of his gaze licked through her.

You could let go of fear and worry, Emma. Put yourself into my keeping. You could trust me to give you everything you need.

A shiver ran through her. She ought to have been shocked. Disgusted.

Instead, his words set off a deep, explosive resonance that

shook the foundations of her being.

'Twas a yearning she could put no words to—an urge so terrifying that for the first time in her life, she'd not only stood down, but fled. Only she couldn't run from herself. From the strange, mortifying, *exhilarating* impulses that Strathaven had awakened her.

She'd dreamed of him last night. Of them, tangled skin against skin. In sleep, she had no control over her will, and she'd let him do everything he'd described to her. His hands, his mouth, his command ... Pleasure had trapped her like a bell jar, and there'd been no escaping the confines of her own surrender. He'd owned her breath, her body, her soul— and she'd never felt more free. She'd awoken bathed in perspiration, the tips of breasts pebbled and throbbing, her sex slick with dew ...

"I don't think I'll have much use for a new wardrobe," Violet droned on. "I'm planning on joining Astley's and becoming a circus performer."

"That's nice, dear," Emma said.

Silence met her words.

She looked up from the bowl. "Sorry," she sighed. "I wasn't listening, was I?"

"Not to a single word I was saying." Vi's golden-brown eyes narrowed. "What *is* the matter with you, anyway? You've been acting strangely all this week."

"Nothing's the matter. I'm just ... preoccupied."

"By what? Making salve?" Vi's gaze rolled upward. "Back in Chudleigh Crest, you did that while tending to Papa, sewing up petticoats for me and Polly, putting out Harry's latest fire, *and* cooking supper. No, something's going on,"— Vi tapped her chin—"and I'd put my money on the duke."

Though her pulse skittered, Emma spooned salve into the waiting jars. "I've cleared up the matter with the magistrates. I'll have no further dealings with him."

Why doesn't that make me feel relieved?

She told herself that things were better this way. She had to admit that she was not as in command of her carnal impulses as she'd believed, and staying away from Strathaven was clearly the safest option. After all, she'd offered to make amends; he'd refused. She'd done what she could. As for furthering her investigative skills, she'd simply have to find another way to convince Ambrose ...

The sound of rustling silk made her turn to the doorway. One look at Marianne's grave expression, and even Violet said in alarm, "What's wrong, Marianne?"

"I've just received some rather disturbing news."

Emma's nape tingled with premonition. "What is it?"

"It's Strathaven," Marianne said. "He's been shot."

Chapter Twelve

If there was anything Alaric despised, it was the sick bed.

He'd spent half his youth in one, the boredom and helplessness nearly as bad as the illness itself. He'd hated the quacks; summoned by Aunt Patrice, they'd arrived to Strathmore Castle in droves, vials of potions rattling in their carrying cases. Some supposed cures had actually made matters worse; after being dosed with a tincture of belladonna, he'd retched for hours. Writhing and shivering in his own sweat, he'd prayed for an end to the suffering.

Lady Patrice had nursed him tirelessly through it all. Having lost her own son to scarlet fever, she wasn't taking any chances with her new ward. Between her, the stifling sickroom, and uncontrollable episodes of pain, he'd felt like an osprey stuffed in a canary cage.

Like Ares imprisoned in that bloody jar.

His gaze went to the painting on the wall, which brought that mythological scene to life in darkly exquisite oils. He'd commissioned the work from an Italian master, and it showed the God of War, his muscles rippling and fists raised against the curved walls of his cell. The artist had captured Ares' expression admirably, and it wasn't a pretty picture. It wasn't meant to be.

To Alaric, it was a reminder: he'd never let himself be trapped again.

"How are we doing today?" came a bright, female voice.

Annabel McLeod entered the room, Will trotting at her

heels. The two had showed up after the shooting—summoned by Jarvis, the old betrayer—and proceeded to nurse Alaric, who'd been too weak to fend them off.

Now he glared at his sister-in-law. She had pulled back the sleeve of his robe without so much as a by-your-leave and was fussing with the dressing on his right arm.

"Are you trying to finish off what the assassin started?" he said.

Annabel narrowed her violet eyes at him. No tepid lass, his brother's wife. Her temper could flare as brightly as her hair. The Scotsman in him respected a woman who could give as good as she got. Of course, this made him think of Miss Kent.

Did she know that he'd been shot? If she did, would she care?

Only insofar as she'd like to finish the job.

"If you'd hold still instead of thrashing like a lamprey, I'd have an easier time of it," Annabel said tartly. "Dr. Abernathy said to check the wound at least once a day."

"He may be Scottish, but he's still a quack," Alaric grumbled.

"You keep your tone civil, or I'll take my leave and my wife with me," his brother growled from the other side of the bed.

Turning his head on the pillow, Alaric inquired, "Oh, you're still here?"

"You bloody ingrate—"

"Enough, you dunderheads." Annabel peeled away his bandage with enough force to make him inhale sharply. Her auburn brows knit together as she peered at his injury. "The wound's oozing, but it doesn't look infected. The mold paste appears to be doing its job."

"The paste was a fine touch, lass," Will said. "Brains as well as beauty. I'm a lucky fellow."

Seeing the smug expression on his brother's face, Alaric thought he might be ill again. For all his brawn, Will was naught but an oversized pup when it came to his wife. What a chump.

Although he had to admit that Annabel had proved rather handy in this instance. The daughter of a country physician, she'd been the one to suggest smearing his wound with the concoction of fermented bread, an infection preventative that her father had used with great success. Dr. Abernathy had been intrigued in her fount of knowledge, and the two had had quite a time of it, debating ways to treat Alaric's injury. He'd felt like a side of beef with two chefs arguing over which was the best way to serve him up.

"I'm the lucky one." Adoration shone in Annabel's eyes as she gazed at her husband.

Devil take it, the two should just find a bedchamber and be done with it.

She set a tray over Alaric's lap. "As for you, Your Grace, you'd best eat something if you hope to regain your strength."

His stomach churned at the sight of the gruel; it brought back memories of the old duke's punishments. Of the tasteless mush he'd been given to cure him of his "malingering." He'd sooner starve than eat a spoonful of such shite again.

"I'm not hungry," he said testily. "I'd like rest and privacy, if you please."

Fists on her hips, Annabel looked ready to argue, but Will intervened. "Not until we talk."

"About what?" Alaric said.

"Who's out to kill you, for starters."

"That's none of your affair." In a moment of weakness—which he chalked up to blood loss—he'd told his brother everything, from the poison in his whiskey to the shooter last night.

Will glowered at him. "We're kin. Of course it's my affair."

Jarvis' wizened head poked into the room. "Your Grace, Mr. Kent has arrived."

"Send him up," Will said before Alaric could answer.

Jarvis—or should he say *Judas*—shuffled out to do Will's bidding.

"What the devil is your partner doing here?" Alaric demanded.

"I asked him to come. He's the best investigator in London." Will folded his arms over his chest. "And something tells me your particular predicament calls for the best."

Before Alaric could argue further, footsteps sounded on the stairs, and, a minute later, Ambrose Kent strode in. He wasn't alone. Miss Kent followed and mayhap Alaric was hungrier than he realized for she looked luscious in a dress the color of summer peaches. An odd spasm hit his chest when he saw the genuine worry in her eyes.

She was concerned ... about him?

"Your Grace. I do hope we're not inconveniencing you."

Alaric's gaze shifted to the owner of the sultry, feminine voice. He hadn't noticed the regal silver blonde who had followed Miss Kent in, though by all rights he ought to have. Mrs. Kent, the former Lady Marianne Draven, was an Incomparable after all. She performed an elegant curtsy. Hastily, Emma followed suit, and her unfussy little bob made him want to smile.

Schooling his features, he tried to discern if Miss Kent's family had any inkling about the escapade at Andromeda's or her visit last evening to his home. Given the fact that her brother wasn't throttling him or calling him out, he guessed she'd kept their encounters under wraps.

Her discretion was surprising—and irritating. Any other virgin would be clamoring for him to do the right thing. But not Emma Kent, the stubborn, high-minded chit. He, a bloody *duke*, wasn't good enough for her. The question flitted into his head—what the hell *did* she desire in a husband?—and he shoved it out just as quickly.

He deliberately turned his attention upon her sister-in-law. "Mrs. Kent," he drawled, "beauty such as yours is never an inconvenience. I'm afraid I'm rather laid up at the moment. Otherwise I'd pay you proper homage."

"You had better not," Will said under his breath.

Alaric got his brother's meaning. Although he'd judged his brother's partner to be a calm, reasonable fellow, the warning scowl on Ambrose Kent's face suggested otherwise. Which went to show that even a rational man could be made a fool over a woman.

Well, if Kent and Will didn't know the difference between idle flirtation and actual intent, that was their problem. The truth was that it required effort to keep his attention upon Mrs. Kent when all he wanted to do was look at Emma. Surreptitiously, he continued to monitor her.

She was taking in his private sanctuary, a line furrowing between her fine brows as her gaze hit the painting. He wondered what she was thinking. To him, she looked deliciously out of place in the masculine bedchamber. Against the backdrop of the striped forest green silk walls and heavy mahogany furnishings, she appeared more like a fresh, juicy fruit than ever.

An image burst upon his brain: Miss Kent naked and tied to his big tester bed, moaning as he buried his face buried between her thighs ...

Beneath the covers, his cock stirred against his thigh. *Get a bloody hold of yourself, man.* Thank God the tray hid his disgraceful state.

"It seems I owe you an apology, Your Grace," Kent said stiffly. "We Kents have misjudged you, and I have come to make amends. The services of Kent and Associates are at your disposal, with my compliments."

Alaric was tempted to tell Kent to take his free services and go to hell ... but as much as it galled him, he did need help. Someone was out to kill him, and the Runners he'd hired were proving worthless. They were flummoxed by the shooting, had made no progress on the poisoning either.

His instincts told him that Kent was a man who could be trusted. And, despite the longstanding animosity between him and Will, the truth was that he knew his brother would never stab him in the back ... however much he might deserve it.

"Your Grace." Miss Kent approached the side of his bed. Fingers knotted together, she said, "I am terribly sorry that my actions led to you being harmed, and I hope you will be willing to forgive the past."

Her beseeching eyes and sincere apology hit him like pellets of sunshine. His antagonism slowly melted. When it came to the misunderstanding over Clara's death, he found he couldn't hold a grudge against Miss Kent any longer. It would be churlish to do so when, in truth, she'd made an honest mistake, and his own actions hadn't been blameless.

"Think no more of it. You didn't shoot me—some blighter did," he said brusquely.

He was rewarded by her tremulous smile.

"Do you know the identity of the shooter?" Kent drew his attention to the business at hand.

"No. But he had a scar. Like this." Alaric drew a finger down the middle of his face, mimicking the zigzagging disfigurement. "It was dark, and I didn't get a good look at the rest of him."

"That's a start." Kent had removed a small notebook and

was scribbling in it. "Onto suspects, then. Who might want you dead?"

"A charming fellow like him?" Will snorted. "You'll need a bigger book."

"Very droll, Peregrine," Alaric said in icy tones. "As a matter of fact, only one person comes to mind. His name is Silas Webb, and he used to work for the company I acquired." He related his history with Webb. "The Runners I hired haven't been able to find any trace of him."

"We'll look into it." Kent tapped his pencil against the page. "Might you have any other enemies related to your mining venture or other business dealings? In my experience, money is a prime motivation for murder."

"Anyone who has invested in my scheme has become richer for it. If blunt were the measure, I'd be rolling in friends," Alaric said.

"Speaking of personal relationships, do you have any, um, intimate acquaintances who might have an axe to grind?" Miss Kent put in. "I've heard it said that poison is a woman's weapon, you see—"

"We're not discussing my private affairs," he said.

He'd be damned if that Pandora's Box was opened in front of an audience. Nevertheless, Miss Kent's conjecture made his chest tighten uncomfortably. After Laura's death, he'd gone on a bit of a sexual rampage, having more than his share of *affaires*; some of them had not ended well. Despite his making his expectations clear, a few ladies had hoped for marriage. Would any of them try to murder him over the disappointment?

It seemed unlikely, to say the least.

"How can we solve the case if you don't tell us everything?" Miss Kent said.

"*You* are not getting involved."

He and Kent traded startled glances—they'd said the

words simultaneously.

She crossed her arms beneath her bosom. "I'm just trying to help."

"Emma does have a point." This came from Mrs. Kent. "Relationships can be deadly. For instance," she said, "have you considered Lord Osgood as a possible culprit? He'd have motive—against both you and Lady Osgood for making him a cuckold."

"Excellent point, my dear," Kent said.

"As far as I know, the Osgoods had an understanding. Lord Osgood had no problem with his wife's ... friendships." Seeing Miss Kent's rapt interest, Alaric searched for a delicate explanation. "As long as she was discreet, he encouraged it because he had his own pursuits."

"He had *friendships* with other ladies?" Miss Kent said, wrinkling her nose.

"Not with ladies, no." He saw understanding dawn for everyone except Miss Kent, who continued to look confused. "My point is Lord Osgood understood and benefited from their arrangement. He wanted a wife on his arm and a marriage to show the world; he had no reason to kill Clara."

"Ah," Mrs. Kent said. To Miss Kent, she murmured, "I'll explain later, dear."

Kent cleared his throat. "As I see it, there are two avenues of investigation with which to proceed. The first is the poisoning. McLeod told me about your runaway maid, and it is a coincidence that cannot be overlooked. Your staff must be interrogated."

"It's been done," Alaric said.

"Not by me."

Said without pride, there was nonetheless a confidence to Kent's words that inspired Alaric's own. For the first time since this murder business began, he felt a prickle of hope.

"Now for the shooting." Kent came closer to the bed.

"After McLeod described the attempt to me, I went to the scene."

So saying, he removed a small drawstring pouch from his side pocket and emptied the contents onto the coverlet.

In disbelief, Alaric picked up the pair of lead balls, studying them. Misshapen and lumpy, they were each the approximate size of his thumbnail. "You *found* the shot?"

"They were embedded in a wooden post behind where you were standing." Kent shrugged. "So we know the weapon was double-barreled. By my guess, a flintlock."

Shaking his head in amazement, Alaric picked up the torn segment of paper next to the bullet. "What is this?"

"Part of a cartridge wrapper, I believe."

Alaric knew that some shops offered pre-assembled cartridges, with the gunpowder and projectile wrapped in parchment for easy loading. When he put down the paper, specks of a sooty substance clung to his fingertips.

"It was caught in alleyway debris a few yards from where you were attacked. The fact that there's still gunpowder residue upon it suggests that the cartridge was freshly used," Kent said.

A memory pushed through Alaric's brain.

"As the carriage was coming toward me, I saw something fly out of the window. It could have been this." He turned the paper this way and that and saw a symbol along the ragged edge. Part of it had been torn away; what remained was half an oval filled with squiggly lines. "Is that an emblem of some sort?"

"I believe it is part of an insignia used by the gun shop. It may lead us to the place that sold the weapon and the shooter himself. If it suits you for our firm to take on your case, I will personally pursue that line of enquiry."

Alaric had to admit he was impressed. "The case is yours—on one condition."

Kent quirked a brow.

"I will pay your usual rate plus any expenses incurred in the course of the investigation. I will not be beholden to anyone," he stated.

Kent exchanged looks with Will, who shrugged.

"As you wish," Kent said crisply. "In addition to the footmen I saw out front, I would suggest that you retain professional guardsmen for your protection."

"I know some fellows," Will said. "Honest, reliable men from the regiment who I fought side by side with and can vouch for. They'd be keen on the job."

Alaric inclined his head. "Hire them on."

"I will keep you apprised of our progress." Kent bowed. "We will leave you to your rest."

"Our wishes for your speedy recovery, Your Grace," Mrs. Kent said.

"May I visit again?" Miss Kent blurted. "To inquire on your health?"

Her request surprised ... and touched him. "If you wish," he said gruffly.

"I'll be here in the afternoons," Annabel chirped up. "So I could chaperone."

Kent's brows came together. "Emma, it isn't safe. After all, the duke has been targeted—"

"You saw the footmen outside, darling," Mrs. Kent cut in, "and now there's to be armed guards as well. This place is more secure than St. James's Palace."

Kent looked as if he might argue further, but his wife took him by the arm and led him toward the door. "I'll accompany Emma the day after tomorrow. Would two o'clock suit, Annabel?"

"Perfectly, Marianne."

To Alaric, the look shared by the two ladies appeared suspiciously ... conspiratorial.

Chapter Thirteen

Accompanied by Marianne, Emma returned to Strathaven's residence two days later. The Palladian townhouse looked even more imposing with the armed guards flanking the entrance. Mr. Jarvis showed them inside, and she saw that his gait was as slow and shuffling as the last time. Removing a jar from the basket she was carrying, she handed it to him.

"'Tis a salve that relieves aching joints," she said. "I thought you might like to try it."

"Right kind o' ye, miss. Much obliged," he said with a wide smile.

As he led her and Marianne through the foyer, she asked, "How is His Grace faring today?"

"He's much recovered. Been through worse. His Grace ain't no dainty English fop, but a Scot through and through."

Emma heard the pride in the butler's voice. "Have you worked for him long?"

"Worked for Strathavens my whole life, miss. I was there that first day His Grace arrived at Strathmore Castle. Nine years old, he was, and the new ward of the former duke."

Emma recalled what Annabel had said about Strathaven being raised apart from his brother at a young age. "Why did he come to live here when he had his own family?"

"His father was a distant cousin to the old duke. When the duke's own son died and he and the duchess couldna have another, he took the young master in."

Emma pondered this as the butler slowly led them up one sweeping wing of the double staircase. "Wasn't he sad to be parted from his family and at so young an age?" Put in his situation, her heart would have torn in two.

"Not every family is a happy one, dear," Marianne murmured.

"Canna say I know much about that. Even as a lad, His Grace was never the sort to wear his heart on his sleeve." Pausing on the landing, Mr. Jarvis looked back at Emma, his rheumy gaze unexpectedly shrewd. "He's got his reasons to protect it, but if you approach with a patient, kind hand, you'll see his bark is worse than his bite."

Before Emma could digest that, Mrs. McLeod came toward them.

"Emma, thank goodness you've come," the auburn-haired beauty said. "Strathaven is in quite the temper today."

"I may not improve that situation," Emma said truthfully.

"Nonsense. He has been asking for you."

"He has?" Her heart gave a silly little hiccup. "He wants to see me?"

"His precise words were *I thought the chit was supposed to be here at two.*" Winking, Mrs. McLeod nudged her toward the door. "Why don't you go on in, dear. I have something to discuss with Marianne, and we'll be in shortly."

With a fortifying breath, Emma ventured into the bedchamber.

Strathaven was sitting up in his tester bed, lounging against pillows, a portrait of sartorial elegance in his black silk dressing robe. At the same time, there were hints of vulnerability, too: his thick raven hair was tousled, and shadows hung beneath his eyes. He studied a letter, then tossed it impatiently onto the pile of correspondence on the bed.

"Good afternoon, Your Grace," she said.

His head jerked up, and pale green eyes roved over her. "You came after all."

"I said I would."

"How rare. A woman who keeps her word," he drawled.

She was about to retort in kind when Mr. Jarvis' words came back to her. Was the duke's surliness a shield of sorts? Had he been hurt in the past—by his family? Or someone else?

Even so, it's no reason for him to snap at me.

With a patience honed from raising four siblings, she counted to ten in her head. "I'm only late because of this." She tapped the wicker basket. "Our chef is territorial when it comes to the kitchen. I had to wait until he went out to the market before I could use it."

His dark brows came together. "Why would you need to use the kitchen?"

"To cook, of course." Spotting the tray on the side table, she went to unpack the basket's contents. She brought the tray over to the bed and placed it over Strathaven's lap.

He stared down as if he'd never seen stew or bread before. "You made that? For me?"

The odd note in his voice reminded her that ladies of the *ton* didn't prepare meals, leaving such menial tasks to the staff. Emma, however, had cooked all her life, and back in Chudleigh Crest, it had been a gesture of goodwill to bring sustenance to sickly neighbors.

"It's just hotchpotch," she said with sudden embarrassment. "Mrs. McLeod said you weren't eating, so I thought you might like to try it. It's quite restoring—my brother Harry always asked for it when he was ill."

Strathaven gave her an unreadable glance. He picked up the spoon and dipped it into the simmered medley of meat and vegetables. Gingerly, he brought it to his mouth.

What was I thinking, preparing a simple country dish for a duke?

He probably had a team of French chefs producing cuisine suitable for his refined palate. She wanted to groan at her gaucheness.

It was too late. He'd sampled the spoonful.

"It's good." He sounded surprised. "Delicious, actually."

Flustered by the compliment, she said, "It probably just seems so compared to the bland sickroom foods you've been eating. I've never understood why a sick person should have to eat food a healthy person wouldn't."

"I've never understood it myself," he said.

He flashed a smile at her—a crooked, boyish one that transformed him, in a blink, from a wickedly brooding duke to a devastatingly handsome man. Her senses reeled.

He waved her to a chair at his bedside, where she sat, further astonished when he proceeded to tear off a piece of the loaf she'd baked, dipping it into the bowl. This was something any member of her family would have done, but he seemed too sophisticated, too *ducal*, to mop up hotchpotch with bread.

Nonetheless, he ate with seeming gusto, and her gaze wandered to the painting on the bedside wall. The dark, grotesque picture depicted a man—an ancient soldier, she would guess, from his crested helmet and gladiator-like garb—held captive in ... an urn? His expression ravaged, the poor fellow pummeled his fists futilely at the walls.

Who in their right mind would want to wake up to that? she mused.

"Can you cook anything else?" Strathaven drew her attention back to him.

She nodded. "My mama taught me. Being the eldest girl, I helped her in the kitchen as soon as I could peel a potato.

After she passed, I took over preparing the family's meals."

"How old were you when she died?"

"Thirteen." Were they having a ... normal conversation?

"That explains it."

"Explains what?"

"Your tendency to take charge."

Her shoulders stiffened. "I do what needs to be done, Your Grace. If you want to call that managing, then so be it."

"You needn't take that tone." He put down his spoon, wiped his mouth with a napkin. "Tell me, Miss Kent, are you always this difficult? Or is it merely with me?"

"No one has called me difficult before you." At least, not to her *face*.

"It's me, then." His mouth curved in the faintest of smiles. "'Tis only fair, I suppose."

"What is fair?"

"Given that you seem to bring out the devil in me, it is only fair that I should have the same effect on you," he said dryly.

She was about to argue that there was no devil in her—but that wasn't true, was it? Since meeting him, she'd interfered with justice, visited a bawdy house, and engaged in a reckless embrace. She'd discovered her susceptibility to wanton impulses; her once sturdy morals lay in shambles. With a feeling of resignation, she decided not to add lying to the list.

"Fine. We bring out the worst in each other," she muttered. "Satisfied, Your Grace?"

He laughed, the husky sound ruffling her senses further. "I believe that this is the first time we have agreed on anything."

Wry humor tugged at her lips. "We agree that we disagree?"

He gave a slow nod. "To celebrate the momentous occasion—and also because it seems ludicrous not do so at this juncture—let's skip the formalities, shall we? My name is Alaric."

"Oh. Well, I'm Emma. As you know." She fought to keep from blushing.

His smile faded, and his gaze grew intent. "Tell me, Emma, why are you being so nice?"

"I'm not acting any differently than usual."

"Let me rephrase, then: why are you being nice to *me*?"

Right. Now that she could see that his health was improving, 'twas time to proceed with the other purpose of her visit.

Alaric was in danger, and he needed help. Ambrose was making some headway, but his interrogation of Alaric's staff had turned up no clues. Desperately, Emma had begged her brother to let her have a go with the maids. He'd adamantly refused.

"You've been far too entangled with Strathaven already," he'd said sternly. (*You don't know the half of it*, she'd thought). "I won't have you involved in this business any further, Em."

There'd been no swaying her brother. Once he made his mind up, Ambrose was as stubborn as an ox. This left her one other option. If she could convince *Alaric* to let her talk to his servants, then maybe she could find a clue to the missing Lily Hutchins—and save his life.

She had to try.

"Since your life is in peril, I thought we should bury the hatchet," she began.

"Consider it buried."

That was easy. Too easy. His expression gave away nothing.

"You know my brother talked to your staff at the cottage—"

"And discovered nothing. As I predicted."

"It can be difficult for women to talk to men," she said diplomatically. "On the other hand, perhaps if *I* were to interview the maids—"

"Devil take it, I should have known." He scowled at her. "You're like a bloody dog with a bone, you know that?"

"I'm only trying to help," she protested.

"Why?"

"What do you mean *why*? Someone shot at you. Your life is at risk—"

"I'm touched by your concern for my welfare. But there's something else, another reason, isn't there?" Beneath his piercing gaze, she found herself squirming. "Spit it out, Miss Kent, or I will drag it out of you."

She huffed out a breath. "I *do* care whether you live or die—God knows why. But, yes, my plan does benefit us both. I tried to explain this to you last time, but you wouldn't give me a chance—"

"Explain now."

"By assisting in your case, I will prove to my brother that I am capable of doing investigative work. Joining Kent and Associates is my calling, and I'm going to fulfill it one way or another." With a touch of defiance, she added, "What do you think?"

"You don't want to know," he grated out.

He'd *known* the chit had something up her sleeve.

Alaric fought to control his anger at being manipulated. Cooking him stew, acting so concerned, being so sweet—all of it was a ploy. She was as cunning as all the females he'd known. To think, he'd been touched that she seemed to care ...

His gut balled as he thought of Laura. How he'd fallen for her words of love. After their wedding, her adoring whispers had warped into insistent demands for his attention. No matter how much he gave, it had never been enough. She'd goaded him, tried to make him jealous, bedded one man after another. All the while, she'd blamed him.

You're a selfish bastard. You have no heart. You don't know how to love.

Aye, she'd been a manipulative bitch—but she hadn't been wrong, either.

He did lack the capacity for softer feelings, and it was a *bloody good thing*. Because they couldn't be used against him. Because no one, not even Emma Kent, could twist him to her will. Her stupid whims. Fury frosted his insides. A *female* investigator? Who ever heard of that?

She shot to her feet, glaring down at him. "You're as bad as Ambrose. Why won't either of you at least give my plan a chance?"

With a curse, he yanked aside the covers.

She backed away. "Have a care. Your injury—"

"Damn my injury and damn your obstinacy." He stalked toward her, backing her into a corner. Through his teeth, he said, "Next time, don't bother with the stew and just say what you want."

"What does stew have to do with this?" She sounded bewildered. "And I *am* telling you what I want!"

"You can't seriously think you can be an investigator," he snapped.

"Why not?"

"We're talking about a murder investigation. A dangerous business and one that you are entirely unsuited for."

She *dared* to glower at him. "And why is that?"

"Because you're a bloody lass—and an innocent one at that!"

She scowled. "I'm not *that* innocent, thanks to you."

Of all the times to remind him of blasted Andromeda's—he set his jaw, struggled to think through his haze of anger and arousal. Why did she always push him to edge? The idea of her hurt because of this mess set off a maddening beat in his blood. Protective instincts he'd thought long dead roared to life and angered him even more.

Why did she stir up his old, stupid dreams?

Experience had taught him that love was just a euphemism for power. In relationships, there were only two options: control or be controlled. He would never be anyone's puppet again.

"You're not getting involved, and that is final," he gritted out.

"You cannot dictate what I do." Her bosom surged.

"Can't I? I believe I proved you wrong two nights ago in my library. Care for another demonstration?" Because he *burned* to give it to her.

"Stop trying to intimidate me with your ... your seductive wiles!"

"So you do find me seductive."

"I do *not*."

"You can't hide the truth from me, Emma." In a swift motion, he caught her wrists in one hand, pinned them above her head. He leaned in, heat sizzling in the sliver of air between them. "You melt for me every time we touch."

"No, I don't—"

In favor of expedience, he kissed her.

She struggled, and he gave her no quarter, holding her in place. He took her mouth, her flavor flooding his senses, his anger exploding into raw desire. Within seconds, she surrendered, yielding with a delicious sigh. Driving his tongue home, he pressed his hard, aroused body against her willing softness.

Restrained, her passion burned even more brightly. Her soft little body stretched tantalizingly against his own hard edges, and he felt like he was on a rack of pleasure as she strained against him, her eyes glazed with desire, her stiff nipples teasing his chest through layers of fabric.

His mind warned him of the dangers; the door was open, anyone could see them.

That only heated his blood *more*.

He tossed up her skirts with his free hand, his lungs burning as he encountered the silken softness of her thighs. He covered her mouth with his own, drinking in her gasp, shuddering as his questing fingers found her damp curls and the slick petals within.

By God, she had the softest, wettest little cunny.

When he circled her pearl, she moaned.

"Be very quiet," he whispered. "Unless you want to get caught."

Understanding widened her eyes. At the same time, her hips lurched helplessly against his hand. She bit down on her bottom lip as he played with her love-knot, stroking it, titillating the bold nub as he held her against the wall. Her color rose, her bosom surging, and he knew she was close to her climax. Rolling her clit with his thumb, he slid his middle finger along her plump cleft.

He held her gaze as he pushed inside her virginal hole.

She was hot, wet, so tight. So bloody *perfect*.

"God, why can't I get enough of you?" he rasped against her ear.

Her lips parted on a soundless cry.

He barely restrained his own groan as she came, the lush flutters making his erection jerk beneath his robe, a spurt of pre-spend scorching his belly. He gritted his teeth, fighting the urge to replace his finger with his cock, to take her here and now—

"Annabel, it's been lovely chatting." Marianne Kent's overly loud voice drifted through the doorway. "I think it's time we go check on Emma and His Grace."

Panting, Emma stared at him in mute panic.

In the next instant, he shoved himself away from her. In the nick of time, he got back into bed and tossed the covers over himself. His heart hammered, his loins throbbed. Every cell of his body hummed with need.

"Emma, are you finished visiting?" Mrs. Kent entered with Annabel behind her. "I have other calls to make today."

"Y-yes," Emma stammered.

"We'll take our leave then, Your Grace." Mrs. Kent took her charge's arm, turned to go.

He collected his wits. "Miss Kent?"

"Yes?" Emma faced him, her color heightening.

"I trust you will not forget our *tête-à-tête* today." He gave her his most quelling, ducal stare. "There's to be no more talk of you sleuthing about. We have an understanding, do we not?"

Annoyance flashed in her gaze. Her chin high, she said, "You have yours, and I have mine." Even her curtsy was defiant. "Good day, Your Grace."

Goddamnit. Frustration and desire roiled in him as she walked out with the other two.

Clearly, Emma meant to meddle further in his affairs. His title, his wealth and power—hell, his *sexual dominance*—none of it intimidated her one bit.

He wanted to bare his teeth.

He wanted to screw her senseless.

He shoved his hands through his hair. Even if he felt the *tiniest* tug of respect for her audacity, no way in hell was he going to let her run amok in his life. He'd have to keep her under watch. If—*when*—her behavior went out of bounds, he would intervene. Swiftly and decisively. He would show her once and for all who was in control.

Anticipation flared in him. The blood of his ancestors drummed in his veins.

That's how you want to play it, lass? Then let the games begin.

Chapter Fourteen

The next day, Emma paid the hackney driver and descended onto Compton Street, a busy thoroughfare near Soho Square. Storefronts lined both sides of the street, and people and horses jostled along the cobblestone. Emma's destination was Number Eight, a two-storey building sandwiched between a bakeshop and a pianoforte maker's store. A small gold placard on the dark green door read simply, "Kent and Associates."

Stepping inside, Emma paused on the threshold. The sun shone through the bow window at the front of the room, glinting off the reception desk and stairwell that led up to the partners' new suites, which had been added in the reconstruction. A small waiting area boasted comfortable seating and newspapers to peruse. The scent of baking bread mixed with the occasional discordant chord of an instrument being tuned.

Something about the office had always reminded Emma of the cottage in Chudleigh Crest. Perhaps it was the coziness, the hodgepodge of sights, sounds, and smells, and the hum of activity. Coming here was like coming ... home.

She couldn't give up. She had to convince her brother to give her a chance.

I am capable of being an investigator, she thought fiercely. *I'll show everyone—especially Strathaven.*

For a brief instant yesterday, it'd seemed as if she and the duke had reached an armistice. She'd discovered his approachable side, a hotchpotch-eating fellow with a heart-melting smile. Then he'd attacked her for no reason, disparaged her goals ... and shown her hot, wicked pleasure, the likes of which she hadn't known existed. Her toes curled in memory of that mind-obliterating bliss.

His carnal whisper shivered over her. *God, why can't I get enough of you?*

As if he ... needed her.

The notion thrilled, confused, and dismayed her. Why did they share this intense physical attraction when they were ill-suited in every other way? Strathaven was nothing like the sort of man she would envision for herself. He wasn't principled or kindhearted; he wasn't a man devoted to his family. *He* was complicated, moody—and a duke to top it off.

The only thing they had in common, it seemed, was stubbornness. He faced *imminent* peril and yet he still refused her help. How could he expect her to stand by and do nothing?

"Miss Kent, what a pleasant surprise!"

Mr. Hobson, the bespectacled clerk, came bounding down the hallway toward her with a tea tray in hand. Around her age, he had a puppyish quality owing to his downy golden-brown hair and cheerful disposition. His eagerness to please was matched only by his innate clumsiness—a fact that exasperated Ambrose and his partners to no end.

If Hobson hasn't spilled or broken something, then the day's not over, Mr. McLeod was wont to grumble.

What Hobson lacked in adroitness, however, he made up for in loyalty, optimism, and unquenchable enthusiasm. One couldn't help but like him. Even if he constantly splattered ink over everything and smashed all the good tea cups.

From experience, Emma knew to keep her distance from the tray in his tenuous grasp.

"Hello, Mr. Hobson. Is my brother in?" she said.

"Indeed." The clerk lowered his voice. "He's with the Mr. Hilliards upstairs. They dropped by unannounced."

"Ah," Emma said.

The Hilliards were the father and son bankers who had provided the loan for the rebuilding of the office. Shrewd businessmen, they popped in now and again to ascertain the health of the business—and their investment.

"I was about to bring up tea. Got cakes from the bakery. Thought they might sweeten the two up a bit," Hobson whispered.

Emma looked at the tray. Two of the cakes had fingerprints embedded on the glaze. The other two had clearly crumbled and been put back together ... oddly. They now resembled haphazard little haystacks.

"I had some trouble getting them out of the box." Hobson's brow pleated. "Do you think anyone will notice?"

She was saved from the need to reply by voices and footsteps coming down the stairs. Ambrose appeared with the Hilliards in tow.

"Emma," he said in surprise. "I wasn't expecting you. You remember the Hilliards?"

She curtsied politely. "Good day, sirs."

"And to you, Miss Kent." Mr. Hilliard Junior bent over her hand. Dressed in somber black relieved only by the white of his shirt, he reminded her a bit of a penguin. He was short and rotund, a younger replica of his father. "Father and I are most impressed with the progress that's been made here, and Mr. Kent tells us you played a hand in things."

"I'm always happy to assist where I can," Emma said.

"A young lady who isn't afraid to roll her sleeves up, eh?" Mr. Hilliard Senior winked broadly at his son. "Don't find many of those around these days."

His son's ears turned red.

"I'll see you out, sirs," Ambrose said abruptly. "Emma,

wait for me upstairs?"

As the men went outside, Emma headed up to the new floor, which was bisected by a main hallway with offices on either side. Ambrose's suite was at the end of the corridor, a comfortable space paneled in oak. Leather seats were clustered by the stone fireplace, and a shelf of books took up one wall. The desk sat by the front window.

She went to look out the curtains and saw Ambrose talking with the Hilliards by their carriage. Idly, her gaze went to his desk ... and landed on his appointment book. Before she could question her actions, she was flipping through the pages.

Her brother had been busy in the last week, making many enquiries on Strathaven's behalf. Leafing through, she found the record of the visit to the duke's cottage and memorized the address in St. John's Wood. Hearing footsteps, she quickly closed the book and dashed to the other side of the desk, plopping herself into a chair. Her pulse thudded guiltily.

"Sorry to keep you waiting, Em," her brother said as he entered.

"Is everything alright?" she said. "With the Hilliards, I mean?"

Ambrose sat across the desk from her, his expression rueful. "As long as we make our monthly payments, they've no basis for complaint."

Emma's guilt doubled as she saw the strain on her brother's face. He was a man who disliked debts; such a large one must sit uneasily on his broad shoulders. She felt an acute yearning for the old days, when he'd shared his burdens with her. When they'd been a team.

"Please let me help," she blurted.

"Don't worry your head over it, Em," he said. "The agency is doing fine. Our clientele is expanding—we'll keep the Hilliards happy."

"But you could use an extra pair of hands. I know Strathaven's case has taken up much of your time. I've been thinking," she plunged on, "about ways I could contribute. For instance, if you'd give me a chance to interview his staff—"

"We've been through this. I don't want you involved." Though quiet, Ambrose's tone possessed an edge of steely finality. "Especially with the Duke of Strathaven."

"I—I'm not involved with him." Her cheeks heated.

"I see the way he looks at you," her brother said flatly. "He's a rake, Emma, an unsavory sort. You're too innocent to understand, but I assure you his intentions are not honorable."

A foreign and mutinous urge crept over her to tell her brother that she not only knew what Strathaven's intentions entailed, she'd already experienced them. *Twice.*

Instead, she bit her tongue and said, "I owe him, Ambrose. After how I misjudged him—"

"I'll take care of it."

Frustrated, she stared at her brother. "You used to trust me."

Surprise flickered in his amber eyes. "I do trust you. But this is men's business, rife with danger. I won't allow you to get hurt."

"There's *nothing* I can say to convince you to let me help?"

Why are you treating me like I'm useless?

"None at all, though I appreciate the offer." He came over and patted her on the shoulder. "Run along, Em. I'm sure you can find something to do at home."

Emma had never willfully disobeyed her brother before, and her heart and head were in turmoil as the hackney entered St. John's Wood. She felt guilty over defying Ambrose, yet her sense of resolution was stronger. She *knew* that both he and Strathaven needed her help, and she couldn't stand by wringing her hands. She was a Kent, after all.

In this case, she would have to act first, apologize later.

Follow the wisdom of your heart.

That advice brought her to Alaric's "cottage," a luxurious Italianate villa nestled within a bucolic setting of woods and flowering plants which seemed a world away from the city. As the hackney rolled up the long drive, she observed the privacy afforded by the towering trees and hedges.

When she rang the bell, a woman in her middling years answered. Her black taffeta dress and firmly secured knot of grey hair announced her as the housekeeper.

"How may I help you, miss?" she said.

"I am Emma Kent." Squelching her guilt, Emma handed over the business card she'd filched from Mr. Hobson's desk on her way out from the office. "Kent and Associates was hired by His Grace to investigate the matter of Lady Osgood."

Frowning, the good lady looked at the card, then at her.

Emma assumed her most professional expression.

"Those gentlemen from your firm were here earlier this week," the housekeeper said.

"I'm following up," Emma improvised. "I have a few more questions."

The woman scrutinized her for a few more moments before standing aside. "I am Mrs. Millbury, the housekeeper, and I've already told the gentlemen what I know about Lily Hutchins, which is very little. If you must, however, you may speak to the maids again."

Emma could barely contain her excitement. "Thank you, Mrs. Millbury."

She was brought to wait in a salon, which had been decorated with an exotic flair. Bronze bamboo-patterned silk covered the walls, and the furnishings were upholstered in a rich shade of Oriental blue. The overall feeling was one of decadence. Thinking of the guests Alaric must entertain here, Emma felt her chest tighten with a foreign feeling ... jealousy?

Surely not. She had no attachment to him, no claim.

You're here to find a murderer. So focus.

Two maids entered, a plump brunette and a ginger-haired girl. Both bent their knees.

"Good mornin', Miss Kent." The brunette was bran-faced, with dimpled cheeks that hinted at a jolly disposition. "Mrs. Millbury said you wanted to speak wif us?"

"Yes, Miss ...?"

"I'm Jenny." Clearly the leader, the brunette jerked her chin at her companion. "And this 'ere is Gretchen."

Gretchen ducked her chin shyly.

"Won't you both sit down?" Emma said.

"Don't mind if I do." Jenny plopped herself on the divan while Gretchen perched on its edge.

Taking the adjacent wingchair, Emma pulled out a pencil and notebook from her reticule. "I understand that both of you knew Lily Hutchins. Would you describe her to me?"

"Ash-blond 'air, 'azel eyes, the kind o' female gents take notice o', if you catch my meaning." Jenny snorted. "Lily started work 'ere about a month ago, but as I told the other investigators, she was too hoity-toity to rub shoulders with the likes o' me and Gretchen. Myself, I wouldn't be surprised if she *were* the one that done the poisoning."

"Why do you say that?" Emma said swiftly.

Jenny tapped her temple. "I *know* people, miss. Worked in more than a few 'ouseholds in my time, and there was somefin' not right 'bout Lily."

"What wasn't right about her?"

"She didn't *know* things, for starters. Once, I caught 'er using silver polish on a *copper* pot."

"When a dash of salt and lemon juice would have sufficed," Emma said, her brow scrunching. Any housemaid ought to know *that*.

Jenny gave her a woman-to-woman look. "'Xactly. Lily made plenty o' other mistakes, too, but got away wif it on account o' 'er charms. 'Ad Billy—'e's the second footman—running in circles doing 'er chores."

"Do you think Billy might know her whereabouts?"

"Nah." Jenny rolled her eyes. "'E was just a pigeon and didn't know 'e were getting plucked. Cried like a babe, 'e did, when Lily up and left."

"Did she mention any places she frequented, anywhere she might have gone?"

Jenny shook her head. "Quiet as a clam, that one. Lily ne'er breathed word 'bout 'erself."

"Actually ... she did mention something once," a timid voice said.

Emma's gaze shot to the other maid, whose cheeks now matched the color of her hair.

"Why didn't you mention it before?" Jenny demanded. "To the master or the investigators?"

"I couldn't say it in front o' gentlemen. It's embarrassing," Gretchen mumbled. "Besides, I'm certain it isn't important."

"Anything you remember could be helpful, Gretchen." Emma gave her a reassuring smile. "Please, I'd like to hear it."

Fingers twisting her skirts, Gretchen said haltingly, "Me

and Lily, we were cleaning up 'is Grace's bedchamber this one time. Suddenly, she curses—on account o' snagging 'er stocking, you see. Since it was just us two, she pulled up 'er skirts to take a closer look, and bless me, if my jaw didn't drop at what I saw."

Emma's spine tingled. "What did you see?"

"'Er stockings, miss. Made o' the finest silk they were, with clocking that stretched from calf to knee." The girl's eyes were as big as dinner plates. "She must have seen me staring, for a strange smile came over her face, and she said, *I'll bet a little maid like you hasn't ever seen something so pretty in all your life, have you?* I told 'er, *No, Lily, I 'aven't.* And then she ... she showed me something else."

"Yes, Gretchen?" Emma leaned forward.

The maid bit her lip. "She made me promise to keep it a secret."

"If she's a murderer, you best not be keeping 'er secrets," Jenny said in stern tones.

In a small voice, Gretchen said, "She let me see ... 'er petticoat. Lord, it was beautiful." Her voice hushed with wonder. "Embroidered with bumblebees and vines and all sorts o' fancy flowers."

Emma's pulse sped up. What was a maid doing with such expensive undergarments?

"Do you know where Lily got the petticoat and stockings?" Emma said.

"Come to think o' it, she did mention a name." Concentration lined Gretchen's forehead. "When I said 'er petticoat looked fit for a queen, Lily laughed and said, *'Tis a king's ransom Madame Marieur charges, but for me, she offers a special discount.*"

Madame Marieur. A lead.

With thrumming excitement, Emma said, "Can you recall anything else, Gretchen?"

"That's it, I swear. I—I didn't think talk o' undergarments was important." The maid's bottom lip trembled. "Am I in trouble, miss?"

"On the contrary, you have been extraordinarily helpful," Emma said. "My thanks to both of you, and now I must take my leave."

Because she had a suspect to find—and a trail to follow.

Chapter Fifteen

Alaric stood before the cheval looking glass in his dressing room. While his valet fussed with the folds of his cravat, Alaric's thoughts returned to the letter he'd received from the dowager duchess. Lady Patrice's spidery cursive had spilled over several pages, with words like "Catastrophe," "Doom," and "Rescue" written in underlined capitals.

His aunt had always had a flair for the dramatic.

The idea of her coming here, filling his house with her nervous, overabundant concern, made him cringe. He'd sent off a reply assuring her that he was fine and telling her to stay put in Lanarkshire. Although he was indebted to Lady Patrice—she'd done her best by him, after all—her constant worries about his health and happiness were draining to say the least.

His plan to find himself a new duchess was, in part, a means to ward her off. Since Laura's death, the dowager had offered tireless support, once again taking over the mistress' duties at Strathmore Castle. Having run the household during her husband's reign, she'd declared it was no trouble at all. Alaric's gratitude had quickly transformed into an intense desire for escape.

Hence, he'd arrived at the solution: find himself a new wife and retire his aunt to the dowager house for good.

Of course, finding a lady who could rub along with his aunt wouldn't be easy. Laura and Patrice had fought like two well-bred cats, polite in public, hissing and clawing in private. An idea had germinated over the last few days, and for an instant, he allowed himself to consider it: how would Emma and Lady Patrice get along?

His ethereal, nervy aunt would likely expire from the shock of Emma's arrow-straight directness.

Yet as mad as the notion was, the idea of making Emma his duchess held a certain ... appeal. Once the possibility had nudged itself into his head, he couldn't help but ponder it. Thanks to her meddling, his search for a wife had been thwarted. Her testimony against him had tainted his reputation, and, even with its retraction, the scandal would take time to fade. He didn't want to waste another Season looking for a wife.

Not when he had a perfectly good candidate staring him in the face.

"The jade or gold cufflinks, Your Grace?"

"Jade," he murmured.

Hell, Emma had made a hash of his marriage plans; she *owed* him a duchess. And marriage would actually give him control over her. She would carry his name. Eventually his child.

His loins stirred at the thought.

Aye, that was the most compelling reason of all: he would no longer have to deny his sexual attraction to her. He could bed her as often, as thoroughly as he wished. Night after night, he could bring about her passionate surrender.

As his valet helped him into his jacket, Alaric told himself not to rush things. Because there would be clear drawbacks to marrying Emma as well—the main one being that he'd never have a moment's peace again. She was the most headstrong, tenacious woman he'd ever met ... yet he had to admit that she was generally not underhanded about it. When Emma defied him, she did so to his face.

In retrospect, he knew it had been unfair to call her manipulative, his reaction triggered by his experiences with Laura. By his dead wife's deviousness, her ability to slyly twist him into knots of guilt and anger.

Despite the dark memory, his mouth suddenly quirked.

One could accuse Emma Kent of being many things but *subtle*? Not so much.

The valet stepped back. "Your Grace?"

Pushing aside his musings, Alaric flicked a look at his reflection. His arm had healed nicely, the bandage barely visible beneath the sleeve of the cutaway. He looked and felt almost as good as new.

"That'll do, Johnston," he said.

The valet bowed, departing as Jarvis shuffled in.

The butler held out a note. "A message arrived, Your Grace. From Mr. Cooper."

Alaric's senses prickled. Richard Cooper was one of the guards he'd hired at his brother's recommendation. Like Will, Cooper had been a scout for the 95th Rifles, and recognizing the stoic ex-soldier's skill immediately, Alaric had assigned him to a special purpose.

Alaric scanned the brief message. The hairs shot up on his nape.

Christ's blood, I'm going to wallop her until she can't sit for a week.

With mingled fury and fear, he pushed by the startled butler, shouting for his carriage.

∞

"How may I assist you ... Mademoiselle Kendall, was it?" The buxom, black-haired proprietress arched a thin eyebrow.

"Um, yes. Eloise Kendall. That's me," Emma said.

Inwardly, she cringed. She hated lying, was terrible at it. Yet as she'd entered the shop located on a hidden lane in Covent Garden, her instincts warned her to keep her true identity and purpose concealed. Something about the place didn't seem quite ... right.

She couldn't put a finger on the reason, however. The boutique was sumptuously decorated in tones of cream and pale bronze. Its wares—ladies' unmentionables that looked as expensive as those Lily had been described as wearing— were artfully displayed.

From all appearances, Madame Marieur ran a successful establishment.

Emma's ears picked up a noise, and her gaze shot to the red curtain at the back of the shop. "What was that sound?"

"Just my girls hard at work. A shop doesn't run itself, you know," Madame Marieur said breezily. "Now how may I help you, *chérie*?"

The dressmaker's polite manner didn't mask the hard impatience in her onyx eyes.

Emma thought quickly. "I'm, um, in need of some undergarments."

"I'm afraid we take clients by appointment only. We are very busy, you understand. Perhaps you will try the modiste on the next block ..." Madame Marieur pushed her toward the door.

Emma dug in her heels. "But ... but Lily said you would help me."

The dressmaker halted, her eyes narrowing. "Lily White sent you? To me?"

Lily *White*? Was that the maid's real name? "Er, yes." Gretchen's words flashed through Emma's brain. "She said you would offer me the, um, *special discount*?"

"I see." Her ploy must have worked because the impatient gleam left Madame's eyes, replaced by one of ...

interest? "I would not have guessed, *petite*, that you are a friend of Lily's."

"We met at a mutual place of employ," Emma extemporized.

"You are an actress at The Cytherea?"

Lily was an *actress*? Had she been hired because of her profession to play the part of a maid in Strathaven's household? Emma's mind spun with new possibilities.

"I met Lily, er ... at a production," she said with thumping excitement. "But I haven't seen her of late. Have you?"

"That one comes and goes, *non*?" Madame shrugged. "I haven't seen her in over a fortnight."

Not since Strathaven had been poisoned. Coincidence? Surely not.

"Do you know where she might have gone?" Emma said.

"You ask many questions." Madame Marieur's eyes narrowed. "You will learn, *chérie*, that discretion is the best policy for women of the world. And you *are* a woman of the world, *n'est-ce pas*?"

"Of course," Emma said hastily.

"*Bien*." The dressmaker's black skirts swished as she went to the counter, crooking a finger for Emma to follow. She opened a ledger with an embossed leather cover and dipped her pen in ink. "Now what will your pleasure be today?"

"I—I'd like a corset and petticoats. And stockings, too. Like Lily's." The more elaborate the ensemble, the more time she'd have to try to finagle information out of Madame Marieur.

"An ambitious little bird, aren't you? You demand the very best my establishment has to offer. As luck would have it,"—a calculating gleam entered the other's eyes—"I happen to have exactly what you seek today."

The dressmaker jotted something down on the page ...

what appeared to be a figure—Good Lord, *five hundred pounds*? For unmentionables?

For an instant, Emma was sorely tempted to negotiate the astronomical figure. But Madame snapped the book shut and headed toward the curtain at the back of the shop.

"Come, *petite*." She beckoned with an impatient hand. "If you wish to complete this transaction, we haven't time to spare."

Emma took a breath. Strathaven had said that he would pay for all expenses incurred in the course of investigation—surely his offer would apply in this situation. At the thought of how he might react to learning of the current intrigue, however, her insides quivered.

She stiffened her backbone and her resolve. *You must act as you know best. You're doing this for Strathaven's own good. Look what you've discovered already.*

Decision made, she went over to Madame, who parted the velvet and opened the heavy door behind it, waving Emma forward into a narrow corridor. The door closed behind them, deepening the shadows. The dancing light of the occasional taper and the deep, musky scent of roses disoriented Emma's senses.

Madame set forth at a brisk pace, Emma stumbling to keep up.

The dressmaker said, "*Le Boudoir Rouge* should do nicely."

Hinges squealed softly, and a door opened, a shaft of light widening into the darkness. With cautious footsteps, Emma followed the other inside. She blinked—for a changing room, this place was opulent, to say the least.

Red beeswax candles diffused a hazy glow throughout the chamber. Their flames swayed in the mirrors that adorned all four walls. Reflections magnified the decadence of the scarlet interior, the walls, divan, and carpeting blending into one lushly wicked hue.

Next to the divan was a dressmaker's raised platform. Plush red carpeting covered the dais and the three steps leading up to it. The customary looking glass was absent; Emma supposed there was no need for it given the field of surrounding mirrors.

"Up you go, *chérie*," Madame Marieur said.

Hesitantly, Emma took the steps up to the dais. As she stood there, images of herself flashed around the chamber, and her breath grew choppy with self-consciousness. The dressmaker rummaged in a cupboard before joining Emma on the stage.

"I have just your size. *Eh bien*, turn around, and we'll get you undressed."

Emma's cheeks burned as the dressmaker proceeded to strip her with the efficiency of a hunter skinning game. Soon her gown, petticoat, and stays lay in a discarded pile. Left only in her chemise and stockings, Emma shivered, wrapping her arms around herself.

"The chemise comes off too," Madame said.

"Surely that's not necessary—"

"*Oui.* Only the closest fit will do."

With no choice, Emma let her arms fall to the sides as her last layer of protection was removed. Lungs pulling for air, she tried not to look at her naked reflection dancing over the walls. Relief came when Madame fitted a corset over her torso.

"Take a deep breath. *Un, deux, trois ...*"

Emma's breath whooshed out as the dressmaker yanked the strings. Her eyes bulged, not from the lack of air but at the sight of herself in the most wicked garment she'd ever beheld. Constructed of fuchsia satin, the corset was trimmed with a column of little black bows down the front and black lace along the edges. It molded her figure into a sensuous shape, cinching her waist and pushing her breasts up so that they nearly spilled from the pleated cups.

"Fits like a second skin," Madame said with satisfaction. "Now for the stockings."

As the Frenchwoman held up the sinful black scraps, Emma focused on breathing in and out.

Do not lose your nerve now. Remain steadfast in your purpose.

She tried to think. "Madame, did anyone accompany Lily here on her visits?"

Marieur tied on one frilled garter—fuchsia to match the corset. "Of course not. That would defeat the purpose of the visit, *non?*"

"Defeat? In what way?"

The other's eyes formed obsidian slits. "You are certain Lily sent you to me?"

Dash it. "Yes, of course. She spoke highly of your services," Emma said quickly. "Said you had exactly what I'm looking for."

Seeming mollified, Marieur finished with the other garter and rose. "Success takes the both of us. You, Miss Kendall, must put in the effort as well. Today is a test: I work only with those worth my time, *comprehendez-vous?*"

Beneath the pleasant tone was a distinct warning. *What does Madame Marieur mean by* test? Emma had the intuition that she was on the cusp of an important discovery. At the same time, goose pimples spread over her bared skin.

Warily, she said, "Yes, I understand."

The other pushed the remaining hosiery into her hands. "Finish with these. I'll return shortly." In a swish of black skirts, she disappeared from the room.

Alone, Emma sat on the edge of the dais. She slipped on the black silk stockings, securing them to the garters. As she sat, her naked bottom against the plush carpeted platform, outfitted in the most debauched ensemble she could possibly imagine, trepidation rolled in with the swiftness of fog from the Thames.

What am I doing? I ought to have gone to Ambrose or Alaric instead of coming here alone ...

She'd gotten carried away by the excitement of possible success, of her impending discoveries. Her gaze swung to the heap of her clothing. There was still time to throw her gown back on. Make a quick escape before the dressmaker returned.

Voices came from outside the chamber. Madame Marieur... *but she wasn't alone.* A wave of panic washed over Emma as she heard low, deep tones that were unmistakably masculine—and they were growing louder, headed toward her room.

Dear God. Have to run, hide. But where?

The door was opening. With a squeak, Emma crossed her legs, slapping her hands over her exposed womanhood. A man strode in. Wintry green eyes bored into her, and relief welled ... followed swiftly by alarm.

"Strathaven," she whispered.

Chapter Sixteen

Alaric stood transfixed, his cold rage swirling into a blazing wall of lust. His hands fisted at his sides. His loins flooded with heat.

"I see you two are acquainted," Marieur said with a smirk.

"Get out," he said.

"*Oui*, Your Grace, but as you have intervened in my, ahem, wardrobe selection for Miss Kendall—"

"I'll take an entire wardrobe for Miss *Kendall* here." Alaric saw Emma wince at his use of her assumed name, and his anger flared white-hot. How *dare* she put herself in such a dangerous position? "See that we're not disturbed."

"Excellent, Your Grace." The bawd scraped and bowed her way out.

The door closed with a click. The tension in the room climbed.

Perched on the edge of the dais, Emma had her hands clamped over her sex. His blood pumped with outrage and hunger. Devil take it, her getup might have been summoned from his darkest fantasies. A naughty red corset held her breasts up like an offering to the Gods, her dusky nipples playing peek-a-boo behind black lace. Displayed in black silk, her shapely, slim legs beckoned with outrageous eroticism.

"This isn't what it looks like," she said.

"No?" Jaw clenched, he strode to her. Stopped an inch

from her knees. "Then perhaps you would be so kind as to explain what you are doing dressed like a bluidy harlot in a bawdy house!"

He caught his slipping accent. Never a good sign. With monumental effort, he held onto his temper. Emma turned even rosier—by *God*, she blushed in the most interesting of places ...

"I didn't *know* this was a place of ill repute. I was following a clue, you see and—"

"Clue? Explain," he said through his teeth.

She fidgeted, and the corset shifted. His breath rammed in his throat. Christ's blood, he had a prime view of her nipples from this angle, and the taut little berries were full, maddeningly ripe. They would taste so sweet on his tongue ...

"I, um, interviewed your staff. Before you get all hot under the collar about it,"—she raised her chin, and his temperature did rise, though lower than where she suggested—"I discovered something extremely useful. Your missing maid was an actress at a theatre called The Cytherea; her real name is Lily White. She was a regular visitor to Madame Marieur's." A furrow appeared between her brows. "Apparently not for the purpose I initially believed, however."

He stared at her. He didn't know what dumbfounded him more: her ingenuity or her recklessness. "You interviewed my maids—and then you came here *on your own?*"

"There's no need to shout. How was I to know that this was a den of iniquity? The sign outside clearly stated that this was a shop for ladies' apparel—false advertising, if you ask me." She had the gall to sound disgruntled. "And Madame seemed quite convincing as a dressmaker."

"Your *dressmaker* is one of the most notorious bawds in

London," he clipped out. "Her matchmaking skills are sought by every light-skirt and courtesan in Town. Just now, she was about to enter the gentlemen's bidding chamber to auction off your favors."

Emma's lashes swept up. "Bidding chamber? *Auction?*"

"Your favors were about to be sold at the starting price of five hundred pounds."

Her pupils dilated. She bit her lip and looked worried. *Finally.*

His hands fisted on his hips, he leaned over her. "If I hadn't arrived when I did, it could have been any man who walked into the room just now. What do you think would have happened then?"

The notion of another man seeing her thus, lusting over her, touching her—

No one lays a hand on what is mine.

As his fury boiled over, he was simultaneously struck by scorching clarity. Like it or not, he wanted Emma Kent. Fighting that fact was a damned waste of time. He'd given her plenty of warnings; she'd ignored them all.

Now it was time for both of them to face the consequences.

"I'm sure I would have thought of something. I'm perfectly capable of taking care of myself." She peered up at him with feminine awareness in her wide eyes, a new breathy edge to her voice. "If you would just, um, hand me my clothes ... "

He took a step forward, his knees parting hers in a forceful movement. She gasped as he insinuated himself between her spread thighs. Her hands sprung upward in an instinctive attempt to ward him off and, in the process, she exposed her womanhood.

Ach, she looked as pretty and soft as she'd felt.

His nostrils flared, and she gasped again, her hands

flying back to shield her little cunny.

"No more hiding," he rasped. "All my warnings have fallen on deaf ears. You've pushed your luck one too many times, Emma."

Her cheeks turned pink. "Stop acting like a heathen. Let me go at once—"

His response was to tumble her back onto the carpeted dais. He kept his weight on his elbows so as not to crush her, yet his aroused body pressed against her every curve. Her softness molded instantly to his rigid form and the result was ... sublime.

A bluidy perfect fit.

"Tell me, pet," he said silkily, "why have you disobeyed me at every turn?"

"I've used my best judgment. You have no right to tell me what to do ..."

She broke off with a whimper when he ground his hips, circling them deliberately against her bared sex. Molten lust poured through him as her dew soaked through the barrier of his trousers. His burgeoned cockhead butted against the confining fabric, straining for home.

"I think you want to be told what to do," he said.

The hitched cadence of her breath told him that, whether or not she realized it, he'd hit the nail straight on the head. Anticipation bloomed in his gut. By God, she was the perfect mate to his desires.

"That's ridiculous. I'm not some weak-minded miss," she whispered.

"You, Emma, are the most stubborn female I've ever met." He rolled his hips again, and her gaze grew unfocused, heavy-lidded. "It takes strength to choose surrender. You've tested me time and again because you know I'm the man who can give you what you need. Because you want me," he said, "as much as I want you."

By all rights, he couldn't expect a virgin to understand the intricacies of power and sex. Or to admit her own carnal impulses. But he would begin as he meant to go on: he would never allow her to hide her passion—hide anything—from him.

She was *his*. The question was whether or not she was ready to admit it.

A myriad of emotions flitted through Emma's wide, clear eyes.

In a muffled voice, she said, "But I *shouldn't* want you. We're wrong for each other."

Triumph surged through him.

"Nay, lass," he said huskily, "let me show you how right we are ..."

He took her mouth, and she gave it to him with an eagerness that underscored his claim. Cupping her jaw, he drank of her sweetness, headier than the finest spirits. He licked into her mouth, leaving nothing unexplored. When she sucked shyly at his tongue, he knew he'd lit the tinder, her inhibitions going up in flame.

Even as he burned for her, he knew that he had to remain in control. He wouldn't take her maidenhead in a rush of unthinking lust the way he had with Laura. At her engagement party to his brother, Laura had seduced him, used his desire against him, and he'd fallen into her trap, betraying Will in the process. He'd not make the same mistake twice.

Then and there, he made up his mind: he wouldn't bed Emma until they were wed. In this relationship, *he* would be in charge. He would gain her submission, make her come again and again until she *begged* to be his duchess ...

He pressed open-mouthed kisses down her neck and shoulders, reveling in the downiness of her skin. Her fingers slid against his scalp, urging him closer. His nostrils flared at the sight of her breasts, the cherry peaks peeping above the line of black lace. He drew his thumb across a stiff bud, and she moaned.

"Like that, Emma? Do you want me to do it again?" he inquired.

"Mmm," she sighed.

"Answer me properly, pet." He gave her nipple a light tweak.

Her breath caught in surprise, yet her eyes melted like chocolate. "Yes ... please?"

"Aye, my good lass." He rolled the plump bud between his thumb and forefinger, and she gave the *sweetest* moan. Damnation, he should have taken this approach with her from the outset and spared them both the trouble. "What pretty breasts you have. I can't wait to taste them."

"T-taste?" Her voice quavered.

Loosening the corset, he yanked it down to free her firm, rounded tits and bent his head. Her startled cry sent satisfaction humming through his veins. Emma was so responsive—she could never hide her response from him, lie to him. She clutched his shoulders, her breaths coming in rapid pants as he tongued her ripe berries. He adored how proudly they stood, how sensitive they were. When he suckled one deep into his mouth, her back bowed off the dais.

He ran his palm possessively up one silken thigh and cupped her cunny. His cock pulsed to find her soaking for him. With reverence, he delved into her little nest, petting her slick folds. She moaned low in her throat when he circled her pearl. He played with her, his touch light, dancing over her delicate flesh, teasing her toward orgasm and retreating when it loomed too close.

In this way, he kept her on desire's edge.

Her head tossed frantically. "Alaric, what are you doing?

Please ..."

"This is mine," he said as he stroked her nub. "Your pearl belongs to me. Say it."

She bit her lip.

He stopped.

"My pearl ... it's yours," she whispered.

He cupped her entire mound, massaging her peak with the heel of his palm. "Your sweet cunny is mine."

She moaned, her hips arching in entreaty. "Yes, yes."

He stilled his hand. "The words, pet."

"My ... cunny is yours," she said bashfully.

He plunged a finger inside her, his bollocks drawing tight as her passage squeezed him like a vise. Christ, this was only one finger. What would it feel like to have his cock buried inside her snug little sheath?

You'll find out after *she's your wife.*

Grinding his teeth, he worked her clit, taking her to the precipice. "Then come for me, sweeting."

Her pants and gasps were a symphony of feminine surrender, the most sensual music he'd ever heard. As tremors shook her limbs, he went to his knees. Spreading her thighs, he leaned in and gave her the kiss that burned in his dreams.

Emma's shocked cry was swept into the wildfire ignited by Alaric's kiss. His hands kept her thighs splayed, pinned to the dais as he put his mouth on the most intimate place on her body. Of their own volition, her hips bucked against his mouth, his searing lips melting away her protests, leaving nothing but a strange, blazing truth.

Who knew that capitulation could be so blissful?

Then her thoughts burned to ashes, and there was only

the moment, the sensations, the bone-melting swirl of his tongue.

"Your pussy is like honey." His guttural lilt thrilled her. "I could feast on you all day."

She would never survive it. Her nerves were taut from her last climax, stretched on a rack of delight. Yet the pressure at her center was already building again.

"Do you like my mouth on you, pet? Do you like me licking you, eating your cunny?"

She couldn't answer that. She couldn't.

"Emma." He lifted his head, and the authority in his glittering pale gaze was oddly ... soothing. Calming. As if she didn't have to fight for pleasure the way she had for so many things in life—she had only to ask for it.

"Yes, I like it," she whispered.

"There's a good lass," he said with husky approval.

Her head flung back as his tongue flicked her sensitive bud while his touch delved inside her. Stretching, opening her to more rippling sensation. The pressure in her belly shot up another notch, and she was *so close* ...

"You're so fucking tight, squeezing my finger," he grated. "Take another and take it deep ..."

He drove into the core of her, and she exploded once more. Heavenly warmth spilled over her insides. She was floating, steeped in relaxation when his deep command reached her.

"Again, Emma."

Is that possible?

His face was above hers, stark with arousal and determination. He continued to work his fingers inside her, her own slickness easing the way. He thrust deeply with sudden force, and the sharp slap of his palm against her mound reawakened her satiated nerves. He did it over and again until she was rocking her hips to meet his touch, panting his name.

Ecstasy rolled over her once more, deeper this third time, an endless, languorous wave.

"Christ, you're bonny." His voice was deep.

Through her euphoric haze, she noticed the sheen on his forehead, the tight lock of his jaw. Once she'd interpreted his control as a sign of a cold, unfeeling nature; now she wondered why such a hot-blooded man would so tightly leash his passions. Whatever the reason, she had a flash of insight into what his willpower cost him—and she wouldn't stand for it.

He grew still when she reached up, brushing away a dark, tousled lock.

"What about you?" she said.

His eyes glittered. "What about me?"

"Don't you want to ... ?" Blushing, she couldn't force out the word.

"Do you want me to come, sweet?"

She gave a shy nod.

His nostrils flared. He shifted onto his knees next to her, his hands going to the waistband of his trousers. His eyes never left hers as he lowered the flap. Her eyes widened as she took in his rampant manhood. His big, thick pole stood boldly erect, the engorged purple crown reaching several buttons up on his waistcoat. Her intimate muscles clenched as he slowly ran a fist from root to tip. As he stroked himself, the turgid shaft jerked with a life of its own, the veins pulsing along its length. At the base, his sac hung like a ripe, heavy plum.

"Have I shocked you, pet?" he said silkily.

Was she shocked? Yes. But even more so, she was *curious*.

Feeling very bold, she said, "May I ... touch it?"

His smile was slow, brimming with sensual promise. "No, this time you watch."

She leveraged herself up on her elbows to get a better view. He handled himself firmly, the motion swift and strong, his bicep bulging beneath his jacket. Arousal sharpened his features, and within his grip, the rosy brown skin of his cock rippled over its rigid core. He was a study of control, of primal male power contained by equally potent self-discipline.

Watching him pleasure himself had a profound effect on her. Her nipples stiffened, her mouth watering at his magnificence. She wet her lips, and his gaze hungrily followed the path of her tongue. When he drew the skin back on his shaft, she watched, transfixed, as dew seeped from the slit in the exposed head. The fluid was swept up by his palm, and more leaked out, quickening his strokes. She could tell he liked the sensation from the way his jaw clenched, as if he were biting back a shout of pleasure.

He looked so powerful—and alone. A solitary, savage god. His loneliness, even in this, pulled at her heart.

"Come for me, Alaric," she whispered. "Please."

He jerked, his eyes blazing with pagan fire. "Feel me then. Feel my seed."

An instant later, he exploded, his teeth gnashing. Her breath stuttered as droplets pelted her breasts, marking her with his heat, his scent so masculine and arousing. One pearly bead landed on her nipple and clung to the hardened tip, before sliding leisurely down the curve.

Heart pounding, she saw his gaze following that languorous trail.

"My God, Emma," he said hoarsely.

Yanking her to him, he claimed her mouth with fierce possession.

Chapter Seventeen

Despite the fact that the velvet curtains had been drawn for privacy, Emma was cognizant of the four burly guards posted atop and at the rear perch of the moving conveyance. It felt surreal to be cocooned in the luxurious carriage with Alaric while the world and its dangers slipped by outside. He sat on the opposite bench, his long legs stretched in front of him, one broad shoulder propped against the wall. His pose was casual, yet the possessive heat in his gaze filled her with a strange, dozy warmth.

Her thoughts were utterly scrambled. She felt disoriented, confused ... and, most perplexing of all, too *relaxed* to care. For the first time in her adult life, all she wanted to do was take a nap.

"We have matters to settle, Emma," he said.

At the glittering resolve in his eyes, some of her languidness faded.

"You gave yourself to me," he said tonelessly, "and now we must discuss the consequences."

Panic dispelled the rest of her torpor. He made it sound as if she'd ceded more than she had.

She sat up. "It was the heat of the moment, and I didn't give ... that is, we didn't *do* anything irrevocable—"

"It's just a matter of time. You can't deny what's between us." His gaze warned her not to. "I'm not going to spend my energy fighting my attraction to you."

He had to *fight* his desire for her? Her chest went as soft as a gently boiled egg.

"With time and proper guidance," he went on, "I'm certain you'll do."

She blinked. "I'll do ... what?"

His eyebrow cocked. "You'll do as a duchess, of course."

It took a second for his arrogant assumption to sink in. Her jaw slackened; her traitorous heart gave a leap. "Is that supposed to be a *marriage proposal?*"

"Pet, the time for proposals is over. You've made your choice. You're mine."

His conceit raised her hackles. "I am *not* yours. One reckless ... interlude doesn't constitute ownership."

"Andromeda's and my bedchamber make three interludes," he said smugly, "and the only reason you're still a virgin is because I wish to respect our wedding night."

Pressure built in her head like water heating in a covered pot. "I never said I'm going to marry you! And Lord knows why you want to marry me. We fight like cats and dogs. We have nothing in common. You're a duke, and I'm a country miss—"

"As I said, you'll learn."

"I have no interest in giving up who I am to be your wedded slave. I have dreams of my own, a purpose to fulfill—"

"The managing of my estates and producing of my heirs should give you plenty to do."

Was he serious? Did he *truly* think he could dictate her future?

"I am going to be an investigator." She repeated this slowly, as if to a daft person. After all, if the Hessian fit ...

The indulgent light vanished from his eyes. "I'm offering you one of the most coveted positions in Society. Do you know how many ladies would give their eyeteeth to be the next Duchess of Strathaven?"

"Then marry one of them."

"I don't want any of them. I want you."

Why, oh why, did the authority in his voice make her thrum with yearning? She told herself she disdained his arrogance. Yet her belly fluttered, some feminine part of her helplessly captivated by the fact that such a beautiful, sensual man would look at her with burning possession in his eyes.

Swallowing, she said, "*Why* do you want to marry me? You ... you don't love me."

"No, I don't," he said dispassionately. "Love is a complication I neither need nor want in my life. What I'm proposing is a marriage of mutual benefit."

How could he be so cynical about love—about life?

"So far I haven't heard any benefits," she managed.

His brow quirked. "Marrying me will endow you with worldly goods, the privilege to do as you please. On my side, I will gain a duchess and someone to provide me with an heir." His voice lowered to a seductive timbre. "Given our attraction to one another, the begetting of the latter should prove a most pleasurable activity."

"That's not enough to build a marriage on."

"I say it is."

"You're not going to bully me into marrying you," she said.

She steeled herself for an onslaught of threats and intimidation. Instead, he scrutinized her for long moments, his eyes as impenetrable as smoked glass. His words took her by surprise.

"You want to negotiate? Let's do it." He gave a cool nod. "Tell me what it will take to make you mine."

Apparently three orgasms hadn't convinced the obstinate

chit that she belonged to him.

Nonetheless, Alaric admitted that Emma had a point: as a tactic, bullying had thus far proved ineffective with her. Clearly, he would have to employ a different stratagem to win her over. This fact filled him not with annoyance but anticipation: his duchess-to-be would challenge, provoke, and test him—she would, however, never bore him.

"You want to bargain with me? Over marriage?" Emma frowned.

It wasn't for nothing that he'd garnered a fortune through his business dealings. He knew how to leverage his assets and exploit the opposition's weaknesses to get what he wanted. Where warranted, he could adapt his strategy to achieve the desired outcome. Time to apply a similar mindset to dealing with his future duchess.

He capitalized on the element of surprise. "Aye. State your terms."

"My terms?"

Her confusion reached some deep, frozen part of him ... warming it. 'Twas as if she'd given no thought to how much she had to gain from marrying a duke. As if her desire was for him and not just what he could give her ...

He ruthlessly cut off that train of thought. He would hold no illusions when it came to this marriage, nor would he allow Emma to do so. He'd been clear about love: there would be no false expectations on either side. As long as she didn't expect more than he could give, they would rub along just fine.

Now all he had to do was secure her hand. It wouldn't be difficult. He knew her Achilles' heel, after all, and would use it to his advantage.

"For instance," he said innocently, "you could barter for a generous monthly allowance, enough to purchase all the jewels and furs a lady could want."

Her brow furrowed. "I don't want jewels and furs."

He knew that, of course. "Then perhaps you'd care for a carriage and yacht of your own, outfitted in the latest style to impress your friends?"

"My friends would not be impressed by such excessive frivolity," she said scornfully.

"Ah." He steepled his fingers. "Then perhaps there's nothing I could offer to entice you to marry me after all ... unless ... wait a minute. No." He shook his head. "You don't need *my* help with that."

"With what?" Her eyes narrowed.

"With your plan. Your goal of being an investigator."

"You would help me with that?" she said with clear skepticism. "When you've said time and again that it's an unsuitable job for a woman?"

"For an ordinary woman. Now for a *duchess*,"—he paused for effect—"it is an altogether different story."

She frowned. "Why?"

"Because a duchess has the power and cache to do as she wishes. What is considered unacceptable behavior for an ordinary woman would be nothing more than a charming eccentricity in Her Grace. No one would dare gainsay you for fear of my reprisal."

"And, hypothetically speaking, you would support your wife being engaged in detection work?" she said suspiciously.

In a manner of speaking. He'd come to the conclusion that it was a better option to let Emma dabble under his watch than to have her going at it pell-mell on her own. At least this way he would know what she was up to. He could keep a rein on her, keep her out of trouble.

"As long as you abide by the rules I set, I don't see what harm it would do for you to have a hobby," he conceded.

"Profession," she corrected. "And what are these supposed rules of yours?"

He told himself to tread with caution.

"Your safety must come first, for one. Although you did uncover a useful piece of information today," he said, noting how she instantly beamed with pleasure, "you also placed yourself at great risk. I'll not tolerate such recklessness."

Her smile faded. When she spoke, her words were surprisingly candid.

"You're right. I did get rather carried away by events," she said, her expression abashed. "For a moment back there, I feared I was in over my head."

"You'll not risk your neck like that again," he said sternly. "You're too important."

"I ... am?"

At the shy yearning in her look, his heart gave an erratic beat. He calmed it. It wouldn't do to be controlled by sentimentality. "Certainly. You are the mother of my future heirs."

"Oh." She blinked, then shook her head. "You speak as if it's a *fait accompli*. It's not."

"Tell me how to make it so," he said with steely determination.

"Shouldn't we get to know one another better before making a permanent decision?"

To his mind, the decision was made. But if he went head-to-head with her, she'd only dig her heels in more. If she needed time to reach the inevitable conclusion, then so be it.

"I'll court you," he said decisively. "How long?"

"I don't know." She nibbled on her lip. "Until we're certain that we're suited?"

"If you still need convincing after what just happened at Marieur's, I would be happy to provide another demonstration. I can still taste your honey, pet, and already I hunger for more."

Her cheeks turned a charming shade of pink. "You oughtn't say such things."

"Why not? You're the one who's always insisting that I tell the truth."

"Not about *that*." She huffed out a breath. "The point is that there is more to a relationship than physical intimacy. We hardly know one another. We come from different backgrounds, have differing views on marriage and—"

"Tell me how your views differ from mine."

Her lips pursed. "I believe in fidelity, for one."

"Agreed. Next."

"Wait—that's it? Don't you want to discuss the issue?"

"What is there to discuss? There will be no other man for you. And I'll be so busy attending to your pleasure,"—he lifted his brows—"that I won't have time for anyone else."

She flushed. "You would be faithful to your vows. Truly?"

She'd obviously heard the rumors about his first marriage. Bitterness rose, yet he told himself that Laura was in his past. His future would be different; he would make it so.

"I was a faithful husband," he said coolly, "regardless of what you may have heard."

"Your first marriage ... what was it like?" she asked tentatively.

He didn't want to talk about his mistakes. Didn't want the trail of filth to follow him into the present. Yet he knew that in order to gain Emma's trust, he had to give her something.

"I was young and foolish when I met Laura, taken in by her beauty and charm. I married her after a whirlwind courtship. Our marriage was not a happy one."

The understatement of the century.

"Why weren't you happy?"

His jaw tautened. "Laura and I did not suit, let's leave it at that. But I was faithful until the day she died. God knows I've been no saint since, but when I marry again, I intend to honor my vows." For some reason, he heard himself ask, "Do you believe me?"

After a moment, Emma gave a brisk nod. "Yes."

"Just like that?"

"You are arrogant, controlling, and manipulative at times. As far as I can tell, however, you've never lied to me."

Unexpected relief ballooned in him. "Thank you," he said softly.

"You're welcome. And ... I'm sorry."

He tensed. "I don't want your pity, Emma."

"There's a difference between pity and empathy. I don't feel sorry *for* you—I'm sorry that you had an experience that sounds dreadful."

"It's over and so is this conversation." He wasn't about to tell her the worst part—his unforgivable disloyalty to Will. He wouldn't risk exposing his faults any more than necessary.

She wrinkled her nose. "That speaks to another difference between us. I won't be dictated to. Any marriage that I'll be a part of will be based on mutual respect."

"Again, I see no problem."

"How can you say that?" she said incredulously. "You want a wife who will submit to you without question. Whereas I am an independent woman who knows her own mind, who has opinions and won't be ordered about willy-nilly—"

"Will you deceive me, Emma? Betray me in any way?"

She frowned. "No. Of course not."

"Then we'll work on the rest."

"People don't change that much," she said dubiously. "I don't see me getting any less independent—or you any less domineering."

"I don't hear you complaining about that when we make love. When you're in my arms, you surrender so sweetly," he murmured. "As if you'll give me anything I ask."

A painful flush stole over her cheeks. "I'm *not* weak," she blurted.

He looked at her in surprise. "No, you aren't. Why would you think it?"

"Because of what you just said. What happens when we're together. I don't know what comes over me, but truly I am not subservient or weak-willed ..."

The crux of what was troubling her dawned upon him. Staring at her embarrassed, wide-eyed expression, he was filled with equal parts desire ... and tenderness. With all his jaded experience, he'd forgotten that true innocence existed.

"Come here," he ordered softly, patting his lap.

He saw the way her muscles quivered to obey even as her mind resisted. She scooted back against her side of the bench. "No, we should talk about this."

To preclude further argument, he simply reached over and scooped her onto his lap. Delightful as her squirming was, he stilled it by tightening his arms around her. "Submitting to me doesn't make you weak," he told her. "On the contrary, it takes a strong, spirited woman to give me what you do."

She stopped struggling. "It does?"

"Aye." He brushed his knuckles against her silky, flushed cheek. "Your surrender is potent *because* of your strength. Because I know what you're trusting me with," he said huskily. "Besides, outside of lovemaking, I know you'll go on doing as you please."

Her brow puckered. "My being headstrong doesn't bother you?"

"Aye, it does—but it also excites and arouses me."

Deliberately, he pressed her down against his erection, and her color heightened even further. "The same way my arrogance excites and arouses you."

She bit her lip. "This is all very confusing."

The carriage was slowing; they were nearly at her home. Time to push his advantage. "So let me court you. We'll explore this together, so you won't be afraid of the passion that burns between us." He nipped her ear. "Give me your answer. Say you'll let me woo you, sweeting."

A tremor passed through her. "I will ... on one condition."

He ought to have expected as much. "What is it?"

"If I respect your rules, you'll let me help with your investigation where it's safe to do so. Please, Alaric," she said earnestly, "I can't stand by and do nothing when your life is at risk."

If he refused, she'd go ahead and do it anyway. Better to contain a fire than be burned by it.

"Agreed—as long as you'll be guided by me. I mean it, Emma," he said with emphasis. "No more harrying about on your own."

She nodded happily. "We have a bargain—"

The sudden wrenching open of the carriage door cut her off. The sun hit Alaric's face, its blaze nothing compared to the fury in the newcomer's gaze.

Emma's brother leaned in, his expression livid.

"What the devil is going on here?" Kent demanded.

Chapter Eighteen

All in all, Emma thought that Alaric was handling his first meeting with her family rather well. After the inauspicious start with Ambrose, he and she were greeted by her sisters as soon as they stepped foot inside the house. Emma hastily made the introductions.

After her curtsy, Violet studied him with frank curiosity. "So you're a duke? I've never met one before."

"Manners, Vi," Thea said in an undertone.

But Alaric only looked ... amused. "I must confess my own curiosity—having never met so many *Kents* before. Beauty and grace must be family traits."

The girls looked at each other ... and giggled as haplessly as debutantes. Emma, who'd never witnessed his gallantry in action, watched in bemusement as he continued to work his charm.

"Thank you for the compliment, Your Grace," Rosie said, dimpling.

"It is only the truth." He smiled at the vivacious girl, then he turned to Polly, who'd been standing bashfully off to the side. Over the latter's hand, he courteously bowed. "I don't envy Kent. He'll have to chase off suitors when you young ladies have your come outs," he said.

Polly turned pink with pleasure, and Emma's chest warmed at Alaric's unexpected sensitivity, at the sight of him teasing and at ease with her sisters.

Ambrose's stern tones broke up the banter. "Go attend

to your lessons, girls. His Grace and I have business to attend to."

After the girls scampered off, Ambrose led the way to the drawing room. Tension set in as they all took up their positions: Emma and Alaric on the settee and Marianne on the chaise longue, Ambrose pacing behind her like a caged tiger. He growled questions one after the other.

Alaric, with a booted foot resting upon one knee, was the picture of ducal assurance as he responded. He seemed to have an answer for everything, maneuvering through her brother's queries like a seasoned hackney driver through London's streets. He glossed over certain details—their lovemaking at Madame Marieur's, for instance—without telling any lies.

Finally, Ambrose turned to her. "What were you thinking, Emma, interviewing His Grace's staff?" he said in bewildered tones. "Going off on your own to this disreputable place?"

"I thought I could help," she said in a small voice. "The maids talked to me. And I discovered Lily's true identity—"

"At what risk? Anything could have happened. You could have been hurt, accosted, or worse."

"I assure you, Kent, she was perfectly safe," Alaric said. "I put a guard on her."

Shock jolted Emma. She'd assumed that his staff at the cottage had told him about Marieur's. Instead, he'd had her *followed*?

Looking as stunned as she felt, Ambrose said, "You did *what*?"

"The better question is why didn't you? She's your sister. You ought to know how determined she is when she sets her mind upon a thing," Alaric said calmly.

His high-handedness was astounding. And he didn't look the least bit apologetic.

She glared at him. "You can't have someone following me—"

"Actually, I can and I did. I told you, pet: I protect what is important to me."

The silver flame in his jade eyes hitched her breath. How could she have ever thought him cold? Beneath that icy authority raged volcanic heat—and it disturbed her to realize that she *liked* this side of him. Liked that she could stir his emotions ... the way he did hers.

"About that, Your Grace." Marianne gave a flick to her jonquil skirts, which were as smooth as her expression. "You understand why we must ask your intentions toward Emma."

"Why was my sister sitting on your bloody lap in the carriage?" Ambrose thundered.

Heat boiled up in Emma's cheeks. "Ambrose, it wasn't—"

"Let me answer, pet. 'Tis a fair question, and I have naught to hide." Alaric regarded her family with cool equanimity. "My intentions toward Emma are honorable."

She didn't mistake the claim in his deliberate and intimate use of her name.

"*Intentions*? Toward my sister? Now see here—"

"Darling." Marianne reached out and touched Ambrose's sleeve. A silent communication passed between them. Amber eyes blazing, he clenched his jaw and let his wife speak.

"You wish to marry Emma, Your Grace?" Marianne said.

"Yes. As soon as possible." His eyes upon Emma's face, he murmured, "As soon as I can convince the lady in question to have me, that is."

Way to throw me beneath the carriage. Emma gave him an annoyed look.

A smile flickered on his lips.

"Emma?" her brother said in disbelief. "Are you truly considering this?"

She took a breath. "His Grace and I have agreed to a courtship period. To help us decide if we are truly suited."

"You see?" Alaric's wide shoulders lifted. "'Tis Emma who is dallying with me and not the other way around."

"No one is dallying with anyone! Emma, I cannot condone this." Ambrose gripped the back of the chaise, his face stark with disapproval.

For the first time, Emma felt a spark of anger. Why was her brother being so unreasonable? She was a grown woman, capable of making her own decisions.

"You're the one who said I should find a husband," she said.

"I meant a suitable one. He ... his past,"—her brother waved a hand at Alaric in mute frustration—"he's not good enough for you."

The unfairness of the statement riled her. "He *is* a good man!"

"A duke being condescended upon by a mere mister—that has to be a first." Alaric arched a dark eyebrow. "Would you prefer it, Kent, if I were a costermonger?"

"'Tis your past and your character I question, not your title. Can't you see how different you and Emma are? She is an innocent girl, devoted to her family. You are an accounted rake, and from what I've seen between you and McLeod, you haven't the first notion of what it means to be a family."

Emma cringed.

The muscle ticked in Alaric's jaw. "You know nothing about my family."

"And you know nothing about mine," Ambrose said. "When it comes to marriage, Kents don't care about money or rank."

"Yes, I can see how you've sacrificed the finer things in life on the altar of matrimony." Alaric's gaze circled sardonically around the well-appointed drawing room.

Her brother's cheekbones turned a dull red.

Intervening quickly, Emma said, "Strathaven and I aren't making any hasty decisions. We're taking the time to get to know one another. Nothing is written in stone."

"Emma knows her own mind," Marianne said quietly to Ambrose. "She always has."

Emma felt a rush of love toward her sister-in-law.

"Someone is out to kill you, Strathaven," her brother growled. "Do you wish to endanger my sister as well?"

"Emma's safety is my primary concern. Which is why we will keep our courtship secret until the murderer is caught," Alaric said evenly. "If you truly wish to guarantee Emma's safety, you might consider actually finding the bloody killer."

"We have made progress." Ambrose's tone was equally hard.

"I'm all ears."

Emma saw the indecision on her brother's face. Clearly, he wanted to go a few more rounds with Alaric. His gaze landed on her, and his mouth tightened. "We'll remove to my study—"

"Emma will hear this," Alaric said. "She has the right to know about the case; it affects my future and therefore hers. Besides, it was through her efforts that we now have a new lead on the maid."

Despite Alaric's overconfident assumption that their futures were indeed entwined, Emma's chest expanded with giddiness. He'd listened to her in the carriage. He was respecting her wishes—had just publicly *acknowledged* her abilities as an investigator.

Catching her eyes, he murmured, "See, pet? I am capable of compromise."

"Emma will find out anyway. As will I," Marianne said. "You might as well discuss the case here, darling."

Ambrose said tersely, "We're not done talking about you and my sister, Strathaven."

Alaric's gaze was cool, level. Clearly, *he* was done.

Her brother raked a hand through his hair and visibly collected himself. When he spoke, it was with brisk professionalism.

"I'll begin with the poisoning," he said. "I discussed your symptoms with a physician experienced in such matters. He suspects that we are dealing with a substance of strong toxicity, one with dose dependent qualities—most likely a wild plant of some kind. He once saw a family, all of whom had mistakenly ingested poisonous mushrooms. The father, who'd eaten the most of the contaminated stew, died, as did one of the sons, who'd had a second helping. Having eaten less, the mother and sisters survived."

"This why Clara died, and I did not."

Despite Alaric's detached tone, Emma knew him well enough now to perceive his self-recrimination. She touched his arm; beneath her fingers, his hard bicep quivered.

"It wasn't your fault," she said. "You didn't know the whiskey was poisoned."

His expression remained harsh, but his chin dipped in a slight nod.

"We don't know that drinking less of the whiskey would have saved Lady Osgood," Ambrose said. "Depending on the individual, the lethal dose can vary to some degree. In the case of the family, a second son, who ate just as much as his brother who died, ended up surviving. My physician friend hypothesized that this was because this boy had survived eating poisonous mushrooms once before and had developed a degree of resistance to the toxins."

Grooves deepened around Alaric's mouth. "I had a digestive illness in my youth, which I later overcame. Perhaps that built up my resistance."

"Perhaps. At any rate, we are dealing with a murderer with some knowledge of poison. He knew enough to choose a weapon with no detectable taste or odor. His mistake was not dosing the whiskey with enough poison to kill you with one drink ... which brings us to the second attempt on your life."

Alaric straightened. "You have news about the shooting?"

"McLeod has made headway with the list of gunsmiths. He's narrowed it down to the last handful, says he should have the shop identified by the morrow."

"I'm going there with you," Alaric said.

"I want to come, too," Emma said.

Silence fell like a guillotine.

"No," her brother and Alaric said as one.

At least the two agree on something. Well, it wasn't as if she didn't expect resistance. Summoning her breath, she prepared to argue, but Alaric headed her off.

"I have kept my end of the bargain. Now you will keep yours. My rules, Emma," he reminded her.

"But I want to help investigate—"

"And so you shall," he said. "I have an assignment. An important one."

"An assignment for me?" She could hardly wait. "Do you want me to go to The Cytherea, track down Lily White—"

"No. Your task is more important than that."

More important? "Yes?" she said eagerly.

"Your job is to infiltrate the *ton*."

"What?" She frowned. "Why would I do that?"

"Remember what you said about poison being a lady's weapon?"

Brows drawn, she gave a slow nod. "But that was just conjecture. We don't have any specific evidence to support—"

"That is where you come in. I want you to circulate amongst my peers. Keep your eyes and ears open for any suspicious activity, particularly where ladies are involved."

"But I don't know the first thing about high society," she protested.

"I need your help, Emma."

With those five words, he had her. How could she deny his request—deny him anything—when he looked at her with such mesmerizing warmth in his eyes?

Swallowing, she said, "What sort of suspicious activity would I be monitoring?"

"Gossip, for one thing. Amongst the *ton*, it is a powerful weapon. It often holds fragments of the truth and may yield clues to the killer's identity." He paused, leveled a challenging look at Ambrose. "If you don't believe me, ask your brother."

Ambrose's brows knotted. After a minute, he said curtly, "It is true that gossip can be a source of important information."

"See?" Alaric's broad shoulders lifted. "I would do this myself, but people don't dare to talk about me to my face. That is why I need you: an investigator with excellent observation skills, someone I can rely upon."

Touched by his trust, she searched his face. "This isn't some ploy to distract me from the real danger, is it? You really think I could learn something important just by listening?"

"Emma, you have the ability to do what your brother and his partners cannot: you can blend in with the ladies, conduct reconnaissance in drawing rooms and ballrooms undetected. And let me be clear: *all* you're to do is listen. You'll take no risks, and you'll report anything you hear directly to me and your brother. Is that understood?" His gaze locked with hers until she gave a nod. "If I am asking too much of you, pet—"

"I'm willing to do whatever it takes to see you safe." She wouldn't have him believing otherwise, not when he was entrusting her with so vital a mission. "I won't let you down."

"Thank you." His slow smile dazzled her senses. "I'll make all the arrangements."

"Wait. What arrangements?"

"You can't go sleuthing about without the proper equipment. In order to operate amongst the *ton*, you'll need a few supplies. I will, of course, bear the expense for them."

Before she could ask what *supplies* he was referring to, he said to Marianne, "You would not mind chaperoning Emma, Mrs. Kent?"

"Not at all." Marianne's lips gave an odd twitch. "Are there any particular, er, investigative opportunities you'd like us to pursue, Your Grace?"

"Start with the Blackwood Ball," Alaric said. "Their parties are guaranteed crushes."

"And quite exclusive," Marianne murmured.

"Lord Blackwood is a friend of mine and can be trusted to be discreet. I'll secure your invitations."

Emma's stomach lurched at the prospect of attending so elevated an affair, but she reminded herself that she'd do anything to help protect Alaric's life—including navigating the *ton*'s treacherous waters.

Alaric addressed her brother. "Kent, I'll expect to be notified when Will identifies the gunsmith."

His expression carved in stone, Ambrose jerked his chin in reply.

Alaric rose, bowing first to Marianne and then taking Emma's hand. When his lips skimmed over her knuckles, longing shivered over her.

"You won't regret our bargain, sweeting." His pale green irises smoldered with silver smoke as he murmured, "Once this is over, I will come to you a free man and make no mistake: we *will* settle things between us."

"Is that a promise or a threat?" She wrinkled her nose.

His lips took on a faint, wicked curve. "Either way, pet, it means you're going to be mine."

Chapter Nineteen

"Papa, may I sleep with the light on?"

Seated at the side of the bed, Ambrose smiled at his seven-year-old son. "There's no need for that. Nothing's going to happen, I promise."

Edward's eyes, the same emerald shade as his mama's, peered anxiously from his small face. "How do you know?"

"Because monsters live only in dreams, and they can't hurt you. You have nothing to fear, lad." Ambrose tucked the blanket around his son's shoulders. "I'll stay here until you fall asleep."

"Promise, Papa?"

"I promise, lad."

A quarter hour later, Ambrose brushed his hand lightly over Edward's tousled dark head, extinguished the light, and headed for the master bedchamber.

Marianne was waiting in bed. Even after eight years of marriage, her beauty struck him anew. With her platinum hair loose around her slim white shoulders and her vivid eyes glowing with love, she was an angel. And he was one lucky bastard.

Setting aside her book, she smiled at him. "Asleep?"

"Aye. Poor fellow." Removing his robe, Ambrose got into bed and took her into his arms. Settling them both against the pillows, he said, "I hope he outgrows the night terrors soon."

"Did he ask about the monsters?"

"I told him they weren't real."

"Not the kind he fears, anyway."

At his wife's pensive tone, Ambrose turned his head to look at her. He saw the shadows in her gaze, as if she were recalling the monsters of her past. Monsters he'd done everything in his power to slay.

"Sweetheart?" he said quietly.

She touched his jaw. "I'm not thinking of my own demons, darling, but of yours."

"Mine?" he said in surprise.

"Monsters come in all guises. Evil people, harrowing events—even something as ordinary as not being able to protect the ones you love."

His muscles tensed. "What are you saying?"

"Ambrose, you're a wonderful brother, but Emma is a grown woman." Marianne's perceptive eyes searched his face. "You cannot protect her any longer, and you *must* not blame yourself for those times when you could not."

The memory of those times rose within him. Those years when he'd barely been able to feed his younger siblings ... when Emma, as the next eldest, had been forced to shoulder all the burdens of their family while he earned a living in the city. One time, she, a sixteen-year-old girl, had travelled all the way to London on her own because calamity had struck their family, and she'd had no one to turn to ...

Old knots tightened in his chest. "She's missed out on so much. She's never had a chance to be young," he said roughly. "She deserves to be happy."

"Yes, she does. But only she can decide what will make her so."

"You can't think Strathaven is a good decision," he said in incredulous tones.

Marianne said softly, "Why not? Because he's a duke? He's rich?"

"No, because he's a *rake*."

"The gossip isn't all true. His dead wife spread some vile rumors about him. And Annabel says that he's got a good heart—that she and Mr. McLeod are in his debt." After a pause, Marianne said, "I know what it's like to be misjudged by Society."

Ambrose tightened his arms around her. "That was different. Your actions were prompted by your desire to find Primrose. You were blameless, sweetheart."

"How do you know Strathaven is not as well? Whatever his past, he cares for Emma."

"What makes you so certain?"

Marianne's lips formed a wry curve. "Why else would he concoct this plan to have her investigate the *ton*? He's keeping her away from the true danger—and saving her from herself, I might add."

That insight did not sit well with Ambrose. Even if Marianne was right, he didn't trust Strathaven's motives. Didn't want a dissolute libertine entangled with his innocent sister.

Stiffly, Ambrose said, "Even if he didn't kill Lady Osgood, he was having a salacious affair with her—a married woman. He is morally corrupt."

His spouse made an amused sound.

"What is so humorous?" he said, frowning.

"You, darling." Still smiling, she kissed his jaw. "By your standard, no gentleman would be good enough for Emma. What man hasn't had an *affaire* or kept a mistress?"

"I haven't," he said.

"You are the exception. That is why I adore you." Her hand glided down his chest, and he felt himself hardening, responding as ever to his wife's touch. "You want to handle Emma with care. You don't want to push her away."

"I can't talk about my sister when you do that," he said

hoarsely.

Marianne smiled her siren's smile. "Will you consider what I said?"

In his work, he prided himself on considering all the evidence before drawing any conclusions. He supposed he ought to do the same in this instance. Objectivity could be dashed difficult, however, when one's own family was involved.

"I will try," he conceded.

"Thank you, darling."

His wife's lips caressed his neck, her hand wandering lower still. Fire ignited in his loins, and rolling her onto her back, he took her mouth in a hungry kiss. She sighed with pleasure, her ardor obliterating his thoughts, and for the next little while at least, all worldly troubles scattered to the winds.

Chapter Twenty

Two days later, Alaric found himself in his carriage with his brother. They were outside Palmer's, a small establishment tucked between Covent Garden and St. Giles. From the window, Alaric saw the weathered sign above the door which bore the gun shop's emblem of a pineapple. Will, seated on the opposite bench, held up the torn cartridge wrapper.

The half oval with the squiggly lines was a perfect match for the fruit on the sign.

"This is the place," Will said with satisfaction. "Kent's on his way from The Cytherea. Once he arrives, we'll go in and question the owner."

Alaric hesitated. A part of him wanted to praise his younger sibling's scouting abilities. Another part felt ... awkward. Too much had passed between them, bricks of hostility and misunderstanding forming an invisible wall.

Yet Will *was* his brother. His only sibling.

He settled for a compromise. "How did you manage to find the shop? It was no small feat, I imagine. There must be dozens of gunsmiths in the city."

"Compared to tracking down spies and scouting enemy terrain, this is child's play."

Pride gleamed in Will's brown eyes nonetheless—and threw Alaric back into a memory. Of the two of them as boys, trespassing on their neighbor's property. The

McGregor had been the stingiest, meanest man in the county, and the wagers amongst the village lads oft involved his infamous tree, which boasted bright red apples the size of small melons.

Any lad who could show a McGregor apple would win undying respect from his peers, and at age nine, Alaric had craved that respect more than his next breath. A single apple was guaranteed protection against the taunting and beatings of the other boys; he'd been prepared to filch the fruit or perish trying. What he hadn't been prepared for was his little brother's insistence on tagging along.

If you don't let me go, I'll tell Ma, Will had said. *Da'll whip you for trespassing.*

In the end, he'd had no choice but to let Will have his way. At first, things had gone well; using a ladder, they'd made it over the tall stone fence, racing through the waving grass fields undetected. Alaric had climbed the tree and tossed the apples down into Will's waiting arms.

I told you I could help, Will had called proudly.

Without warning, a shotgun had fired.

The idyllic summer afternoon exploded with cries of panicked birds. The next instant, Alaric jumped to the ground, hissing *Run* at his paralyzed brother. When Will didn't move, Alaric yanked him by the arm, dragged him back through the fields, apples scattering as they ran for their lives. When Will stumbled, crying, Alaric hauled him up and towed him along.

The fence came into sight, the promise of safety. Just as Alaric reached the top, he heard his brother's whimper behind him.

It's too high. Will's chubby fingers slipped against the stones, and he slid to the bottom, his eyes wide and shimmering. *I can't get over.*

Cursing, Alaric dropped to the ground. Going down on

one knee, he linked his hands and boosted his brother over.

It worked—*too* well. Will had gone sailing over the top, landing hard enough to break his arm. Alaric could still see the accusing looks on their parents' faces.

What were you thinking, involving my boy in your shenanigans? his stepmother had cried.

By God, you're a bad seed, his da had spat. *No son of mine would hurt his own kin.*

Alaric had received the whipping of his life.

Not only that, but he hadn't even an apple to show for it.

"Kent's hackney just pulled up." Will's voice pulled him back to the present. "You're certain you want to go in with us?"

Jaw taut, Alaric said, "I'm not hiding in the carriage like some lily-livered coward."

"Suit yourself." Will shrugged. "Stay close, and I'll take the lead."

His brother might have been a pain in his arse during their youth, but Alaric had to admit a growing respect for the adult William's expertise. Will looked as seasoned and fierce as one of their ancient Highland ancestors as he led the way from the carriage, his eyes roving in a ceaseless scan, his brawny posture ready for anything.

Kent descended from a hackney and joined them. From the investigator's terse greeting, Alaric assumed that the other hadn't yet come to terms with Alaric's involvement with Emma.

Too damn bad for him.

Entering the shop, Alaric was assailed by the scent of oil, leather, and gunpowder. It was a humble, rather gloomy premises compared to Manton's on Davies Street, the gun maker favored by the *ton*. Here, dust blanketed the counters, and pistols hung in crooked lines over the walls.

A round-faced clerk greeted them at the front counter.

"Afternoon, gents," he said, wiping his hands on his leather apron. "How may I be o' service?"

Will placed the torn cartridge wrapper on the counter, tapped his gloved finger on it. "This one of yours?"

The clerk peered at the paper. "Aye, that's from a cartridge for our double-barreled flintlock. I can tell by the quality o' the paper." He pinched it between finger and thumb. "Extra heavy, see, to carry the weight o' the powder and shots. Costs extra, but it's worth the—"

"And this?" Will set down the pair of bullets Kent had found. "Yours too?"

"Could be. But harder to say—shot ain't that distinctive." The clerk's expression grew wary. "Er, what was it that you said you wanted?"

"We're looking for the customer who bought a double-barreled flintlock and that cartridge. A fellow with a scarred face," Will said.

The clerk's gaze jumped nervously, his face reddening. "I'm sorry, sirs, I didn't sell nothin' to a scarred gent. Now if you'll excuse me, I've got to get back to work ..."

"Babcock, you lazy bugger, what are you jawing about?" A man with stringy salt-and-pepper hair emerged from the backroom.

"N-nothing, Mr. Palmer," the clerk stammered.

Palmer's eyes formed slits as he regarded Alaric and the others. "Who're you?"

Kent stepped forward. "Ambrose Kent, at your service." He handed over his calling card. "My colleague and I are investigating a crime. We're looking for a man with a scarred face who might have purchased a double-barreled flintlock and cartridges to go along with it."

Something slithered through Palmer's eyes. He crumpled the calling card in his grease-stained fist.

"Didn't see no scarred man," the gunsmith said. "Now if

there's nothing else, I've got a business to run."

Will jerked a thumb at Alaric. "Do you know who this is?"

Palmer eyed him up and down and sneered, "Some nob, by the looks o' 'im."

"The nob happens to be the Duke of Strathaven. And someone, using your shot and your gun, attempted to assassinate him a week ago. So, unless you want to be carted off to Newgate as an accomplice," Will growled, "you will tell us what you know."

"Already told you. Don't know nothing," Palmer said belligerently.

Alaric noticed sweat trickling down one of the clerk's temples. "You—Babcock, is it?"

"Y-yes, your lordship."

"Have you seen a disfigured man in the shop? One with a scar down the middle of his face?"

Babcock darted a terrified gaze at his employer. "N-no, sir—I mean, your lordship."

"That's a bluidy lie," Will said, his hands balling.

Alaric held his brother back. "If either of you remembers anything, there happens to be a sizeable reward," he said coolly.

The clerk wetted his lips, his Adam's apple bobbing.

"Ain't nothin' for us to remember," Palmer spat. "Now get out o' my shop afore I toss you out."

As the carriage rolled off, Will said in frustrated tones, "Both of them were lying through their teeth. I could have gotten the truth out of them."

"By beating them?" Alaric smoothed his gloves in place. "Palmer still wouldn't talk. My guess is that he has some personal connection to the shooter."

"We'll have Palmer tailed," Kent said. "He might lead us to the suspect."

"If Babcock doesn't come to us sooner." Alaric's instincts told him the clerk was more than ready to fly his employer's coop. "He wants that reward."

"Blunt doesn't buy everything," Will said.

"Anyone who believes that doesn't have enough of it," Alaric replied. "Kent, any progress at The Cytherea?"

"I confirmed that Lily White was indeed an actress there—the term "actress" being applied loosely," the investigator said. "By the look of things, the theatre is a step up from a bawdy house, with skimpy outfits and skimpier talent."

"Got a good look, did you?" Alaric drawled.

"I have no interest in such depravity." Kent shot him an irritated look. "According to the manager, Miss White up and left the company around the time she started as a maid at your cottage. No one at the theatre has seen her since, and they haven't any notion where she might have gone. Apparently, she kept to herself."

"That's what my staff claimed as well—until Emma somehow got them to talk." With an odd mixture of ruefulness and pride, Alaric had to acknowledge the truth: his future wife was a force to be reckoned with. Fortunately, he knew how to put her energies to good use.

"Do *not* bring my sister into this," Kent said through his teeth.

"She's already in it."

"Aye, and I don't like it." The investigator glowered at him. "What are you up to, Strathaven? Why are you sending Emma on a wild goose chase through the *ton*?"

"You have a better idea for keeping her out of trouble?"

The look of impotent frustration on Kent's face spoke

louder than words.

Will's brow lined. "What wild goose chase? Why is Miss Emma involved?"

"She is determined to be part of the investigation and, more specifically, to protect my life." Emma's loyalty and concern reached a dark, frozen corner inside him. There it was again, that dangerous spark of hope ...

Don't be a fool. He could lust after Emma, do what it took to make her his. But he would never lose control over his heart or his head. Never set expectations that would only lead to disillusionment and pain.

In cool tones, he said, "I'll leave it to Kent to explain why his sister disobeys commands and does exactly what she pleases."

"I'm her brother not her keeper," Kent snapped. "Aye, Emma is independent and headstrong; she has had to be. She has managed our household since she was a girl, saw our family through poverty and loss."

"A fact that I admire. If you can't protect her from herself, however, then I certainly will," Alaric said calmly. "We both know that Webb is our main and only suspect at this point, and he's hiding somewhere in the stews. Thus, if Emma is determined to muck around, the *ton* is the safest place for her to do so."

"I'm not daft, Strathaven, I know what you're doing," Kent growled. "You're circulating her amongst your sort on purpose—grooming her to be your next duchess."

Alaric didn't bother denying it. Part of Emma's resistance to marrying him had to do with her perception that they came from incompatible worlds. Which meant that getting her comfortable within his social stratum was essential to furthering his cause.

"Mrs. Kent was preparing to launch her anyway." He gave an insouciant shrug. "With my backing, Emma will not only be a guaranteed success, she'll land the Season's biggest catch."

"I don't give a *damn* about your title. You don't have what it takes to make Emma happy."

Will, who'd been watching the exchange with an air of mute fascination, burst out, "You ... and Miss Emma? Bluidy hell," he said, looking stunned, "Annabel was right."

"My sister has not agreed to anything," Kent said sharply.

"Not yet," Alaric said.

Will's face split into a sudden grin. "Lass wouldn't have you? Turned down the great Duke of Strathaven himself?"

"Shut it, Peregrine." Alaric narrowed his eyes at his brother. "Emma *will* have me."

"Not if I have anything to say about it," Kent vowed.

Alaric's patience snapped. "Just what do you have against me? Other than the wealth and privilege I intend to bestow upon your sister, that is?"

A heartbeat passed. Kent said, "Do you love her?"

Pinned by the other's keen gaze, Alaric felt the ghosts within him swirl. Da's furious brown eyes, the lecture he'd delivered between the stinging swishes of the belt. *No son of mine would endanger his own brother. You're a disgrace to the McLeod name. You have no part in this family ...*

Laura's beautiful face contorted with feverish anger. *You don't love me. You're not capable of love. Well, one day soon you'll know what you've lost—*

"I didn't think so," Kent said coldly.

Alaric tried to ignore the pressure at his temples. "I will take care of Emma. She will want for nothing."

"Except for the one thing she needs most. Your philandering is common knowledge. My sister will give you her heart, her trust, and in return what do you have to offer?"

You're nothing. A useless invalid. His guardian's deathbed words sliced through him. *I never should have taken you in …*

"I am a *duke*," he bit out.

Kent shook his head in disgust. "You don't even understand, do you?"

Will cleared his throat. "Kent, far be it for me to interfere, but Strathaven, well, he's my kin after all. Now I'm not saying he's perfect, but he ain't as bad as all that …"

Alaric took refuge behind a wall of anger. He didn't need this investigator's judgment, his brother's condescension.

The righteous fools don't know me. Devil take them both.

"I am marrying Emma. Get used to it or don't, Kent—I don't give a damn," he said in chilling accents. "In the meantime, however, I'm paying you to find a murderer. If you cannot carry out your duties, say so now, and I'll hire someone else."

White-lipped, the other man said, "I will do my bloody job, Your Grace. If for no other reason than to put an end to this case and my sister's involvement with you."

Will looked as if he might speak … and then shook his shaggy head and looked out the window. Silence descended upon the cabin, and whilst Alaric maintained an icy facade, his mind spun like the carriage wheels. He knew how much Emma valued her brother's opinion—hell, she looked up to him as if he were a bloody saint.

What would she do if Kent forbade the match? What choice would she make?

Alaric's hands clenched with sudden ferocity. *There's only one choice. No one is going to take her from me. Emma is mine.*

Chapter Twenty-One

"Good afternoon, Miss Kent," Jarvis said as he ushered her into the foyer.

"Hello, Jarvis. How are your knees today?" Emma said.

Beneath his beetled brows, his eyes twinkled. "Much better, thank ye kindly. Your salve is nothing short of a miracle."

"I'll bring more the next visit," she promised. "Is the duke at home?"

"Indeed, miss. But His Grace has a meeting at the moment—"

"I'll wait. I have an important matter to discuss with him," she said with determination.

"Of course. Right this way."

Jarvis put her in the drawing room, leaving to fetch refreshments. Alone, she paced over the Aubusson, impatient to see Alaric so that she could take him to task. Ever since she'd agreed to spy on the *ton* on his behalf, an unending stream of so-called *supplies* had arrived on her doorstep. His extravagance had been staggering: evening gowns, frippery, every kind of accoutrement—all of it in the latest fashion and every item fitting her perfectly.

Rosie and her sisters had *oohed* and *aahed* over each lavish gift, and even Marianne's brows had risen at the item currently residing in Emma's reticule. Emma, however, was not impressed. As she faced the prospect of her debut reconnaissance mission at the Blackwoods' tomorrow night, she had to wonder if Alaric had something other than investigation on his mind.

An ulterior motive that had little to do with her helping to track down a villain—and everything to do with getting his way.

When she heard his deep, distinctive tones in the distance, she could wait no longer. She headed in the direction of the voices ... and stopped short. Not because of Alaric—who appeared, as usual, effortlessly virile in a burgundy waistcoat and buff trousers—but the familiar pair of men standing with him.

"We are grateful for your patronage, Your Grace," the senior gentleman said.

"As ever, we are at your service," his younger replica added.

Alaric wasn't looking at them, however. His eyes had locked on her. His guests followed the direction of his gaze.

"Ah, Miss Kent. What a surprise." The speculative glance that the elder banker threw in Alaric's direction confirmed her sudden, blazing suspicion. "Good afternoon."

"Mr. and Mr. Hilliard," she said. "What a coincidence it is to see you here."

"Er, yes. Coincidence, of course." The younger Mr. Hilliard cast an uncertain look at Alaric. "'Tis a pleasure to see you, but Father and I must be getting along. Appointments, you know."

"Don't let me keep you," she said.

After they left, she turned to Alaric, who emanated tension. Her intuition told her the cause of his unease. Yet if her hunch was correct, why would he want to hide such a thing?

He rubbed the back of his neck, scowling at her. "What are you thinking, coming here unchaperoned? There's a murderer on the loose, not to mention proprieties—"

"You arranged the loan for Kent and Associates, didn't you?"

She saw him flinch; he recovered instantly. "My business affairs do not concern you."

If he thought hauteur would shield him, he was wrong.

It was too late for that; she'd seen him for what he was.

And she *liked* it. Liked it so very much.

"After the fire, no bank would lend the agency the sum at a reasonable percentage. So you made it happen," she said steadily. "You've been looking out for your brother all along."

He took her by the arm and steered her down the corridor to his study. His hounds leapt up to greet her, but he evicted them from the chamber with a sharp command. Closing the door, he backed her into it. With his hands planted on either side of her, he leaned in and said, "You are not to say a word of this. To anyone."

She looked up at his handsome, annoyed visage—and tenderness filled her. What a complex man he was, his motivations and desires hidden behind a facade of arrogance. He could be moody, brooding, deserving of his moniker. Yet now she knew what her instincts had sensed early on: the proud, powerful duke had a true and loyal heart.

"Why don't you want Mr. McLeod to know that you've done this for him?" she said gently.

"That's none of your concern. Just do as I say and keep your mouth shut."

"But why don't you want Mr. McLeod—or my brother, for that matter—to know that you're their secret benefactor? You're their guardian angel—"

"I'm no angel. Ask anyone." The wild, pale fire in his eyes dared her to disagree.

Quietly but firmly, she said, "I say you are. Why do you try to hide it?"

With a ragged breath, he pushed away from her, stalked toward his desk.

She followed him.

"Why are you here?" He shuffled irritably through a pile of papers. "You're risking your safety—never mind your reputation—coming here on your own."

"With Mr. Cooper following me like a hawk, I'm perfectly safe." She canted her head. "Why are you avoiding my question?"

"Why are you avoiding mine?" he shot back.

With a hint of exasperation, she said, "Fine, I'll answer first. I'm here to return this." From her reticule, she withdrew the black velvet jewelry box and placed it on his desk.

His gaze smoldered into hers. "You don't like it?"

"That's not the point. I can't accept it."

"Why not?"

"It's too expensive. Too *much*."

"It's perfect for you. You'll wear it." He returned to sorting his correspondence as if the subject was closed.

"I will not." She lifted her chin. "Our bargain was for me to scout the *ton* for you, not dress up in jewels that could feed a family for generations. I'm beginning to wonder if you aren't sending me on a fool's errand to keep me occupied. To keep me from doing real detection work. From continuing to track Lily White at The Cytherea—"

"You agreed to this plan, and you'll stick with it."

Riled by his dictatorial tone, she said, "I can back out at any time. There's nothing binding me to our agreement."

His head snapped up. "What did you say?"

The ominous glitter in his eyes made her recognize her mistake immediately. "I mean, I agreed to let you court me, but nothing is written in stone ... remember?"

The last word emerged with a breathy edge as he

rounded the desk toward her. She held her ground, even as he towered over her, more than six feet of lean, bridling male.

"Oh, I remember. And I'm realizing that I've been too lax with you."

The silky menace in his voice spread tingling awareness over her skin. Beneath his civilized exterior, the savage God had awakened, preparing to do battle. And heaven help her, every part of her responded. Beneath the pale yellow muslin of her bodice, her nipples budded, her core blooming with humid heat.

"You don't own me," she said. "You can't tell me what to do."

"That you believe that proves that I've chosen the wrong tactic with you. By negotiating with you, I've led you to think that you can manage me. That you can tame me like a lapdog and run roughshod over me."

The idea of this virile, dangerous male as a lapdog was ludicrous. "I don't think that."

"I've agreed to let you investigate. I've agreed to court you. I've indulged you to make you happy," he went on with deadly calm. "In return, you pester me about matters that don't concern you, question my motives, and won't even wear a bloody necklace."

She knew him well enough now to recognize the stillness of the predator the moment before the strike. Yet she couldn't resist saying, "*Pester* you? I'm trying to communicate with you—that's what people do when they're courting. How will we know if we're suited if we can't carry on a normal conversation?"

"You want us to communicate?"

She gave an emphatic nod.

"Bend over my desk."

"Pardon?"

"I believe I was quite clear." His eyes gleamed with challenge. "Face my desk and place your hands there. Do not move them unless I give you leave to do so."

His sensual authority released a shivering excitement. With blinding honesty, she recognized that she'd been longing for this since their last encounter. Alone in her bed, she'd fantasized about him—about the two of them, bound by nothing but each other and the wicked passion that burned between them. He'd told her that her submission didn't make her weak, and the knowledge of that paradox fanned the flames of her curiosity.

With him, she was discovering that passion *was* a form of communication. With every intimate game they played, they opened up to one another a bit more. Trust was a two-way street. To gain his confidence, perhaps she would first have to demonstrate her own faith in their developing relationship.

On a shaky breath, she turned. Placed her bare palms flat on the hard surface.

"Good girl." He removed her fichu, the scrap of lace-edged lawn landing carelessly on the desk. His breath gusted warmly against her bare nape. "Was that so difficult?"

"You try having someone order you about—"

The rest of the sentence died in her throat as he nipped the tender ridge between her shoulder and neck. Her head arched back at the scrape of his teeth, the scorching suction as he licked the small hurt with sinuous laps that made her fingers curl against the wood. From behind, his erection pressed into her, his arousal unmistakable despite the layers between them. His hands slid up her bodice, cupping and squeezing her aching breasts. When she moaned, he again suckled her neck with delicious force.

"You're so responsive, sweeting," he murmured. "Tell me, are you wet for me?"

Her cheeks flamed.

"Still shy, I see. There's no room for modesty between us. Can you feel how hard you make me,"—he ground against her—"how big my cock is, how it throbs for you?"

Her eyelids grew heavy. Oh, she could feel him. She could.

He swept his arm across the desk, sending objects crashing pell-mell to the ground. "Lean down all the way." With his hand at the small of her back, he pushed her upper torso flush against the desk. "Stay just like that," he said.

With her palms and cheek supported by the cool wood, Emma felt a luxurious calm wash over her. That decadent stillness anchored her as he raised her skirts, layers of silk and linen skimming against her stockinged legs, her bare thighs. The material swished softly over her waist, and she shivered at the kiss of the cool air against her exposed backside.

"Christ, you're lovely." His reverent growl curled her insides with pleasure. "Spread your legs farther apart. Show yourself to me, pet."

Shamefully stimulated, she widened her stance, feeling his rapacious gaze on her, on her wet, quivering sex. Heartbeats passed. His silence, his control stretched her nerves like a clothesline. She squirmed against the desk in helpless anticipation, his steely discipline maddening her, making her arousal unbearable. Why didn't he touch her?

The realization came as a stroke of lightning. This was a battle, a contest of wills. And the way to victory was ... surrender.

"Please." The word left her in a whisper.

"Please what?"

"Touch me," she begged.

He smoothed his palms over her buttocks, running them along her thighs, and she purred.

"My kitten likes to be petted." His words were husky with approval. "Tip your pretty bottom up for me higher."

Eagerly, she did so, gasping when his fingers slid through her intimate folds.

"Ach, Emma, you're drenched. Coating my fingers with your sweet honey."

His guttural tone, the emergence of his lilt, betrayed the fraying edge of his control, and that *thrilled* her. Wantonly, she circled her hips against his touch. "It feels so good when you touch me."

"I love petting your soft, wet pussy. Stroking your pearl."

Her eyes squeezed shut as he followed through on his lusty litany, finding that spot of exquisite pleasure, rubbing and circling, winding the coil in her belly ever tighter. The muscles of her pussy fluttered, clutching on emptiness.

"Do you want more, Emma?"

"Yes," she breathed. "Give me more."

His swift incursion, thick and deep, made her moan. "Push your tight little cunny against me," he instructed. "Fuck yourself on my fingers."

The rawness of his command inflamed her. Panting, she rocked her pelvis back, impaling herself on his long, thick fingers. His dark praise spurred her wanton ride. *Your pussy is so greedy. So hungry. Take me even deeper ...* Desperately, she obeyed, the tension inside her building with each filling thrust, each slap of his palm against her mound. The glittering precipice neared, surges of pleasure propelling her closer and closer.

She gritted her teeth, resisted going over the edge.

His body curved over hers, his breath heating her ear as his fingers drove deep. "What do you want, love? Tell me. Whatever you need, I'll give it to you."

"With you, Alaric," she gasped. "I want to go over *with you*."

In the next instant, she was spun around. He sat her up, her bottom landing on the edge of the desk. She glimpsed the desperate hunger in his gaze the moment before his mouth sealed over hers. His tongue stabbed inside, and she responded with eager abandon, sucking on what he offered, drawing him in deeper.

He took her hand, and her breath stuttered when her fingers wrapped around his hot, pulsing cock. She could barely encircle the thick girth of his shaft, the silky skin a riveting contrast to the iron core.

"Touch me, Emma." His eyes were hooded and hot. "Like this."

His hand covered hers, tightening her fist, plunging it from the tip of his member to the root and back again. Aroused beyond anything, she took up the rhythm with reckless delight, tugging on his engorged stalk, rubbing her thumb over the seeping head, desperate to share the wild pleasure with him.

"Christ, sweeting, your hands were made to frig me," he rasped.

"I like frigging you," she whispered back. "Like sharing this, together ..."

He devoured the rest of her words at the same time that his fingers delved between her thighs, titillating her pearl and driving into her sheath. They panted, straining together toward bliss. She reached the pinnacle first, and he swallowed her cries before shuddering with his own fulfillment, his release lashing hotly over her thighs.

His arms closed around her, and she sagged against him like a rag doll. The sound of their tattered breaths filled the silence. She floated, buoyed by a delicious contentment.

"Don't deny me, Emma. Don't push me away."

Surprise percolated through her languor. Lifting her head from his chest, she saw the stark set of his beautiful face. "I'm not pushing you away."

"You question my motives. Won't accept a simple gift. You want to back out of our agreement."

Despite the mechanical delivery of his words, she glimpsed raw agitation in his eyes. That hint of vulnerability was utterly at odds with the self-assured duke, and it made him ... human. He'd said that he didn't want love, called it a complication—but was it possible that he secretly desired her affection? When he looked at her the way he was doing so now, she felt as if he *did* need her. And that feeling made it difficult to deny him anything.

"I'm not reneging on our bargain. But I do want us to be honest with one another. Trust one another," she said earnestly.

"I want you, Emma. I'm not letting you go."

"I want you, too, Alaric." She cast a pointed look at the desk. "Obviously."

His expression relaxed a fraction. "Good. Then you'll marry me."

"You can't rush this." When he stiffened, she cupped his hard jaw and looked in his eyes. "We'll get there if you give us time."

"I am there. You're the one who needs to make up her mind."

Taking a breath, she said, "I'd get there faster if you told me why you don't want anyone to know that you're the secret benefactor of Kent and Associates."

"Devil take it, you're as obstinate as a mule."

She risked a small smile.

His chest heaved. "I'm no benefactor. I owe my brother, and I'm merely making amends."

"Because you married his intended, you mean?"

He stared at her. "You know about that?"

"Annabel mentioned it awhile back," she admitted. "She

blamed Lady Laura for making trouble between you and Mr. McLeod."

"My sister-in-law is too generous. I made the choice to betray my brother. Fate paid me back by giving me the marriage I deserved, but it's not enough—not for what I did." Self-recrimination weighted his words even as he shrugged. "All I have to offer is money. I funneled the funds through the Hilliards because I know my brother's pride. I didn't want William to feel obligated to me when it is I who can never right the wrong I did to him."

Alaric's guilt, the depth of his remorse, squeezed her heart.

"You have much more to give than money," she said softly. "And family forgives."

"Your family, perhaps." His bleak expression reminded her that he'd been parted from his true kin at an early age. "There's too much bad blood between William and me. More than just Laura. And before you ask—yes, I'll tell you about it. Not today, however."

He'd exposed more to her today than he ever had. Something had changed, deepened between them. Hope bloomed in her for their future.

"Thank you for sharing this with me. I won't tell anyone," she promised.

"You don't despise me, Emma, for betraying my own brother?"

Suddenly, she understood. "Is that why you wouldn't answer me when I questioned you about the Hilliards earlier? Because you thought I'd despise you?"

At his curt nod, her chest constricted. Did he believe her regard of him so conditional? Then again, she hadn't exactly been steadfast in their relationship. She cringed, thinking of how she'd first misjudged him, how noncommittal she'd been since.

"I don't hate you. I couldn't. I ... I care for you, Alaric."

Goodness, it was *more* than that. Was she ... falling in love with Alaric? He, who'd told her he didn't want or need her love?

"Then wear my necklace." His knuckles grazed her cheek, his eyes silvery and intense. "'Tis my gift to you, a token so that you might think of me when we're not together."

How could she refuse such a request?

"And you say *I'm* stubborn," she muttered.

"It takes one to know one, pet."

She debated for a moment—and hit upon the perfect compromise.

Meeting his gaze, she smiled. "I'll wear the necklace ... if you'll do me a favor in return."

Chapter Twenty-Two

"I cannot believe I agreed to this," Alaric said.

Emma beamed at him. "'Twas a fair bargain, Your Grace."

She looked as smug as if she'd haggled with the butcher and secured a prime cut at a steal of a price. Certainly, she seemed to have no qualms whatsoever about being in a third-rate, ramshackle theatre several blocks from Drury Lane. "Actresses" were milling about, and their skimpy robes and painted faces suggested that The Cytherea's main source of income was not the ribald plays it put on, but the entertainment it offered to male patrons afterward in the "visiting" chambers.

As usual, Emma was too focused upon her goal to take any notice of the impropriety of her being in such a place. *What would she do without me to protect her from herself?* Alaric wondered wryly. He'd taken the precaution of posting guards around the theatre and greased the palm of the manager to let him and Emma backstage.

"Who should we approach first?" she said.

His lips twitched. Truly, she looked like a child in a confectionary, her eyes wide and shining as she considered all the options.

"You're the one who wanted to come here and investigate. I thought you had a plan," he said.

"Of course I do." She pulled her shoulders back. "Just, um, follow my lead."

Because he found her determination to help him so damned adorable—and coming in her sweet palms had put him in an indulgent mood—he complied. In her primrose walking dress, she was a blast of sunshine in the windowless space. She meandered between the rickety vanities that served as primping stations for the cast. She stopped at one and, clearing her throat, tapped the shoulder of a ginger-haired actress who sat powdering her face before a cracked looking glass.

The tart eyed Emma in the reflection. "Gor, 'oo are you?"

"My name is Emma Kent," she began. "I'm looking for an actress who used to work here by the name of Lily White."

"I don't know nothin'—which is what I told that other investigator who showed up askin' questions about Lily earlier this week." The woman turned her attention back to the powdering.

"But it's vital that you speak with us. You see, Lily may be involved in a crime and—"

"She could be involved wif the King o' England for all I care. I don't poke my nose where it don't belong. Now I got a show to ready myself for."

Alaric stepped forward. "Excuse me, Miss ...?"

The actress turned in her seat to face him. Her sooted eyelashes fanned, and she readjusted the neckline of her robe, showing more of her twin assets.

"Well, 'ello, luvie," she purred. "Didn't see you there. The name's Miss Bloom, but you can call me Daisy."

Out of the corner of his eye, Alaric saw Emma frown.

"Miss Bloom," he said, "finding Miss White is a matter of some urgency. Anything you recall would be helpful, and I will be happy to compensate you for your time."

"What kind o' compensation do you 'ave in mind,

'andsome?" she cooed.

"He means with *money*." Emma's hands fisted on her hips.

Alaric hid a smile. It was nice to know his kitten felt as possessive over him as he did over her. For an instant, the memory of Laura's crazed jealousy raised its malignant head—and he pushed it aside.

This was different. *Emma* was different.

She had every right to defend what was hers; if the situation were reversed, he wouldn't countenance any man propositioning her.

He removed a small purse from his pocket and saw Daisy's ears perk as the coins within jingled. As she reached for the bag, he kept it just out of reach.

"For your assistance," he said.

"I like a man who drives a *'ard* bargain." Winking, she said, "Onto business, then. Lily worked 'ere for about six months before she upped and left well o'er a month ago."

"Do you know where she went?" Emma said.

"We weren't bosom friends. In competition, weren't we, for the best, ahem, *patrons*." Daisy sent him an arch look. "Lily couldn't act worth a farthing, but she 'ad the kind o' talent coves admired, if you know what I mean."

"Was anyone here close to Lily?" Emma asked.

"Like I said, she was close to plenty o' gents. But you might try Peter Dunn—four-eyes o'er there." She angled her head toward a gangly bespectacled fellow standing next to a set of plaster columns. "'E's the playwright. Lily had 'im wound round 'er finger so that he'd write 'er good parts."

"Thank you," Emma said.

Daisy aimed a pointed gaze at the coin purse.

When Alaric gave it to her, she cooed, "Come alone next time, luvie, an' I'll give you a private showin' o' The Cytherea's main attractions." She wriggled her shoulders, causing said attractions to nearly tumble free of her robe.

Emma took hold of his arm and tugged him away. Out of earshot of the actress, she muttered, "You can close your mouth now."

Amused, he arched a brow. "You're not jealous?"

"Of course not. I just think it's rude to be staring at a woman—anywhere below her face," she said primly.

"First of all, I wasn't staring at her. Second, I look at you all the time below your face. And when I'm really lucky," he murmured, "I get to do more than look."

She blushed. He hoped she never grew out of that charming habit.

As they approached the playwright, she said in a brisk undertone, "I'll do the talking."

"I wouldn't dream of interfering with a professional at work," he said.

She slid him a narrow-eyed glance, and he bit back a smile. He had to admit that sleuthing with Emma was rather ... fun. He hadn't enjoyed himself this much in, well, he couldn't recall the last time. His amusement only grew as they neared Peter Dunn, who was trying to instruct a buxom actress on her accent.

"Repeat the line after me," the lanky bespectacled fellow said. *"The heavens weep and I submit/ to the hail of the Gods upon my bosom."*

"The 'eavens weep and I submit," the actress began.

"Heavens," he repeated.

"That's wot I said. 'Eavens."

"Heavens and *'eavens*—can't you hear the difference?"

"I can *'ear* just fine." The actress pouted and flipped a black lock over her shoulder. "Now can we get on wif it?"

"Go on," Dunn said with a sigh.

"The 'eavens weep and I submit to the ... the 'ail o' the Gods 'pon ..." A notch formed between her brows before she finished triumphantly, "my tits!"

Alaric choked back a laugh.

"It's *bosom*." Dunn looked ready to rip his hair out.

The actress jutted a hip. "I know a good rhyme when I 'ear one—and it ain't *bosom*."

"Mr. Dunn?" Emma said.

"What is it?" The playwright swung around to face her, and his expression went from aggrieved to enchanted in a way that set Alaric's teeth on edge. Dunn smoothed his blond hair in place and gave a flourished bow. "Egad, if it isn't Aphrodite, walking amongst mere mortals."

"Actually, my name is Emma Kent. Miss Bloom said you might be able to help me."

"I would be delighted to be of assistance," Dunn said. "And to be freed of the labors of Sisyphus."

"Gor, you ain't got no right to call me a sissy puss—or whate'er that bad name was," the actress put in sulkily.

"I wasn't—never mind. We'll work on the lines later." Dunn gave an impatient wave, and the actress flounced off. He flashed a dazzling smile at Emma. "How can I be of service to you, fair maiden?"

"You can start by not calling her fair maiden," Alaric said.

Dunn blinked, pushing up his spectacles. "Pardon. I didn't notice you, sir."

"We're looking for Lily White," Emma said, shooting Alaric a warning look, "and we understand that you knew her better than most."

Dunn gave a dramatic sigh. "She was my muse, my guiding star. Then one day she abandoned me, left me in the fading twilight of love."

"I'm, er, sorry to hear it," Emma said.

"Your kindness is a balm to my heart." Dunn reached for her hand.

"Touch her, and you will be requiring balm for other bodily parts," Alaric warned.

Dunn's hand fell to his side. "Like that, is it?"

"Yes," Alaric said.

Emma's gaze cast heavenward. "Look, Mr. Dunn, we really need to know where Lily went."

"Why?"

"We have reason to believe that she is involved in dangerous business. We must find her to ascertain the truth and prevent further harm from occurring."

Alaric had to admire Emma's truthful yet tactful reply.

"Lily's mixed up with a bad lot, is she?" Dunn surprised Alaric by saying.

"Why do you say that?" Emma said quickly.

Dunn snorted. "I may be a playwright, but my head ain't in the clouds. One day Lily is as poor as a church mouse and the next she's swimming in blunt. She said it came from a windfall, some dead relative she never met, but I didn't believe her."

"Why not?"

"Because she was right jumpy, desperate even, to leave London immediately. As if she were running from trouble. Fool that I was, I let her convince me to go with her. Got the tickets, made the plans, and packed up everything to run off to Brighton with her," Dunn said darkly.

Brighton. Alaric met Emma's gaze and saw his own excitement reflected in her eyes. Finally, they'd picked up the maid's lead.

"You went to Brighton with Lily?" Emma said eagerly.

Dunn shook his head. "Never made it that far. We weren't halfway there when she met some rich cove travelling in our coach. Next thing I knew, she threw me over and ran off with that bounder."

"How long ago was this?" Alaric demanded. "Do you

know where they were headed?"

"It was nearly three weeks ago and, as far as I know, they were continuing on to Brighton. I came back here and was lucky that I could get my old job back. All I have left of Lily is this." Reaching inside his jacket, he pulled out a miniature of the maid. "I carry it as a reminder of love's cruelty."

Emma exchanged looks with Alaric.

"We're going to need that portrait, Mr. Dunn," she said.

Chapter Twenty-Three

The next afternoon, Alaric leaned back in his chair, rolling a smooth crystal paperweight from hand to hand. Sun streamed through the tall windows, brightening his study and his already optimistic mood. The tides were finally turning in his favor. He and Emma had informed Kent of their discovery concerning Lily White; although displeased by his sister's involvement, Kent had given his partner Mr. Lugo, a stalwart African gentleman, the portrait of Lily and tasked him with hunting down the actress.

Mr. Lugo was presently on the way to Brighton.

Progress was being made—on all fronts.

For, bit by bit, Alaric was also winning Emma over. Not only was their passion burning more fiercely with each encounter, he sensed her resistance to marriage was waning. And, despite his dominant tendencies, he had to admit that letting her take the lead at the theatre had deepened his admiration for her. With her intelligence and determination, she would make him an excellent duchess. Once the business of his murderer was settled, he'd claim her for good.

And now his present visitor had come bearing more good tidings.

"The situation with the investors has stabilized," the Marquess of Tremont said, crossing his long legs. "It seems your scandal has already become last week's news."

"Gossip can't beat out the lure of profit," Alaric said.

"A few wags like Mercer continue to forecast doom for

our venture, but they are in the minority. Thank God."
Tremont's grey eyes were rueful. "I must confess I'm
breathing easier now that our plans are once again secured.
As you know, I've got a fair share of my personal holdings
tied up in United Mining. I'm afraid I'm rather depending
on it to go through."

Quietly, Alaric said, "If you're short on funds, I'd be
happy to—"

"No, thank you," Tremont said.

Knowing the other's pride, Alaric did not pursue the
subject further. "No matter," he said instead. "In a fortnight,
we'll get the expansion vote passed at the General Meeting,
and the value of shares will go through the roof. You'll be a
rich man."

"That was the plan." The lines around Tremont's mouth
eased. "Onto more important matters—how goes the search
for the fiend who shot at you?"

"We're making progress. It's only a matter of time
before we catch the bastard."

"I am relieved to hear it, old chap. Murder puts a damper
on one's plans." Tremont paused. "At least with our venture
going smoothly, you can spend what's left of the Season
focusing on your wife hunt."

Alaric put down the paperweight with studied
nonchalance. "Indeed."

Tremont, however, must have caught some betraying
sign. "Egad, don't tell me you've managed to find a duchess
with all the mayhem that's been going on?"

"Nothing's settled yet," he muttered.

"But you do have an iron in the fire." A slow smile
spread across Tremont's face. It shed some of his years,
made him look more like the roguish lad he'd been at
Oxford. "By God, I've always said you're the most efficient
fellow I've ever met. Do I know her?"

"I doubt it."

"A mystery woman not from our circle. Now I am intrigued." Tremont's tawny brows shot up. "Is she a scandalous opera singer perhaps? Or a beautiful merchant's daughter—"

"Get intrigued over some other female," Alaric said irritably.

Tremont's grin deepened. "Is that the twang of Cupid's bow I hear?"

Alaric was saved from answering when a knock sounded, and Jarvis peered in. "Please excuse the intrusion, Your Grace. You have a visitor."

"You can see I'm busy," Alaric said.

"I would not have disturbed you, but this, ahem, gentleman, claims you invited him to call. His name is Babcock."

Anticipation rolled through Alaric. *Some days are just better than others.*

"Put him in the drawing room. I'll be there shortly," he said.

"Sounds important. I shan't keep you." Rising, Tremont said, "Before I go—don't I get at least a hint about the object of your undying affection?"

To his consternation, Alaric felt his cheekbones heat. "Devil take you, Tremont."

The marquess laughed.

"Are you sure you don't need my help with your undergarments, Miss Emma?" the ladies maid said anxiously from the other side of the door. "At least to tighten your corset strings—"

"I'm fine for now, thank you. I'll ring when I'm ready to

put the ball gown on," Emma said in bright tones.

As soon as she heard the maid shuffle off, Emma released a breath. She was sitting in front of her vanity, a high-necked robe bundled around her. She'd put that on after removing the high-necked frock she'd worn all day. Undoing the belt, she parted the lapel and blushed to see that nothing had changed since she'd last looked.

The red mark still blazed at the side of her throat.

She brushed her fingertips against the evidence of Alaric's kiss. She had no doubt that he had put it there on purpose. Recalling the branding scorch of his lips as he'd bent her over his desk, heat prickled over her insides.

At the same time, her reflection wrinkled its nose.

"Devious man," she muttered.

It could be no coincidence that he'd placed his mark in that particular place. Given the low cut of her fashionable ball gown, she would have *no choice* but to cover it with the jewelry he'd given her. She gave an exasperated huff at his unnecessary high-handedness. She would have worn the necklace anyway—to uphold her end of the bargain after he'd taken her to The Cytherea.

Her irritation turned to excitement as she thought of their discoveries at the theatre, the excellent headway they'd made in the search for Lily. Moreover, Alaric had demonstrated his support of Emma's dreams, and she had to admit that working together with him was even better than going at it on her own.

They were becoming true partners, equals capable of give and take. At The Cytherea, he'd let her take the lead with questioning the witnesses. Right before that, when they'd made love on his desk, she'd surrendered to his control. A giddy feeling swept over her. In both instances, she'd felt connected to him body and mind. She'd once wondered if she was capable of a passionate bond with another, and now she knew the answer.

I've fallen in love with Alaric.

Somehow, despite their disastrous first meeting and subsequent conflicts, she'd lost her heart to the duke. A dictatorial man whose icy cynicism hid a passionate nature. A man with more layers than an onion. How many would she have to peel back, she wondered, before she reached his heart?

Wistfully, she lifted the choker from its black velvet box. The triple strand of flawlessly matched pearls slid against her fingers. The centerpiece—an enormous pink diamond set in a dazzling frame of diamonds—nestled itself heavily in her palm.

It was a necklace fit for a duchess—or rather, a *queen*. According to Marianne, this particular piece had occupied the center display at Rundell, Bridge, and Rundell, London's most prestigious jeweler; it was said to have once belonged to the wife of a great Maharaja.

Shaking her head at Alaric's extravagance, she secured the diamond-studded clasp and looked in the mirror. Her heart stumbled in her chest.

Oh. My. Goodness.

She'd never been overly concerned about her appearance. Pretty is as pretty does, after all. Yet now she marveled at her reflection, the way the necklace imbued her with glowing vitality. She didn't recognize the bright-eyed woman with skin as lustrous as the pearls and lips as vividly blushing as the rare diamond. The choker seemed to lengthen her neck, inject her carriage with grace. She didn't look like the country spinster she was.

It's perfect for you, Alaric had said.

Could it be that he saw her this way—as this exotic, bold, confident creature?

"Emma, may we come in?"

Her sisters' voices broke her reverie. When she let them in, Thea's hazel eyes widened. "The necklace looks beautiful on you, Emma."

"That diamond is as big as the egg I had for breakfast," Violet declared.

Touching Alaric's gift, Emma felt her cheeks warm. "Is it too much?"

"You're glowing," Polly said simply.

"Thank you, dear." Emma smiled. "Help me dress, will you?"

Closing the door behind them, her sisters clustered around her at the looking glass. With an efficiency borne of practice—growing up without the benefit of maids, they'd always dressed one another—the girls set to work. Vi helped her pull on her unmentionables, Thea worked on the corset strings, and Polly crouched to adjust the skirts of her petticoats.

"Just like the old days," Vi said.

"Do you think about Chudleigh Crest?" Emma said.

"I do. On the count of three now." Thea's deft tug on the laces whooshed the air from Emma's lungs. "As exciting as London is, I sometimes miss the simplicity of country life."

"Not me. London is the tops," Vi decreed. "One never knows what will happen next."

"Are you going to marry the duke, Emma?" Polly blurted.

In the reflection, Emma saw her sisters grow still, their faces bright with curiosity.

Meeting Polly's aquamarine eyes, she said, "Would you mind if I did?"

"No," Polly said. "I like him."

Her youngest sister's approval buttressed Emma's own feelings. If there was anyone whom she trusted as a judge of character, it was her baby sister. Gifted with an intuitive nature, Polly was wise beyond her tender years.

"The question is whether or not *you* like the duke, Emma," Thea said gently.

"I do." It was a relief to admit the truth. "He can be stubborn and overbearing, and he *always* thinks he's right. Yet beneath it all he has a good heart."

"Sounds like someone I know," Vi said, grinning.

"Who?" Emma said.

Her sisters looked at each other and burst out laughing.

Emma rolled her eyes. "That's different. You lot required a firm hand. I *had* to be managing to keep you in line."

"We know that, dear." Thea's eyes sparkled. "But let's face it, you're no wilting violet. You need someone with a will to match yours—and His Grace certainly fits the bill."

"I hope that doesn't mean the duke and I are destined to a lifetime of locking horns."

"Father always said love involved compromise," Thea said.

"Well, Strathaven and I *are* learning to negotiate and work together," Emma mused, "and he even supports my assisting in his case."

"I think it's smashing that you're working with Ambrose. I wish he'd let me help, too," Violet said.

Uh oh. What have I started?

Seeing the spark in her sister's eyes, Emma said, "I, er, thought you were enjoying your lessons and the delights of Town."

"I am, but what you're doing sounds *more* fun."

"It isn't a game," Thea chided gently. "The duke's life is at stake. You mustn't pester Ambrose and distract him from serious work."

"You're such a spoilsport." With a good-natured sigh,

Violet went to fetch Emma's ball gown from the dressing screen.

Emma had the feeling that the conversation was not quite finished. Like the pot, however, she couldn't very well call the kettle black. Perhaps Violet's sudden interest would go the way of so many of the dear girl's impulses. A while back, after seeing a performance at Astley's, Vi had decided to become an acrobat.

Whatever the case, we'll cross that bridge when we get there, Emma thought.

Thea said, "Well, I, for one, am happy that you've found someone who appreciates you, Em. And you'll make a fine duchess."

"How difficult could that be?" Vi returned with the eggshell satin cradled in her arms. "All you have to do is wear a hideous turban on your head and refer to yourself in the first person plural." She mimicked in a nasal tone, "*We do not find the dessert to our liking. We are not amused at being served plum pudding when we specifically requested a chocolate gateau.*"

Polly giggled.

Even Thea's lips twitched as she helped Emma into the gown.

"I don't care about being a duchess. I care about ... him." Emma tried to put into words what she knew in her heart. "I can't explain it, but I thinks he needs me. From what I've gathered, his first marriage was rather horrid. And his mama died when he was young and then he was separated from Mr. McLeod at an early age. I don't think he's ever felt a part of a true family."

"Gadzooks," Violet said with sympathy.

"Poor man," Thea murmured.

"He's lonely," Polly whispered.

If there was anything a Kent understood, it was the

importance of family.

"Well, if you marry him, then he'll become a member of *our* family," Vi said stoutly. "No one's ever lonely when we're around."

"Thank you, dear, but nothing is settled yet. We have a murderer to find. Moreover, I need to be certain that we truly suit and can live in the same world."

"Turn around and look in the mirror," Thea suggested.

Emma did—and her breath stuttered.

The ivory gown left her shoulders bare, the bodice glimmering with the subtle sheen of seed pearls embroidered in a swirling vine pattern. The waistline followed the current trend, nipping in at her waist and flaring subtly at her hips. The hem was caught up at regular intervals by ribbons fashioned to look like tiny, magenta butterflies, the bright splashes of color echoing the brilliance of the necklace.

Bemused, she said, "I do look different, don't I?"

"Oh Emma," Polly said, "you look like a *duchess*."

Chapter Twenty-Four

Dusk had fallen, making the alleyway in the Seven Dials even darker. The stench of human waste filled the fetid air, tempting Alaric to cover his nose with a scented handkerchief. The only reason he didn't was because he wouldn't give his brother the satisfaction. Parked against the adjacent wall, Will was monitoring the tavern across the street.

"You're certain Babcock said The Thirsty Ox?" he said for the umpteenth time.

"There's nothing wrong with my hearing," Alaric replied. "Babcock told me two facts. One, our shooter's name is Clive Palmer, and two, he visits this tavern every Friday."

"I'm only asking because public houses can all sound the same. Coming from Mayfair, you might not appreciate the fine distinction between The Thirsty Ox, The Drunken Ox, The Thirsty Bear—"

"Christ's blood, William, I'm a duke not a dunce," Alaric said icily.

"Touchy, aren't we?"

"If by touchy you mean ready to pummel you with my fists, then yes."

Will grunted. "As if *you* could pummel *me*."

"Care to have a go?"

"Lads," Kent said from behind them. "Can the bickering wait until after we catch the criminal?"

"He started it." Will jabbed a finger in Alaric's direction.

"For Christ's sake." Blowing out a breath of disgust, Alaric resumed the watch.

The street was crowded with people and hawkers' barrows. Rowdy customers stumbled in and out of the tavern in a steady stream, their drab clothes making them nearly indistinguishable from one another. Luckily, the streetlamp by the entrance shed light on their faces as they passed. No sign of the scarred shooter as yet.

"Perhaps we should check in with Cooper," Alaric said.

Cooper and other guards were posted at the back entrance. Alaric was taking no chances at letting Palmer escape. Initially, he'd proposed storming the tavern, but Kent had pointed out the risk in taking on a building full of drunk, armed cutthroats, and Alaric had conceded the other's point.

Kent lifted the whistle that hung on a string around his neck. He'd equipped the guards with similar devices. "Cooper will sound the alarm if he has the suspect. Right now, he's watching and cooling his heels like we are."

Alaric did not like to wait. Especially not in this cesspool of an alley.

Will smirked. "Perhaps you'd be more comfortable in the carriage, Your Grace?"

"I'm fine where I am," he said curtly.

Silence fell again. Kent took up the main watch, and Will and Alaric hung behind him. Standing beside his brother, Alaric returned suddenly to another time they had waited together in the dark: at their father's wake. At sixteen, Will had cried openly by the side of the casket, his grief streaming free; Alaric hadn't shed a single tear, pain and anger bottling inside him.

Why didn't you care for me, Da? Why wasn't I your son, too?

Now, to his surprise, he found that his father's

indifference had lost much of its sting. The impact had faded through the years until he bore only the invisible bruises of acceptance. What did feel fresh, oddly enough, was his brother's grief. The younger Will's brokenhearted expression haunted Alaric here in the shadows. He knew his brother's loss had been intensified by his refusal to take Will back to Lanarkshire with him after their father's funeral.

At the time, he hadn't wanted to explain his reasons. Pride had made it impossible to explain to the golden boy, the perfect son, that rejection had followed Alaric all the way to Strathmore Castle. That there must be something so despicable about him that he invited cruelty wherever he went. Nay, he hadn't been able to say the truth aloud, so he'd done the next best thing: he'd protected Will—by pushing him away.

The old duke's cold eyes pinned him, the belt raised. *You deserve to be punished, you deficient weakling!* Even as Alaric's gut knotted in memory, Emma's voice reached him through the darkness.

Family forgives, she'd said.

His guardian and parents were all dead. His closest living kin was his brother.

Alaric glanced at Will, who was monitoring the street with an eagle eye. Who was trying to protect him despite all the bad blood between them.

Taking a breath, he said in an undertone, "It wasn't because I didn't want you at Strathmore."

"What?" Will's gaze swung to his.

"The regiment was the safer place for you to be."

"Why do you speak of this now?" Even in the shadows, he could see his brother's incredulous expression. "After all this time?"

Alaric wasn't quite sure himself. He gave a slight shrug. "You deserve to know."

"Know what? That facing down enemies with bayonets, scouting enemy terrain," Will said with rising ire, "*that* was safer?"

Alaric's fists clenched, yet he kept his voice low, for Will's ears only. "Compared to living under the duke's tyranny and suffering his brand of punishment? Aye," he said roughly.

Will stilled. "Our uncle, he ... hurt you?"

"I'd rather have taken on an entire battalion," Alaric said succinctly.

After a moment, his brother said in hushed tones, "Why didn't you say anything?"

"It wasn't a topic for polite conversation. And we haven't exactly been on good terms."

"But you're my brother. I would have ..." Will trailed off.

"Exactly. You could have done nothing. It's over; I just wanted to clear the air." Alaric returned his gaze to the tavern, signaling an end to the conversation.

To his surprise, Will said softly, "I had wondered why you seemed different. On the rare visit home, I mean. Ma thought it was because of your illness, but I knew you weren't yourself."

His brother had noticed? An odd spasm gripped his throat. "The illness was only a part of it. The sicker I was, the more the duke punished me."

"Bluidy hell, Alaric, I never knew—"

"Attention, lads." Kent's furious whisper broke the spell of the moment. "Scarred man leaving the premises. Can you identify, Your Grace?"

Alaric pushed from the wall, strode to the mouth of the alley. He spotted the figure instantly. While the burly figure and greasy, overlong hair could have belonged to anyone, there was no mistaking the jagged mark that bisected the man's face into two menacing halves.

"That's him," he said grimly.

"Do you wish to wait here?" Kent began.

Alaric didn't bother answering. Pulling his hat down low, he started toward Palmer. Kent and Will's bootsteps sounded behind him, and from the corner of his eye, he saw them fan out, mingling with the throng. Taking his cue from them, he slowed his pace; when Palmer suddenly swung around, Alaric halted at a barrow. He felt the other's gaze on him, his heart thudding as he pretended to study the peddler's offerings.

"That cup's made o' sterling, guv," the gap-toothed hawker said cheerfully. "Ruin may rot your gut, but it won't tarnish that lovely piece."

Alaric fought not to look at Palmer. "How much?"

"A quid, guv, an' that's on account o' my generous 'eart."

Alaric risked a sidelong glance ... and saw Palmer's back fading into the distance. He took off after him, the hawker's voice ringing behind him. "'Alf a crown, guv, an' that's my best offer!"

Kent and Will were gaining on Palmer, flanking him on two sides. Alaric quickened his steps and kept to the middle of the road, pushing past drunks and painted whores, dodging carts of goods. His eyes and nose stung from the smoke of scorching chestnuts. He was almost upon the fiend, and Will and Kent were nearly parallel: their triangle formation was poised for attack.

He met Kent's gaze, saw the other nod, and his muscles bunched, ready to propel him toward the target.

In that instant, Palmer turned his head.

Recognition flashed across the disfigured face, and the cutthroat broke into a run.

He turned right, and with beefy momentum, plowed through Kent, the investigator sprawling to the ground. The villain vanished into the nearest alleyway, Will on his tail,

Alaric just behind his brother. Alaric heard the shrill of a whistle cut through the thudding in his ears before he was enveloped in darkness. The labyrinth of the rookery engulfed him, the walls widening and narrowing, a twisting path of disorientation.

"Up ahead," Will shouted. "There's a dead end. We've got him."

That his brother knew the stews with such acuity astounded Alaric, and he could only be grateful to have the other as a guide. Energy pumped through his veins, the battle instincts of his ancestors kicking in. He *thirsted* for his enemy's blood.

The darkness grew lighter as the low-hanging eaves gave way to the night sky. He saw a faint glimmer paces ahead: a stream of moonlight striking off stones ... a wall. Palmer scrambling to get over.

A few steps ahead of Alaric, Will raced forward, shouting, "Stop! You can't escape."

Palmer spun around. Steel glinted in his hands.

"Down, Will!" Alaric yelled.

He threw himself forward, knocking his brother to the ground as twin shots whizzed past him, blasting through the night. Breathing hard, he pushed to his feet in the next instant, saw Palmer struggling to reload the pistol. He charged into the cutthroat, sending the firearm scuttling into darkness. Red filled his vision as he slammed his foe into the wall. Pinning the other by the throat, he drove his fist into the bastard's face again and again.

"No one shoots at a McLeod," he growled.

"Strathaven, I've got Palmer covered." Kent had arrived, positioning himself to Alaric's left, panting and aiming a pistol at the villain.

Caught in the grip of bloodlust, Alaric didn't give a damn. He drew his fist back again.

Palmer gasped, "Bloody 'ell, stop ... I give ..."

"Who paid you to kill me?" Alaric slammed Palmer against the wall. "Give me his name."

"Don't ... know." Blood streaked down Palmer's face, trickling into his scar. "'E ne'er told me. Just paid me five 'undred quid ... for the job."

"What did he look like?"

"Black 'air, pudgy face—like a babe's. Wore sp-spectacles."

Silas Webb.

"Where can I find him?" Alaric demanded.

"If I tell you, you'll let me go ..."

"If you don't, I'll kill you." Alaric squeezed Palmer's throat.

"He will, you know." This came from Will, who now stood shoulder-to-shoulder with him. "We Scotsmen keep our word."

"Alright ... alright," the bastard choked out. "I followed 'im once—like to know where my blunt is comin' from. 'E's got a place ... in Whitechapel."

"Take us there," Alaric said.

⁓≍◦

The tenement was part of a sagging pile of misery at the heart of the East End.

"That's the room." His hands manacled behind his back, Palmer could only jerk his head toward the peeling door of the apartment. "I remember it on account o' it being next to the stairs."

"Take him back to the carriage," Alaric said to Cooper. "Keep an eye on him."

The guard nodded and hauled Palmer away at gunpoint.

Kent tried the knob. The easy click raised the hairs on

Alaric's nape.

Wordlessly, Kent withdrew a pistol from his greatcoat, and both Will and Alaric followed suit. Kent pushed the door harder, and the squeal of rusty hinges spurred Alaric's heartbeat. Darkness greeted them, the air musty and dank, and there was an indistinct noise ... a buzzing. An unsavory odor caught Alaric's nose, and his stomach gave a queasy surge.

Kent held up his lantern, and shadowy light spilled over the cramped interior.

"I think we've found our man," he said in grave tones.

A figure lay face down on the table in the middle of the room. As he approached, Alaric saw the flies swirling, the stain beneath the head. Will lit another lamp, and brightness flared above the dead man's head—what remained of it anyway. A gaping hole had been blown out the back; a pistol lay on the ground near the man's dangling hand.

With a detached professionalism that Alaric could only admire, Kent turned the corpse's head to the light.

"Silas Webb?" the investigator asked.

Alaric grimaced. "Aye."

"By the state of decomposition, I'd say it's been several days since the bastard blew his brains out," Will muttered. "Damned messy way to go."

Bending, Kent fished a sheet of paper from the pocket of Webb's jacket. Creases deepened around the investigator's mouth. "It's a signed confession. Webb says he acted out of revenge but now repents." Kent passed Alaric the note. "Can you verify the handwriting?"

Alaric scanned the brief lines. "It looks like Webb's signature."

He wondered why he didn't feel relieved. As he looked around the room, he didn't see signs of anything untoward— no evidence of a struggle, of this being anything but what it appeared to be: a sinner succumbing to his conscience. Yet Webb had never struck him as a man of strong morality or the type to end his own life.

Alaric took a step forward, intending to look around, and something crackled beneath his boot. Bending, he found wire spectacles, the lenses cracked—and the glint of something else in the shadows. Reaching beneath the table, he retrieved the small object nestled against Webb's boot.

"What have you found?" Kent asked.

Alaric showed him the cuff link. Made of onyx and gold, its workmanship fine, the expensive piece was clearly out of place in the dingy environs.

Swiftly, Kent checked the corpse's wrists; both brass links were intact. The three men commenced searching through Webb's meager belongings, and to no one's surprise, the twin to the onyx cuff link did not emerge.

Icy premonition gripped Alaric's gut. "The cuff link didn't belong to Webb. Someone else was here."

Kent's gaze matched the brightness of his lantern. "So it would seem."

"Over here," Will called.

They went to join him by the hearth where he'd unearthed the charred remains of a ledger.

"Looks like an appointment book," Will said.

When he opened it, ashes drifted to the ground.

"My guess? The true murderer destroyed this to hide his identity," Kent said. "Do you know of any men Webb might have had dealings with, Your Grace? A wealthy man. One with a penchant for fine accoutrements such as the cuff link?"

Alaric shook his head. "As far as I knew, Webb had worked solely for United Mining for years. Until I dismissed him, that is."

"We'll come back in the morning," Kent said decisively,

"and canvas the neighborhood. Perhaps someone saw Webb with our mystery man."

"I appreciate your diligence," Alaric said.

"We Kents do not concede until the matter is resolved." An unexpected hint of a smile relieved the somberness of the other man's expression. "I believe you know something about that, Your Grace."

Chapter Twenty-Five

As *ton* affairs went, this ball was definitely better than Emma's first experience.

Emma had no doubt that Alaric had pulled strings to make her feel comfortable at this lavish affair. The hosts, Lord and Lady Blackwood, personally greeted her and Marianne as if they were longtime friends.

Lady Blackwood, whose raven-haired beauty suited her name, kissed the air near Emma's cheeks. "What a divine necklace," she said warmly. "From Rundell and Bridge's, is it not?"

"Er, yes. I believe so," Emma mumbled.

"It was a gift," Marianne said smoothly.

"Ah." Lady Blackwood's gaze turned speculative.

"Now don't go giving my wife any ideas," Lord Blackwood said wryly. With short hair of polished bronze, he possessed a soldier's bearing and kind eyes. "Lady Blackwood is prone to extravagance as it is."

"For that comment, I shall expect a bracelet to match the emerald earrings I purchased," his wife said saucily.

"I am ruined." Blackwood regarded his lady with clear affection.

"As if a bracelet could ruin you, my dear." Lady Blackwood turned to Emma. "Well, let's not keep you in the corner, Miss Kent. Shall I introduce you to some of the other guests?"

"Yes, please," Emma said, more than ready to embark on

her mission.

For the next hour, under Lady Blackwood's wing, Emma circulated amongst the glittering throng. She made an effort to converse; after all, her goal was to determine if any of these guests could be guilty of murder, and to do that, she needed to establish rapport. To her surprise, some of the lords and ladies were not as haughty as she had previously assumed.

Some ladies even discussed such mundane topics as household remedies and unruly children, and Emma found herself quite naturally contributing to the conversation. At the request of a dowager, she provided her recipe for joint salve; at that of a countess with a fussy, two-month-old babe, she shared the tonic she'd used to calm Polly's colic.

It was quite strange to find herself fitting in.

Two hours of conversation and dancing passed pleasantly enough, yet Emma discovered nothing even remotely suspicious. She headed for the refreshment table, the oasis of gossip at any social gathering. Accepting a cup of champagne punch from a footman, she discreetly posted herself behind a potted palm and eavesdropped on the surrounding voices. Alaric's name soon cropped up, and she peered through the fronds at the backs of the chattering trio.

" … it appears as if Strathaven truly is Croesus," said a grey-haired gentleman. "The price of stock in that joint venture of his has increased threefold in the last week. Everything he touches turns to gold."

"Should have bought shares myself," said a short balding fellow.

"I wouldn't act too hastily." The drawl came from a tall blond man whose black jacket was meticulously fitted to his figure. "You never know what will happen with speculation. As I understand it, Strathaven doesn't have his investors' confidence. If the vote to expand the venture doesn't go through in a fortnight, the shares will plummet once more."

Obviously, the man doesn't know Alaric, Emma thought. Strathaven would never leave something like a vote up to chance.

"Speculation is a young man's game," Grey Hair said. "I've always said that the only wealth a gentleman can depend upon comes from land."

As the men's talk drifted to other topics, Emma found her attention hooked by another conversation, this time between a gaggle of ladies standing by the champagne fountain to her left. Emma had a clear view of their bobbing plumes as they spoke in titillated tones.

"They say Strathaven means to resume his duchess hunt," said a plump brunette.

"Given his scandal of late, I wonder at his temerity," said her friend in rose silk.

"He's never lacked for temerity and well you know it." The arch tones came from a third lady with a smirking expression. "I have no doubt he'll get what he wants—he always does, after all. Anyway, his search for a wife is old news. What intrigues me is when he will be on the market for Clara Osgood's replacement."

"Lady Julia, how perfectly wicked of you!" the first lady whispered in delight.

"You were thinking the same thing, Lady Lauren. *I* just said it aloud."

"Well, I confess I am intrigued by rumors of his prowess. You have heard what they say about his personal, ahem, endowments?" Lady Lauren giggled. "Apparently they match his financial ones."

"And that's to say nothing of his stamina and control," Lady Julia purred. "I've heard our duke is as deliciously dominant in the bedchamber as he is in out of it. Why, it's said that a certain Lady M. enjoyed a rollicking afternoon *on his desk …"*

As the ladies tittered, Emma turned away, her cheeks burning. She knew, of course, about Alaric's past and his proclivities, yet hearing other women talk about him in such an openly lascivious and covetous manner caused hurt and, yes, *jealousy* to burgeon.

Images flooded her: Alaric tying Lady Clara up in the garden … him making love to nameless, faceless beauties on the *same desk* where he'd made love to her …

Up until this moment, the passion she shared with Alaric, while undoubtedly wicked, had also seemed … special. Precious. That others had known the raw intensity of his lovemaking made her chest ache. Her throat cinched, his gift suddenly heavy and constricting.

"Hello, miss," said a hesitant voice. "I was wondering if you would mind some company?"

She turned and found herself looking into the blue eyes of a plump, ginger-haired pixie.

"I beg your pardon?" Emma said blankly.

The girl, who looked barely eighteen, turned as red as her hair. "You were standing there alone, and I'm alone … well, not exactly, I do have my chaperone, but she's busy with the other duennas, and I … dash it all, I'm talking too much, aren't I?" she finished miserably. "It's a terrible habit of mine, and Papa says it makes me awkward. As if I could be *more* awkward …" Her self-conscious shrug caused the ribbons to flutter on the many tiers of her gown. "Never mind. I'm sorry for disturbing you. I'll just be—"

Emma took an instant liking to the girl. "No, don't go. I was just woolgathering, and I'd love some company. I'm Emma Kent."

"I'm Gabriella Billings, but everyone calls me Gabby." The way the girl's smile lit her face reminded Emma of Polly. "It is lovely to meet you. It's so tiresome to be a wallflower that even other wallflowers won't pay any attention to. Truly, I'm more of a wall*weed*."

Emma stifled a smile. "Surely it isn't bad as all that? You're perfectly charming."

"Only because you're a decent sort. I can always judge a person's character, you know, just by looking at them," Gabby said cheerfully. "Being a businessman's daughter, I've inherited the ability to size someone up at a glance."

"Really?" Emma said, amused. The girl's irrepressible spirit now reminded her of Violet.

"Take you, for instance. You have a kindly disposition, yet there you were hiding behind that palm, so I surmised that you didn't fit in here either. I thought you might be a middling class sort like me. No offense," Gabby added quickly.

"None taken. It's true."

"Your gown is delectable. And your necklace has the ladies green with envy. So even if you are a Cit like me, you have oodles more style," Gabby said in consoling tones.

Emma had to smile. "I wouldn't mind being a Cit. But actually I'm from the country."

"Really?" Gabby said with interest. "I've never been outside London. Papa owns a bank, you see, and he's too busy to take me anywhere."

"What about your mama?"

"She died in childbirth. The only things I have of her are a dowry and this." Gabby tugged on a bright curl. "Unfortunately, carrots aren't in fashion this Season. Or ever."

"I think your hair is lovely and unique," Emma said.

"Truly? You aren't just saying that?"

"Not at all. As for fitting in, my papa said that the rarest of jewels shines the brightest."

"My father says the nail that sticks out gets the hammer."

"Ouch," Emma said.

"Exactly." Gabby sighed. "Unfortunately, it seems I can't help but stick out no matter what I do. And tonight, especially. Not that I'm surprised—I'm more or less an act of charity."

"How so?" Emma said curiously.

"Papa has a client—a gentleman of consequence—who owed him a favor." Gabby wrinkled her nose. "Clearly it was a *big* favor as the fellow had to secure a spot for *me* on the exclusive guest list. An invitation, however, is no guarantee of success. Papa will be quite disappointed when he discovers that I was not asked for a single dance."

"Dancing isn't all that it's made out to be. My toes are still sore from being trod on."

"You're very kind. It would be nice, however, to have made some friends," Gabby said wistfully. "You're the first person who has spoken with me all evening."

"Would you like to call upon me some afternoon?" Emma said on impulse. "I have sisters your age, and I have a feeling you will rub along famously with them."

"Oh, I'd love to, ever so much." Gabby's blue eyes shone.

Emma fished a calling card from her reticule. "Here is my direction."

"Dash it, I know I have mine in here somewhere ..." Rummaging in her lumpy evening bag, Gabby triumphantly produced one bent-eared card.

As Emma was tucking the card away, a liveried footman came up to her.

"Pardon. Miss Kent?"

"That's me," Emma said in surprise.

"I was instructed to give you this, miss."

She took the note from the footman's salver and, unfolding it, read the succinct message.

Meet me in the gallery on the third floor.

There was no signature, but the slashing imperiousness of the handwriting gave away the identity of its sender and made her pulse race. Then she remembered what she had overheard earlier and, with a huff, wondered if she should go running to obey His Grace's command.

Apparently, he was all too used to having females at his beck and call.

"Is everything alright?" Gabby said.

"Yes. But I have to attend to something," Emma said, sighing. "I shall see you soon, I hope?"

Gabby gave a merry nod. "You can count on it."

Chapter Twenty-Six

Emma found the door to the gallery unlocked, her skirts whispering against the Aubusson runner as she entered the long rectangular room. Paintings framed in gilt lined the navy silk walls, and benches and curtained alcoves with window seats were conveniently placed for contemplation or conversation. The lush drapery and carpeting provided a hushed quality to the space, which was a welcome relief from the brouhaha of the ballroom downstairs.

Awareness prickled over Emma's skin. As ever, her senses reacted instinctively to his presence even before she saw his leanly powerful figure in one of the alcoves. He was staring out the window, his hands clasped behind his back. His head turned immediately in her direction, and the intensity of his gaze sizzled through her.

In several strides, he crossed over to her. A faint smile edged his lips as he touched the choker, his finger running over the pearls, causing the strands to clack softly against one another.

"How beautiful you look," he murmured.

"What are you doing here?" she said. "I thought we couldn't be seen together."

"I came in through a private entrance. No one saw me." He caressed her jaw. "Hasn't anyone told you never to accept a *rendezvous* with a stranger?"

Given the many trysts he'd apparently had, he was one to talk.

Lifting her chin, she said, "I thought that was why unattached ladies attended these functions in the first place. To find a beau."

His eyes darkened. "You are not unattached."

The gossip she'd heard continued to sting. She gave a slight shrug. "That is a matter of opinion. Now, Your Grace, what are you—"

The rest was lost in a gasp as she was yanked into his embrace. His lips claimed hers in a hot, demanding kiss. Desire rose in her, drowning out the protests of her wounded pride. She clung to his hard shoulders as he ravished her mouth, his tongue plundering, luring hers into a primal dance.

When he ended the kiss, they were both breathless.

Eyes gleaming, he said, "That settles that. It seems I can't leave you alone for a day without you forgetting who you belong to."

"I don't belong to you," she retorted. "At least, no more than all the other women you've dallied with."

His eyes narrowed. "What are you going on about?"

He wanted her to report on the *ton*'s gossip? Fine. She told him.

When she finished, his face was utterly devoid of expression. She frowned. Did he not care? Where was his reaction? She'd expected embarrassment, perhaps, or even anger. Instead, he was eerily ... still.

When she could stand the silence no longer, she said, "Well?"

"Well, what?" he said evenly.

"Is it true?"

"I'm no saint and never claimed to be. I don't see what the problem is."

"The problem is I thought that what passed between us was different." She had to force the words past her cinched throat. "Yet you've done the same things with other women."

"What happens between you and me has nothing to do with other women."

"How can you say that?" she said, her voice trembling. "When you made love to some Lady M. on the *same desk* where we made love?"

That fact, she realized, bothered her the most: he'd taken her in the same place he'd taken other women. As if she didn't have a special place in his life. In the heart he professed not to have.

The world tilted with disorienting speed. Before she could catch her breath, he'd deposited her none too gently on the padded bench of the alcove. She scooted away, her back wedging up against the window as he leaned over her, his velvet-encased shoulders blocking out everything. All she could see was the savage flame in his eyes.

Suddenly, she realized that he wasn't indifferent at all. He was *furious*.

"First of all, Lady M. and I did not make love. We fornicated—which is different from what you and I do. Second, I did not fuck her on the same desk. I do not invite casual bed sport to my home. You'll recall I retain a cottage for that purpose."

Relief unfurled in Emma at his clipped words. At the same time, feminine wariness arose at the tension vibrating from his muscular frame.

She wetted her lips. "I thought—"

"You made it quite clear what you thought. Now let me make it clear that I will not tolerate baseless accusations," he bit out. "I will not be controlled or manipulated by jealousy—I've had enough of that to last a lifetime."

"The accusations weren't baseless. I heard people talking about you," she protested.

"You could have asked me about it rather than flinging it in my face."

Her indignation abruptly fizzled. He did have a point.

"That was unfair of me, wasn't it?" Releasing a breath, she said, "I'm sorry."

"You're sorry." He spoke without inflection.

"Well, yes. I shouldn't have assumed the gossip was true. It's just that it ... hurt," she said miserably, "to hear people talk about you. To think that what we shared wasn't special."

He stared at her. "How could you think that?"

The truth struck her fully for the first time.

"I suppose I've never been special to anyone before. As a sister and friend, yes—but not as a woman. A lover." She gave him a rueful look. "And here you are: a duke who apparently every lady covets. Why should you want me when you could have anybody?"

He curled a finger beneath her chin, forcing her to meet his gaze. "Because there's no else like you, Emma."

"What you said earlier ... about having been manipulated in the past." She hesitated. "Were you referring to your wife?"

He straightened, took a step back from her. His expression iced over.

"After we wed, Laura constantly accused me of infidelity, was jealous of every female who crossed my path from the maid to the neighbor's daughter," he said tonelessly. "There was nothing I could do to convince her that I was faithful."

Heart thumping, Emma waited.

"Finally, I got tired of defending myself. She would rant at me, throw fits of hysterics, yet I stopped caring what she believed. Or what she did. She accused me of not giving her attention, not loving her as she deserved—and I suppose she was right. Any affection I felt for her died the moment she took her first lover."

"She betrayed you?" Emma whispered.

Tight-lipped, he gave a nod. "She needed attention more than she needed her next breath, and if I didn't provide her with it, she found it from others. In her deluded mind, she thought that if I saw how desirable she was to other men, I would want her more."

"That's madness."

"That's not all of it. She slandered me to all and sundry, played the role of the injured party—which, in her sick mind, I suppose she was."

"Why—why didn't you divorce her?"

"I'd made her a vow." His broad shoulders rose and fell. "And there was my son to think of. I didn't want Charlie to think poorly of his own mama."

It was the first he'd spoken of his son.

Quietly, Emma said, "What happened ... to Charlie?"

Alaric's eyes were empty and cold as he looked out into the darkness beyond the pane. Into the endless stretch of night.

"Laura and I had fought, and she'd threatened to leave me. I didn't take her seriously," he said. "She'd given ultimatums countless times and never once acted on her words. Then one day I came home and found her gone. I could have lived with that—if she hadn't taken Charlie."

"Where?" Emma whispered.

"She'd secured them passage on a ship bound for France. I believe she wanted me to chase after her, to show my undying devotion. Instead, the ship went down in a storm that night." His voice was flat, devoid of emotion. "There were no survivors."

She had no words for such a loss. Emma rose and wrapped her arms around his lean waist, giving him what comfort she could. Slowly, his arms came around her. Although he said nothing, his embrace was suffocating. His heart thundered beneath her ear, a shudder passing through his large frame. She held on even tighter.

"Don't ever question my desire for you," he said in guttural tones. "Or compare it to what I've known in the past. I have never wanted anyone the way I want you, Emma."

Her heart skipped a beat. It was the closest he'd come to saying that he cared for her.

"I didn't mean to stir up old memories," she said softly, "and I'm sorry I jumped to unfair conclusions. I'm not trying to control or manipulate you. I just want to be ... special. I want to be different from all the other women you've known."

"*That* you definitely are."

Relieved to hear the note of wry humor in his voice, she tipped her head back and said tremulously, "I'm glad you came here tonight to see me."

His expression turned grave. "That wasn't the only reason. We found Webb."

He sat them both down on the alcove seat and filled her in on the details. At his conclusion, she said admiringly, "How clever of you all. The murderer thought to pull the wool over your eyes, and instead you're even closer to catching him. The noose is tightening around his neck."

"Bloodthirsty thing, aren't you?" he murmured.

"Better his neck than yours."

"Miss Kent, I do believe you're flirting with me."

She was about to reply when voices drifted in from the corridor. Before she could react, Alaric was on his feet, yanking the curtain across the alcove. The dark velvet panels obscured them from the rest of the gallery and just in time. The voices—male and female—grew louder, followed by footsteps into the chamber. A soft click signaled the closing of the door.

Heart racing, Emma looked helplessly at Alaric. Standing by the curtain, his figure tensed, he put a finger to his lips. Perhaps he was right. Perhaps if they just remained silent, the guests would take a quick tour of the gallery and leave without discovering them.

"What luck to find this door unlocked," came a man's voice. "Privacy at last."

His companion giggled. "Privacy for what, my lord?"

The rustling of skirts was followed by a sensual moan. Blood pulsed in Emma's cheeks.

"That's what, minx. That'll teach you to tease a blooded bull, eh?"

"But I thought you liked it when I teased," was the coy reply.

"Egad, you're a hot piece," the man said in strained tones. "Greedy for my cock, are you? Give us a nice stroke then—mmm, tighten your fist. Ah, that's it ..."

Her breaths shallow, Emma glanced at Alaric. Moonlight from the window highlighted the flush on his high cheekbones, the hard, sensual jut of his jaw. His chest rose in surges beneath his waistcoat and lower ... Her pulse sped up as she saw the growing bulge between his strong thighs. It made her keenly aware of her own arousal, of the wicked need gathering inside her.

The masculine groans beyond the curtain stirred up the images she'd seen at Andromeda's. Of women ... servicing men. A naughty notion took root: what would it be like to instigate their lovemaking for once? To drive Alaric mad with passion? To give him that same uncontrollable ecstasy that he gave her every time they were together?

Desire heated her blood, the fantasy as irresistible as a siren's call.

As stealthily as she could, she lowered herself to her knees in front of Alaric. She looked up into his startled gaze and placed her palm over the ridge in his trousers, squeezing gently. His nostrils flared, his pale irises blazing in the moonlight. His hand clamped on hers, and she waited with bated breath. Would he allow her to take the lead? Did he trust her enough?

Slowly, his hand lifted. Went to his waistband. His gaze never leaving hers, he undid the fall.

Her core tightened at the sight of his bold virility. Glazed by silvery light, his cock was big and thick, veins twisting along its tumescent length. Like a heavy branch, it bobbed under its own weight. The fact that this part of him was exposed while the rest of him was so urbanely attired struck her as utterly erotic. Looking into his eyes, she wrapped her fingers around him.

His shaft jerked in her palms as she ran a fist from root to tip, his skin gliding with velvet softness over the poker-stiff core. She drew the skin back and exposed the eye at the bulging crown.

"Take me in your mouth."

The guttural demand came from the other side of the curtain, yet it sent a sizzling current through the sheltered alcove. Alaric's jaw visibly clenched, his hands fisting at his sides. His cock thickened even more, its throbbing girth testing the limits of her grip. A pearl of liquid welled up at the slit.

Excitement swirling in her veins, Emma leaned forward and licked it off.

The force of his shudder travelled through her, emboldening her. She mouthed the blunt tip, and not sure what to do next, gave it a cautious suck. His masculine musk spread over her tongue and aroused her even more. She placed kisses along the throbbing length, lost in her desire to know every inch of her duke ... and determined to show him pleasure he'd never known before.

Surely, a man couldn't die of pleasure.

Yet as Alaric watched Emma on her knees before him, her lips skimming so sweetly along his rod, he thought it might indeed be possible to expire from sheer want. Even in this she demonstrated her unique ability to push him to the limits of his self-control. It was clear that she had no idea what she was doing, and, paradoxically, her innocence made her explorations all the more potent.

Her delectable sucking had weakened his knees. Now, as she reached the base of his shaft, her tongue flicked out, and he nearly lost his seed at the exquisite torture of his future duchess lapping delicately at his balls.

Women had performed fellatio on him before. No one had ever made love to his cock. Had ever worshipped him with such sweet and generous ardor.

"Take my prick deeper," the bastard growled on the other side. "I want to feel your throat."

The fact that only a panel of velvet separated them from an audience brought an explosive edge to Alaric's arousal. It required all of his self-restraint not to groan aloud as Emma apparently took inspiration from the other's command. With awkwardness as endearing as it was erotic, she proceeded to cram as much of his cock as she could into her mouth.

She choked a little, and he almost shot his seed then and there.

Dark, dominant urges roared over him. He'd let her play long enough. After all that he'd disclosed to her this night, he required quid pro quo, and he would take it in the form of her sensual submission.

Hooking a finger inside her choker, he drew her from his prick. She released him with a barely perceptible *pop* that seared his nerve endings. In the moonlight, her eyes were fathomless jewels, a thousand times more brilliant than the diamond at her throat. Her hands fell to her sides, and she waited, her cheeks flushed, her surrender utterly perfect.

Wordlessly, he wrapped a hand around his cock. The other he placed at the back of her head to guide her. Silently, he mouthed, "Open."

Her lashes fluttered. Then, obediently, she parted her lips.

Satisfaction roared through him—and that was *before* he slid inside. Her mouth enveloped him like hot silk, and his jaw clenched against a hiss of pure bliss. He forced himself to go slow, feeding her an inch of his cock at a time, getting her used to taking him this way. The sight of his shaft disappearing betwixt her lips made his seed rise, his balls pulsing, yet he reined in the impulse to thrust as deep as he could go. Instead, he kept the pace slow, easy. Drawing in and out, each time going deeper.

When he felt her tense, he palmed her jaw, urging her to relax. Somehow she understood him perfectly, her muscles softening, and he plunged in farther. Suddenly the constriction disappeared altogether, his fingers gripping her scalp as he went all the way in, his sensitive head butting her silken throat. Panting, he withdrew at once ... and her hands clutched his hips, urging him back inside.

Christ Almighty.

Everything around him blurred as he succumbed to his animal urges. The frenzied sounds of the other couple faded to the wild drumming in his chest as he drove into her mouth, fucked it, and she took everything he gave her, everything he was. Her hot, selfless giving incinerated his defenses. The warning sizzle shot up his shaft, and with his last ounce of sanity, he tried to pull free of her kiss.

She wouldn't let him. Her hands gripped his hips, her gaze held his, and his world turned inside out. He bit down to prevent himself from shouting, tasted the tang of blood as pleasure detonated. He shuddered, shooting uncontrollably, pouring himself into her.

Over his galloping heartbeat, he heard shuffling, whispered words and laughter, the door opening and closing, leaving them alone. Emma tucked him back into his trousers; after the raw eroticism of their exchange, her prim efficiency made his lips twitch. He helped her to her feet, and when she smiled at him, another part of his anatomy twitched as well.

With his thumb, he wiped away the glistening dew at the corner of her mouth.

"Missed a drop," he said hoarsely.

She flushed to the roots of her hair; she looked adorably pleased with herself.

"Practice makes perfect," she said.

Her prosaic tone rustled a laugh from his chest. "If you get any more perfect, you'll kill me." Drawing her close, he kissed her, and the trace of his salt on her lips made him harden with shocking speed. "I haven't yet returned the favor."

Her cheeks grew even pinker. "You needn't. I enjoyed that as much as you did."

"I'm certain that's not possible."

"I wanted to give you something special. And you let me." She caressed his jaw. "That is a gift in itself."

The tenderness in her eyes, her touch, swamped him with pleasure. *Relax and enjoy this. She's different. Not like the others.*

At the same time, inexplicable panic surged. *Don't let her see who you really are. Don't make the same mistakes. Stay in control.*

"Thank you," he managed. "Your gift was as unique as you are."

A grin tucked into her cheeks. "I'll take that as a

compliment, Your Grace."

Chapter Twenty-Seven

The next morning found Emma in the carriage with her brother. They were on their way to Silas Webb's tenement in Whitechapel, and the very fact that she'd been included on the excursion filled her with happiness.

"Thank you for bringing me along, Ambrose," she said.

Her brother shifted his gaze from the window to her. "I'm still not certain that it was a good idea. But I seem to have little choice about it."

Guilt needled her insides. She'd campaigned rather fiercely to be included. "Ambrose, I—"

"I cannot very well exclude our most successful investigator from the case, can I?"

It took a moment for his words to sink in. For her to recognize the faint smile in his golden eyes. "Do you mean that? Truly?" she said.

"I can't deny the facts, Em. You got information from Strathaven's maids and those theatre folk that I could not. You are undoubtedly skilled."

Joy bubbled through her. "Thank you, Ambrose."

"You're welcome." His smile faded a little. "I want you to know, however, that it was never your ability that I doubted. I've always known how capable you are, Emma."

"If you're worried because of the danger, I'll take every precaution—"

"Even if you do, I'll always be concerned. I can't help it. I'm your brother." Ambrose studied the pleat on his trousers.

"The truth is there's another reason as well."

"Because it's not proper for a female to be an investigator?" she guessed.

Her brother gave her a wry look. "When has a Kent ever cared about convention?"

He had a point.

"What is it then?" she asked.

"Do you recall the time you came to London on your own? When the cottage caught fire, Father was ill, the family was about to be evicted, and you somehow made it here to get help?"

"I remember." How could she forget? It had been an adventure, terrifying and thrilling. "But why do you bring it up now?"

"You were only sixteen, Em. You should *never* have gone through that."

His quiet vehemence startled her.

"It couldn't be helped," she said. "I did what needed to be done."

"Had I earned a better living, been able to take better care of the family, you would have been spared that ordeal." His jaw clenched. "It was my job to protect all of you."

Looking at her brother's face, she saw how genuinely earnest he was.

"You did everything you could," she protested. "You were working yourself to the bone to support us all. Ambrose, you cannot possibly blame yourself."

"Marianne tells me the same. Logically, perhaps it is true. But here,"—he placed a hand to the place over his heart—"here I'll always wish that I'd done better. Especially for you, Em."

Her throat thickened. She'd had no idea that her brother had carried this burden.

"This is why I want you to have the freedoms, the

choices you missed out on as a girl," he said quietly. "I want you to be happy."

"I am," she said tremulously.

Her brother hesitated. "With Strathaven?"

She nodded.

He sighed. "I cannot say I like the man, but I will admit that I may have misjudged him in one regard. The other night, he risked his own life to save McLeod."

When Ambrose went on to describe Alaric's heroics during the capture of Palmer, it didn't surprise Emma one bit. Nor did the fact that Alaric had made no mention to her of his own valiant behavior. One of her father's sayings echoed in her head.

Virtue doesn't call attention to itself; it is its own reward.

"Strathaven is a good man," she said when her brother finished, "but a little complicated."

"A little?"

Tentatively, she said, "Do you think you could bring yourself to like him?"

"Does it matter?"

"I want you to like him. To like each other," she admitted.

A pause.

"If that is what will make you happy, then yes, Emma," Ambrose said gently. "I will try."

Her heart swelled. "You see, big brother? You've always done your best by us. By me."

Ambrose gave a gruff nod, and she caught the sheen in his eyes before he turned back to the window.

Soon thereafter, they arrived in a part of town she'd never visited before. As they drove through the Whitechapel slums, her heart constricted at the weary resignation she saw on the sooty faces of women and babes dressed in rags. Their carriage stopped in front of dingy tenements, and they were met by Alaric, Mr. McLeod, and a coterie of guards.

Alaric bowed to her, his gaze as possessive as any touch.

"Hello, Miss Kent," he murmured. "Recovered from your adventure last night?"

She knew that he referred not to the ball itself but what had transpired in the gallery.

"As a matter of fact," she said, "I feel quite invigorated."

His lips curved.

"We've scouted the place," Mr. McLeod said brusquely, "and secured the perimeter. We can start questioning the neighbors. Miss Kent, Cooper and I will escort you."

"As will I," Alaric said.

Knowing the brothers' combative relationship, Emma winced at Alaric's peremptory tone. To her surprise, however, Mr. McLeod's face split in a grin.

"Never thought I'd see the day. Ach, but you're a McLeod through and through, brother."

Alaric gave him a stony stare. "Meaning?"

"Meaning we Scotsmen stake our territory and don't give up what's ours." Mr. McLeod buffeted his brother in the shoulder with enough force to knock any other man off his feet.

Although Alaric didn't budge, color washed over his high cheekbones.

"If you're done flapping your lips, Peregrine, let's get on with it," he muttered.

"Gladly, Your Grace." Mr. McLeod was still grinning.

Emma marveled at the lighthearted banter. Recalling what Ambrose had told her in the carriage, she wondered if Alaric's selfless act had triggered the healing of old wounds.

"Miss Kent?" Alaric offered his arm.

As they moved toward the tenements, she murmured, "Are things alright? With you and Mr. McLeod, I mean?"

Alaric hesitated. In a low, bemused voice, he said, "Aye. I

think they may finally be."

The team split into several groups, going door to door through the tenements. The most common response to their enquiries was a suspicious glare, accompanied by some variation of, "I mind me own business and don't know nothin'." A few inhabitants spouted tales that were obviously fabricated, based on a desire for reward money rather than reality. And no one seemed surprised or concerned by the fact that one of their neighbors had been found dead.

After an hour of fruitless canvassing, Emma found herself back on the first floor by Webb's apartment. She idly surveyed the dusty street. The other side was almost a mirror image of the one she was standing on, with tenements directly across the way. A movement caught her eye: laundry fluttering on a line, the whiteness of the linen a stark contrast to the dirty exterior of the building.

On a hunch, she put a hand on Alaric's sleeve. "Let's go over there. To the tenement with the clean laundry."

"See something, pet?" he said.

"Call it an intuition."

"That's more than anything else we've got thus far," he said wryly.

Accompanied by Ambrose and Mr. McLeod, they went over and knocked. From within came the squeals of children and a dog barking, the scent of simmering food. A minute later, the door opened, revealing a sturdy matron with rosy cheeks and clothes that were old and darned but washed and pressed. Her cap sat neatly atop salt and pepper curls.

"Whate'er you're peddlin', I ain't buyin'," she said.

"Pardon, ma'am." Ambrose doffed his hat. "We're investigators looking into a matter concerning a man who lived across the street—"

"Don't know 'im, an' don't want to know 'im. Now I got a pepper pot o'er the fire an' no time for palaverin'—"

"Excuse me, ma'am." Nudging her way forward, Emma dropped a curtsy. "My name is Miss Kent. Who do I have the pleasure of speaking to?"

"Mrs. Gibney's the name," the woman said reluctantly.

"We'll only take a few minutes of your time. And I'd be happy to compensate you for it," Emma said. "If you'd rather, I can come in and talk with you while you attend to the stew. The gentlemen can wait outside."

The woman frowned, but her gaze went to Emma's reticule. "Compensate?"

"Say, five pounds?" Emma said.

The woman's eyes grew big. "How do I know you're not pullin' my leg?"

Opening her reticule, Emma counted out five sovereigns and offered them. "Here you go. Now may I come in?"

"You're supposed to give the money *after* you receive the information," Mr. McLeod muttered from behind her.

The woman, who had stretched her hand toward the money, now snatched it away as if burned. Glaring at the Scotsman, she said, "I ain't a thief. If that's what you're suggestin', you can take your blunt an'—"

"No one's suggesting such a thing, Mrs. Gibney," Emma said quickly. "The money is for your time, fair and square. Please take it."

Finally, the woman relented. Pocketing the coins in her apron, she waved Emma inside.

Alaric followed.

Mrs. Gibney blocked his path. "The miss said only she was to come in."

"I'm not leaving her alone," Alaric said. "Kindly step aside, madam."

Something in his tone made even the assertive matron back down. The three of them entered the cramped space, which consisted of one main room where a tangle of children were playing with a puppy. Despite its small size, Emma noted how lovingly the home was kept and how clean and well-nourished the little ones were. A cracked vase of wildflowers and herbs adorned an all-purpose table on which fresh vegetables lay ready for chopping.

All of this fit with what she'd deduced about Mrs. Gibney. This was a proud, hard-working woman, one who might not trust strangers, but who would not lie to them. One who believed cleanliness was next to Godliness—and if the whiteness of her linens was any indication, that meant she had to be out of doors often, hanging up and taking down the laundry before it got dirty again from the sooty air and muck from the streets.

Ergo, this would put Mrs. Gibney in frequent, front and center view of Silas Webb's dwelling.

"Who're they, Ma?" A boy of six or seven trotted up to them.

"Mind your manners, Tommy," Mrs. Gibney scolded.

"I'm Miss Kent," Emma said, smiling at the child, "and this is the Duke of Strathaven."

"A duke? In our 'ouse? Pull me other leg, miss," Tommy scoffed, "it's shorter."

"*Manners,*" his mother said. "Go play with your brothers and sisters or start scrubbin' the chamber pots—'tis your choice."

Tommy scampered off to the former option.

"You have lovely children," Emma said sincerely, "and keep a lovely home."

"It ain't Carleton House," Mrs. Gibney snorted, "but it'll do." She went to the hearth, stirred the black iron pot over the fire. "Now what do you want to ask me?"

Emma gestured at the vegetables on the chopping board. "Shall I?"

The matron shrugged. "Suit yourself."

Aware of Alaric's amused regard, Emma began to deftly slice the carrots and onions. "A man was found dead across the street," she said. "His name was Silas Webb."

"Don't know 'im."

"Perhaps not by name," Emma acknowledged, "but he lived just across the way. In the tenement that directly faces yours."

Mrs. Gibney said nothing and continued stirring.

"We're looking for any information about him—in particular, any associates he might have had." Emma started on the potatoes. "Webb was a villain, you see. He attempted twice to murder Strathaven here."

Mrs. Gibney's eyebrows inched toward her cap. "Murder, you say?"

"Aye," Alaric said.

"Anything you might have noticed would be helpful. A man's life is at stake," Emma said.

Mrs. Gibney set her spoon down on the table. "Perhaps I did see a man visit there once."

Emma's nape tingled. "Yes?"

"Little o'er a week, it was. I was puttin' up the washing, and a carriage drives up. A fine one like 'is." Mrs. Gibney jerked her chin at Alaric—proving Emma's theory that the matron didn't miss much.

"Could you describe the carriage? Did it have any special markings?" Emma asked.

"It was black and shiny, that's all I recall. A cart 'ad o'er turned that day, blockin' the other side o' the street, so the driver parked right in front o' me place. Blocked out the sun, 'e did, and what was I supposed to do with all me wet things an' no sun to dry 'em? Driver took no notice, o' course." Mrs. Gibney chuffed with indignation. "Just said to me, *Be off*—as if I should leave me own 'ome so that Lord So-and-So could do 'is business in a public thoroughfare."

"Did you get the gentleman's name?" Emma said eagerly.

Mrs. Gibney shook her head. "But I didn't trust that driver worth a farthin'. Kept me eye on the carriage from me door—an' that's when I saw a man come runnin' across the street. From that tenement you mentioned."

"What did the man look like?" Alaric said tersely.

"Short. Black 'air, meat on 'is bones. An' spectacles."

"Silas Webb," Alaric confirmed.

Trying to contain her excitement, Emma said, "What else did you see, Mrs. Gibney?"

"Well, the carriage door opened, an' I think the nob inside 'ad yellow 'air—but I only got a glimpse, mind you, before that Webb fellow climbed right in an' shut the door. The curtains were pulled so I didn't see what they were up to. 'Bout ten minutes later, Webb comes out, and I 'ear 'im say,"—Mrs. Gibney's forehead scrunched—"*I'll take care o' Palmer. You handle Billings.*"

Emma could scarcely breathe as pieces of the puzzle fell together. Palmer. *Billings.*

"That Webb fellow went back to 'is place an' the carriage took off wif the nob inside." Mrs. Gibney gave a decisive nod. "I ain't got more to say than that."

"You've been incredibly helpful, Mrs. Gibney," Emma said. "Thank you."

Shrugging, the matron peered over at the vegetables that Emma had prepared. "Thank *you*, missy. That's as fine a chopping job as any."

Alaric came forward and discreetly deposited a banknote on the table.

With a bow, he said, "Thank you for your time, madam."

"Already paid me for it. We Gibneys don't need charity." It was a measure of the woman's pride that she didn't even glance at the amount of the bill.

Emma did, however, and her heart swelled at Alaric's generosity.

"It's a gift, Mrs. Gibney. For the little ones," she said.

The matron hesitated, then gave a gruff nod. "I thank ye, then."

Outside, Alaric and she were met immediately by the others.

"Well?" Mr. McLeod said. "Did you learn anything?"

"Indeed, thanks to Miss Kent's ingenuity. Let's talk in private," Alaric said.

Once the four of them were inside the carriage, Emma blurted, "We have a new lead. Mrs. Gibney saw Silas Webb with a gentleman—blond, she thinks. She overheard Webb say that he would take care of the business with the shooter while our mystery man was to deal with Billings."

"What sort of billings? Is our murderer a man of business?" Mr. McLeod said, his brow furrowing.

Emma frowned—then she understood. "I don't think he was referring to the settling of accounts but to a person. Someone by the *name* of Billings."

"What draws you to that conclusion, Em?" Ambrose said.

She told them about meeting Gabby Billings at last night's ball. "It could be a coincidence, of course, but Gabby did mention that her father was a banker. And that she had been invited to the Blackwoods through some influential patron who owed her father a rather large favor." As possibilities tumbled through her head, Emma bit her lip. "I do hope Gabby's father isn't mixed up in this. She's a lovely girl."

"'Tis as you always say, Kent," Mr. McLeod said. "Follow the money."

"Let us pay the banker a visit," Alaric said.

Chapter Twenty-Eight

Billings Bank was located on a small lane a convenient distance from the Bank of England and the 'Change. The squat, grey stone building was unprepossessing, as if designed to be overlooked. As Alaric entered with the others, however, he saw the affluence of the interior. Fine furnishings clustered around a marble hearth, and an ornate bronze chandelier bathed the reception area in a luxurious glow. Beyond, Alaric saw a carpeted corridor leading to a suite of private offices.

A uniformed clerk hurried over and inquired about their business.

"We're here to see Billings," Kent said.

"Do you have an appointment, sir?"

"Tell him that the Duke of Strathaven wishes a word," Alaric said.

"Yes, Your Grace. Very good. Please have a seat,"—the clerk gestured to the waiting area, bowing low—"while I let Mr. Billings know that you are here."

Alaric accompanied Emma to a chair. He remained standing, casually assessing the other patrons. Billings clearly catered to rich clientele of a certain class—specifically, the underclass. Though the other clients were dressed in expensive garb, their ruthless expressions and armed guards suggested that they'd earned their wealth the hard way and would do what was necessary to keep it.

The clerk hurried back and announced that Mr. Billings

was ready to see them. The suite they entered was spacious, outfitted in mahogany and shades of burgundy. Billings rose from his desk; short and wiry, he had dark, keen eyes and sharp features. His expression was politely smooth, his accent polished.

"Welcome to my humble establishment." He waved them into the seats facing him. "Tea?"

"Thank you, no," Alaric said. "We've come on an urgent matter."

"Indeed? I'm not sure how I can be of assistance."

"We need information on one of your clients," Kent said.

Billings' gaze flickered; other than that, he remained perfectly composed. "I'm afraid I'm not at liberty to discuss my clients. We at Billings pride ourselves on the utmost discretion and confidentiality. I'm sure you understand."

"And I'm sure *you* understand that if you don't talk to us now you'll find yourself in bluidy Newgate," Will said.

"On what charge?"

"As an accomplice to murder," Kent said.

"That's absurd." Billings' laugh was brittle. "I'm not involved in any murder."

"You may not be, Mr. Billings, but I think you know someone who is." Emma's gentle yet firm tones drew the banker's attention. "I met your daughter at the Blackwood ball."

"Gabriella?" The banker's countenance darkened. "What does she have to do with this?"

"She told me that one of your clients sponsored her to the affair. A rich and influential gentleman who owed you a large favor." Emma paused. "We need to know the identity of that man. We believe that he may be involved in the assassination attempts on His Grace."

"My business was built on the precept of confidentiality.

I have a reputation to protect," Billings said stiffly. "The clients who seek me out—let us say they are not the most forgiving of men."

Alaric had enough of beating around the bush.

"Neither am I, Billings," he said with cool menace. "Tell me who this bastard is or I will use my power and influence to ruin you. I will take this bank apart brick by brick. I am not an enemy you wish to make."

The banker's eyes darted like a pendulum as he made internal calculations.

"I will tell you," he said with clear reluctance, "but you didn't hear it from me."

"Spit it out, man," Will growled.

"Lord Mercer," the banker said. "He was the one who owed me a favor."

Alaric's stomach clenched. Goddamnit—the bloody *fop* was behind all this?

"What did you do for Mercer?" he demanded.

"About five months ago, he came to me. He asked me to broker a deal for him." The banker straightened a pen on his desk. "It involved stock in United Mining."

"Didn't you take over the venture around that time?" Will asked Alaric.

Alaric gave a terse nod. "Why would Mercer want to kill me? If he bought shares, I've made him rich since I took the helm. After the expansion vote goes through, he stands to make a mint."

"Well, that's just it, you see. Mercer didn't bet on the price of stock going up—he wagered on it going *down*."

Comprehension sent ice floes through Alaric's veins.

Of course. The sneaky, brilliant bastard.

"I don't understand," Emma said, her brow pleating.

The banker set about explaining in the pedantic tones of a schoolmaster.

"Mercer and I entered into an arrangement wherein he 'sold' shares to me and I paid him the selling rate at the time. In other words, I gave him money for shares he did not yet own, and in return, he signed a promissory note to present me with the actual shares within a specified timeframe—with an extra percentage added, of course. Do you follow?" Billings said.

Emma nodded.

"This happened a few weeks before Strathaven formed the venture. At the time, United Mining was a sinking ship," the banker went on. "Mercer was certain that the price of the stock would continue to go down so he planned to use the money I gave him to purchase actual stock later, when the prices had fallen even further. In that way, he could pocket the difference and replenish his fortunes."

"But then I took over and the prices went up," Alaric said, "which means Mercer has been falling deeper and deeper into debt."

"Precisely. Lord Mercer has managed to hide the fact that he's in Dun territory up until this point, but now?" Billings shrugged. "He's utterly on the rocks. And per our contract he is obligated to provide me with the actual stock certificates by the end of the next fortnight."

"How much does Mercer owe you?" Kent said.

"At today's price of United shares, approximately thirty thousand pounds," Billings said. "That's to say nothing of when United's expansion vote goes through. From the talk I've heard, the stock prices will go through the roof. Mercer's debt—it will be astronomical."

"And you'll have made yourself a tidy profit," Alaric said.

Billings didn't bat an eyelash.

"Mercer thought that if he did away with Strathaven, United would fail once more," Will reasoned grimly, "and all his financial troubles would be over. It's definitely motive for murder."

"I know nothing about that. I'm just a banker," Billings said.

"But you're not surprised, are you, that Mercer would resort to killing a man?" Kent said.

Billings' lips formed a hyphen.

"Do you know Silas Webb and his connection to Lord Mercer?" Emma asked.

Despite the heinous revelations, Alaric felt his lips quirk at her shrewdness. She might look like a pretty miss with her glossy curls and big brown eyes, but his Emma never missed a step.

"Mr. Webb accompanied Lord Mercer to one of his appointments here," Billings said. "He didn't say much, but I believe they are business partners."

"They were partners," Alaric said. "Webb is dead."

"Dead?" the banker said.

"Shot through the head. Aye," Will said, "*that* is how Mercer thanks his associates."

"I can take care of myself." Billings flicked a piece of lint off his sleeve. "I'm an important man to important men, and my clients—they don't like losing their deposits to a thief. If Mercer reneges on his debt, half of the underworld will be out for his blood."

In the carriage, Emma said, "That Mr. Billings wasn't a very nice man, was he? Strange, because his daughter was lovely. I hope Gabby doesn't land in hot water because of all this."

Frowning, she wondered if she should try to send Gabby a note.

"Aye, I would not use *nice* to describe the banker

extraordinaire to the underworld." Mr. McLeod snorted. "No wonder Mercer's on the run. If we don't find him, Billings' cutthroat clients will."

"Where will we look next? Lord Mercer's residence?" Emma said.

"If by *we* you are referring to Will, Kent, and me, then yes," Alaric said. "*You*, however, are going home."

"What?" she said indignantly. "We've discovered the murderer. I'm not leaving now, in the middle of an investigation."

"My rules, pet. You agreed to them."

At his autocratic tone, she stiffened, ready to argue, but he cupped her chin in his gloved hand.

"You have been a great help." His husky words sent waves of delight through her. "But I will not risk anything happening to you. What remains is dangerous business, and I cannot afford to be distracted by my concern for your safety."

She chewed on her lip. Blast it, he was ... right. Her physical prowess was no match for the brutal, murderous strength of men like Mercer. The last thing she wanted was to compromise the mission.

Swallowing, she said, "What about your safety? That of Ambrose and Mr. McLeod?"

"We'll be armed and have guards with us," he said. "We'll be fine."

"Strathaven's right." This came from her brother, who'd been quietly watching the interplay. "You can help best by being with the family."

"Don't worry, lass," Mr. McLeod added, winking, "I'll look after your duke."

Emma blushed. "I hope you will all look after each other."

Alaric drew the back of his hand across her cheek, the

gesture so casually tender that her chest hurt with all the love she felt for him.

"This will soon be over and then you'll give me your answer about our future." Though his words were cool, peremptory, she heard the yearning beneath. "Promise me, Emma."

How could she resist those pale irises gleaming with intensity and raw need? He made her feel as if she were the only woman in the world for him—as he was the only man for her.

Her certainty blazed like a bright star. She knew what her answer would be.

"I promise," she said. "Be safe. I'll be here. Waiting for you."

Chapter Twenty-Nine

"That bastard Mercer has more brains than I gave him credit for." Will stabbed his knife into the roasted pheasant, cut off a chunk, and chewed vigorously. "I can't believe he managed to elude us all bluidy day."

Alaric had to agree—Mercer was diabolically gifted at evasion. Somehow the blighter had gotten wind that the game was up, and he'd taken off like a hunted fox. Alaric, Will, and a team of constables and guards had tracked the earl to his residence, clubs, even a bawdy house he was known to frequent; he'd remained one step ahead and just out of reach.

With his usual efficiency, Kent had organized teams to keep up the search for Mercer around the clock. After twelve hours, Alaric had reluctantly conceded that respite was in order. Will had insisted on escorting him home, which had led to Alaric inviting his brother in for a late supper.

To his surprise, Will had accepted.

Now the two of them were seated in the dining room at one end of the long table. Will had slung his jacket and cravat over the back of his chair and looked perfectly at home. The two of them were eating and talking ... generally acting like normal brothers might.

It was altogether odd.

And ... not unpleasant.

Alaric sampled the chestnut stuffing, found it moist and flavorful. He attributed that both to his French chef's talent and the fact that chasing down killers apparently piqued one's appetite.

"Where do you think Mercer will go next?" he said.

Will washed down his food with a swig of wine. "I suspect he'll try for safer shores. Gut tells me France. He's a nob after all, and they like to dock there."

"According to Kent, you've got the most accurate gut in the business."

Will dropped his fork, clutched his brawny chest. "Sweet Child of Mary, was that a compliment from His Grace?"

Alaric's lips quirked. As a boy, Will had been playful and irreverent; apparently, he'd never outgrown those tendencies.

"Your buffoonery offends the ducal presence," Alaric said with mock hauteur.

Grinning, Will picked up his silver. "The ducal presence better grow a thicker skin if he's so easily offended."

"The ducal heir better get ready for a pummeling if he continues with this baiting."

"As if you could pummel me." Will shoveled in a forkful of asparagus *à l'amande*. Chewing, he said, "Ach, this is good, isn't it?"

"The French know their cuisine."

"I don't mean the asparagus—I mean the two of us. Supping together. Talking instead of being at each other's throats."

Habit put a sardonic reply on Alaric's tongue. Instead, he said, "Aye, 'tis a welcome change."

Will paused, his hand on his wine glass. "I believe I owe you an apology, brother. I misjudged you." His chest heaved on a breath. "All these years, I've blamed you for denying me sanctuary when instead you were … protecting me."

The sincerity in his brother's brown eyes put Alaric at a momentary loss for words.

"You don't owe me anything," he said finally. "Not after Laura."

To his surprise, Will merely shrugged. "I'm not so certain that wasn't Fate intervening. After all, I ended up with the lass of my dreams. Couldn't imagine being happier than I am with my Bella and our bairns."

Will seemed to have no lingering animosity over Laura, his acceptance of the past genuine. Seeing that, Alaric felt a shifting inside himself: 'twas as if a boil had been lanced, the festering guilt draining free. His next breath came easier for it, his entire being somehow ... lighter.

Leaning back in his chair, he mused, "Will the calf love ever end? In all my life, I've never seen a man so happy to be leg-shackled."

Will gave him a sly grin. "Well, you have seen my lass—what do *you* think?"

"That you are one lucky bastard," Alaric said sincerely.

"Aye, I am. Then again, it seems Fortune smiles upon the McLeod brothers when it comes to women. You've found yourself a fine, spirited lass, eh?"

Heat crept up Alaric's jaw, and a foreign feeling puffed up his chest.

Pride.

When he thought of Emma's plucky determination, her warmth and intelligence, he was astounded that he'd found her. She would make him a fine duchess, provide him with beautiful, feisty children and create a stable, caring home for them all.

As long as you don't bollix things up.

He pushed aside the doubt that had been plaguing him since the steamy interlude in the gallery. He told himself that such concern was natural seeing as how he was facing the prospect of marriage once again. But this was Emma, not Laura. And this time he knew what he was up against—what he was and wasn't capable of.

He'd been clear with Emma. She wouldn't expect his love.

Wouldn't expect him to be more than he was.

They would have passion and laughter, even affection. After the debacle of his first marriage, it was more than he expected to find with any woman. He wanted his ring on Emma's finger as soon as possible.

"When this business with Mercer is done, I'm going to marry her," he said.

Will gave a knowing nod. "Don't worry, we'll find the bastard soon. With Kent tapping his old Thames River Police cronies to help scour the ports, we've got tabs on the water routes—"

A commotion outside the dining room cut him off. Jarvis entered with unusual haste.

At the unflappable butler's ruffled expression, Alaric frowned. "What is it?"

"Your Grace, you have a visitor …"

"I'm not a visitor, you old fool," said soft, imperious tones. "I am *family*."

Alaric shot to his feet, Will following his lead.

A diminutive figure dressed in a brown velvet travelling ensemble entered the room. Beneath the brim of the feathered leghorn hat, her bright blue eyes latched onto him. She gestured him over with a regal wave.

When she held out her hand, Alaric bowed over it out of habit. He kissed the translucent, veined skin above her large carnelian ring.

"My dearest boy," she said, sounding out of breath, "I've heard all the news, and I could stay away no longer. In fact, I would have been here earlier had it not been for a broken axel. Such inconvenient things, carriage wheels. Now are you well? Have you been ill? I've brought the medicines—"

"I'm fine, Your Grace." Recovering from shock of her sudden arrival, he said, "I don't believe you've met my brother."

"Your brother?" Her gaze swept over Will, lingering on his open collar and shirtsleeves, before returning to Alaric. *Sotto voce* she said, "Not much of a family resemblance is there, my dear? But I suppose all McLeods are not created equal. Different stock, you know."

Will turned ruddy.

"Since William and I share a father, we are from the same stock," Alaric said tightly.

Her blue eyes shimmered. "Oh dear. I've thought of you as my own for so long that sometimes I forget. Forgive me?"

The familiar mix of guilt and annoyance knotted his insides. Reminded him acutely of the failings Laura had accused him of. For despite all that he owed the lady before him, he'd never been able to feel more than gratitude toward her. A sense of obligation.

"There is nothing to forgive," he said curtly. "May I present to you Mr. William McLeod? Will, say hello to Lady Patrice, the Dowager Duchess of Strathaven."

An hour later, Patrice finally went upstairs to bed, leaving Alaric to bid goodnight to Will.

In the foyer, Will said in a low voice, "She's quite an, ahem, interesting lady, your aunt."

"She's your aunt, too," Alaric said irritably.

"Right." Will cleared his throat. "Is she always this … full of energy?"

"Hysterics are part of her daily regimen." The minute Alaric said it, shame tugged at him. "She means well," he amended. "During the years when I was ill, she cared for me as if I were her own. Nursed me day and night."

Then why don't I feel true affection for her?

Laura was right about one thing: I am a coldhearted bastard.

"Can't blame her for worrying after you, I suppose." Pausing, Will said, "You have enough on your plate as it is, what with Mercer still on the loose. How do you plan to manage her as well?"

Alaric's temples throbbed just thinking about it. In spite of the lateness, Lady Patrice had insisted on summoning the housekeeper to review the week's menus; she'd wanted to ensure that the meals suited his delicate constitution. Then she'd directed two maids to change his old bedclothes to the new ones she'd brought because Scottish flannel would help him sleep better. She'd had those same blurry-eyed maids search through her mountain of luggage to locate a satchel of white sage. Apparently, some quack had sold it to her, claiming that burning the herb would ward off evil and keep Alaric safe.

As usual, she brushed off his objections by simply ignoring them. Or growing tearful.

Obligation or not, one hour in her presence was already driving him mad. With the hunt for Mercer, he had enough to contend with. The last thing he wanted was to deal with an anxious, overbearing dowager.

Then it struck him. *He* wouldn't have to deal with Patrice.

Because he'd found someone else perfectly suited for the task.

"We'll rendezvous at Kent's tomorrow morning," he said. "I have a plan."

Chapter Thirty

"You want *me* to entertain your aunt?" Emma said.

"Just for a few hours." Alaric put on his most charming smile. "It'll be good for you to get to know the old girl. You talk about the importance of family, after all. Don't you wish to be acquainted with mine?"

They were in a private parlor of the Kents' townhouse. Alaric had arrived moments before and asked to speak with Emma in private. The door was open, Mrs. Kent just outside. Which was unfortunate because Emma looked delectable in dotted muslin trimmed with lavender ribbon. She reminded him of a bonbon, and he would have dearly liked to savor every bit of her. Instead, he'd had to settle for a quick kiss that only made him hungry for more.

Time for that later, he told himself. *Deal with the problem at hand—or, rather, the one waiting in the carriage.*

"I've never had tea with a duchess before." Emma nibbled on her lip. "What if I say or do something wrong?"

"Just be yourself. You're perfect."

She eyed him suspiciously. "Why are you pouring on the butter boat?"

"It is the truth." Taking her hand, he played his trump card. "It would relieve my mind, pet, knowing that Lady Patrice is here with you. Until we hunt Mercer down, I need to know that the ones I care about are guarded and safe. It will allow me to focus on catching the villain."

"I'll take care of your aunt," Emma said instantly. "You

can entrust her to me."

"Thank you, sweeting." He paused; in all good conscience, he couldn't leave without tipping his hand a little. "You recall I had a digestive illness in my youth?"

"You mentioned it when we were talking about the family who ate the poisoned mushrooms." Emma tilted her head. "Why do you bring it up now?"

"At times, the disease was quite debilitating, and Aunt Patrice devoted herself to my care. Tirelessly. I owe her more than I can say." Treading with care, he said, "She is, however, possessed of a ... nervous disposition. She can be rather lively."

"Livelier than a bunch of Kents? I doubt it. Don't worry about a thing."

Her nonchalance relieved him. Curling his finger beneath her chin, he said, "I knew you were the one for the job, pet."

She wrinkled her nose. "I'd rather help hunt down Mercer than be a nanny for your aunt."

"That wasn't the job I was referring to."

"Which one, then?"

"The one of being my duchess. You *are* going to take me on, aren't you?" he murmured. "I find that I cannot wait to have your answer."

Her eyes were so clear that he could read his future in those tea-colored depths. His breath held in anticipation. To be so close to what he wanted ...

"Yes, Alaric," she said. "I will marry you."

A feeling flooded him like sunlight. It took him an instant to recognize it as ... happiness.

"Thank you," he said, his words hoarse with wonder.

He was about to draw her into his arms when Mrs. Kent's discreet voice came through the open door. "Ahem. Her Grace got tired of waiting in the carriage. She's in the drawing room."

"We'll be right there," Emma called. To him, she said in hushed tones, "Let's not share our news just yet. We must not distract everyone from the business at hand."

He wanted to shout it from the rooftops ... which was as embarrassing as it was absurd. What had happened to his much vaunted self-control?

Begin as you mean to go on. Discipline yourself. Don't make the same mistakes.

"As you wish," he said with a bow.

When they entered the drawing room, Aunt Patrice was perched upon a curricle chair, her hands folded upon her tan skirts. Tea sat untouched in a cup next to her. Her eyes went from him to Emma, and her brows inched toward her beige turban.

"Is this who you kept me waiting for, dear boy?" she said. "Well, don't dally. Introduce us."

"May I present Miss Emma Kent?" he said.

Emma curtsied. "Good morning, Your Grace."

"Prettily done," Aunt Patrice approved. "I've always said that manner is more important than a title. And your maturity is so refreshing," she added in conspiratorial tones, "for chits fresh out of the schoolroom can be a dreadful bore."

"Thank you." A line appeared between Emma's brows. "I think."

Alaric coughed into his fist and thanked his lucky stars when Will and Kent strode in. After the men paid their respects to the ladies, he said, "Where shall we start today?"

"Just heard from Cooper," Will said. "He's tracked down one of Mercer's who—" He cut himself off suddenly, darting a look at Patrice. "One of his, er, female acquaintances, I mean. She may have some information."

"Excellent," Kent said. "Let's start there."

"Strathaven, I had better accompany you," his aunt interrupted. "With your delicate health, you need someone to look after you—"

"I will be fine. You must stay here and visit with the ladies."

"But surely I could—"

"I should enjoy chatting with you, Your Grace," Emma said. "I am curious to learn more about Scotland and the home that Strathaven grew up in. Please, won't you keep us company?"

Patrice looked from him to Emma. Gave a reluctant nod.

"Thank you, Aunt," Alaric said with satisfaction.

He kissed Patrice on the cheek and took Emma's hand.

"I'll see you soon," he said. "Take care, pet, and don't get into trouble."

"That goes double for you," she said.

"She's an odd duck, isn't she?" Violet whispered.

Standing by the sideboard with her sisters, Emma shot a worried glance at the dowager. Luckily, Lady Patrice was chattering away feverishly with Marianne and didn't seem to have overheard.

"Alaric says his aunt is a bit high strung," Emma replied in hushed tones. "But she's a good sort and looked after him when he was a boy."

"I'm sure she's just anxious about the men's mission," Thea said softly. "As we all are."

Vi snorted, piling an assortment of cheeses and sliced meats on her plate. "She's a *bit* high strung? She makes the horses at the Ascot seem sedate by comparison."

Emma had to admit Lady Patrice's conversation was an unending ricochet, a fusillade of words that bounced from topic to topic with no apparent connection. Seeing Marianne discreetly hide a yawn, Emma felt a prickle of guilt. Little Edward's nightmares had kept his mama up last night, and Marianne showed signs of being peaked, which was unusual for her.

Going over, Emma said, "Marianne, don't you have an appointment this afternoon?"

Marianne's emerald eyes lit up . "My ... appointment. Yes. I nearly forgot."

"Don't let me keep you, Mrs. Kent," Lady Patrice said generously. "The girls can keep me company. I've yet to talk about Strathmore Castle, which Miss Emma has expressed interest in."

As Marianne made a graceful exit, she paused behind their guest. She mouthed to Emma, *Thank you*. Emma managed a discreet wink in reply.

"Now what would you like to know about Strathmore?" Lady Patrice said.

"Is it really a castle?" Vi said, popping cheese into her mouth.

"Indeed. It has grand towers and turrets, a magnificent crenellated profile, not to mention a lovely drawbridge," the dowager said proudly.

Emma tried to think back to her father's history lessons, when he'd taught them about the tumultuous relationship between the English and the Scots. "Was it built as a fortress to defend against border invasions?" she asked.

"No, my dear. It's not that kind of a castle."

"Oh. What other kind is there?"

Lady Patrice's azure eyes blinked at her. "Well, the kind that *looks* lovely, of course. Strathmore embodies the majesty of a bygone era and was designed by one of the foremost architects of the Romantic Revival."

"It's a ... fake castle?" Vi said.

"Young lady, there is *nothing* fake about Strathmore." The lace on the dowager's bosom quivered. "The papa of my own dear duke spent a king's ransom building it. It is the noblest house in the county—I daresay in all of Scotland."

Vi looked unimpressed. "But there's never been any sieges there? No battles or bloodshed?"

Thea nudged her. "Your home sounds very grand, Your Grace."

"I can't expect you to understand," the dowager sniffed. "Coming from Chuffy Creek ..."

"Chudleigh Crest," Emma said. "It's a small village in Berkshire."

"Yes, well, you can't be blamed for not comprehending the grandeur and sophistication of our family seat. Not everyone can understand—unlike my dear Alaric." The storm left her eyes as suddenly as it had come, replaced by a misty, faraway look. "He took to life at Strathmore like a fish to water. He adored it at first sight, and well he should: 'tis in his blood, after all. Coming to my dear duke and I—well, it was like coming home."

"It was kind of you to take Strathaven in," Emma ventured.

"It was my husband's idea. He knew how terribly I missed our son and wanted to give me comfort." Lady Patrice's bottom lip quivered. "Alaric filled a void in our lives—and, I like to think, we in his. He suffered a grave illness, you know, and I nursed him through it."

"He speaks of your great care and devotion to him," Emma said sincerely.

The dowager gave her a beatific smile. "Does he?"

"Most definitely."

"I do worry about him. His health. And now this murder business." In a sudden blur of motion, Lady Patrice rose to her feet and began to pace. "I wonder how he is. I should not have let him go alone. What if something happens ...?"

"I'm certain he's fine. He's with our brother, Mr. McLeod, and the others."

The dowager did not seem to hear Emma's reassurances, her agitation feeding upon itself. She wrung a handkerchief between her hands, darting from place to place, her movements like that of a crazed hummingbird. Clearly, she was worrying herself into a frenzy.

"Gadzooks," Vi whispered, "*do* something, Em."

"Er, perhaps you'd like a stroll in the square, Your Grace?" Emma said.

"A stroll?" the older lady said blankly.

"Fresh air can be very calming to the constitution," she said.

The lines smoothed from Lady Patrice's expression; her smile jolted like lightning through thunderheads. "That sounds lovely. Let us go."

❧

Pleading fatigue, Thea stayed home, leaving Emma and Vi to accompany Lady Patrice. Jim the footman followed at a discreet distance, and Emma began to relax into the beauty of the summer afternoon. The park in the middle of the square was tranquil, a leafy green oasis filled with birdsong. If it were not for the surrounding townhouses, she could almost imagine that she was on one of her old walks through the countryside.

Vi scampered off, her coltish stride unable to accommodate a sedate pace. As Emma walked more leisurely along the pebbled path with Lady Patrice, the latter seemed to calm.

"How charming," the dowager said with a sigh. "Back at Strathmore, I take a daily morning constitutional on the banks of the loch. There's something very soothing about the water. Strathaven adored it when he was a boy."

"What was he like when he was a boy?" Emma said.

"Oh, he was handsome and clever," the other said, smiling. "He takes after my own dear duke, you know. Strathaven men are always ambitious. They don't sit on their laurels, content with the title and what they've inherited. They want more. They thrive on success and power."

Sounds like Alaric, Emma thought wryly.

"And they marry ladies who support their noble aspirations. My husband and I used my dowry to add two new wings to the castle," Lady Patrice said proudly.

Emma hadn't considered what wealth she'd bring to Alaric; to her, he hardly seemed to need *more* money. But maybe, as far as the upper classes were concerned, one could never have too much. Ambrose would certainly not allow her to go to her future husband empty-handed, yet any dowry of hers would definitely not add a wing to an ancestral home.

Emma felt a sudden pang as she imagined the advantages to Alaric if he married an heiress, a lady of his own class.

"Oh dear. I've spoken too candidly." Lady Patrice bit her lip, her eyes clouded. "Forgive me, Miss Kent. My words have a way of running away from me. I hope I have not offended you."

"You haven't. I just hadn't given much thought to the connection between money and marriage," Emma admitted.

"Which is most charming and refreshing. And why, I think, Strathaven has taken such an interest in you." When Emma blushed, Lady Patrice said indulgently, "Oh yes, my dear, I can tell which way the wind blows. And if I may be so bold ... do you return his regard?"

Emma gave a shy nod.

"I am glad to hear it. I like you, my dear, much more than his last duchess." The dowager gave a soft harrumph.

"Laura might have been rich and beautiful, but she was also a spoiled, demanding chit. My poor boy did what he could to please her, but it was never enough. For that reason alone, I could not like her."

"Of course," Emma murmured.

"He needs someone to nurture him, to devote herself *entirely* to his happiness and the care of the family estate. My boy deserves nothing less. You will do that for him, won't you, Miss Kent?"

The other's fervent scrutiny was rather unnerving. Emma didn't think now was the time to share that, in addition to her wifely duties, she planned to pursue her passion for investigation.

"We've certainly discussed the merits of partnership," she hedged. "Of respecting and supporting one another—"

A rustling sounded behind them. Some sixth sense made her turn around ...

... in time to see a dark-garbed villain bash Jim in the head with a cudgel. With a groan, the footman crumpled to the ground. The cutthroat advanced toward Emma and the frozen dowager. Emma grabbed onto Patrice, dragging her backward. Only to collide into a brick wall of a chest—another cutthroat had snuck up behind them.

A thick piece of cloth muffled Emma's scream. She struggled against her captor, a sweet pungent smell burning through her nostrils, her throat. Her strength floated from her, and the world dissolved into a cloud of darkness.

Chapter Thirty-One

Miss Kitty Germaine, Mercer's mistress, occupied a small, neat house on Henrietta Street. Clad in a filmy, flesh-colored robe, she received Alaric, Will, and Kent in a parlor done in a palette that strategically complimented her brunette coloring. By Alaric's reckoning, this was a woman with a calculating bent. Despite her classical looks, he sensed a hardness to Miss Germaine, a cynicism that was beginning to etch lines around her eyes and mouth.

The profession of a mistress was, undoubtedly, a difficult one.

"Mercer's not here," she said matter-of-factly after they'd been seated. "And to save you the trouble: no, I haven't the faintest notion where he's gone."

"How do you know we're here because of Mercer?" Will demanded.

"Well, now, are you here for another reason, love? Because I do have a weakness for strapping men." Her dark gaze encompassed all of them, lingering on Alaric. "And, my, what fine specimens you are."

"We know Mercer was here," Will said doggedly.

"He was." Her shoulders lifted lazily. "Now he is not."

"He is wanted for murder," Kent said, "and unless you want to be charged as an accomplice—"

"Murder?" The languidness fled her expression. "The earl?"

"He has attempted to kill me twice," Alaric said, "and

shot another man in cold blood. He is not the sort of protector a woman would wish for."

Beneath her subtle, artfully applied paint, Miss Germaine's cheeks paled. "He isn't—my protector, I mean. We parted ways a month ago."

"Then why was he here?" Alaric said evenly.

"He said he'd run into a spot of trouble and needed a place to spend the night." Her throat bobbed. "I didn't have any cust—company planned, so I let him stay."

"You have no idea where he's headed?" Kent said.

"He left before dawn. Didn't say goodbye." Licking her lips nervously, she added, "My maid said she looked out the window and saw him with some unsavory characters. Apparently, they all took off in a coach together, and the top was packed with trunks. That's all I know."

Alaric didn't detect any falsehoods. "Why did your arrangement with Mercer end?"

"Money," she said succinctly. "Specifically, his lack thereof. Some conniver bilked him of his fortune—he'd turn apoplectic whenever he talked about it."

Alaric exchanged grim glances with the other men. Apparently Mercer had rewritten history to make himself out to be the victim—perhaps he even believed his own false tales, used them to justify all the evil that he'd done. There was no telling what such a man was capable of.

Urgency and frustration filled him. He had to find Mercer, put an end to this chaos.

Then he could start a new life with Emma.

Her poise returning, Miss Germaine said coyly, "Being as selective as I am about my friendships, it has not been easy to find a truly rich and powerful patron."

"I wish you luck." Bridling with impatience, Alaric rose. "Thank you for your time."

"Leaving so soon? Perhaps you'd like some

refreshment—"

A pounding sounded on the front door. A minute later, Cooper entered the room, and Alaric's insides chilled when he saw the bleak set of the guard's features.

"What is it, Cooper?" he said.

"Mercer's kidnapped Miss Kent and the dowager," the guard said tersely, holding out a note. "He's demanding ransom."

The world came slowly into view. In the dim light, Emma made out wooden walls, a shuttered window, a table and stool … she was in a tiny cabin of some sort. And it was … rocking?

Where am I?

Emma registered that she was laying on a cot. She managed to sit up and get woozily to her feet. She stumbled a few steps, heard the clanking of metal, felt a jerk on her ankle. Looking down, she saw that a manacle and short chain anchored her right foot to the bed.

She and the dowager had been *kidnapped*.

Memories returned in hazy snippets, accompanied by the sweet, sickening scent of ether. A carriage ride through darkness. Being hauled up a gangway … Yes, she could smell the tang of sea air now. She was on a ship.

Dear God, where was Lady Patrice?

A faint sound made her look up. There was a bunk above her own, a small figure upon it. Standing on her tiptoes, Emma verified with relief that it was indeed the dowager. Other than the rise and fall of her thin chest, the lady lay still as death, the stone of her ring gleaming like blood upon her waxen hand.

"Lady Patrice," Emma whispered urgently.

No reply. The poor thing was heavily drugged. The bastards—how could they treat a defenseless elderly woman in this despicable manner?

Footsteps approached. Before Emma could return to the cot, the door opened, and a tall blond man holding a lamp stepped inside. As he set the light on the table, its flickering glow gave his handsome face a demonic cast. His cravat was elegantly knotted, his wool overcoat lavishly embroidered. She recognized him from the Blackwood ball—one of the men who had disparaged Alaric's venture.

"You're Lord Mercer," she said, her gaze narrowing.

He smiled thinly and bowed. "Welcome aboard my vessel, Miss Kent."

"You had better release us this instant." She angled her chin up. "If you don't, you'll regret being born when Strathaven and my brother find us. And I promise you they will."

"Oh, I'm counting on it, Miss Kent. You are my insurance, you see, and my ticket to a new life. I've been watching Strathaven, and I know he'll do anything to have you." Mercer smirked. "That is, if he hasn't already had you."

Emma stumbled back when Mercer came toward her, trapping her against the frame of the bed. His pungent cologne wound into her nostrils, and she shrank away, her skin crawling as he pressed himself up against her.

"I wonder," he said, his breath hot against her cheek, "what talents could a country miss possess to enthrall a man like Strathaven? I have a mind to see for myself."

"Get away from me, you bounder!"

Her lungs seized as he fingered a fallen tress of her hair. She felt a revolting poke against her thigh, the thing hard and ... sharp? The realization struck her: the object prodding her wasn't his manhood—but a ... *key.*

He let her go. "Time to sample your charms later. For now," he said with a sneer, "I have a welcome to prepare for your erstwhile duke. He should be arriving anytime now."

Emma thought quickly. "He won't fall into your trap. He's too clever for that."

Mercer turned a livid shade. "He'll dance like a puppet on strings if he wants you and his aunt alive." His manicured fingers curled like claws. "*I* am dictating the terms now—not him."

Sensing the crazed fury beneath the polished facade, Emma knew she'd hit upon his weakness. She had to use his vanity to her advantage. *Just have to get him closer ...*

"Strathaven is going to crush you," she taunted. "You don't stand a chance."

She yelped when Mercer grabbed her by the hair. He yanked hard, jerking her face up, forcing her to meet his eyes, which were dilated with fury. She feigned fear, twisting as if to get away from him, angling her hand toward the pocket of his overcoat ...

"Shut your mouth, bitch," he spat. "If it weren't for the interfering bastard, I'd be a rich man by now. My scheme was brilliant; I stood to make a *fortune*. But Strathaven ruined it all. Thanks to him, not only did I lose my money— now I have Billings' underworld criminals after my blood."

"It's your own fault." *Almost there ... keep him distracted ...* "You made a bad business decision. You compounded that by trying to murder Strathaven—and by killing Silas Webb."

"Webb was a spineless fool. He didn't have the stomach for greatness and would have given me up when he was caught. No," Mercer said craftily, "Webb left me no choice."

"What about Strathaven? It's not his fault you took a reckless risk."

"*Everything* is his fault!" Mercer's eyes were reptilian

with hate, his words hissing. He pushed his face into hers just as her fingers closed around metal. "He left me no resort but to flee like some common criminal. Well, he's going to pay to the tune of fifty thousand pounds. If he doesn't, I'll send you and his aunt back to him—piece by lovely piece."

Heart hammering, Emma let her shoulders sag as if in defeat; at the same time, her hand slipped behind her back, clutching her prize. "You really have thought of everything."

"I will be victorious. Like a phoenix, I will rise from the ashes on French soil. Who knows?" A nasty gleam lit Mercer's eyes. "If you please me, I might keep you alive to see to my pleasures."

Emma swallowed. "But I thought … aren't you going to ransom me?"

Mercer's laugh was short and brutal. "I'm going to get my money. And then I'm going to put an end to Strathaven once and for all."

"You're a dishonorable cad!" she cried. "Strathaven is smarter than you—he'll never fall for your trap!"

Mercer shoved her violently onto the cot, her back smacking the thin mattress. Panting, she kept a firm grip on her stolen treasure.

"He already has, you little whore. He'll bring me my blunt at nine o'clock sharp—and I'll put a hole through his heart," Mercer snarled. "And after I deal with him, I'll be back for you."

The door slammed behind him, his barked order filtering through. "No one goes in or out—see to that by any means necessary."

"Wif pleasure, m'lord," replied a leering voice.

Instantly, Emma sat up. Looked at the key in her hand. Sending up a prayer, she reached for the manacle on her foot.

Chapter Thirty-Two

Alaric and the other men reached the appointed destination before dawn. He'd rented out two stage coaches to convey the team of investigators and guards from London to Portsmouth at record speed, so that they could arrive a few hours prior to the meeting with Mercer. Will and his comrades had already taken off on a scouting mission. Disguised as porters, the four ex-soldiers were presently conducting reconnaissance on the dock.

Their goals: to find Mercer's vessel and locate Emma and Patrice.

In the meantime, Alaric and Kent took a suite at an inn. They were guarding the trunks of ransom money and awaiting the arrival of some mysterious associate Kent had said might be helpful to the cause. From the second floor balcony, Alaric watched the ribaldry in the street below. How clever of Mercer to choose this place to conduct his nefarious business.

With all the lawlessness and depravity going on, who would care about two women being held against their will? Who would even notice?

Outside the gate of the old town, Portsmouth Point was known as "Spice Island," not only for the scent of imported spices that came from the harbor but also for the piquant activities so clearly on display. Whores plied their trade openly in the alleys, sailors and dockhands stumbled in and out of the public houses that lined both sides of the street.

Brawls broke out with regularity, cheered on by drunken bystanders.

Alaric's hands fisted with impotence. *If Mercer so much as touches a hair on Emma's head ...* He was unwilling to contemplate that possibility. He was going to get her and his aunt back. Then he was going to tear the earl apart limb by limb.

Slowly.

Kent came to stand beside him. "McLeod will find my sister and your aunt. He's the best there is when it comes to scouting."

"Aye. But time is running out." Alaric gave a terse nod at the sky over the harbor.

Already, the horizon was losing its dark opacity. He could make out the forest of masts bobbing on the black water and the fleet of small barges that zipped between the larger ships, ferrying passengers and goods back and forth from the docks. The Byzantine activity of the scene frustrated him further. Which one of those hundreds of ships held Emma and Aunt Patrice prisoner? What was Mercer's ultimate plan?

"We should review the strategy for the exchange. I still don't like the idea of you meeting the villain alone," Kent said.

"Mercer made it clear in the ransom note that I'm to follow his instructions to the letter," Alaric said starkly. "If I don't bring the gold to the quay alone and unarmed at nine o'clock, he's going to kill Emma and Patrice. I won't take that risk."

"He might kill them anyway. You as well."

Alaric saw emotion flare in the other man's eyes. Fear. Fury. The same feelings that ran molten through his own veins.

"Whatever it takes, I will see your sister safe," he vowed.

"It's me Mercer wants."

"You'd trade your life for Emma's?"

"Whatever it takes," he repeated.

Kent studied him for a moment. "My wife was right after all."

"About what?"

"You truly do care for Emma."

Alaric's cheekbones heated. He felt suddenly exposed—and he didn't like it. "I told you my intentions were honorable," he said stiffly.

"There's a difference between an honorable marriage and a loving one."

A knock on the door cut short the conversation. Alaric tensed.

Kent checked his watch. "Right on time."

The investigator opened the door and ushered in a fellow dressed in the loose jacket and trousers of a man who worked on the water. The newcomer's most distinguishable feature was the curly auburn hair beneath his cap. His freckled face split into a grin. He and Kent exchanged bows—and then slapped each other on the back like old friends.

"As I live and breathe, six years and you don't look any different, sir. Except your clothes—quite dapper now, ain't you?" The stranger winked. "Told you a wife would do you good, didn't I?"

"Indeed you did, old friend," Kent said with a faint smile. "But time to reminisce later. As I mentioned in my message, I'm afraid I'm here on urgent business."

"I'm at your service, sir."

"I'm deeply grateful to hear it." Kent turned to Alaric. "Your Grace, this is John Oldman, a former colleague of mine at the Thames River Police. He moved to Portsmouth six years ago."

"Call me Johnno. Everyone does," the man said cheerfully.

"I beg your pardon," Alaric said, "but how is it that you're to help us?"

"Kent says you need a way to hide in plain sight on the water. I can provide that."

"How?"

"Johnno and his brother-in-law operate one of the largest barge services here in Portsmouth," Kent explained. "A third of the barges that travel between ship and shore are theirs. With Johnno's help, we'll surround the quay where you're to meet Mercer." The investigator's eyes burned with a fierce light. "Unbeknownst to that blackguard, we'll block his escape route. We'll capture him—and get Emma and the dowager back."

Finally, Lady Patrice stirred.

Emma had begun to lose hope, her desperation mounting as pale light seeped through the shutters of the window. She could hear the activity above, the shouts and heavy bootsteps as the villains readied themselves for Alaric's arrival.

For the ambush.

She had to free herself and Lady Patrice before Alaric arrived. Before he fell into Mercer's deadly clutches.

"Lady Patrice," she said as loud as she dared, "please, open your eyes."

The dowager's lashes fluttered against her pale cheeks. Slowly, her head turned toward Emma. "Miss Kent? Where—where are we?" she said in a trembling, befuddled voice. "What has happened?"

Emma wanted to weep with relief. Instead, she said in

calm tones, "We've been kidnapped, Your Grace. Mercer is holding us hostage—and he means to kill Strathaven when he brings the ransom money. We must stop the villain, and I need your help."

"Kill Strathaven?" Lady Patrice pushed herself to sitting and though she weaved a little, she said firmly, "We cannot allow that to happen. Tell me what you want me to do."

"Remember we'll be watching from the barges," Will said. "One wrong move from Mercer and we'll move in, cut off his escape."

"Aye," Alaric said.

The two of them were standing on the quay Mercer had designated for the exchange. Besides him and Will and the trunks of ransom, the dock was abandoned, positioned within a small isolated cove. Near the entrance of the cove, he saw two of Johnno's vessels patrolling the waters. They appeared like the other ubiquitous barges, and he prayed that Mercer would be fooled.

"It's a quarter to nine. You'd best go before the bastard shows up," Alaric said.

Will didn't move. Gruffly, he said, "Don't get yourself killed, alright? I'd hate to lose my only brother."

Alaric's chest tightened. "If anything happens to me, you're the last of the Strathaven line. Take care of the title."

Will's eyes widened. "Don't talk like that."

"Promise me."

"I don't want the bluidy dukedom—"

"I know," Alaric said simply. "But promise me you'll look after it anyway."

"Nothing's going to happen to you." Will raked a hand through his hair. "But ... aye. Have no worry, Alaric, but that of saving your lass."

Alaric clasped his brother's shoulder in silent thanks. He was startled to find himself pulled into a rough hug. The embrace ended just as abruptly.

His face ruddy, Will muttered, "I'll be watching from the barge."

After the other left, Alaric turned his attention back to the mouth of the cove. Minutes later, he saw a small covered vessel approaching, moving steadily toward the inlet, churning a white line in its wake. It passed through the entrance of the cove and minutes later arrived at the quay.

Alaric's muscles tensed as a figure disembarked onto the wharf, his face shielded by the brim of his hat. The bastard looked up.

Alaric's gut clenched. "Where's Mercer?"

The dark-haired ruffian casually withdrew a pistol, pointed it at Alaric. He crossed over and, searching Alaric's pockets, removed the firearm. He made a *tsking* noise as he tossed the weapon into the water.

Shaking his head, the brute said, "Nobs ne'er are any good at followin' instructions." He gave a short whistle—and two more cutthroats emerged from the barge. "Boys, have a look inside those trunks."

The pair opened the lids, and Alaric saw the avarice glittering in their eyes.

"I've brought the ransom," he said evenly. "Give me the women."

"You ain't in no position to make demands, yer lordship." To his comrades, the cutthroat ordered, "Tie 'im up, boys. We're bringing 'is Grace back to the main ship."

On a barge near the cove's entrance, Ambrose swore

softly. He'd been monitoring the events on the quay through a telescope.

"I don't see any sign of the women or Mercer," he said. "The villain sent his lackeys to get the money."

"Those bastards have Alaric now," McLeod growled. "We've got to head them off before they leave the cove."

"We can't," Ambrose said in frustration. "If Mercer doesn't get his gold, Emma and the dowager will die."

"If we don't stop them now, my brother will!"

"We have no choice. Strathaven was willing to the risk, and we must see this through." Cursing, Ambrose pounded his fist on the barge's railing. "Johnno," he said in clipped tones, "signal the other barges. We'll have to follow the bastards to their ship, but we cannot, under any circumstances, be seen."

"Just like the old days. Don't worry, sir," Johnno said, "I haven't lost my touch."

Jaw clenched, Ambrose prayed that he was making the right decision. The lives of three people—one of them his sister—depended upon it.

Chapter Thirty-Three

"Help! Someone please! She's not breathing!" the dowager cried.

Emma heard a curse from outside the door, the guard's key inserting into the lock. Heart pounding, she stood at the ready, arms raised, behind the door.

It opened, and the guard rushed in. "What the bleedin'—"

Stepping out behind him, Emma brought the stool down with all her might. The heavy wood cracked against the back of his skull. With a groan, he toppled to the ground.

She set down her weapon and crouched next to him.

"Did I ... is he dead?" she said, her voice trembling.

Squatting on the other side of the fallen figure, Lady Patrice shook her head. "He's breathing. He won't be out for long."

With hands that shook, Emma searched the guard's body, removing a pistol and a vial of clear liquid, which she passed to the dowager. Just as she was reaching for the rope on the man's belt—she planned to truss him up—a beefy hand gripped her wrist. She jerked, her gaze flying to the guard's face. His eyes were open, and he bolted upright, his expression menacing.

A scream rose in her throat—

A small hand with a red ring slapped fabric against the brute's face. He let out a moan and fell backward, his head whacking against the floor. This time he didn't move.

"See how you like a taste of your own medicine," the dowager said.

Emma saw that Lady Patrice had dumped the contents of the vial onto the hem of her petticoat, using it to subdue the cutthroat.

Emma's brows rose. "Your Grace, I didn't know you had it in you."

"I may be a duchess, but I am Scottish," the other replied tartly. "Now how are we getting out of here?"

Emma clasped the pistol. "We'll locate the lifeboat. If we can escape before Alaric arrives, he needn't bargain with that monster."

"An excellent plan."

Emma led the way out of the cabin and into the dark and narrow corridor. Listening to the pattern of footsteps overhead, she headed in the direction away from the activity. Minutes later, she saw steps up ahead, light filtering in from a trapdoor at the top.

Emma crept up the steps and carefully pushed the trapdoor open, just enough for her to peer out. Daylight shocked her pupils, momentarily blinding her. When the dots cleared, she could see that they were below the quarterdeck. She spotted a pyramid of barrels just paces away—possible cover. Boots suddenly crossed her line of vision; she let the trapdoor fall immediately, her heart thumping like a rabbit's.

A minute or so passed. She cracked open the door once more.

The way looked clear.

"I'll have to go out and look for the lifeboat," she whispered. "Wait here, Your Grace."

The dowager nodded.

Inhaling for courage, Emma pushed the door open and scrambled out, making a dash for the barrels. Pulse racing, her back against the curved containers, she waited for a bark of discovery. None came. Scouting the environs, she estimated about a half-dozen yards to the side of the vessel, where a lifeboat might be located. Her muscles readied to make the sprint.

Mercer's voice in the distance made her freeze.

"Welcome aboard, Strathaven," said the earl in snide tones. "I have been expecting you."

Alaric took quick stock of the situation.

Mercer and six cutthroats, plus the other two bringing the trunks up from the barge.

Nine villains in all—not the best of odds, especially since Alaric's hands were bound and he was flanked by a pair of brutes. Yet if he bought some time—distracted Mercer—Will and the others might yet arrive. He didn't dare scan the surrounding water to see if Johnno's barges had managed to follow the cutthroats' snaking path to the present ship. If Will and Kent had lost the trail, finding Mercer's ship amidst the flotilla of vessels in the harbor would be akin to searching for a needle in a haystack.

He couldn't worry about that now.

You have to trust Will and Kent. Stay focused. Be on the lookout for Emma and Patrice.

Coolly, he said, "This wasn't our agreement, Mercer."

The earl gave a harsh laugh. "There is no agreement, Your Grace. In case you haven't noticed, I hold all the cards. You'll do as I say."

"I brought the money," Alaric said evenly. "Count it, if you wish. But you must honor your word as a gentleman and release Miss Kent and the dowager duchess."

Mercer stepped forward and backhanded him. Alaric's

head snapped to the side.

"You've ruined me. Thanks to you, I'm not welcomed in Society any longer." The earl's urbane face contorted with rage. "You've destroyed everything!"

"You did that to yourself. Or perhaps you needed help even for that," Alaric said in tones designed to goad. "Perhaps Webb came up with the stock scheme, and you were merely his lackey, following his orders."

"The plan was *mine*, damn you! *I* recruited Silas Webb, not the other way around. I saw United's failing prospects and hired Webb to help topple it from the inside. The company's demise was inevitable. A sure thing. But then you came along, ousted Webb, and turned the venture into a bloody success. I've lost everything because of *you*."

"You lost everything because you made a bad investment—and compounded matters by having me poisoned and shot."

"What poison?" Mercer snarled. "What are you—"

"Get away from him!"

Alaric's gaze jerked in the direction of the clear, feminine tones. Relief exploded in his chest—replaced instantly by bone-deep fear. *What the devil is she doing?*

Emma came toward them like some avenging angel, her unbound hair sweeping past her shoulders and a pistol in her small hands. She aimed it at Mercer.

Mercer gave a nasty laugh. "You're not going to shoot."

"Aren't I?" Emma said calmly. "Your henchman underestimated me as well. Now he's below deck—and he's *no longer moving*."

At her declaration, the seasoned cutthroats exchanged uneasy looks, a few shaking their heads. Alaric interpreted the silent male message: *Females—they're an unpredictable lot.*

"Untie Strathaven." Emma's finger tightened on the trigger; she was within several feet of Mercer now. "Or I'll put a hole through your heart."

After an instant, Mercer snapped, "Do as she says."

The lackey next to Alaric untied his wrists. Before the rope hit the ground, Alaric swiveled, securing Mercer in a chokehold and simultaneously grabbing the pistol from the earl's belt. He pressed the barrel to Mercer's temple.

Emma hurried to his side, her gun now pointed at the band of ruffians.

"You can't shoot all of us," Mercer gasped. "Put down the gun, and I'll spare you and the women."

"Drop your weapons," Alaric growled at the cutthroats.

Mercer's henchmen looked at one another, their expressions uncertain. Then the dark-haired brute, the one who'd met Alaric at the quay, guffawed.

Stepping forward, he said, "I don't think so."

Alaric dug the gun in deeper, making Mercer wheeze with fear. "I'm serious. I will shoot."

"So go ahead—kill 'im," the leader said with a sneer. "With the bugger gone, that'll mean more gold for me an' my men. You're just savin' me the trouble o' killin' 'im meself, isn't that right, boys?"

Assent rose from his crew, and they came to stand behind him with ominous solidarity.

Bloody Christ. A mutiny.

"What?" Mercer spat at his employee. "You infidel! You foul betrayer!"

"I've 'ad enough o' you lordin' it o'er me an' the boys. You 'aven't paid us 'alf what you promised, ye bloody skinflint, an' I'm tired o' waitin'," the leader snarled, levying his own gun.

Acting on pure instinct, Alaric released Mercer and dove for Emma. He knocked her to the deck, covering her body with his as a blast tore through the air. Heart thundering, he looked into her pale face.

"You alright?" he rasped.

"Yes. You?" she said.

He jerked his chin, looked back and saw—

Mercer still standing, his expression stunned.

The cutthroat leader, his mien equally startled as he looked down at the scarlet blossoming over his chest. A second later, he crashed to the deck like a felled tree.

"Aboard, men!" came a guttural cry.

William.

More gunshots rang out. The ship shook as barges bumped it on all sides. Through the haze of gunfire, Alaric saw the guards jumping aboard, his brother leading the charge. A familiar lanky figure leapt onto the ship.

"Kent," Alaric shouted. "Over here."

The investigator ran over. "Emma?"

"I'm fine," she assured her brother.

"Take care of her," Alaric told the other man. "I've got to help Will."

"Be careful, darling," Emma called after him.

He entered the fray, which had turned into a vicious free-for-all. He spotted Will by the mast, wrestling with two burly brutes. The one behind Will had him by the throat; the one in front reached down and pulled a knife from his boot.

Alaric took aim and fired.

The blade-wielding villain jolted and collapsed to the ground. In the seconds that it took Alaric to run over, Will had already freed himself of the remaining ruffian. He sent his foe into oblivion with a powerful hook to the jaw. Alaric didn't have time to compliment his brother's technique for another pair of brutes advanced upon them, circling, blades flashing.

The brothers stood back to back.

"I'll take the bigger one," Will said.

"Like hell you will," Alaric said.

The larger bastard made the decision for them, charging Alaric, who feinted left at the last moment, plowing his fist into his attacker's belly. The brute bowled over, and Alaric wrenched the other's arm, forcing the villain to drop the knife. He hauled his foe up and finished the job with a facer that sent the other sprawling.

A minute later, Will dispatched the other cutthroat.

Meeting his brother's gaze, Alaric cocked an eyebrow. "What took you so long?"

"Always have to be the best, don't you?" Will grumbled.

Alaric scanned the deck, counted the enemy subdued by his team. His nape went cold.

"Where the devil is Mercer?" he said.

"Bluidy weasel," Will said. "We'll search the ship. He can't have gone far."

They rounded up the free guards and split the search through the vessel. Accompanied by Cooper, Alaric went to the lowest deck. His shoulders brushed the walls of the narrow corridor, his muscles bunching at each creak and rattle of the aged ship. He and the guard searched each cabin along the way—no sign of Mercer.

Mid-ship, he heard a scuffling from below. He gestured to the trapdoor in front of them.

"He's down in the hold," Alaric mouthed to the guard.

Cooper nodded. Crouching, he yanked the door open by its iron ring.

The shot punched the guard against the wall. Blood spurted from his upper arm. With a curse, Alaric dragged Cooper out of harm's way and ascertained the damage. Luckily, it appeared to be a flesh wound; he bound it quickly with his cravat.

"This'll hold until the others get here," he said.

"You should wait for them, Your Grace—"

Ignoring the guard, Alaric approached the trapdoor again. He stopped at a safe distance and unhooked his watch fob. Taking aim, he tossed it through the open hole, heard it skitter down the steps—

Another shot blasted from the hold.

The next second, Alaric launched himself through the trapdoor, landing in musty darkness. His gaze swung left and right, caught the limned outlines of crates, barrels, sacks—

Mercer.

He lunged at the earl, who was fumbling to reload. He tackled the bastard, slamming his opponent's body against a crate. The pistol clattered out of sight, yet Mercer fought back with feral desperation. The bastard landed a low blow, and stars streaked across Alaric's vision.

His grasp loosened, and Mercer wrestled free. As Alaric sought to regain his breath, he saw something flash in his opponent's hand right before Mercer charged at him, knocking him to the ground. He thrust his hands out, catching the earl's arm, blocking the downward arc of the blade. The lethal point hovered inches above his throat; his muscles strained against the other's maniacal strength.

"I'm going to slit your throat open, you ignorant Scot," Mercer shouted.

Like bluidy hell you will.

Power surged through Alaric. Leveraging his lower body, he gave a mighty shove, rolling over and taking his enemy with him. Now with the upper hand, he grabbed the other's wrist, gave it a sharp twist, and Mercer released the blade with a cry of pain. Bloodlust took over, and Alaric drove his fists into the other's face, bone crunching against bone. He didn't stop until the other lay bloodied and insensate.

Only then did Alaric rise, his chest heaving.

"Alaric!"

He turned to see his brother descending into the hold.

Pistol in hand, Will said tersely, "All you alright?"

"Aye," Alaric said between breaths. "Everyone else?"

"Cooper's getting bandaged by Miss Emma and the dowager." Will paused. "I'm not surprised by Miss Emma's fortitude, but apparently our aunt has got a spine of steel as well."

"Patrice is stronger than she looks." Alaric grimaced as he tested his knuckles.

"Must run in the bloodline. For a duke, you held your own."

"For a little brother, you didn't do so poorly yourself."

A pause. They grinned at each other.

Alaric said, "Let's get some rope and tie up—"

"Behind you!" Will shouted.

Alaric pivoted in time to see Mercer rushing toward him, face bloody and demented, hand raised and wielding a knife. On instinct, he went low, kicking out, and the earl flew forward, crashing headfirst into a tower of crates. One by one, the wooden boxes toppled onto him.

Alaric and Will approached, the latter with his pistol aimed at the prone figure. Cautiously, Alaric pushed the heavy containers off Mercer; with his boot, he rolled the earl over.

Mercer's gaze was unseeing. Scarlet bloomed around the stem of steel in his chest.

The bastard had fallen on his own knife.

"A fitting end," Will said.

"Aye." Alaric exhaled. "It's over."

Together, the brothers left the bloody scene and went to join the others.

Chapter Thirty-Four

A week later, at an intimate gathering of family and friends at his townhouse, Alaric mused over the changes that the last few days had wrought. His enemy was dead, his life no longer in danger. Yesterday, at the meeting of the United Mining venture, Alaric and Tremont's expansion plans had received unanimous support from the shareholders, and the price of stock was soaring.

Most important of all, Alaric had publicly announced his engagement to Emma.

He watched as his betrothed mingled with their guests in the drawing room. Tonight was their engagement supper, and she was radiant in a cerise silk gown that draped enticingly over her curves and slender waist. The choker he'd given her circled her throat, and now a matching pink diamond ring glittered on her finger.

She was, every inch, a duchess. *His* duchess.

He could hardly wait the eight weeks until she walked down the aisle of St. Paul's toward him. Lady Patrice had insisted that two months was the minimum acceptable time for an engagement; any earlier would cause talk about the reason for the haste. He knew that Emma was anxious about getting on in the *ton*, and for her sake, he wanted no blemish on her reputation.

He was determined that, this time around, his marriage would be free of scandal. He wouldn't rush into anything. The key to contentment was to remain in control.

"She'll make a fine duchess, Strathaven." The dowager came to stand beside him. She adjusted her feathered turban, her ring catching the glimmer of the chandelier. "I must confess I had my doubts, but now I understand your interest in her. She is unlike any lady of my acquaintance. Her family is rather ... unique as well."

Alaric stifled a smile. Over supper, the Kents had proved to be an entertaining, lively bunch. Presently, Dorothea was playing the pianoforte in one corner, and he noticed that his friend Tremont appeared quite captivated by her performance. Violet and Polly were at a card table, the former drawing chortles from a curmudgeonly earl with her card tricks. Surrounded by eager bucks, Primrose Kent held court at the center of the room.

All in all, Alaric thought he could grow fond of Emma's family.

"Indeed, Aunt," he said.

"No wonder you are besotted. Don't bother denying it," Lady Patrice said, wagging a finger at him, "for your heart is fairly hanging on your sleeve."

Alaric flicked a sardonic glance at the pristine black velvet arm of his jacket. "I'm sure you exaggerate, Your Grace."

"I'm sure I do not. The entire *ton* is agog with how the mighty have fallen. You're on the road to proving that adage true: reformed rakes *do* make the best husbands."

Heat crept up Alaric's jaw. It was one thing for him to admit to himself that he desired Emma—quite another for the *beau monde* to snigger behind their fans about it. Especially since these were the selfsame gossips who'd labeled him a faithless rake during his last marriage.

"Is it the past that disquiets you, my boy?" The dowager's inquisitive gaze searched his. "I do not think Miss Kent will betray or manipulate you as Laura did."

Alaric said stiffly, "I don't wish to discuss the past."

"I've upset you, haven't I? Forgive me. I don't mean to say the wrong things. You must know I want only your happiness."

At the glimmer in his aunt's eyes, he sighed inwardly and bowed over her hand. "I know. If you'll excuse me, I must circulate amongst my guests."

"Don't worry about me." The dowager gave him a small smile. "Be happy, my boy."

He wound his way through the drawing room, stopping to accept felicitations from various guests, including the Blackwoods, on his engagement. He finally reached his betrothed, who was chatting with their respective brothers and sisters-in-law. He slid a proprietary arm around Emma's waist as he joined the circle.

"Enjoying yourself, pet?" he said.

She smiled up at him, and the warmth in her tea-colored gaze dispelled the unease triggered by the conversation with his aunt. *Emma is nothing like Laura*, he told himself.

Since their engagement, they'd managed to steal only snippets of privacy. The last such occurrence had happened after he'd escorted her to the Opera, and Mrs. Kent had obligingly allowed him to take Emma home.

Those hot, steamy minutes in the carriage rose up now, fogging his brain, making another part of his anatomy stiffen in anticipation for his wedding night. Christ, to feel her luscious sheath clench around his cock the way it had his fingers, his tongue ...

Another eight weeks of this would be pure torture.

But he would bear it—because he could. Because he was in control. Almost.

"We were just talking about wedding plans," Emma informed him, "and the importance of details."

"I don't think Alaric gives a damn about the flowers,"

Will said knowingly.

Alaric narrowed his eyes at his brother. Just because they were getting on these days didn't mean that Will couldn't be a pain in the arse.

"Did *you* notice the flowers at your own wedding?" Alaric said with cool irony. "As I recall, the entire affair passed in a flash. You pushed your guests out of the house before cake was even served."

Annabel turned rosy, but Will merely grinned and draped an arm around his wife. "I had the wedding I wanted—with the lass I wanted it with."

Alaric couldn't fault that. In a way, he envied his brother's freedom, unencumbered as it was by a dukedom and the accompanying expectations. Will's wedding had been small and intimate, a dozen guests or so; Alaric's would number close to a thousand.

"My apologies for mixing business with pleasure," Kent spoke up, "but I thought you should know that I received a message from Lugo today."

Despite Mercer being dead, the African investigator continued his quest to find the missing maid. Kent and Associates did not leave loose ends. Alaric respected that.

"Any new developments?" he said.

"Miss White apparently attracts admirers like bees to honey. Lugo has been following a trail of broken hearts," Kent said dryly. "He thinks he'll have her soon."

"Please convey my gratitude for his persistence," Alaric said.

"And please tell Mr. Lugo that he is invited to our ..."

Emma broke off, her gaze drawn to the gentleman who'd just entered the room. The fellow bore an incongruous mix of characteristics. Tall and broad-shouldered, he had the fit build of a man who enjoyed physical activities. At the same time, his wire spectacles and rumpled hair and clothes gave him the absent-minded air of a scholar.

Frowning, Alaric said, "Who is that?"

"*Emma*," the stranger said simultaneously.

In disbelief, Alaric watched his fiancée *run* toward the newcomer, flinging her arms around him. Her embrace was returned with equal enthusiasm. The pressure in Alaric's veins shot up dangerously.

"Harry!" Violet bounded up to the pair. "You made it! I wasn't sure when my letter would reach you."

Harry Kent—Emma's *brother*. Alaric's fists loosened at his sides. As the Kents gathered around their newly arrived sibling, he saw that the family resemblance was unmistakable.

"I left Paris for London as soon as I received it," Harry Kent said. "When I got home, Pitt gave me this address, said you were all here." Frowning, he studied his eldest sister. "Are you alright, Em? Vi wrote that you'd been abducted—"

"I'm perfectly fine. I'm sorry your studies got interrupted, but I *am* glad to see you. There's someone I want you to meet." Taking her brother by the arm, Emma tugged him over to Alaric. Beaming with pride, she said, "This is my brother Harry. Harry, this is the Duke of Strathaven, my fiancé."

Harry blinked owlishly at his sister. "You're getting married?"

Alaric bowed. "Your sister has bestowed a great honor upon me."

Hastily, Harry returned his courtesy. "It's a pleasure to meet you, sir—I mean, Your Grace." The look he shot Emma clearly said, *You'll have to fill me in.*

"Welcome home, lad," Kent said. His eyes shone with pleasure as he shook his brother's hand. "You've sprouted even more since we saw you last."

"You're just in time, too," Mrs. Kent said, smiling as

Harry kissed her cheek. "There's much to be done for the wedding—starting with fittings at the tailor. You and Ambrose must make a trip to Old Bond Street on the morrow."

The Kent brothers looked at each other ... and groaned.

Emma's heart could not be fuller. The evening was going swimmingly, and Harry's appearance had been the icing atop the cake. Surrounded by family and friends, she brimmed with joy. Her engagement party was everything she could have wanted.

Yet as Thea began a haunting rendition of Master Beethoven's *Moonlight Sonata*, Emma became aware of a stirring restlessness. She realized that she hadn't seen Alaric for at least a quarter hour; scanning the room, she saw no trace of him. Following impulse, she slipped out to find him.

The door to his study was open, and she saw him standing by the windows, looking out into the dark garden. Phobos and Deimos were at his feet, the deerhounds' feathery ears perking with interest at her arrival. She entered, closing the door behind her.

His jade gaze locked on her, and she was struck anew by his masculine beauty ... and by wonder. At times, it felt like a dream that this wickedly attractive duke wanted her. She could scarcely wait for their wedding day—and night—to arrive.

"I wondered where you'd gone," she said.

"I just wanted a moment to myself." His smile was rueful. "I'm not used to being around so much ... family."

"I understand," she assured him. "Shall I go ...?"

"No, pet. Your presence is welcome." He held a hand out to her, and when she went over, he pulled her into his embrace. Pleasure hummed through her as he nuzzled her earlobe. "I miss you, Emma."

She didn't pretend to misunderstand. "I miss you, too."

His answer was a scorching kiss, one that instantly kindled her desire to an overwhelming flame. She tangled her tongue eagerly with his, pressing into his lean, hard length, wanting to be even closer. His hands cupped her bottom, molding her to him, lifting her against the virile bulge that she could feel through the layers of her skirts. She rubbed herself against him with unabashed hunger, her core fluttering with emptiness, a wanton need that only he could fill.

"Christ, I want you so badly," he said in ragged tones. "I don't know how I'm going to wait eight more weeks to make you mine."

The realization burst inside her. In truth, the seed had been germinating ever since she'd been kidnapped by Mercer. Life was too short, too precious and tenuous, to waste.

"I don't want to wait," she whispered.

He gazed at her, his slashing cheekbones ruddy with arousal. "I'm not taking you until we're wed, Emma. I'm going to do this right."

She loved him for it. Loved how he treated her, the effort he was making with her family and his own, how determined he was to give her the wedding of any woman's dreams.

I love him so much, she thought wistfully.

She was tempted to tell him so—but she had decided to wait until their wedding night, to seal that special moment with a declaration of her feelings. She didn't know how he would respond; he'd been honest about his views on love, after all. Yet in her heart she believed that he cared for her, and she felt confident that one day soon he would return her words.

Taking a breath, she said, "Then let's get wed."

"Pardon?"

"Let's elope," she said simply. "Gretna Green is on the way to your estate, isn't it? We could have our honeymoon at Strathmore."

Desire flared silver in his eyes, yet he shook his head—as if to himself as much as to her. "You deserve a grand wedding, and you'll have it."

"I deserve *you*," she said, kissing his jaw, "and I don't want to wait."

"Your family—"

"They'll be happy that I'm happy. We can invite them to visit us at Strathmore, can't we?"

"Our home is theirs. But sweeting ..."

He trailed off when she linked her arms around his neck. Standing on tiptoe, she whispered against his ear, "Please? I don't want to waste another moment. I need to be yours, Alaric."

She saw shadows flicker in his eyes, his shoulders stiffening as if he were fighting some inner battle. Surely propriety couldn't mean that much to him?

Then his arms closed hard around her, crushing her to his chest.

"You are mine," he said roughly. "Oh, Emma, you *are*."

Around noon the next day, Marianne found her husband in his study working on a report. As he scribbled, he absently rubbed the back of his neck, a habit she found endearing even after all these years of marriage.

He rose immediately when he saw her, the smile in his eyes softening his somber mien. "You're a welcome sight.

Did you get enough rest, sweetheart?"

"Yes." Going over, she straightened the lapels of his coat. "Last night's party didn't go that late."

She was stalling ... and cursed herself for her foolishness. She was known for her directness. Yet this was Ambrose, the man she loved, and she knew he wouldn't take well to the news she had to deliver.

"I wasn't referring to the party," he murmured as he bent to kiss her cheek.

Her skin warmed at the memory of their private celebration *after* the party ... but she could delay no longer. She decided to let the facts speak for themselves. Wordlessly, she handed him the letter she'd discovered moments earlier on Emma's neatly made bed.

"What's this?" Furrows deepened on Ambrose's brow as he scanned the brief lines. "Bloody hell—they've *eloped?*"

"Emma must have slipped out before the servants awakened. I'd assumed that she stayed abed to rest after the party—I should have known better," Marianne said wryly. "When I went to check on her just now, I found the note."

"*We'll be travelling by Mail Coach, which promises to get us to Gretna Green within three days,*" Ambrose read aloud. "*I hope you will forgive my impetuousness, but the truth is I could not wait. Please share in our happiness. Will you visit us soon at Strathmore Castle? I look forward to welcoming you all to my new home. Your loving sister, Emma.*"

He crumpled the letter. "Goddamnit, even if I leave immediately, they have a half-day's lead. I won't catch them in time."

Marianne put a hand on his shoulder. "You mustn't interfere, darling."

"But eloping—it's not proper!"

"Once Emma is a duchess, it won't matter how the marriage took place. Trust me, anyone who dares to gossip about her will face the wrath of Strathaven. In case you haven't noticed," Marianne said with a touch of amusement, "he's quite protective of her."

"I've noticed." Ambrose swiped a hand through his hair, said darkly, "I was beginning to get used to His Grace, too—until this."

"You can't blame a man in love for being impetuous."

"And you're certain he loves her?"

Marianne touched her finger to the divot between her husband's brows and said huskily, "Darling, he looks at her the way you look at me."

Ambrose exhaled. "I hope you're right."

"I know I am." She linked her arm with his. "Let's go tell the rest of the family. I have a feeling they'll be quite eager to visit Scotland."

Chapter Thirty-Five

It was amazing how something as mundane as supper could be transformed into a thrilling activity when shared with one's new husband.

Sitting at a cozy table by the fire, in a suite that the innkeeper had declared his "verra best," Emma studied Alaric as he sipped his wine. He'd changed into a black brocade dressing robe, his throat bare, his midnight hair curling and damp from his bath. They'd both cleaned up after arriving at the inn an hour ago. A half hour before that, they'd pledged themselves to each other over an anvil in a ceremony as short as it had been sweet.

Now Emma was officially Mrs. Alaric James Alexander McLeod.

And also the new Duchess of Strathaven.

Picking her hand up from the table, her new husband rubbed his thumb over her plain gold wedding band, clearly pleased with the sign of his possession. As he wore a wider masculine version on his hand, a symbol of *her* claim, she had no complaints.

His eyes a beautiful smoky jade, he murmured, "Had enough to eat, pet?"

"I'm stuffed to the gills," she said truthfully. The remnants of their feast—roasted venison and Scotch pie, potted haugh and assorted local cheeses, raspberries topped with whipped cream—still lay on the table before them. "The innkeep sent up enough to feed an army."

"He wanted to make sure we keep our energies up."

Alaric's slow, wicked smile made Emma's cheeks warm, her heartbeat quickening.

"I don't expect stamina will be a problem," she said.

During their speedy two and a half day journey to Gretna Green, they'd been alone together in the mail coach Alaric had procured exclusively for their use. The drivers and guards up top had made the situation less than private, however, and Alaric had insisted on being circumspect.

They had spent most of the time talking instead, sometimes about lighter topics such as their favorite foods— Scotch pie (his) and almond tart (hers)—and places they'd been and wanted to go. They'd also discussed weightier subjects. She'd talked about the poverty she'd known as a girl, the ever-present fear of an empty larder or rent past due. She'd shared her deepest joys, too: being part of a family that stuck together through thick and thin, that valued laughter and each other more than worldly things.

For his part, Alaric hadn't disclosed his past as readily, yet he'd answered her questions, giving her sufficient detail to piece together a lonely childhood and an adolescence overshadowed by his illness. She'd already known that his mama died when he was young. From the little he said about his father and his guardian, she gathered that neither was a nurturing sort. When it came to his aunt, he spoke with distant appreciation for all she'd done for him.

He was more willing, however, to speak of the time after his guardian's death. Upon receiving a small stipend from the Strathaven estate, he'd invested it, parlaying it into tuition and living expenses at Oxford. After his studies, he'd continued to accumulate wealth through his investments; he'd been on his way to building a financial empire when, one by one, the heirs to Strathaven passed away, leaving him to succeed as duke.

At eight-and-twenty, Alaric had inherited an expensive castle, ill-managed estates, and little income to maintain the properties. With his business acumen, he'd turned things around, invested in modernization. During his tenure, he'd refilled the Strathaven coffers and brought prosperity to his lands.

Emma hadn't known this side of Alaric: the hard-working man beneath the jaded aristocrat. It made her admire him even more. The journey to Gretna Green had fostered further closeness, and Emma had no doubt that they belonged together. As a result, she was more than ready to explore and deepen their physical intimacy. To give herself to her husband, body and soul.

Alaric pushed his chair back, patted his thighs. "Come here, pet."

With prickling excitement, she obeyed. She wore nothing beneath her pink flannel robe and thus could feel the taut sinew of his thighs, the ridge of his growing arousal. He kissed her softly, and she sighed, drinking in the taste of him sweetened with mulled wine. They sipped at each other, tongues lapping and twining, a kiss of tender lust.

He loosened the belt of her robe, parting the panels, and she blushed as he gazed upon her bared self with raw possession in his eyes.

"Look at you," he said. "So beautiful and you're all mine. You trust me, Emma?"

"I do." A thrilling echo of the words she'd used to commit herself to him forevermore.

"Say you'll let me do whatever I wish. Say you're mine," he commanded.

Her breath hitched as he cupped one breast, giving it a proprietary squeeze. She understood the importance of these words to him, a man who'd been betrayed by his first wife. Who'd been alone for so much of his life.

Was it any wonder that Alaric needed certainty—that he needed *her*?

"I'm yours," Emma pledged. "To do with as you wish."

The familiar, exhilarating freedom soared within her, and she saw his nostrils flare, his pupils darkening with excitement. When it came to lovemaking, she needed to let go as much as he needed to be in control. They were a perfect match.

Reaching to the table, he dipped his finger into his wine goblet. Her breath grew choppy as he painted the cool liquid over her nipple, circling the areola, teasing it to a hard peak. Her neck arched as he bent his head and tongued the pouting bud. The sensation shot straight to her center, and her pussy dampened in a warm rush.

"You like that," he murmured after lavishing the same attention on her other breast.

"Yes," she sighed.

"Did it make you wet?"

Blushing, she nodded.

"Show me."

She blinked.

"Touch yourself, darling," he said huskily.

He took her hand and placed it between her thighs. Her pulse raced as their joined fingers combed through the plump folds, which were very slick indeed. He guided her touch upward, to her hidden knot, circling and stroking until a moan broke from her lips. Her embarrassment faded to the hot sensuality of their combined touch.

"Feels good, doesn't it?" he crooned. "Frig yourself for me. Make yourself come while I suckle your pretty tits."

Supported by his arm, her spine bowed as his tongue swirled her nipple, erotically mimicking what her fingers were doing down below. It was outrageous, depraved ... deliciously so. Her touch grew faster, the pressure inside her building as he went back and forth between her breasts, sucking and lapping. When his teeth grazed a sensitive peak, pleasure exploded, and she cried out his name.

He swept her up in his arms, his kiss soothing and sweet while her lungs pulled for air. He sat her down on the edge of the bed and removed her robe and his own. Despite the aftermath humming in her veins, her belly grew molten as he stood before her, his body revealed to her in its magnificent entirety for the first time.

He might have been carved from marble, so perfectly rendered was his form. The firelight licked over his muscular shoulders and hard-paved chest, the rippling ridges of his belly. His hips were taut and hollowed, girdled by a prominent vee of muscle. Everything about him—from the dusting of dark hair over sleek sinew to his enormous erection—radiated flagrant virility.

"You put a statue to shame," she said in wonder. "You're so beautiful, Alaric."

His lopsided grin was surprisingly boyish. "You shouldn't flatter me so. Such encouragement might go to my head."

"I think," she said, aiming her gaze at the swollen tip of his cock, "it already *has*."

"What a naughty minx I married," he said with a husky laugh.

"May I touch you?"

"Aye, lass. Put your hands on your husband."

Since he was standing and she perched on the mattress, all she had to do was reach out. Wrapping both hands around his thick stalk, she pumped reverently, reveling in having all that masculine power contained within her palms.

"The way you touch me—it's so bluidy good." Arousal stained his cheekbones, deepened his lilt. The dew that leaked from his cockhead was further evidence that he was speaking the truth.

"I love touching you," she confessed.

"Ach, I can't take much more of this." He groaned, his hands sliding into her hair, guiding her head toward his turgid shaft. "Make it wet, darling. So it will fit more easily into your tight little cunny."

She eagerly did as he instructed. Tonguing his cock, she lubricated its steely length. When she arrived at the bulging crown, she parted her lips, taking him deep, and his breath hissed through his teeth.

His hands tightened in her hair, stilling her. "That's enough. Lie back now and spread those pretty legs for me."

His lordly command sent flames of desire licking over her skin. She obeyed, placing her head against the pillows. He knelt between her thighs, and her bosom surged with anticipation—and just the tiniest smidgen of anxiety—as the broad head of his cock lodged against her vulnerable flesh.

Alaric looked upon his Emma and knew how Ares must have felt when gazing upon Aphrodite. Desire. Covetousness. Fierce possessiveness tempered by an equally fierce dose of tenderness. Yet Ares, that wretched Olympian, could only claim Aphrodite as his lover for she'd been wed to another god. Emma, on the other hand, was all Alaric's, and he would never, ever let her go.

He told himself that he'd done the right thing in eloping with her. In giving in to her sweet request. Why delay the inevitable? Now she belonged to him, and the torment of waiting was over. His cock strained to make the ultimate claim, yet first he had to be sure his duchess was ready to take him.

Taking his rigid member in hand, he teased them both

by running the burgeoned tip through her damp petals. He groaned at her lushness, her cream coating his head. Withdrawing, he found her opening with his fingers, eased his middle digit inside. Her little passage clenched him immediately.

"You're delicate, pet." He fingered her, drawing out her wetness, not wanting to hurt her. "It might sting a little at first."

"I'm not afraid. I want you, Alaric," she said steadily. "Come inside me."

Unable to hold back any longer, he lowered himself onto her giving softness, notching his cock to her slit. He pushed slowly between her dewy lips. A strangled sound left him at the snug fit, the decadent squeeze of her virginal sheath around his invading cock. She stiffened beneath him, and it took all of his willpower to hold still, to not thrust all the way home as his every instinct clamored to do.

"Sweeting?" he said, looking into her eyes.

"It feels strange," she said breathlessly. "Is the fit always this ... tight?"

Perspiration misted on his brow as he battled for control. "'Tis only because it's your first time. You'll get used to me."

"Are you, um, all the way in yet?"

He looked down—a mistake. The sight of their joined bodies, of her pretty pussy stretched around the thick meat of his shaft nearly undid him.

"About halfway," he managed. He was definitely overestimating, but he didn't want to frighten her.

"Halfway?" she said with clear dismay. "You're too big."

At the mention of its size, his vain beast puffed up even further. "You'll adjust to me in a moment," he said, gritting his teeth. "Try to relax, pet."

"Maybe if I move a little ..."

Before he could dissuade her, she tipped her hips up, the

motion making him slide deeper into her heat. She gasped; he groaned at the torturous pleasure. His cock was halfway buried in the hottest, tightest quim he'd ever had—*and he couldn't move.*

"It doesn't sting as much now," she said. "Can you try again—but go slowly?"

He wanted to sing Hallelujah with the angels.

"Aye, pet." He rocked his hips. "Whatever you want ..."

He moved back and forth carefully. Seeing that she didn't show any signs of pain, he went a little deeper the next pass and the next. He could feel her flowering around him. She let out a sigh, her lushness surrounding him, gripping him. Lungs burning, he finally sank himself to the hilt and held.

"How is that, darling?"

Her eyes were heavy-lidded. "Mmm, quite ... nice."

"We'll have to do better than nice," he said huskily.

Leaning down, he suckled her nipple as he began moving again. When she moaned, her hands tangling in his hair, he knew her discomfort had passed. He quickened his thrusts, groaning as her hips began to accompany his movements, lifting naturally, perfectly, to take him even deeper. When her head began to toss restlessly on the pillow, he gripped her soft bottom and plunged, angling his prick to graze her pearl, grinding against the sensitive peak. Over and again, he did this, circling his hips, using the unyielding root of his cock to maximize her pleasure and ratcheting up his own in the process.

He was wild for her, a hair's breadth from spending harder than he ever had in his life. She writhed against him, their bodies straining together, slick with sweat.

"Oh my goodness," she gasped.

"That's it," he rasped, increasing the ferocity of his thrusts. "Spend for me. I want to feel you come around my cock."

"*Alaric.*"

"Yes, sweetheart," he groaned. "Christ, you're milking me so hard I can't—"

His climax roared over him. Waves of heat boiled up from his balls. He shuddered with ecstasy as his seed jetted hotly inside his wife, as her fulfillment wrung him of his own.

Afterward, he rolled them both onto their sides so that they faced each other, their bodies still joined. He kissed her forehead and ran a possessive hand over her hip.

"How do you feel?" he said softly.

"Wonderful." Eyes dreamy, she whispered, "I love you, Alaric."

He went still. Even as wild wings of pleasure beat in his chest, an equally strong panic set in. The past bared its feral claws, humiliation gutting him as he recalled the times he'd spoken of love, how Laura had extorted countless such professions from him. How desperate he'd been for her affection and how in the end it hadn't been enough. How *he* hadn't been enough.

You're a selfish bastard. You're not capable of love—or deserving of it.

Sudden anger chilled his insides, banishing the afterglow. He'd been clear with Emma, honest from the start. She couldn't expect his love when he had none to give, and lying would only make matters worse in the long run.

Suspicion pierced him. *Does she think she can manipulate me? Because she convinced me to elope with her, does she think she has me wrapped around her finger?*

That misconception *had* to be nipped in the bud.

"Thank you, pet," he said coolly, "but it isn't necessary."

The lazy contentment in her eyes faded. A myriad of emotions flitted across her face, and he tensed for the inevitable backlash. For the accusations and tears.

After a moment, she laid a hand on his jaw. Her eyes steady and clear, she said, "I know."

When she said nothing else, profound relief trickled through him. She wasn't trying to ambush him, control him. Shame spurred his heartbeat, yet he didn't know how to apologize ... so instead he kissed her. The ready sweetness of her response flummoxed him, and despite their recent coupling, desperate hunger rose in him again.

Tumbling her onto the pillows, he let his need take over, intent upon showing her that passion was enough to build a marriage on.

Because it had to be.

Chapter Thirty-Six

On her fifth morning at Strathmore, Emma decided that she'd had enough.

Not of her new home, which turned out to be magnificent despite it not being an authentic castle. She was certain her sisters would be tickled pink over the grand turreted towers and the view of the rolling green hills and shimmering loch from the battlement.

She didn't even mind her new role as duchess, which was not as intimidating as she'd imagined. Returning from London, Jarvis had offered felicitations with a twinkle in his eyes and then proceeded to introduce her to the staff. Emma took pains to remember everyone's name and was relieved to find them an efficient, no-nonsense bunch. She especially liked the cook, Mrs. Murray, who'd generously shared the recipe for the duke's favorite Scotch pie.

Overall, Emma thought she was settling quite nicely into her new life—with one exception: her husband was driving her mad.

As she descended the sweeping staircase, she reflected that her present state of exasperation wasn't due to his cool reception to her words of love. His reply had smarted—but, truthfully, it hadn't surprised her all that much either. He'd told her his views on love, and she didn't expect him to change overnight, especially knowing what she did of his history.

Her love was a gift; she'd offered it without strings.

At the same time, she didn't expect him to *block her out* because of it.

Ever since their wedding night, Alaric's behavior had been ... strange.

On the one hand, some of his old impassiveness had returned. 'Twas as if the progress they'd made before their marriage had eroded. Any time she brought up a more intimate topic of conversation, he regressed to politeness. Or shut her out with excuses—he had tenants to visit, correspondence to dictate.

Paint to watch dry on a wall, perhaps?

Her fear that she'd made a mistake in her marriage might have turned into full-fledged panic ... if Alaric hadn't expressed his need for her in other ways.

Because even as he withdrew from her emotionally, he couldn't seem to get enough of her physically. When they were together, he couldn't keep his hands off of her. Yesterday, they'd had a picnic in one of the estate's wooded glens, and blood rushed beneath her skin as she recalled their lusty frolic outdoors. How he'd bade her to sit atop his mouth, his tongue impaling her as she writhed in helpless pleasure. After her bursting climax, he'd pressed her onto her hands and knees, entering her swiftly from behind, the passionate sounds of their coupling echoing through the forest ...

Then he'd brought her home to his bed and made love to her until dawn.

There were the tokens of his affection as well. He showered her with *things*. Everything from baubles to bonbons—and yesterday he'd given her a beautiful silver-white mare that he planned to teach her to ride. The day before that he'd bought her a desk inlaid with mother-of-pearl and had it set up for her in his study so that they could work in each other's company.

Emma was patient, but Alaric's contradictory behavior was testing even her limits. She was a practical sort and didn't require words to tell her that he cared for her, enjoyed her company—his actions in this regard spoke clearly. Why, then, was he simultaneously trying to erect a wall between them?

Perhaps he was adjusting to being a husband.

Well, she'd given him five days. That was long enough.

Arriving at the door to his study, she marched in, ready to do battle if necessary to get her answers.

"Good morning, pet." Rising from his desk, he came to her. The smile that warmed his eyes turned her knees to water. "You look good enough to eat."

Her wits scattered. Breathlessly, she said, "So do you."

"I've created a monster. Lucky me," he murmured as he drew her in for his kiss.

The entry of a footman—followed by his hasty apology and retreat—made them come up for air.

"Goodness, what will the servants think of us?" Emma said with a flustered laugh.

"They'll think I'm a red-blooded Scotsman with an itch for his wife."

As tempted as Emma was to give into the seductive gleam in his eyes, she knew they had matters to address. She smoothed her skirts and, to distract herself from licentious impulses, wandered a safe distance over to the shelves that covered the far wall of the room.

As she tried to marshal her thoughts and strategy, her gaze caught on an object. Sitting alone on a shelf and encased in a glass box, the Grecian urn looked ancient: its ebony glaze was crackled, one of the two curving handles missing. Nonetheless, the red-brown drawings on its surface remained intact and raised goose pimples on her skin.

She recognized that figure. The soldier with the crested

helmet, his anguished expression, those raised fists pounding against the walls of the urn for eternity.

She'd seen that same character depicted in that horrid painting in Alaric's bedroom.

Intuition flashed: what significance did this suffering soldier have for Alaric? Why did this ravaged figure invade his innermost sanctuaries?

"Who is that?" she said, pointing at the urn. "The man, I mean. He's the same one in that painting you have in London, isn't he?"

Silence. For an instant, she thought he might not respond.

"That's Ares. The Greek God of War," Alaric said tonelessly. "The painting and urn depict a myth about him."

Foreboding crept over her. "What is the myth about?"

"According to legend, Ares was born of immaculate conception. His mother, the goddess Hera, conceived him on her own to gain revenge on her unfaithful husband Zeus. Not surprisingly, Zeus felt no kinship toward Ares, who was not of his blood." Alaric retreated behind his desk, shuffling papers as he continued to tell the story with cool detachment. "After giving birth, Hera's vengeance was accomplished so she, too, was indifferent to the child. Thus, when Ares one day went missing, neither of his parents noticed—or cared particularly."

Emma's throat cinched. "What happened to him?"

"Being a lad, he liked to play with his friends. It happened that he chose his friends poorly." Alaric shrugged. "He got caught up with a pair of Giants—twins with a nasty sense of humor. For fun, they trapped him in a bronze jar and locked the lid. They held him captive for years, and the isolation almost made him lose his mind."

She couldn't bear the bleakness of his tone. She crossed over to him, yet the wintry cast of his eyes warned her not to approach too closely.

Facing him across the desk, she said, "How did Ares get out?"

"Another god ended up freeing him. Ever since that incident, however, Ares was filled with uncontrollable fury and a taste for destruction. He was mindlessly aggressive—it wasn't for nothing that he became the God of War. Needless to say, the other gods didn't like him much."

"He was misunderstood," Emma said fiercely. "All he needed was love and compassion."

"He was a bastard—unloved and unwanted." To her disbelief, Alaric turned back to his papers. "Now if there's nothing else, I have work to—"

"Why does Ares matter to you?" she said.

Alaric flicked a glance at her. "I don't know what you mean."

"He's in your bedchamber, your study. You named your deerhounds after his companions. Surely there must be a reason for it."

"Perhaps I merely find his story interesting."

"Perhaps you could do me the courtesy of telling me the truth."

The indifference fled his eyes. He quickly masked it with distaste. "Emma, I'm busy. I don't have time for this nonsense."

Her simmering temper boiled over. "Our *marriage* is not nonsense. Stop shutting me out—I won't stand for it."

"You're giving me an ultimatum?" His expression hardened.

"I am *not* your dead wife," she said in annoyance. "What we're having is known as a conversation. It's what married people do."

"And if I don't want to talk?" he said icily.

"Then be a coward and hide in your blasted jar!"

"What the devil is that supposed to mean?"

He was white-lipped, livid. She was too angry to care.

"It means that *you're* the one putting up the wall between us," she snapped. "If you're too afraid to tell me what's really going on, then you deserve to stay right where you are."

A hush fell over the study.

"You want to know?" he said with menacing softness. "Fine, I have something to show you."

On the way over to the banks of the loch, he questioned himself again and again.

Do you really want her to know the truth?

He'd never taken anyone to the cave. Not Laura—not even Charlie. Yet something in him would not relent, and it was too late anyway; Emma had issued the challenge, and he could not back down. The looming dread that he'd been battling since their wedding night now suffused him completely. Perhaps it was better this way. The waiting—the anticipation of the blade's descent—was too much to bear.

Best to get it over with.

Best to be done with illusions of love once and for all.

So now he found himself with Emma at the loch, its blue surface gently rippling and studded with diamonds of sunlight. A rock-strewn beach ringed the water, and green hills rose all around. His steps grew heavier and heavier, yet he trudged on until they reached the place that he was looking for: the opening to the cavern that time and tides had carved into the bank.

"A secret cave?" she said.

He helped her over the boulders and into the sheltered grotto. Although he hadn't been there in years, it was exactly how he remembered it. Humid and dark, the silence was buffered by the sound of lapping water and wailing gulls. He smelled moss and earth and remembered loneliness.

Emma was looking at him, her head canted. Waiting for him to speak.

"This was the place I escaped to as a lad." The words emerged matter-of-factly. "When I could manage to get away from my uncle's cruelties, I came here." He placed a palm against the mossy wall, remembering how he'd huddled against that stony pillow, retching, gutted by pain. "Sometimes I prayed the water would rush in. That it would cover everything. End everything."

He heard Emma's sharp intake of breath.

Now she would see how weak, how disgustingly pathetic he'd been.

Ruthlessly, he forced himself to forge on. "When I got sick, my uncle believed I was faking my symptoms to gain attention. He said I was a weakling and a liar. He valued strength and perfection above all else—and he despised me for being a failure on both counts."

"Did he … hurt you?"

"I preferred the beatings to his other punishments," Alaric said flatly. "To the isolation, starvation, and scorn. There wasn't a day that went by without him telling me how contemptible I was. How worthless."

"Why didn't your aunt stop his abuses?" Emma's voice quivered.

"She worshipped her husband and never went against his wishes. Not that it would have mattered if she did. His will was law."

"What a horrid man! He had no cause to treat you so." Emma tugged on his arm, and he turned, meeting her eyes, the unexpected fire in them fighting back some of his inner frost. "How was it your fault that you had an illness, for God's sake? The fact that you survived and regained your health—that's a testament to your strength and courage."

Her conviction was like a beacon in the darkness. His beautiful Emma—his soul hungered for her light, her warmth. Yet he couldn't go on letting her believe that she loved him when she hadn't seen all that he was. His dark inadequacies and failures.

"Then why did my father and stepmother want to be rid of me? Why was my mama unhappy until the day she died?" The words were razors in his throat. "Will—he was always loved. But not me."

"I didn't know your family, so I can't explain why they acted as they did." Emma gripped both his arms. "But I know *you*, Alaric McLeod, and you are strong and clever and honorable. That is why I love you."

Those words ... sweet cruelty when they were all he wanted and could not have.

"You've a loving heart, Emma," he said roughly. "You could love anyone."

"That's untrue." She stared at him, gnawing on her lip. "If my love doesn't convince you, think of all the other ladies who have wanted you through the years. From what I've heard," she said, her tone dry, "that accounts to hordes."

"What do they know about me?" he said with a dismissive shrug. "They see the title, the money. They do not see me."

"I see you," Emma said fiercely, "and I love you."

She's going to find out sooner or later. Better to face her disappointment now. She'll hate you less in the long run ...

Bracing himself, he said, "Laura claimed that I wasn't capable of love. That I took her love for granted. The last time we argued she said I'd only understand if ... if I lost everything. That was why she took Charlie with her when she left."

The last time Alaric had come to the cave was after

Charlie's funeral. Alone, he hadn't been able to shed a single tear. Had just sat there as cold and numb as the surrounding stone. What kind of a man didn't weep over the loss of his boy?

I failed you, Charlie. Because I couldn't love you enough.

He forced himself to say what history had proven. "The truth is, I'm not deserving of love—because I'm not capable of giving it."

The dark walls surrounded him, closed him in.

Chapter Thirty-Seven

Emma's heart broke at the pain, the unrelenting guilt in Alaric's voice. He couldn't even look at her, his gaze fixed on the wall of the cave. His expression was worse than ravaged, it was *resigned*: as if this were a stone prison that he could never escape.

A more refined lady might have approached him with caution, politely given him time to collect himself. *Emma* was too forthright, too furious to hold her tongue.

"For God's sake, you can't honestly believe that drivel?" she demanded.

His head snapped up. "Pardon?"

"That self-serving nonsense your previous duchess fed you." She glared at him. "You cannot think it is true."

"Well, I ..." He broke off, blinking.

"You married her, remained faithful to your vows even when she did not. You could have divorced her or abandoned her, but you didn't. You stayed and gave her the protection of your name." Emma poked him in the chest. "What is that, if not love?"

Alaric stared at her. "It was ... my duty. She was my wife. My responsibility. And even if I'd once had feelings for her,"—he shook his head—"they died."

"Because *she* killed them. She didn't deserve your love—which, by the by, isn't just about words." Emma was working herself into a fine rage and didn't even care. "It's about actions. It's ridiculous that you think you aren't capable of love when you show it every single day."

"I … do?"

"Of course. You haven't said you love me, but I'm quite certain you do. Because you demonstrate your affection for me in ways other than words."

He looked dumbstruck.

"Alaric," she said in exasperation, "you've filled my closets with finery fit for a queen, given me more jewelry than I could possibly wear in a lifetime, installed me in a castle—"

"That's just money," he said starkly.

"You listen to me," she persisted, "and respect my opinion even if you don't agree. For goodness' sake, you support my desire to be an investigator—how many husbands would do that?"

"I'm not going to stand in the way of your dreams."

"Exactly. Because you *care* about my happiness. So much so that you're making efforts to get to know my family because you know how much they mean to me."

Was it her imagination or did his eyes flicker, some of the desolation fading?

"I like your family," he said gruffly.

"And they like you. How could they not?" She laid a hand on his taut jaw. "You're wonderful."

She saw hope spark … and then he shook his head. "So wonderful that I got you kidnapped and nearly killed."

"Stop it," she said hotly. "You are *not* going to blame yourself for that lunatic Mercer. What happened was not your fault."

"All my life, people have scorned me—hated me." His lips twisted. "If that's not my fault, whose is it?"

"*Theirs*. Your family's because they didn't understand you. Your guardian's because he was an evil tyrant. Yes, he *was*," she said when he remained broodingly silent. "How he treated a sick young boy was despicable."

"I didn't cry ... when Charlie died." Alaric's voice was gravelly with emotion. "And as much as my aunt's done for me, I don't love her."

"Everyone experiences grief in different ways. My papa—he didn't cry much either when my mama passed, but he nearly went mindless with sorrow," Emma said gently. "As for Lady Patrice, I can't say I blame you. She's an odd bird, isn't she?"

She saw yearning and panic flare in his jade eyes. She sensed how badly he wanted to believe her. How afraid he was to do so.

"Mercer," he said, clearly grasping at straws. "True, he was an evil lunatic, but the fact is that he hated me enough to try to kill me. Twice. Why am I always the target of attack?"

Tenderness cinched her throat. With both hands, she reached up and cupped his jaw. "Mercer was jealous of you. Your success, who you *are*. Alaric, don't you see it?"

"See what?"

"How special you are. How loving and deserving of love. Not because of your title or money or position—but because you look out for your younger brother and help him, even though you won't let him know it. Because you've survived hardship and loss, and it's only made you stronger. Because you see something special in me, a managing, independent spinster—and you make me feel beautiful and cherished." Her voice broke a little. "I love *you*, Alaric."

For a long moment, crashing waves filled the silence.

"Christ, Emma," he said, his words raw and ragged, "I love you so much it hurts."

Joy burst within her. "I know."

Because she did.

His arms closed like a vise around her, his lips descending with crushing force. She answered his desperate love with her own. She licked his thrusting tongue, sucked upon it, wanting him closer. Wanting to share her body, her breath, everything that she was with her duke. Her love.

No trace of ice was left in his eyes, the irises burning with silver fire. He stripped away her clothes with savage haste, rendering delicate cloth, scattering buttons over the sandy floor. He backed her into the wall of the cave. Locking her wrists above her head, he devoured her mouth, owning her with his kiss. After all he'd laid bare, she understood his need to be in control once more, and she melted for him, gave him anything he asked. Her back arched against the mossy stone as his lips captured her nipple, sucking deep.

"I'll never get enough of you. My duchess, my love," he rasped.

Her answer emerged as a whimper for he was caressing her pussy, smearing her wetness over her pearl, plunging into her aching hole. He drove deep, his long fingers curling, stimulating an exquisite spot high inside. Shocks of pleasure shot down her legs; already, an orgasm was blooming.

"Your cunny is so wet and greedy. Tell me what it needs," he commanded.

"You, my love," she breathed. "I need you inside me. Always."

He opened his trousers, and a heartbeat later, she was lifted up against the wall. Her feet dangling off the ground, she was held aloft by his strength, by the upward thrust of his big cock. He impaled her completely, and she screamed as she came.

He shuddered as Emma's climax pulsed around his rock-hard shaft. Her slick muscles clutched at him, the voluptuous massage drawing his bollocks up tight. He withdrew and drove deep, her cream easing his way. Driven by an animal need to possess, he slammed into her over and again.

"You feel so bluidy perfect," he grated.

"Oh, Alaric," she sighed, "so do you."

"I could fuck you forever."

"Good, because I don't want you to stop ..." Her lashes fluttered over her gloriously dazed eyes. "I think I'm going to ... *oh* ..."

She stiffened, and the tides of her second climax rippled over him, making his eyes roll back with bliss. In the next second, he had her on the floor, spreading her beneath him on the mattress of sand. Pushing her knees back, he drove into her, groaning at the depth of the angle, at how totally she received him.

"Take me," he said between serrated breaths. "All of me."

"I'm yours." Her beautiful eyes held him as sweetly as her body. "Forever."

Her acceptance shredded his control. His balls slapped her pussy again and again as he lost himself in the unrivaled joy of being one with his wife. The mate to his soul. Fire licked up his spine, his cock, and his seed climbed with volatile pressure. This time he didn't hold back, surging deeply, shuddering as he brushed her womb. He heard her cry out and then his own groan exploded against the walls of the cavern.

He pumped hotly into her again and again, his release without end. She clasped him, milked him, her culmination emptying him of everything he'd been. Shattering and rebuilding him with ecstasy.

When he could move again, he rolled her atop him. Threading his fingers reverently through her tumbled tresses, he let out a contented sigh. "You were made for me, lass. Everything I've ever wanted."

A smile tucked into her cheeks. "You wanted a duchess who makes love in caves?"

"I wanted a wife to love." Tenderly, he rubbed his thumb over her kiss-swollen lips. "One who would love me in return."

"You've definitely got yourself that."

"Don't ever leave me."

"Never," she said.

Her kiss was as warm and sweet as her promise, dissolving the last of the frost inside him.

Chapter Thirty-Eight

The dowager arrived from London the next morning with luggage and servants in tow. Emma received her in the castle's main salon and placed a dutiful kiss on the lady's powdery cheek. After ringing for tea, she took a seat on the adjacent chaise.

"Where is Strathaven?" the dowager said immediately.

"He's caught up in a meeting with the land manager. He'll be out shortly."

"Well, you two have been naughty children,"—Lady Patrice wagged her finger, the rust-red stone upon it gleaming dully—"but I forgive you. Impetuosity is the privilege of the young."

"There was no sense in waiting," Emma said prosaically. "We both knew what we wanted."

Lady Patrice studied her with alert blue eyes. "One can't blame you for jumping at the chance to be a duchess."

Annoyance flared in Emma. "That isn't why I married him."

"Why then?"

"I love him," Emma said, "and he loves me."

"Well, that is a different story. One that I hope shall not be a repeat of Strathaven's last marriage." Shadows flitted through the dowager's gaze.

Emma's irritation waned. Lady Patrice was just being protective of Alaric. Knowing Alaric's past as she now did, however, Emma found that she couldn't quite forgive the dowager for failing to protect a vulnerable boy from the old duke's abuses. Yet what good would it do to hold a grudge against an elderly lady?

"I will do my utmost to make Alaric happy," Emma said.

At that moment, the subject of discussion strode in, and Emma wanted to sigh at the sight of her husband. He was so handsome, his Prussian blue jacket and buff trousers molded to his muscular form. More than that, it was the love glowing in his jade eyes, softening the wicked perfection of his face. He looked younger, happier.

And he was all hers.

Picking up her hand, Alaric pressed a warm kiss on her wrist. "Manage to sleep in, love?"

She nodded. For once, she'd slept past dawn, and she'd awoken to find him gone, a single red rose next to her pillow. Who would have thought Strathaven would turn out to be such a romantic?

"I'm glad you got some rest." Turning, he greeted his aunt and said, "I've been instructing Emma on the duties of the duchess. I must say she is an apt pupil and most willing to learn. She's been applying herself most … vigorously."

Emma narrowed her eyes at her husband. His expression remained impassive; his eyes, however, danced with the devil's merriment.

Oblivious to the by-play, Lady Patrice said in approving tones, "I'm glad that you appreciate the importance of your new position, my dear."

"As it turns out, Emma can adapt readily to any position," His Grace said outrageously. "I am indeed a lucky man."

The dowager frowned. "Is something the matter, Emma dear? You're looking rather flushed. Perhaps Strathaven has been working you too hard?"

Cheeks afire, Emma tried not to look at Alaric whose

shoulders were silently shaking.

"Actually, I've enjoyed learning the ropes here," she said, "although *certain* aspects of Strathmore are rather complicated and exasperating to manage."

"As I was the mistress of the keep for many years," Lady Patrice said mistily, "perhaps I could be of assistance?"

"Are you free on the morrow, Aunt?" Alaric said. "I just met with the land manager. The storm that blew through here last month apparently did damage to some of the cottages, and I'll be out late tomorrow surveying the repairs." He smiled at Emma. "You ladies can keep each other company and talk about Strathmore."

Lady Patrice's lips curled. "I would dearly love a chat. Would you care to meet me at the dowager house—say at two o'clock?"

Emma told herself that there was naught to be gained from holding onto animosity, especially against a lady who, as Alaric had said, had been powerless to stop her husband's cruelties.

"Thank you, Your Grace," Emma said. "That sounds lovely."

The next day, Emma arrived at the dowager's residence at the appointed hour. Lady Patrice's home was situated on a slight rise overlooking the loch. It was an impressive building, echoes of the castle in its neo-gothic stone facade and small decorative turrets. To Emma's surprise, the dowager met her at the door.

"I gave the servants the afternoon off," the lady said, her putty-colored skirts swishing as she led the way to the drawing room. "After the long journey from London, they deserved it. I hope you don't mind that we'll be fending for ourselves."

She gestured toward the tea tray on the coffee table.

"I don't mind at all." Emma smiled as she sat adjacent to her hostess. "I've been fending for myself for most of my life."

"How very industrious. Now I hope I shan't bore you by starting with the history of the Strathaven family?"

"I'd love to hear it."

"Excellent." The dowager beamed. "Let me pour you some tea, and we'll begin."

Sipping the brew, Emma listened as Lady Patrice told a tale of a powerful clan with roots reaching back to the thirteen century. Over the years, different branches of the clan flourished, although there was plenty of bloody history within the family as well. Conflicts pitted one branch against another, and the winning side did not take kindly to the losers, harassing their people and pillaging their lands.

Despite the fascinating topic, Emma had to stifle a yawn. Perhaps it was the dowager's voice—it had a mesmeric drone to it. Feeling groggy, Emma drained her cup in hopes that the tea would revive her.

"Our branch was particularly astute," Lady Patrice said fondly. "When it came to the wars with the English, we made sure to have family supporting both causes. By playing both sides of the field, we were always assured of a winner. In this way, we secured the Duchy of Strathaven and the lands we hold to this day."

"How ... clever." Emma couldn't stop the yawn this time. "I'm sorry. I—I must be more tired than I realized."

"I know. You have been busy after all. Taking my role, my boy away from me."

Emma blinked as the dowager's smiling face split into two. "P-pardon?"

"Don't fight it, dear. You must be feeling tired. Just lay

your head down."

The room grew blurry, the dowager's voice slow and distorted. Emma's lashes felt as heavy as lead, and she couldn't keep her eyes from closing. Gentle hands guided her down into an abyss of darkness.

On horseback, Alaric galloped through the fields back toward the castle. He'd completed the task at the cottages ahead of schedule. Dusk was falling, the sun sinking toward the horizon, casting blood-red streaks into the sky. He wondered if Emma was watching the sunset, thinking of him as he was of her.

His lips curved, and he urged his stallion to go faster.

As he neared the gates of the estate, he saw approaching plumes of dust. Riders ... two of them. Strange, he wasn't expecting visitors.

He halted his mount for their approach.

His surprise deepened when he recognized the faces.

"Kent? Will? What are you doing—?"

"Where's Emma?" Kent said tersely.

For Emma's sake, Alaric had hoped that her family had accepted their decision to elope. That they'd accepted *him*. Jaw taut, he said, "We're wed. There's no changing—"

"The dowager poisoned you," Will cut in.

Alaric jerked. "*What?*"

"That's why we're here. Lugo tracked down the actress. Lily White confessed that it was Patrice who hired her to lace your whiskey."

No. No, it can't be.

Panic punched Alaric in the gut.

"We'll explain the rest," Will said. "First we need to know that everyone is safe. Where's your lass?"

Alaric was already spurring his horse toward the house. "With Patrice," he shouted.

Chapter Thirty-Nine

According to Jarvis, Emma had left the castle before two in the afternoon and had not yet returned. Frantically, Alaric rode through the darkening dusk to the dowager house, Kent and Will flanking him. He barged through the front door, bellowing Emma's name.

No response.

No *servants*.

Fear worse than any he'd known gripped him.

"I dinna like this," Will said grimly, echoing his own thoughts.

The three split up, searching the house. Alaric tore through the duchess' bedchamber, and disbelieving fury roared over him when he found a leather satchel housing a collection of vials. The purpose of each vile potion was labeled in Patrice's spidery hand.

Pain. Sedative. Endless Sleep.

He shouted for the others. Showed them the dowager's diabolical arsenal.

"Where would Patrice take Emma?" Kent bit out. "If she intends to harm her?"

"She will probably try to make it look like an accident," Will said.

Alaric's hands balled. He looked out the window into the night, toward the shadowy movement of the water. Terror thudded in his chest. "The loch."

In her dream, Emma drifted.

Surrounded by inky waves, she couldn't resist their cool, silken pull. They lulled her, drawing her deeper and deeper into their embrace.

Yet something stopped her.

Don't leave me.

She clung to the voice, yet the darkness was so strong. Overwhelming. The tides of oblivion rose quietly, inexorably around her …

Alaric saw the rowboat on the mist-shrouded loch. Glazed by moonlight, it floated, a silver leaf upon the glassy black surface. It was sinking.

He sprinted toward the water, stripping off his jacket and boots as he ran. He passed Patrice, didn't stop, her voice following him with the eeriness of a spectre.

"It's too late. You can't save her."

The hell I can't.

He dove into the icy water, slashing the waves with sure strokes. *Hold on lass, hold on,* his heart thundered. The tides grew choppier, washed over his head, yet he pushed on, spitting water, kicking out against the churning depths. His muscles strained. His lungs burned. A single imperative drove him on.

Get to the boat and save his woman.

He saw the boat yards away, wrapped by tendrils of mist, its sides half-submerged. He battled the waves with renewed vigor, surging forward with powerful kicks. His hands closed on the wooden edge, and he hauled himself up.

Emma. The water was just closing over her face.

He yanked her up by the shoulders, shouted her name.

Limp, lifeless, she didn't respond.

He wrapped an arm around her, nestling her back against his chest. Vigilantly keeping her head above the water, he fought the currents with his free arm. The fog grew thicker, obscuring the way to safety, bearing down upon him. Fatigue turned his muscles to stone. Emma remained slumped in his desperate grasp.

"You stay with me, Emma," he gritted out. "We do this together. Either way."

"Strathaven! Where are you?"

Kent's voice reached him, a buoy in the darkness.

"Over here!" Alaric shouted. "I've got her."

Moments later, a yellow glow burned through the mist, followed by the bow of a boat. Kent dropped the oar and reached out, hoisting Emma aboard. Chest heaving, Alaric followed and knelt beside her.

"How is she?" he said raggedly.

In the light of the single lantern, Kent's face was bleak as he covered his sister in his jacket. "She's breathing, but her pulse is weak."

Panic seized Alaric. He cupped her chilled face. "Wake up, love."

She didn't reply, didn't so much as flicker an eyelash at his plea.

His terror burgeoned until he could barely breathe.

"Devil take it, Emma," he choked out, "you made me a bluidy promise, and you *will* keep it. You come back to me right now. You fight this!"

Was it his crazed imagination—or did her bosom rise on a fuller breath?

"Don't leave me, love." His voice cracked, and he cradled her to his chest, saying in an agonized whisper, "I'm not letting you go. Wherever you go, I'm coming with you ..."

Emma coughed. Sputtered out water.

"Darling?" he said in a torment of hope.

Her lashes lifted. "A-Alaric?"

"Aye, lass." His eyes stung. "I'm here."

She coughed out more water. "Your aunt ... she *drugged* me."

Even as tears scalded his throat, his lips twitched at her indignation.

"I know, and I'll be dealing with her shortly." He smoothed a damp tendril from his beloved's cheek. "You're safe now. I'm never letting you out of my sight again."

"You gave us a fright, Em," Kent said gruffly.

Emma turned her head in his direction. "Thank you for rescuing me, Ambrose."

"That's what brothers are for. Although 'tis your duke here who deserves most of the credit."

Emma looked up at Alaric, her expression so adoring that his throat burned once more.

"I love you," she whispered.

"I love you," he said hoarsely. "So damned much."

He kissed her reverently, and in the warm vitality of her response, his fear receded.

When they reached the shore, Will was waiting. He had Patrice under his watch. As Alaric faced their aunt with Emma in his arms, he knew it was time for a reckoning.

He bit out a single word. "Why?"

The dowager's plaintive smile made his gut roil. "Because, my dear boy, I was trying to save you, care for you, as I've always done. She,"—the bitch pointed a finger at Emma, and Alaric's muscles bunched protectively—"would have hurt you. Just like Laura did."

"You tried to kill my wife. Tried to kill me and murdered Clara Osgood instead," he said through his clenched jaw.

"Lily White confessed that it was you who hired her to put poison in my whiskey."

Emma stiffened in his embrace. "I *knew* the maid was important."

Patrice's expression turned pleading. "Lady Osgood was an accident. How was I to know that she would drink your whiskey and so much of it? I wasn't trying to kill you, dear boy, but to make you understand that you need me. You were pushing me away, Alaric. Distancing yourself." Her eyes glittered with tears of madness. "I calibrated the dose perfectly to give you a reminder of your illness—what we had been through together, all those days and nights I spent nursing you. I never intended to harm you permanently. I planned to come to London and *save* you."

At Emma's gasp, Alaric knew that she'd reached the same nefarious conclusion as he had.

Insides churning, he said, "There was no illness, was there? It was you all along. All that I suffered—it was at your hand."

His aunt licked her lips. "It wasn't my fault. I had no choice."

"No choice?" Emma choked out. "You crazed *witch*—"

Alaric held his wife back. "Let her finish."

"It was my husband's fault," the dowager said, her lips trembling. "I loved my Henry—gave him everything—yet he betrayed me. With your whore of a mother."

Shock jolted Alaric. He heard Will's chuff of surprise.

"It was at a house party at Strathmore. We'd invited our poor relations to see the castle. And how did they repay us?" Rage lit Patrice's eyes. "The slut seduced my duke—her own husband's cousin—and got herself with a bastard."

Pieces began to fall in place. Created a picture with sickening clarity.

"That's why Da hated me." The words left Alaric

numbly. "Because I was not his."

"To avoid scandal, we all agreed to keep it a secret. The truth would have accompanied us to our graves if my son hadn't died. After that, everything changed." Tears leaked down Patrice's cheeks, her voice bloated with grief and self-pity. "Henry and I tried, yet we couldn't have another child, and that made him turn from me. Made him remember that he while he had no legitimate issue, he had a bastard with his blood. Without my consent, he made up his mind to take you—the spawn of a harlot—into *our* home."

Alaric felt Emma's arms squeezing around his waist, lending him strength.

"Under the guise of guardianship, Henry was going to raise his by-blow in *my* house. I couldn't allow it." Cunning curled Patrice's lips. "So I hit upon the perfect solution. For I knew my duke well, knew how he despised weakness above all else. I gave him what he deserved: a frail, useless bastard, one that could never take my own son's place."

"You took your jealousy out on an innocent lad!" Will snarled. "Alaric had naught to do with any of it, you underhanded bitch!"

"I know. That is why I spent countless nights tending to him." Malice melted to anxiety, the maniacal shift terrifying to behold. Alaric felt nauseated as his aunt looked upon him with glowing fondness. "The more my husband despised you, the more I loved you. I'd lost his affection, but I could have yours—and I could remain mistress of Strathmore ... if certain obstacles were removed," she said dreamily. "You were fourth in line to inherit, after all. And since your father obligingly died in that carriage accident, there were only two hurdles to surmount. Two childless, weak cousins who had never amounted to much. Their deaths were hardly noticed."

Holy hell.

He said in disbelief, "You poisoned them ... your husband's kin?"

"I did what needed to be done to secure your legacy." She smiled with horrible pride. "So we could be together, my dearest boy."

A hideous thought seized him. "Laura, *Charlie* ..."

"I had no hand in that. At first, I'll admit I was concerned after your whirlwind marriage to that Jezebel," Patrice said airily, "but when I met her, I knew that she posed no threat. It was clear the passion between the two of you would quickly sour. Laura didn't need my help to destroy your marriage—she did it all by herself. But Emma here,"—the dowager shook her head morosely—"she was different, her hold on you too strong. She left me no choice but to take action."

Alaric's arms tightened around Emma. "You'll never get near my wife again. We're handing you over to the magistrates, and you are going to pay for your crimes."

"She belongs in Bedlam," Emma said.

"*No.*" Patrice stumbled backward. "I'm not going anywhere. I belong *here*."

"There's nowhere to run," Kent said. "You cannot escape justice."

A mad, sly smile crossed Patrice's features. "There's always an escape."

She twisted her ring; the carnelian flipped open. In a blink, she brought the hidden compartment to her lips, downing the contents. Her eyes bulged, and she fell to the sand.

"Bluidy hell," Will exclaimed.

Kent crossed over and, crouching, placed a hand on the dowager's neck. He shook his head.

Alaric didn't know how to respond. Cold numbness spread over him as the revelations swirled in his head. Death, pain, and suffering. His aunt—a crazed murderess, perpetrator of countless ills ... who lay dead before him. So many betrayals. It was too much to take in. He could sense the dark walls curving over his head, the past trapping him ...

"Alaric?"

Emma's steady voice reached him through the darkness. Her face came into focus, became his only focus when he saw the fierce love in her eyes. Her flame vanquished the prison walls, turned them into smoke.

"I'm here, my darling." She cupped his jaw, and her warm strength seeped into him. "Everything will be alright."

"Because of you," he said hoarsely. "My love."

He pulled her into his arms and held on tight.

Chapter Forty

At week's end, Emma stood next to her husband as they bade farewell to Ambrose and Mr. McLeod. With his dark hair gleaming and virile form dressed with effortless elegance, Alaric appeared much like his normal self. At least on the surface. She knew the wounds inflicted by the dowager would take longer to heal, and she was determined to accompany him on that journey, no matter how long it took.

To her relief, he wanted her there by his side.

Talking long into the nights, he'd spoken of memories, feelings so hotly poignant that all she could do was hold him tighter. They'd discussed his realization: there *was* nothing wrong with him. The rejection he'd suffered—from his mama, his da, even the cruel man who'd been his biological father—none of it had been his fault. The lack of love he'd received hadn't been because he was unlovable or ugly, stupid or weak.

The truth was terrible yet liberating: he'd been the unlucky product of an illicit affair and the target of a deranged woman.

Alaric had shed tears; so had Emma.

When even that had been insufficient, they'd made love with a frantic rawness that forged them body and soul. The scorching intimacies of the previous night spangled warmth over Emma's skin, and when she slid a look at Alaric, she saw the answering smolder in his beautiful eyes.

"Well, Kent and I had best be off," Mr. McLeod said.

"Bring your families for a visit soon," Alaric said. "We welcome their company."

"Thank you, Your Grace." A smile in his eyes, Ambrose pulled her aside. "Is there any message you'd like me to pass onto the family, Em?"

"Just this." Emma rose on her tiptoes and hugged her brother fiercely. "Thank you," she whispered in his ear, "for everything. I'll miss you."

"Be happy, Em," he whispered back.

Next to them, the McLeod brothers eyed one another warily.

Mr. McLeod spoke first. "I guess this is goodbye then."

"For now," Alaric said quietly. "If you change mind, if you want to take up what is rightfully yours—"

"Nay, you were the one who suffered for it. You've worked to make the dukedom what it is. I wouldn't know how to be a duke and wouldn't want to learn," Mr. McLeod said. "In my eyes and that of the world, you *are* Strathaven."

After a moment, Alaric gave a terse nod.

Extending his hand, Mr. McLeod said gruffly, "Seems a pity, though. Just when matters were settling between us, it turns out we're not brothers after all."

"You're my brother, William," Alaric said, "in every way that counts."

Heat prickled Emma's eyes as her husband took his sibling's hand—and pulled the other into a fierce hug. The embrace between the two big Scotsmen lasted approximately half a second before they broke apart.

Mr. McLeod coughed into his fist. "I'll, ahem, be seeing you then."

"Aye," Alaric said, equally red-faced.

"Give our love to everyone," Emma said.

Alaric put his arm around her, and together they waved

as their family departed.

When they were alone, she turned to look at her husband. Touched a hand to his jaw.

"How are you?" she said softly.

He nuzzled her palm. "Never better."

"After everything with your aunt and now Mr. McLeod leaving—"

He placed a finger against her lips, stemming the flow of words. "Don't fuss, love. I'm better. Better than I can recall ever being. You see, I came to several realizations this morning."

Searching his brilliant gaze, she tipped her head to the side. "What were they?"

"The past is over. Patrice is dead, and her soul will be judged for her sins. I don't want to be imprisoned by hatred—it's not my cross to bear."

"No, it isn't." Emma's throat thickened at his courage. Despite all the suffering he'd known, he was choosing freedom, the higher path. "She can't hurt you anymore."

"Aye. Even better, when I woke up this morning, you were there beside me." He rubbed his thumb over her bottom lip. "You held me through the night, were so soft and wet and ready for me when I made love to you at dawn. And do you know what I realized then?"

The wonder in his voice made her eyes sting. "What, my darling?"

"Somehow all of this brought me to you. You've freed me, Emma," he said tenderly. "Because of you, I know what it is to love and be loved."

How could she resist this man?

"You've always known how to love—you just didn't get enough in return. Never fear," she said with a sniffle, "I shall make up for it. I'm going to be the duchess of your dreams."

"You already are. Although, now that you mention it,

there do remain several variations to your position that we've yet to explore." His slow, wicked smile sent love and desire tumbling through her. "Care for a demonstration, Your Grace?"

"Always, Your Grace," she said.

He kissed her with a passion that left her breathless. Sweeping her up in his arms, he carried her upstairs. And while her duke proceeded to teach her thrilling new ways to love, she proved, as always, that she was a duchess up to the task.

Epilogue

Other men might fear finding their wives in compromising situations.

Alaric anticipated it—a good thing, given who he was married to.

Stalking through the winding hedges, he arrived at the edge of the moonlit garden, and his blood heated as he spotted the familiar figure of his duchess. She was in the gazebo; she had her back turned to him—and she was not alone.

Soundlessly, he approached. Cleared his throat.

Violet, who was standing on the gazebo *railing*, spun around with the ease of an acrobat. A telescope dangled from one of her hands. "Gadzooks, you startled me!"

"Your Grace." This came from Thea, who curtsied and hastily jammed a pair of opera glasses into her reticule. "We weren't, um, expecting you."

"Darling, I didn't think you were coming tonight." Smiling, Emma stood on tiptoe and brushed her lips against his jaw. "I thought you and Tremont planned to have a late night of cards."

Recently, Alaric had been concerned about his friend, who didn't quite seem himself. Emma had encouraged him to spend the night with Tremont at the club. Halfway through the evening, however, instinct had told him to seek his wife out. Or maybe he just missed her.

Either way, he should have known that she was up to

something.

"If I may be so bold," he said, "what is going on here?"

His cool, polite tones had their intended effect. Violet hopped down from the railing, landing with the grace of a cat on her slippered feet. Grabbing Thea by the arm, she pulled the other out of the gazebo, saying cheerfully, "Marianne will be looking for us, so we'll leave the explaining to Emma. Good evening, Your Grace!"

He bowed to his wife's departing sisters. Then he turned to face his errant duchess.

He quirked a brow. "Well?"

"Now, Alaric, it's not as bad as it looks," she began.

"Does it look bad?" he inquired. "To find one's wife in a dark garden—spying and taking notes?" He dropped his gaze to the notebook jutting out of her pearl-encrusted evening bag.

"I was just doing a little observation," she said brightly. "You see, at a soiree earlier this week, I came upon a lady weeping in the retiring room. She thought her husband might be having an affair with Lady De Burgh. Since I happened to have an invitation to the party next door to the De Burghs, I promised her I'd take a look."

"And you didn't think to mention this to me?"

She peered up at him through her lashes. "I didn't know if anything would come of it. I didn't want to concern you over naught. If I saw anything tonight, however," she said virtuously, "I was definitely going to tell you."

"And did you, my love?" he said calmly. "See anything, I mean?"

She wrinkled her nose. "No. Someone did enter the bedchamber, but Lady De Burgh took the precaution of drawing the curtains before we could ascertain his identity."

"She and Lord Galveston didn't want an audience, no doubt."

"Galveston?" Emma exclaimed. "How do you know it was him?"

"Because he and I do business together. When we meet at the club and he gets into his cups, his tongue loosens. He's been having an *affaire* with Lady De Burgh for several weeks."

Emma's face fell. "Oh dear. I shall hate breaking the news to my clien—I mean, Lady Galveston."

"Indeed." He curled a finger under his wife's chin, searching her clear eyes. "Now tell me why you didn't trust me enough to inform me of your new case."

That was his true concern. He'd made it clear that, as long as Emma didn't compromise her safety in any way and kept him apprised of her activities, he supported her investigative pursuits. Not too long ago, in fact, he'd assisted her and Kent with a case. His financial knowledge had helped them to track down their client's dowry, which had been ferreted into secret funds by a villainous uncle.

"I do trust you," Emma said instantly. "You're the best of husbands."

"I am, of course, relieved to hear it."

Reaching up, she smoothed his lapels, fiddled with his cravat pin. "I planned to tell you about my newest case after I told you ... my other news."

He stilled.

"You've noticed that there hasn't been any, um, interruption to our marital activities as of late?"

"*Emma.*" Heart thudding, he grabbed her hands. "Are you ... are we ...?"

Eyes sparkling, she nodded.

"My dearest love," he breathed, "what the devil are you doing *spying* in a garden when you're increasing—with my heir, no less?"

"We don't know that it's going to be a boy; it could very

well be a girl. And any daughter of ours wouldn't mind a little adventure ... Alaric," she said breathlessly, "what are you doing?"

"I'm getting you out of here."

"I noticed. But I can walk."

"Not as fast as I can." He strode through the hedges with his duchess in his arms. "You shouldn't be out in the night air. You should be resting, eating, whatever it is ladies in your condition do—"

"You're not going to be like this the entire seven months, are you?"

He shot her a look.

She sighed. "I'm a Kent, darling. We're robust, remember?"

"As to that, there's to be no more sleuthing until our son is born."

"You can't be serious."

"Can't I?"

Instead of arguing, she smiled. "You *are* happy about this, aren't you?"

"Darling, I'm overjoyed." Halting, he gazed into her eyes and saw his future so clearly and beautifully reflected. "Everything I've ever wanted, you've given me. And now we're going to have a bairn as well."

"I love you so much," she said.

Words he'd never tire of hearing or saying. Because she'd taught him they were true.

"I love you, Emma." He kissed her with all that was in his heart.

When he raised his head, she whispered, "Let's go home."

"I am home. With you, my love," he said tenderly, "I finally am."

Please enjoy a peek at Grace's other books ...

The *Heart of Enquiry* series

Prequel Novella: *The Widow Vanishes*
Fate throws beautiful widow Annabel Foster into the arms of William McLeod, her enemy's most ruthless soldier. When an unexpected and explosive night of passion ensues, she must decide: should she run for her life—or stay for her heart?

Book 1: *The Duke Who Knew Too Much*
When Miss Emma Kent witnesses a depraved encounter involving the wicked Duke of Strathaven, her honor compels her to do the right thing. But steamy desire challenges her quest for justice, and she and Strathaven must work together to unravel a dangerous mystery ... before it's too late.

Book 2: *M is for Marquess*
With her frail constitution improving, Miss Dorothea Kent yearns to live a full and passionate life. Desire blooms between her and Gabriel Ridgley, the Marquess of Tremont, an enigmatic widower with a disabled son. But the road to love proves treacherous as Gabriel's past as a spy emerges to threaten them both... and they must defeat a dangerous enemy lying in wait.

Book 3: *The Lady Who Came in from the Cold*
Former spy Pandora Hudson gave up espionage for love. Twelve years later, her dark secret rises to threaten her blissful marriage to Marcus, Marquess of Blackwood, and she must face her most challenging mission yet: winning back the heart of the only man she's ever loved.

The *Mayhem in Mayfair* series

Book 1: *Her Husband's Harlot*
How far will a wallflower go to win her husband's love? When her disguise as a courtesan backfires, Lady Helena finds herself entangled in a game of deception and desire with her husband

Nicholas, the Marquess of Harteford ... and discovers that he has dark secrets of his own.

Book 2: *Her Wanton Wager*
To what lengths will a feisty miss go to save her family from ruin? Miss Persephone Fines takes on a wager of seduction with notorious gaming hell owner Gavin Hunt and discovers that love is the most dangerous risk of all.

Book 3: *Her Protector's Pleasure*
Wealthy widow Lady Marianne Draven will stop at nothing to find her kidnapped daughter. Having suffered betrayal in the past, she trusts no man—and especially not Thames River Policeman Ambrose Kent, who has a few secrets of his own. Yet fiery passion ignites between the unlikely pair as they battle a shadowy foe. Can they work together to save Marianne's daughter? And will nights of pleasure turn into a love for all time?

Book 4: *Her Prodigal Passion*
Sensible Miss Charity Sparkler has been in love with Paul Fines, her best friend's brother, for years. When he accidentally compromises her, they find themselves wed in haste. Can an ugly duckling recognize her own beauty and a reformed rake his own value? As secrets of the past lead to present dangers, will this marriage of convenience transform into one of love?

The *Chronicles of Abigail Jones* series

Abigail Jones
When destiny brings shy Victorian maid Abigail Jones into the home of the brooding and enigmatic Earl of Huxton, she discovers forbidden passion ... and a dangerous world of supernatural forces.

About the Author

Grace Callaway's debut novel, *Her Husband's Harlot*, was a Romance Writers of America® Golden Heart® Finalist and went on to become a National #1 Bestselling Regency Romance. Since then, the books in her Mayhem in Mayfair series have hit multiple national and international bestselling lists. She's received top-starred reviews from *Love Romance Passion*, *Bitten by Paranormal Romance*, and *Nightowl Reviews*, amongst others.

Grace grew up on the Canadian prairies battling mosquitoes and freezing temperatures. She made her way south to earn a Ph.D. in Psychology at the University of Michigan. She thought writing a dissertation was difficult until she started writing a book; she thought writing a book was challenging until she became a mother. She's learned that the greater the effort, the sweeter the rewards. Currently, she and her family live in California, where their adventures include remodeling a ramshackle house, exploring the great outdoors, and sampling local artisanal goodies.

Grace loves to hear from her readers and can be reached at grace@gracecallaway.com.

Other ways to connect:
Newsletter: www.bitly.com/CallawayNews
Website: www.gracecallaway.com
Facebook: www.facebook.com/GraceCallawayBooks

Printed in Great Britain
by Amazon.co.uk, Ltd.,
Marston Gate.